BLOWBACK
DENIS KILCOMMONS

BANTAM PRESS

LONDON · NEW YORK · TORONTO · SYDNEY · AUCKLAND

596862

All of the characters in this book are fictitious, and any
resemblance to actual persons, living or dead, is purely
coincidental.

TRANSWORLD PUBLISHERS LTD
61–63 Uxbridge Road, London W5 5SA

TRANSWORLD PUBLISHERS (AUSTRALIA) PTY LTD
15–23 Helles Avenue, Moorebank, NSW 2170

TRANSWORLD PUBLISHERS (NZ) LTD
Cnr Moselle and Waipareira Aves,
Henderson, Auckland

Published 1990 by Bantam Press
a division of Transworld Publishers Ltd
Copyright © Denis Kilcommons 1990

The right of Denis Kilcommons to be identified as the
author of this work has been asserted in accordance with
sections 77 and 78 of the Copyright Designs and Patents
Act 1988.

British Library Cataloguing in Publication Data

Kilcommons, Denis, *1941–*
  Blowback.
  I. Title
  823.914 [F]

  ISBN 0–593–02048–0
  ISBN 0–593–02057–X pbk

Typeset in 12/13 pt Baskerville
by Colset Pte Ltd, Singapore
Printed in Great Britain
by The Guernsey Press Co. Ltd,
Guernsey, Channel Islands.

For Sian

'Secrecy breeds fantasy, and fantasy, feeding on itself at a high altitude of self-importance, can breed more fantasy.'

Hugh Trevor-Roper
Regius Professor of Modern History
at Oxford, 1957–80

Prologue

Stockholm's Arlanda Airport was ten minutes flying time away and Amos Fowler nerved himself for another landing.

Hell, it shouldn't be like this at his age and after all he'd been through. This was the comfort of business class in a Boeing airliner, not floorspace on an Air-America Chinook. His fellow passengers carried briefcases and there wasn't a grenade launcher in sight. He'd even lay odds the pilot was sober.

But he still worried. He always did, these days, despite the statistics that said he was safer here than crossing the road. Well, safer than some roads.

He closed his eyes and encouraged the memories to take his mind off what was ahead. The memories. They were always there, ready to be invoked.

In Indo-China he had been known as the Quiet American. He had been given the nickname by a Vietnamese drugs baron with a fondness for English and American fiction. Most of the people who had used it thought it was original and made no literary connection. Most of them didn't read anyhow, except maybe comic books.

Fowler, like his namesake, had lived with a Vietnamese girl in Saigon. She had been an oasis where he could escape the pressures of what he termed business.

Kieu was seventeen and beautiful and told him she loved him, although he knew it wasn't true. The alternative to being his woman, living in his apartment, and being able to keep her family of seven with what he paid her, was going back to being a bar-girl at the Dreamland.

He didn't mind the lie. She was loyal, subservient in her

9

domesticity, compliant in bed, and, after a while, he thought that maybe she did, at least, like him.

Kieu was always there when he returned from trips into Laos or Cambodia, to Bangkok, Sydney or Hong Kong. No matter if he was away two days or two weeks, she was always there to greet him and serve his needs. She told him she was faithful in his absence and, in this, he believed her.

Fowler enjoyed their relationship although they both understood its limitations. She knew it would cease to exist when the time came for him to leave permanently. She knew he would not take her to the United States as a wife. She probably thought he already had one, but he hadn't. Women had always been too demanding, considering the line of work he was in. Until he had met her.

He really was a Quiet American. He had worked in the unhealthiest trouble spots in the world and had discovered it was wisest to keep his own counsel, watch his own back and do his job with the minimum of fuss. Afterwards, when business was over, he had relaxed by buying a woman and getting drunk.

Drinking had been popular in his line of work.

Fowler and Kieu were together for ten months and it was the longest time he had been with anybody. It ended, one afternoon, when she went to visit her family. He heard an explosion a street away and went looking.

The official reports, that he read later, said a bomb being carried on the back of a motor scooter by a fifteen-year-old Vietcong boy, had gone off prematurely. Kieu had been unlucky enough to be nearby and a piece of the machine had sliced off her arm at the shoulder and dug a hole in her neck. She had died of shock and loss of blood before he got there.

She was one of four victims, not counting the scooter rider, one of whom was an officer in the Army of the Republic of Vietnam, so maybe the Cong had counted it a success.

He had stood by her body in the dust until her family came for her.

Their grief was big enough for all of them and, anyway, he didn't know how to grieve. It was an emotion he had lost years before, in Special Operations above the DMZ. The joke then had been grab the gooks by the balls and their hearts and minds would follow. Some joke. He looked at the faces of Kieu's family and their eyes looked through him. Their grief was their own and there was no place for him.

He had gone back to his apartment and made a telephone call and arranged another deal. He had packed and gone away on business for three days. When he returned, the loss of Kieu had been compartmentalized and he refused to let it bother him. That first night back, he had gone to the Dreamland and got drunk. But he had done it quietly.

Fowler wondered exactly when he had lost his belief and laughed at himself. It was a question he had posed so many times it had become rhetorical. What the hell did it matter? It had happened and it had left him living inside a shell. The one compensation was it had also made him rich. He now worked only because he wanted to.

The killing fields had changed in the last fifteen years. There had been South and Central America, the North-West Frontier of Pakistan, the Lebanon, Cyprus and Israel. Now it was Europe: Athens, the Hague, Stockholm. A more civilized way of death.

He felt the wheels bounce and the engine noise change as the aircraft came down in one piece and he gulped with relief that it was over.

Other people's death, civilized or barbaric, he could handle, but the possibility of facing his own in an aircraft over which he had no control was something else.

Chapter 1

Jim Brady was a fat, fifty-three-year-old freelance photographer from London, who walked into an unexpected society scoop in a schnitzel house in Vienna.

The years had not been kind to Brady. He was going seriously bald, suffered from fallen arches and disillusionment, and was a bad size for ready-made suits.

The glamour of taking photographs for national newspapers had been asphyxiated an aeon before in the smoke-filled unsocial hours of a hundred different drinking dens. It was a lifestyle that bred cynicism and wrecked marriages. Brady didn't mind the cynicism but had been determined it would not wreck his marriage. He and his wife Sheila had found an unlikely salvation in music.

Soon after their marriage, twenty years before, they had begun to make annual pilgrimages to Vienna every spring. The visits had served as a renewal of their relationship. He had never confessed the trips to his colleagues. It made them even more special.

Sheila had died of cancer five years ago. Brady had increased his drinking and smoking, but had not stopped coming to Vienna. The visits were now a double pilgrimage.

Even though he was on holiday, he took his camera with him everywhere. It was the only time he used it for creative photography. He was not looking for news pictures in a city more famous for its middle-class wealth and coffeehouses than for paparazzi opportunities, but when one presented itself as he worked his way through a double wienerschnitzel, the lure of a lucrative sale overcame any reservations.

It was an informal restaurant of small rooms on different levels with a blackboard menu and waiters in long white aprons. His table was in an alcove near the door. The place was already busy with early evening diners and he only noticed the woman because she swore in English. She was on the far side of a partition and he saw her face when she stood up to brush something she had spilled from her dress.

She was striking rather than beautiful, and he recognized her immediately. At the same time he noted that her handsome companion, who had also got up to help, was not her husband.

He was dark enough to be southern European, perhaps Italian, and Brady smiled and visualized headlines about Latin lovers as he continued eating, and tried to evaluate how long it would be before the couple finished their meal.

The woman giggled at something the man said and they sat down again out of sight but Brady decided to take no chances. He left half his second schnitzel, finished the glass of white wine and signalled the waiter, who looked disapprovingly at his plate.

'Very nice,' Brady said, 'but there was too much.'

He patted his stomach and compensated by leaving a bigger-than-normal tip.

The restaurant was in one of the narrow alleys behind St Stephen's Cathedral. Lighting was poor but, where the alley met the street, there was an overhead lamp and the brightness of shop windows.

Brady crossed to the other pavement and took up position in a shop doorway on a corner. He could look at the Afghan carpets in the window and keep watch for anyone leaving the alley at the same time. As he waited, he set his Nikon camera at 125th at f2.8. The film was 400 ASA black and white and he changed the lens for the telephoto in his pocket.

The couple took longer than he expected and he began to wonder if there was another exit. When they did appear, he was surprised to see they were accompanied by a second man, a regulation minder, who looked up and down the street before walking to a parked car.

The couple were alone and bathed in the light from the lamp. Brady pointed and fired and got off half a dozen shots. With the motordrive it took only seconds. The circumstances were not ideal, but he could compensate when processing. The pictures would be grainy but usable.

The couple hadn't noticed his interest, but the minder had.

Brady left the shop doorway and walked away up the street. After twenty yards he glanced back over his shoulder. The two men were standing on the corner watching him; the woman was not with them. He went another ten paces and looked back again. The men had begun to follow him.

What had started as a snatched picture that could earn him a few bob, was turning into aggravation he could do without. Even so, he was loath to give it up without a struggle.

As he walked, he rewound the film in his camera electronically, but dare not make the switch until he had a moment out of sight. There was a bar on the other side of the street that would be ideal and he crossed and went inside.

The room was long and thin. The bar ran along the wall on the right, with high stools in front of it. Tables were set along the wall to the left. A young couple occupied the table by the window and two young men leaned on the bar and talked to the girl behind it. He asked her for a beer before sitting at a table. He held his camera in his lap out of sight, opened the back, removed the film and put it in a small inside pocket of his jacket, and replaced it with a fresh cassette.

As the girl brought the beer, he held down the exposure button on the camera and let the electric drive run the new film through. An old trick, but it had worked before.

The man who had been the woman's companion entered the bar. He wore his light-coloured trenchcoat on his shoulders like a cloak. He was in his early thirties and conscious of his good looks. The second man stayed outside.

The smoothy shook his head at the girl to indicate that he wanted nothing and sat opposite Brady.

15

'That was very bad,' he said in English.

The photographer gave a resigned grin and held up his Press card.

'I'm sorry if I invaded the lady's privacy. I'm on holiday, but old habits die hard.'

The man nodded sympathetically and held out his hand.

Brady picked up the camera from the seat alongside him, opened the back and took out the film, exposing it completely in the lights of the bar. He offered the ruined film and the man took it.

'From now on I'll stick to sightseeing,' he said, talking too much because he was nervous. He shrugged. 'You can't win them all.'

The man smiled and said, 'That's true. You can't.'

They both nodded to confirm they understood each other's position, before the young man got up and left. Brady patted his pocket where the unexposed film was and leisurely drank his beer.

The evening had been very satisfying. He had enjoyed both his dinner and snatching the picture. Keeping it had been a bonus. Brady's build and personality had meant that for most of his life he had been an also-ran. Outsmarting the smoothy had given his ego a charge.

He left twenty minutes later. The night was mild and he would enjoy the stroll back to his hotel on the Währingerstrasse. That was one of the things that was nice about Vienna. It was a small city and most places were within walking distance. It saved money on taxis. The streets were quiet, but he felt safe. That was another thing. Vienna was respectable, its citizens orderly and law abiding. There was no graffiti, no vandals.

Brady followed the road until it became pedestrianized and led into the square where St Stephen's Cathedral with its multi-coloured tiled roof was still attracting tourists. He crossed the square and took short cuts through streets that became progressively less busy, the further away he moved from the city centre.

He and Sheila had often walked the streets at night.

16

They had always stayed in hotels outside the Ring where prices were cheaper. He kept up the tradition and had a room at the place they had discovered two years before she died. It was budget-priced, but it had character and provided good quality, three-star service that the holiday brochure pretended was four star.

The street he was on was cobbled and curved to link two squares. He had gone halfway along it before he realized the echoes of his footsteps belonged to someone following him. When he looked over his shoulder, he saw the minder.

Running for it was out of the question. He was in no condition for any sort of physical exertion. He sighed, this time with genuine resignation, as, right on cue, the handsome half of the duo stepped out of an alley a few yards in front of him.

They'd rumbled the switch.

No-one else was about, there were no cars and the tall buildings provided plenty of shadow. The smoothy in front of him motioned to the alley, but Brady shook his head. They could have the real film, but he was not prepared to step into the darkness and suffer a good hiding into the bargain.

As he reached the young man, he held up his hands to admit defeat. The knife that entered his back was a surprise. The thrust was angled to miss the spinal column and the blade pierced upwards towards the heart.

I don't believe this, Brady thought in the split second before he died. I'm on my holidays. Sheila?

Chapter 2

The room in the House of Commons had been borrowed for the meeting. It was lined with cupboards and glass-fronted bookcases. A table was positioned in its middle with four hard-backed chairs around it. A roll-topped desk and another chair were beneath the window that looked out over the river. Carpet would have been out of place and the floor consisted of bare and dusty boards. They creaked as Hector Rossington-Hall turned from the window, went to the central table and laid upon it the large brown envelope he carried.

The Deputy Director of MI6 was a small, neat man. He had maintained his military moustache through twenty-five years of secret service and he wore his suits as if they were uniforms.

His immaculate appearance was to compensate for his lack of height – he was five feet six – and his embarrassing initials. It was less than amusing to be known as HRH, an appellation he discouraged among less senior colleagues, but one he had to endure from peers and superiors.

His imagined disadvantages made him exceptionally thorough at his job and an expert at career protection. That was one of the reasons he was at the House.

The Director General had put him in personal charge of a file that had the potential to be a bastard. He was here to dilute the threat by sharing it. Rossington-Hall knew what had to be done, but he wanted his minister to share the responsibility for doing it.

He looked at his watch. Four o'clock. He had been waiting fifteen minutes.

The door opened abruptly and Roy Selwyn, the Foreign Secretary, burst in.

'Hector. Sorry I'm late.' He dumped a briefcase on the table. 'I was waylaid by the media.'

He beamed as he came forward to shake hands, overweight and larger than life, full of energy, still performing even though the cameras were no longer there. The grip was firm, but the palm was sweaty.

Rossington-Hall smiled tightly in return. He had no time for false *bonhomie*. His manner stressed the seriousness of their business.

'Minister. Thank you for seeing me at such short notice. And,' he glanced round the room, 'in such anonymous surroundings.'

The Foreign Secretary caught his mood, discarded the beam and gestured towards the table.

'Shall we sit?'

They sat facing each other on either side of the table. Rossington-Hall had met Selwyn on three previous occasions, but was more familiar with his distinctive mane of wavy grey hair and the gestures that mobilized his shoulders, from the man's many television appearances. He had seen him so often on television that he looked smaller in the flesh.

'Now then,' Selwyn placed both hands flat on the table in front of him and raised his shoulders like a rugby player about to scrum down. Rossington-Hall recognized the nononsense stance. 'Let's cut the pleasantries. This has to be important. Tell me.'

The Deputy Director removed a large, black and white photograph from the envelope and placed it in front of the minister without speaking. The minister took half-moon spectacles from a waistcoat pocket, put them on his nose and leaned forward to inspect it.

'Sarah Mathieson.' He looked at Rossington-Hall over the half-moons. 'It is Sarah Mathieson, isn't it? No point us being here if it isn't.'

'It is Sarah Mathieson.'

He lowered his gaze again and continued to stare at the photograph. Eventually he looked up, shaking his head.

'Don't know the chap. Who is he?'

'Aldo Capaldi. Italian, aged thirty-four, single, charming, heterosexual and a known terrorist.'

'Terrorist? Has Sarah been kidnapped?'

'No. It's worse than that. She appears to be a friend of his.'

'Good God! Are you sure?'

'It seems likely. We believe Capaldi was prepared to kill to prevent the photograph being seen.'

'But we have seen it. You'd better explain.'

'It was taken in Vienna. It was on a roll of film found on the body of a British holiday-maker, one James Brady. Brady's occupation was freelance photographer. He worked mainly for the tabloids, so it is a fair assumption that he would know Sarah Mathieson by sight.'

'No doubt about it. If he fed the gossip columns, he would know our Sarah. She's never been one to hide her lust for life.'

'Until now. Brady was professionally killed. A single stab wound in the back.'

'Why did they leave the film?'

'We presume they did not know he still had it.'

'How did we get it?'

'From the Austrian police. Brady's body was found in an alley. Missing were his wallet, passport and the camera he took everywhere with him. The film was in a second inside pocket, the sort of pocket where one might keep loose change. The sort of pocket that could be missed by a killer in a hurry. Brady was identified from his Press card. His belongings were handed over to the duty officer at the British Embassy.

'The police developed the roll of film, but failed to notice its relevance. Mr Brady had taken many pictures. They were of street scenes, by day and by night, of people who were aware they were being photographed and people who were not. Café shots through windows, tram interiors.'

He shrugged. 'Sarah and Capaldi are pictured as lovers in lamplight. It's artistic. A photograph without threat. The police had already decided the motive was robbery and it's likely they have relegated Mr Brady's death to their unsolved file. Vienna is a staid old lady, these days. She still enjoys civilized intrigue, but the murder and robbery of a tourist is not something the authorities like to make too much fuss about.'

'When did this happen?'

'Mr Brady was killed five days ago. His belongings – and the photographs and film – were handed to the embassy yesterday. Our man at the embassy recognized Sarah and sensed a possible embarrassment. We identified Capaldi this morning.'

The minister remained silent while he thought over what he had been told.

'You think Brady took the picture and was killed to keep him silent?'

'That appears to be a reasonable assumption. The pictures of Sarah are the last on the film. They killed him and took his camera. Unfortunately for them, he had already removed the film and put it in his pocket.'

'Do you think Sarah knows?'

'About his death? Probably not. The daughter of the Home Secretary may have a reputation for moral lassitude, but not for terrorism or murder.'

The minister shook his head.

'The silly bitch. She may be reaping wild oats, but she should be more selective. Perhaps it's the whiff of danger that excites her. Do you think she knows who this Capaldi fellow is?'

'Again, probably not. She may suspect he is a high-class crook. It's possibly as you say. The whiff of danger.'

'My God. I wish she'd settle for something more acceptable. Like rape by Afghan tribesmen. If this gets out, it will ruin her father.' He chewed the inside of his mouth. 'Wouldn't do the Government much good, either.'

Rossington-Hall could understand Selwyn's concern for

21

the Government, but knew his solicitude for Reginald Mottram, the Home Secretary, was less than sincere. The two had always been rivals and both still had their eyes on the premiership of the country. In other circumstances, he suspected, Selwyn would be delighted with the news.

The element that tainted the delight was Selwyn's own involvement. He would need guidance as to what action to authorize, which was exactly what Rossington-Hall was prepared to give.

'You can understand, Minister, the sensitivity of the situation. The possible consequences. Mrs Mathieson could be used unwittingly or become the target for blackmail. We had no wish to present this to the Joint Intelligence Committee or the Permanent Secretaries Committee. The fewer who know about it, the easier it will be to contain. But as it involves the daughter of a member of the inner cabinet, it was deemed essential that certain discreet channels be pursued. We feel the PM should be warned, but, of course, we leave the extent of the warning to you.'

Selwyn nodded sagely. Obviously he was balancing the benefits of the information that could remove his colleague permanently from contention to high office, against the dangers of possessing it.

Rossington-Hall added another consideration.

'There is also the question of whether or not the Home Secretary should be informed.'

The statement caused Selwyn to look at the Deputy Director with eyes that widened despite his media training. Then he dropped his gaze to search the photograph for an answer. He garumphed to clear his throat, but still said nothing. Eventually he began to tap the table-top with the forefinger of his right hand, but Rossington-Hall still didn't help. He was enjoying the indecision. At last Selwyn looked up.

'Well?'

'We would advise not doing so. The Home Secretary might be tempted to resolve the situation himself. That would be understandable, but it would impede our efforts to minimize any damage. It is in the national interest that he is not told. With good fortune, he may never need to be told.'

The politician nodded again.

'How do you suggest the damage be minimized?'

'We discover the extent of Sarah Mathieson's involvement with Aldo Capaldi and then we have a discreet chat with her and persuade her to relinquish the relationship. Capaldi and his associates will also need persuading that it is over. We must assume that there may be such things as audio and video tapes, photographs and letters that will need clearing up. Of course, the relationship may have been fleeting, purely sexual and politically innocent. The murder of Mr Brady suggests otherwise.'

'All right. We assume the worst. Can you do all that clearing up?'

'There is a possibility it can be done, but there are too many imponderables to project a success-failure ratio.'

'What?'

'We don't know the odds.'

'Good God, man, that's not very reassuring.'

Rossington-Hall smiled.

'We also have a compromise solution.'

'I don't like the sound of that. Compromise is not a popular word with the PM.'

'This one, I think, will be acceptable, Minister. If we achieve only partial success we pre-empt any scandal by recruiting Mrs Mathieson into the Secret Intelligence Service. A Press leak will ensure maximum positive publicity. We let it be known she has been working undercover for Six in a bid to infiltrate European terror groups.'

The minister looked startled.

'Would it work?'

'Of course. The Press love a beautiful heroine. And the fact that her position will have been compromised by the publicity, means she can be honourably discharged from service. Everyone's reputation will be safe and only a select few, including you and the PM, will know the truth.'

He could tell the minister liked it. The best of both worlds were on offer. He could quietly ruin a rival's career and take credit for turning a possible national disaster into a popularity coup for his party.

'Whatever is decided, minister, is, of course, totally off the record. In a need-to-know situation of this kind, no-one need know anything. This meeting has not been minuted. This conversation has not taken place. But your guidance is necessary.'

The Deputy Director picked up the photograph and replaced it in the envelope, thus removing the only item that linked their collusion.

Selwyn began to regain his public poise as he assessed his position and found it satisfactory. He stood up, his chair scraping on the bare boards, and placed his left hand on his briefcase. Rossington-Hall followed his example and got to his feet neatly, placing the chair backwards so that it made no noise.

'It's been a pleasure, as always, Hector.' Selwyn smiled and stretched a hand across the table. Rossington-Hall took it. It was still sweaty. 'You know you have my full confidence.'

The minister relinquished his hand and the small man let it drop to his side. He disliked fat people on principle and fat people who sweated even more so. He surreptitiously wiped his palm on his thigh.

'Thank you, minister.'

'You'll keep me informed?'

'At the appropriate time, minister.' When it was all over, minister.

Selwyn hesitated at the door.

'This Capaldi fellow. He'll need quite a bit of persuading, won't he?'

'Quite a bit.'

'Do we have the right chaps to do it? Discreetly?'

'Yes, minister. We have chaps of all persuasions.'

The minister nodded, chuckled and left the room.

Chapter 3

Peter Lacey lit another Gitanes and wondered why trouble always came on Friday afternoons.

The weekend had been carefully planned. He and Susan were to drive to the coast the next day for two nights in a quiet hotel. They had booked a room with a view and a double bed, and he was looking forward to a break with no other distraction than his wife. But that had been before the telephone call from HRH.

At least he hadn't been asked to go to Century House for the briefing. The headquarters of The Firm was a place he avoided at all costs these days. Neither his face nor his old school tie had ever fitted during the time he spent there pursuing a non-career. He had been the spare part that was always sent on the assessment assignments no-one else wanted. The most he had ever achieved was the nickname Oddjob.

The Deputy Director General was the man who had sent him to D14a, an unlisted department that occupied the top third floor of a Victorian office block in Charing Cross Road. 'It's a small section; they're all misfits,' he had said. Lacey knew HRH had meant it to be banishment. He had taken delight in thriving and gaining promotion.

The section was self-contained with security provided by retired gentlemen from the SAS who manned the electronically-operated entrance. Eddie, whose expressionless face hid the torment and unpredictability of recurring haemorrhoids, was duty man until eight every evening. Lacey knew better than to attempt to engage him in conversation, unless he was interested in learning desert survival techniques that included drinking his own urine.

25

He had learned the SAS were an earthy lot with a sense of humour all their own, that usually involved death or bodily functions.

Most of the others had gone home. Malcolm, the self-confessed asexual, to his cats in Bow; animals whose habits Malcolm was beginning to acquire in late middle age. He was precise, arrogant and detached, all qualities that made him a perfect analyst, although Lacey kept expecting to find him licking himself clean after the tuna fish sandwiches he invariably had for lunch.

Natalie was also a good analyst, although it had taken Lacey time to accept that someone so beautiful could be so intelligent. He had been relieved to discover that her intellect had proved a barrier to sexual attraction. Instead, she frightened him. She had left early too, but he couldn't imagine why.

A weekend of erotic delight seemed unlikely. She appeared to be more interested in facts and figures, pros and cons, probability flows and converse effects. He couldn't imagine her having a boyfriend. An IBM memory bank, maybe, but not a boyfriend.

Even Harry Ryburn had abandoned his computers and headed home to his wife and kids. It was not like Harry. His computers meant everything to him, but Mrs Ryburn was expecting again and about ready to drop and duty had dragged him away. He had gone reluctantly, muttering excuses to his machines as if they were his mistresses.

The only occupant of the general office was Roland Devere, twenty-seven, handsome, public school and a funny name. He was a newcomer to the department and represented most things Lacey didn't like. Being six feet two, for instance, having the right accent, and being twenty years younger than Lacey. Being blond, indifferent and totally self-assured. He would have classified him as an upper-class prat except that he, too, had to be a misfit. He knew Devere had entered the Secret Intelligence Service from the Army, but he didn't know what he had done to be sent here and he hadn't asked.

26

Lacey passed the time by filling his office with tobacco smoke. Everybody in the general office were non-smokers and let him know it. Personal relations had been difficult until he had been made deputy section head and acquired the spare room.

It was big enough for a swivel chair, desk, two hard-back chairs and a large ashtray. There was also a small filing cabinet behind him which contained a bottle of Jim Beam sourmash bourbon and two glasses. He kept it there to remind himself he didn't need it any more.

Eddie buzzed him.

'The boss is on his way up.'

'When he gets here, make the bastard show his identity.'

Eddie would be watching the progress of the Deputy Director on closed-circuit television. Cameras monitored the second floor as well as the landing outside their suite of offices.

'I can't do that, Mr Lacey. He'll have me guts.'

'Go on, Eddie. Prove you've got a sense of humour. I thought you hooligans were frightened of nothing.'

Lacey knew that Rossington-Hall was a fastidious man. He waited until he heard the inner door of the office open before he lit another cigarette and put his feet on the desk. On the executive floor at Century House the Deputy DG could ban smoking to his heart's content. But here, he was on Lacey's turf.

He heard Devere say, 'He's in there.'

The door opened and Rossington-Hall looked round it.

'Lacey,' he said.

Lacey smiled, removed his feet and stood up slowly.

'Sir,' he said.

Neither offered to shake hands.

Rossington-Hall glanced round the room dismissively before placing his briefcase on top of the desk. He sat down. His mood was brittle. Lacey resumed his own seat, but this time he didn't put his feet up.

The Deputy DG opened the briefcase without speaking and took from it a plain brown folder. He closed the briefcase and placed it on the floor beside him and weighed the folder in his hand. Finally he threw it across the desk to Lacey.

'Bryson still away?'

Lacey renewed his smile. The little bastard knew very well that the section head was away. The comment was meant to convey disappointment at having to deal with him.

'For two weeks.'

He let the file lie in front of him until Rossington-Hall explained it.

'It's baby sitting and retrieval,' he said, and folded his arms. 'It's all there, including a briefing paper on what is required of you. You'll run the operation with minimal fuss. I want no waves, particularly ones that might cross the pond. The Americans may be informed of it later. They may not. Ideally, they will not need to be informed.'

'Who's the baby?'

'Sarah Mathieson. She has been rather . . . indiscreet.'

'Who with?'

'Aldo Capaldi.'

It was a sizeable indiscretion. Lacey knew Capaldi as an assassin who hired out his talents to those terror groups who were willing to pay.

'Where's Capaldi now?'

'Last seen in Vienna.'

'Has he been working recently?'

'Nothing definite. His last job was probably eleven months ago. The American service bus that was blown up in Frankfurt. A Jihad group took the credit, but they had at least two European professionals in the team.'

'What about possibles?'

'None. The only recent activity in Europe has been caused by Red Dawn. They're another Red Brigade splinter, the sort who do their own dirty work. They wouldn't hire a freelance. It would be against their principles.'

'What was Capaldi doing in Vienna?'

'Sarah Mathieson, presumably. Beyond that, we don't know. Requests for information about his present location have been made, to our own people abroad, as well as allies. In itself, that shouldn't raise eyebrows. He's known. People like to keep track of him, even when they haven't got the evidence to arrest him. He crops up from time to time in Paris, the Côte d'Azur, Amsterdam.' He shrugged. 'All traffic will be diverted here, but there are two possible leads: a former mistress in Izmir, Turkey, and an old friend who runs a bar in Arras, France.'

'You want him removed?'

Rossington-Hall pursed his lips and chose his words with care.

'We would like his discretion to be guaranteed.'

The terminology made Lacey smile.

'And what do you want retrieved?'

'Anything that could prove embarrassing.'

Lacey opened the file and took out black and white photographs of Sarah Mathieson and Capaldi together. They were night-time street scenes.

'Who took the snaps?'

'A British journalist.'

'Who's going to guarantee his discretion?'

'That's already taken care of.'

The finality of the tone made Lacey look up.

'What do you mean?'

'He's dead. It's in the file.'

'Who killed him?'

'We believe Capaldi killed him.'

'Because . . . ?' Lacey held up the pictures.

'Yes. It's in the file.'

The death gave a new emphasis to a mission that the pompous little prick had described simply as baby sitting and retrieval. Whatever relationship Capaldi had with Sarah Mathieson, he had been prepared to kill to keep it secret, and assassins only practised their profession for money or a very good reason.

Was Rossington-Hall aware of all this, Lacey wondered, or was he playing it down on purpose?

'If we wait for a sighting of Capaldi, we could wait a long time,' Lacey said. 'Sarah Mathieson is a better bet.'

'Quite so.'

'Where is she?'

'Back in Britain.'

'When can I have her?'

'Monday morning. She's out of town for the weekend.'

'Does she live alone?'

'Yes. She has a house near the river in Wapping.'

'Can we send the plumbers in while she's away?'

'No. That could be embarrassing. A telephone intercept would have to be authorized by her father, the Home Secretary. At the moment, we don't want him to know what's happening.'

Lacey shook his head.

'If we're to do the job right, we need the place bugged and the phone tapped.'

'So ask her. Then you won't need authorization. I'm sure she'll co-operate.'

'What makes you think that?'

Rossington-Hall uncrossed one leg, smoothed his trouser crease, and crossed the other.

'We view Sarah Mathieson's . . . dalliance . . . with extreme seriousness, but we do not see her as a major threat to the western world. She has been stupid, she needs chastising, and the mess she has made needs cleaning up. There is no reason for her not to co-operate, and every reason that she should do so.'

Lacey took a final drag on his cigarette before leaning forward to stub it out.

'What time scale are we on?'

'Obviously, we would like the matter dealing with as quickly as possible, but we don't envisage it causing immediate problems. In any case, we will be providing a cover story that will mitigate any damage if Capaldi makes anything public.'

'Mitigate damage?'

'Yes.'

'You mean damage as in bad publicity?'

'Yes.'

'As opposed to damage as in national security?'

'Don't try to annoy me, Lacey. She may be a lot of things, but it's doubtful she's a traitor.'

'So what is she?'

'As from Monday, she's an SIS operative who has just completed an undercover mission in Europe.'

Lacey laughed and sat back in his chair.

'What if she's not just screwed Capaldi? What if she's sold her country?'

'That's highly unlikely, although it has to be considered, of course. Her family, her background, are impeccable. She went to Benenden.'

'Anthony Blunt was keeper of the Queen's pictures.'

'Don't be facetious, Lacey.'

'I'm not. I'm being realistic.'

'You're talking about a breed of traitor that no longer exists. Blunt, and the rest, were 1930s' intellectuals who saw Soviet socialism as the only hope against fascism. Sarah Mathieson grew up in the sixties, and she's hardly intellectual. Her opinions were formed in swinging London, not meetings of the Comintern. She became a hedonist, not a communist.'

'But if . . . ?'

'If!' Rossington-Hall's interruption was incisive. 'If she has been foolish, we'll deal with it with minimum embarrassment.'

'Another free pardon for silence?'

Rossington-Hall's voice dropped several degrees. The brittleness became ice sharp.

'You never know when you've gone too far, do you, Lacey? It's a lack of class. One of these days, that chip of yours is going to break your back. I'm not trying to save a traitor. I'm trying to save the country from scoring an own goal. I'm the one who's dealing in realities rather than looking for victims to stamp on.'

He uncrossed his legs and picked up his briefcase before

adding: 'All you need to know is in the file, including a number where you can reach me over the weekend. Arrange a safe house and call me on Sunday night. You can have Sarah Mathieson on Monday morning. Nine o'clock, the coffee shop at the Scratchwood service station on the M1.'

The Deputy Director stood in readiness to leave, and looked on the desk to see if he had left anything. Lacey remained seated.

'How do you know Sarah will still be in the country on Monday?'

The small man stared down at Lacey, as if in challenge. His eyes didn't blink.

'Because I'm spending the weekend with her. We're attending the same house party. Can you think of anything more secure?'

Lacey shook his head in disbelief at Rossington-Hall, who smirked as if he'd won a debating blue at Cambridge.

Sarah Mathieson would wait until Monday, and she would be safe enough, and HRH would continue to make all the right career moves towards an early knighthood.

Rossington-Hall was probably right. Lacey was well out of his class, and happy to be so.

Chapter 4

Lacey would have been the first to admit that Brighton was a less-than-original choice for a weekend away with a married woman, even though the married woman was his wife. But it was accessible, it had sea walks and it had hotels that breathed discretion.

'They'll think we're having a dirty weekend,' Susan had said, when he had told her their destination.

Lacey had chuckled.

'They won't be far wrong.'

'Don't be awful.' Susan had punched him. 'Where did the romance go?'

'Oh, it's still there.'

It was, too, and it was still a surprise to him, to them both, although he couldn't remember, with honesty, whether they had ever indulged in romance, even at the start. Their courtship at university had been built around little money and lots of sex. Looking back, it would be easy to confuse lust and love, and view it all as very romantic.

They had been compatible because they had enjoyed each other physically, Susan had the social graces to which he had aspired, and she had confused him with the strong and silent type upon whom she wished to rely. Marriage had followed because her father died.

He couldn't even remember if they had tried to make their marriage work at the beginning. Like most young people, they hadn't thought effort was necessary.

At first, they had survived on youthful enthusiasm and a decent income, but when that palled they had dropped into suburban role playing. It had suited Susan's sense of respectability, but he hadn't acknowledged his own reasons until recently. At the time, he had discovered his career was destined to go nowhere. The last thing he had needed was to be faced with another failure at home.

They had cohabited more as a social exercise than as a relationship, and his frequent trips abroad on courier and relief assignment had helped. Periods of absence didn't make the heart grow fonder, but it saved them from domestic bickering and it rekindled passion, if only for a few days, each time he returned.

His sideways move from Century House cog to covert operations had been the catalyst that had revived something that perhaps they had never really had.

Violent events had made them face up to what their lives had become and they had decided upon one last attempt at making their marriage work. In the process they had fallen in love. Not a singing-in-the-rain sort of love, but a mature passion. They could still get on each other's nerves, but were now sensitive to the fact. More than anything, they were finally at ease with each other instead of at odds. They had started out trying and ended up caring. Perhaps maturity was the key; perhaps they had grown up.

The occasional weekend trips were part of the process of ensuring they continued to make the effort. They were meant to be total escapes from the office, Susan's shop and business partner, and any social commitment that might sneak up on them unawares. The trips worked, and they both looked forward to them.

Lacey picked Susan up from the shop in Bromley at three o'clock. The window was well stocked with bric-à-brac that her partner, Lucy, called antiques, but the interior was bereft of customers. Susan was watching out for him, so that his visit to the shop would be as brief as possible. It wasn't that he had anything against elephant-foot umbrella-stands, just that Lucy didn't approve of him. But that was all right; he didn't approve of her, either.

Lucy was a self-proclaimed liberated wife who was trapped in a pink boilersuit time-warp. For her, reality was still a polytechnic summer in the 1970s. She was married to a bearded English teacher and their two offspring were being brought up by a child-minder so she could concentrate on personal fulfilment, although what fulfilment she got from a shop full of high-priced tat, he couldn't see.

She was sitting on the high stool in the office at the back of the shop, when he opened the door. The jangle of the bell made her lower the *Guardian* to look at him. She smiled at him mechanically, but he didn't bother. They exchanged brief greetings and he noticed her moustache was getting heavier. Susan grabbed her handbag and made a quick exit.

'I'm always on edge when you two are in the same room,' she said, as they walked to the car.

'There's no need. I wouldn't dream of rattling her cage.'

Susan didn't laugh.

'Actually, she's going through a bad time.'

'Not pregnant again?'

'No.'

He knew she was exasperated because he wasn't being serious, but Lucy-baiting was one of life's pleasures.

'Well, she looks pregnant. She always looks pregnant.'

'Peter!'

He gave her a lop-sided grin by way of apology.

'All right. What's wrong?'

'Michael is thinking of leaving her.'

'Michael?' He hadn't thought he'd have the gumption. 'But what about their two point three Tobias and Tabatha? Who gets custody of the Great Dane?'

'It's not a joke. She's quietly devastated.'

'How can you be *quietly* devastated?'

'You know what I mean.'

He opened the car door for her and watched appreciatively as she swung her long legs into the front.

'Maybe if she didn't look pregnant all the time. Maybe if she tried shaving. Maybe . . .'

Susan slammed the door to shut him up and he grinned and walked round to the driver's side.

They drove in silence while he negotiated a roundabout and nosed out towards an open road.

'You said *thinking* of leaving. He might well have been thinking about it a long time, but it's not something you drop into conversation over the cornflakes. Why hasn't he done it? Why hasn't liberated Lucy kicked him out for thinking about it?'

'It's not as easy as that.'

'It never is. But why declare something that might not happen? Is he hoping the child-minder will arbitrate?' He gave her a quick look. 'It's not the child-minder he fancies, is it?'

'Good God, no. Have you seen her?'

'Anything would be an improvement.'

'Lucy's not that bad—'

'Yes, she is.'

'—anyway, she's supposed to be my friend.'

'No, she isn't. She's your business partner.'

'She thinks I'm her friend.'

'That's because she doesn't have any.'

'She says she has lots.'

'Contradiction in terms.'

'I still feel a certain responsibility towards her.'

'Why?'

'Because I work with her; that's a sort of closeness. Because she's a woman, because I've been through it—'

'Not the same.'

'—because she's got nobody else.' She shrugged. 'Probably because she's so helpless.'

Lacey softened and placed a hand on her knee.

'I'm sorry.'

He was sorry at being unsympathetic for Susan's sake, not Lucy's, but his hand of sympathy began to develop into something else.

'Stop it.'

She laughed and pushed her skirt back down.

'Well, we *are* going to Brighton.'

'Wait until we get there.'

36

He concentrated on driving and tried to put Lucy's problems out of his mind. If divorce did happen she was the sort who would adjust her attitudes accordingly, change the child-minder's hours and get on with personal fulfilment. The breakdown would be her husband's fault, she would feel no guilt and probably have no further need for male company. She had been fertilized twice and that no doubt had been enough. She had had children, perhaps now she would take up night classes and learn another skill.

His own experience of relationships had made him aware of how complex they could be, with infinite levels of understanding and commitment. Many marriages started as superficial and ended the same way. Some simply survived and a few grew and developed. God knows how Lucy's had started out, but it was no surprise it had floundered and no surprise that her situation evoked no compassion. Whatever compassion he had, he saved for those who tried, like that poor sod Jim Brady, the photographer, who had been killed in Vienna.

He had read the file last night and again this morning and it was Brady who had stayed in his mind.

The other players had chosen their roles. Sarah Mathieson, a spoiled rich brat from birth, enjoyed screwing around the world, and Aldo Capaldi, son of a wealthy Roman lawyer, had opted for murder rather than the family business.

By contrast, Brady had been the innocent who had walked into accidental death, because he took a photograph of the wrong people, at the wrong time, in the wrong place. He had been in Vienna only because that was where he and his wife had spent holidays of escape, much like the weekend trip to Brighton being taken by Lacey and Susan.

The photographer had not been the most prepossessing of men and there had probably been occasions when he had made himself totally offensive in the course of doing his job. But among the possessions found at his hotel was a

37

diary he had written to his dead wife. In it, Brady had told her where he had been and the concerts he had attended, and he had recalled memories they both had shared. The diary would have caused him terrible embarrassment if it had been found while he was alive. In death, it became a touching memorial.

Lacey had to be unsentimental when working on assessments or in the field, but the diary had affected him. About the only thing the fat photographer had had going for him during his lifetime was a love affair with a woman called Sheila. It had survived her cancer and death. Lucy's couldn't survive a seven-year itch. Was there any wonder he felt less than devastated about her predicament and more determined than ever to work to protect what he and Susan had?

He touched Susan's knee again, in companionship, and she covered his hand with her own, and he counted the miles to Brighton.

Chapter 5

Dan Beckindale nursed a Scotch on the rocks and tried unsuccessfully to melt into the background. At six feet two, eyes of blue and a parade-ground stance, it was difficult.

He felt conspicuous in black tie and patent leather shoes and would have preferred combat fatigues and camouflage paint. He would also have preferred the jungles of Nam or Grenada and all the acceptable dangers that were to be found there, to the acres of carpet, overstuffed furniture and overstuffed people that now faced him.

It was a minefield of small talk and social niceties that he had to survive without making embarrassing gaffes. He avoided this sort of gathering back in Washington, but had been unable to duck this one in the heart of rural England. This one was necessary because of the guest list.

The small man in the well-cut dinner suit who strutted like a turkeycock spotted him and came over.

'Ah, Beckindale. Daniel, isn't it?'

'Only on Sunday, sir.'

'I beg your pardon?'

'I'm usually known as Dan.'

Rossington-Hall forced a laugh.

'Of course. And never mind the sir. Call me Hector.' He took a sip from the sherry glass he held. 'You're the new boy at Grosvenor Square?'

The small man had to look up to speak to Beckindale and he adopted a pose of putting his head on one side, which made him look like a sulking budgerigar.

'I've been there two months.'

'Yes. First visit to London?'

'No.' Beckindale knew they were going through

39

formalities, but these were the polite sort of moves that forged useful aquaintanceships. 'I met my wife here. In seventy five.'

'You married an English girl?'

'She was American. She worked at the embassy. I was here for three weeks.' He smiled at the memory, despite himself. 'I guess it was what you would call a whirlwind romance.'

Rossington-Hall frowned.

'You used the past tense, old boy. I don't wish to pry, but . . . ?'

'That's OK. I lost her in an accident.' He shrugged and pulled the shutter down to close his mind and his face. 'One of those things.'

'Oh, I say. I'm terribly sorry. Forgive me.'

'It was a long time ago.'

The small man nodded in sympathy and then turned to survey the other people in the room, as if looking for something else to talk about.

'Do you know many people here?'

'I've met Melvyn Crawshaw before.'

'Of course. Crawshaw.' Rossington-Hall spotted his opposite number from Five across the room. 'Well, you'll find the rest of them a mixed bag. One or two can drone on a bit, but most have redeeming qualities.' He smiled. 'But they wouldn't be here if they hadn't. Do you have your sights set on anybody in particular? Anyone I can guide you towards?' He indicated groups with his glass. 'The Honourable Nigel Wilkins from the Ministry of Defence, James Weldon, Leader of the Opposition?'

Two women entered the room, one laughing loud enough to suggest a pre-dinner drink too many, and took their attention.

'Ah.' Rossington-Hall's enunciation was cautionary. 'Now there's one honourable I would advise handling with care. The Honourable Felicity is between husbands. Without being unchivalrous, she would have done well in Greek mythology, enticing boatloads of sailors to a fate worse than death. In fact it's rumoured she has. Now the other lady . . .'

'The other lady I know. Sarah was a friend of my wife's.'

'Ah . . .'

Beckindale thought that for someone who was supposed to be a senior member of Britain's Secret Intelligence Service, Rossington-Hall talked too much. Or maybe he was trying too hard to be friendly.

The Honourable Felicity joined the Junior Defence Minister; Sarah Mathieson continued across the room towards them. She wore her black hair pulled away from her face and piled high on her head, a style that accentuated the strength of her features. Her dress was black silk, cut in a simple classic style, that gave her body fluidity and enhanced her natural elegance.

'Sarah.' Rossington-Hall called his greeting while she was still yards away. 'You look charming, as ever.'

'Hector.' She gave him a smile that was gushing and false and turned her attention to Beckindale, taking his free hand in her's. 'And Colonel Beckindale.'

'Hello, Sarah.'

'You two are old friends, I believe?' said Rossington-Hall.

'Yes.' She continued to gaze up into the American's face. 'We've known each other a long time.' Then she chuckled and looked at the smaller man, using him as an audience. 'Do you know what they called him in the Army? Captain America. The All-American hero.' She looked back at Beckindale. 'Do they still call you that in Washington?'

'Not in Washington. Not many people know my name in Washington.'

'Just the ones at the top? The ones that matter?'

He smiled, tolerantly.

'I'm not that important, Sarah. I just do my job.'

Rossington-Hall said, 'Look. You two probably have things to talk about.' He pointed across the room. 'I'll

41

mingle. Leave you to it. Talk to you later, old boy.'

'Fine. Thank you.' He looked back at Sarah and wondered why her eyes sparkled so much. He retrieved his hand and put it behind his back, out of harm's way. 'What are you on, Sarah?'

She pouted and glanced around in an exaggerated pretence at secrecy.

'Colonel, what on earth do you mean?'

'You know what I mean. And you know it's not good for you.'

She poked him in the chest with a finger.

'A little snort never hurt anybody. Anyway, it's essential for gatherings like this. I only come to keep Felicity company. Have you met Felicity? She's your hostess with the mostest. If you're a good boy, she'll probably show you most of it later on. After reveille. Or is it the Last Post?'

'Sarah. It's not good seeing you like this.'

'Oh, loosen up. I'm fine. Just taking the piss out of your moral rearmament.' She shed the flightiness and appeared in total control of herself. 'I'll even introduce you to the old duffers and then discreetly excuse myself so you can swop secrets. And I'll hold your hand at dinner.' She grinned again, teasingly. 'Show you which knife and fork to use.'

'I know which knife and fork to use.'

'Then you can show me, if I have too much to drink.'

'I'm here on business. I don't have time to nursemaid.'

'You're too serious by far. Life goes on, you know. You should try it, sometime.'

He looked straight into her eyes.

'You recommend it?'

The cutting edge of his voice bridled her.

'Don't be pompous.'

'Then stop being a fool.'

'A fool?' She gave him a quizzical look. 'I suppose I am, for thinking you might change. But you haven't. You always were a soldier, weren't you, Dan? Always full of spit and polish and bullshit. Always were, always will be. It's a hell of an excuse for a life.'

'It's my job.'

'And is it all you need?'

'Yes.'

Sarah opened a black evening bag and took out a gold cigarette case and lighter. She put a black Sobranie cigarette into her mouth and lit it, and blew the smoke into his face.

'I feel sorry for you, Dan. It must be terrible to be that empty.'

He smiled.

'You should know, Sarah.'

They continued to stare at each other until the Honourable Felicity was suddenly between them.

'Sarah, darling, stop trying to hide this delicious hunk of manhood and introduce me.'

She was in her late thirties, an English blonde with pale complexion and delicate features. The *décolletage* of her blue dress just about contained her bosom. Her face was upturned towards his, her eyes flashing and lips making coy promises.

Beckindale smiled politely and, as Sarah made the introduction, proffered his hand. She took it as if it were a gift and held it tight, her finger scratching, almost absent-mindedly, in his palm.

Rossington-Hall had not been unchivalrous, after all. Perhaps for staging these select house parties, she was allowed to choose her own spot prize.

'You're wasting your time, Felicity. He's only interested in God, one indivisible people and the star-spangled banner.'

'I don't mind. I'll wear a star-spangled banner.'

Beckindale couldn't tell if the Honourable Felicity was for real or playing games.

'You've got a beautiful home,' he said.

'I've got a beautiful everything. Why don't I show you? Later.'

Sarah laughed and Beckindale smiled.

'I don't get much free time, I'm afraid.'

43

'Oh, don't be afraid. I won't bite. Unless you want me to. And then only in places that won't show.' She flashed her eyes and made him chuckle. 'The night is young and there are no group activities planned between midnight and seven. Only grope activities.'

'It's no use, Felicity.' Sarah had regained her good humour. 'The last time I propositioned him he said he was going to bed with the good book. I thought he meant Jeffrey Archer. He meant the Bible.'

'Ooh. But I never could resist a challenge.' Felicity released his hand to feel the muscles of his forearm. She looked at him wistfully. 'Confession, you know, is really very good for the soul. Think what you could confess in the morning? Your soul would glow with righteousness. Afterwards.'

'It sounds like a neat idea, but I have to say no.' He grinned at her. 'Regulations stipulate no fraternization.'

'Told you,' said Sarah. 'His second purple heart was for celibacy.'

'Oh dear, what a shame.' Felicity finally let go of him. 'I'm sure it would have been so stimulating.' She glanced around the room. 'I suppose I should go and try somebody else. It is, after all, one's duty to fulfil the expectations of one's guests.' She flashed him a smile between themselves.

'Hector's free,' Sarah said.

'Hector's a little shit. There are occasions when one means it.' She gripped Beckindale's arm briefly. 'And occasions when the little shits of this world think you mean it. Who's that bald-headed man that looks like a walrus?'

'Cyril . . . something. Foreign Office.'

'I've never had a Cyril and I'm not sure I want to start now. It's such a non-name, don't you think? But then, I've never had a walrus, either. Do you think he'd have to do it in the bath? Excuse me, Colonel. It's show time. But if you change your mind . . . ?'

'I'll tell you.'

The Honourable Felicity headed off towards another victim.

'I like her,' Beckindale said.

'You amaze me.'

'Why? She's fun. She doesn't take herself seriously.'

'Meaning I do?'

'I've never seen anybody chase excitement with such intensity as you do, Sarah.'

She smoked her cigarette and they stood in silence for a few moments.

'Perhaps we can talk later?' she said.

'Maybe we should.'

'Without lectures?'

'Without lectures.'

'Captain America to the rescue again.'

'I do my best.'

She took his hand.

'Come on. I'll introduce you to Jim Weldon before dinner.'

Chapter 6

Franz Haber had always regretted the time and place of his birth. The year had been 1948 and the city, Munich.

True, Munich was the capital of Bavaria, it was beautiful and it had a heritage of art, architecture, festivals and music. True, it had provided the incentive to develop his own talent, and it was also true, that its citizens had lauded him with honours.

But if he had had the chance to choose the particulars of his birth, the time would have been the late eighteenth century and the place, Vienna.

Haber's artistry as a concert pianist had won him acclaim and riches. He had played the capitals of the world, from New York to Moscow; he travelled first class; he had reached an audience of millions through radio, television and records.

But he would have exchanged all his modern fame and fortune to have been alive in this city, when Mozart, Beethoven, Schubert and Haydn had all lived here, breathed its air, walked in its parks and composed their music.

If he ever retired, it would be to Vienna, to forget the discipline of touring and dieting, and to wallow in the indulgences of pastries and abundant good music.

He strolled in the Stadt-park every day when he was here, in the early morning when it was still quiet. The mornings and the evenings, he had long ago decided, were the interesting parts of the day. Dawns and dusks were dramas to be enjoyed. The lame middle period of afternoons was for sleeping. It was pleasant to be able to set his own rules.

The sun was bright, even though it was before seven o'clock, but it lacked warmth and he wore a cashmere scarf with his light overcoat when he left the Imperial on the Kärntner Ring and headed east. The Imperial always put him in a good mood. Its marble corridors held the memory of such illustrious guests of the past as Wagner and Sarah Bernhardt, and the possibility of bumping into such guests of the present as Placido Domingo or Luciano Pavarotti, while directly behind it was the Musikverein concert hall where he was to appear that night. It was a fitting hotel with old world style. He wore in his lapel the red rose the waiter had brought with his breakfast.

He strode into the Schubert-Ring, alone with his thoughts but for a personal assistant in a dark suit and dark glasses who walked ten paces behind.

Haber was built like a tenor and was prone to put on weight like one. His marketing agent had told him that being bulky was acceptable, even masculine, but being gross would affect the public image that had made him such a saleable commodity and a welcome chat-show guest on four continents. Diet was important.

He had a home near Munich for family reasons, a second home in New York for business reasons, and a third home on the Costa del Sol for no reason except that he liked the sunshine. His wife and three children lived mainly in Germany, although they sojourned during the holidays at the villa in Spain.

Times had changed since he had struggled for scholarships as a student and been too poor to ask girls out. Now he had money, the power that money brought, and the celebrity profile that attracted female admirers.

He had a personal manager who toured with him to watch what he ate and guard against scandal, a business manager in the United States, a financial adviser in Geneva, an artistic producer, a publicity agent and a musical arranger.

They all took a percentage. They all looked to him for at least part of their living. They were leeches to his talent, eating at it, encouraging him to dilute it by performing work designed to appeal to an even cruder mass market. He needed Vienna to recharge his soul.

Haber entered the Stadt-park and made for the statue of Johann Strauss the Younger. He would pay his respects at the shrines of the other composers in the park later. He walked leisurely along the curving path, enjoying being alone. The mild spring had caused the trees and shrubs to bud and filled him with optimism. The statue came in sight, a delicate bronze Strauss playing his violin within an arbour of white marble.

As always, Haber climbed the grass bank and the three steps that brought him close to the monument. As always, he removed the red rose from his lapel and placed it at the feet of the statue.

Yes, he would exchange it all for a different age, a different challenge. The time of Mozart, or, later, when Brahms, Mahler, and the Strauss family were composing, conducting, playing. How would he have made out then? How would his talent have been assessed by the greats?

The sound of the motor cycle intruded into his daydreams. At first he dismissed it, waited for it to fade away along the main road, but it didn't.

God! It was in the park and coming this way.

The realization angered him and he turned to face the path from where the noise grew louder. He inflated his chest and prepared for a verbal battle with the young hooligan responsible, and, perhaps, even a physical exchange to force home a lesson of respect and reverence for the park's memories and solitude, as well as in retribution for totally disrupting his own meditation.

Haber sensed that his personal assistant was moving closer in support and he looked forward to pressing his point.

The engine of the motor cycle revved and came into sight from the direction of the Kursalon, the open-air concert pavilion.

The rider drove his machine slowly round the path and

stopped just ten yards away. He wore a tan suit that had been cut to perfection, a cream shirt and burgundy tie. His socks, that showed as he put his feet on the floor on either side of the machine, were cream and looked as if they were silk, his shoes were soft brown leather and very expensive.

The concert pianist, who lived with luxury, noticed all these things in the two or three seconds they faced each other, and he realized they were not the clothes of the sort of lout he had been expecting.

He stared at the black crash-helmet, trying to see beyond the smoked glass of the visor, to judge the age of the rider, but all he could see were the reflections of the trees.

'Herr Haber . . .'

His personal assistant moved on to the grass verge and raised his hand in a gesture that urged caution but Haber, bolstered by years of self-importance, refused to be intimidated.

'You there!' he shouted. 'What do you think you are doing?'

The rider didn't reply. His left hand revved the engine, his right moved inside his jacket, as if to scratch his armpit.

'You oaf!'

Haber took a step forward and the rider removed his hand from beneath the jacket. It held a gun.

The pianist stopped and stared. The situation had changed in a way that was startling and sudden and he didn't know how to react. Fear was a strange experience he had almost forgotten. The gun was an alien item, something he didn't understand and couldn't relate to. It robbed him of will-power.

He didn't know that the gun was a Russian made 9 mm Makarov pistol or that the bullets had been modified to make them dum dums that would explode on impact. He didn't know that it was a favourite weapon of European and Arab terrorists. He only knew that he had to assert himself to stop the situation deteriorating further.

'What . . . ?' he said, but the man in the black visor

didn't let him finish. Instead, he raised the gun, as if he were pointing with it at Haber's head, and fired.

The first bullet hit him full in the face. Parts of his brain splattered over the statue of Johann Strauss the Younger and drops of scarlet blood fell across the white marble plinth in counterpoint to the rose. The second bullet was an assassin's *coup de grâce*, even though it was unnecessary, and was to the heart.

Haber's personal assistant ran along the path and through the shrubs, but the rider ignored him. He put the gun away, revved the engine of the motor cycle, and rode it along the path and across the foot-bridge over the Danube canal.

Franz Haber had been unable to choose the time and place of his birth. He had been unable to choose the time and place of his death, as well. But at least it had been Vienna.

Chapter 7

Breakfast had been nice, but afters had been nicer.

They had eaten in their room, showered and relaxed in towelling robes, with a sea view and a couple of gulls for company on the window-ledge outside. The Sunday papers had been a deterrent to rushing into anything as extravagant as a walk down the Marine Parade, and Lacey had opted to continue browsing through the colour sections while Susan got dressed.

Afterwards, she said he had planned it that way, and he had levelled the same charge at her.

'It was your fault. You knew exactly what you were doing,' he had said.

What she had done was come out of the bathroom ready to face the world with her hair styled and in make-up and high heels. The fact that she had omitted to put on her dress hadn't seemed to bother her; it had bothered Lacey.

She wore grey silk underwear and stockings to match. Lacey never had a chance.

'The older you get, the more you want,' she had whispered, as he had pushed her towards the bed.

'Then we've got more than a pension to look forward to,' he had whispered back.

It was almost noon when they got up for the second time. Lacey lit a Gitanes and walked naked to the window. The gulls, if they were the same ones, flew off.

'You've scared the birds away.'

'I always did.'

'You didn't scare me away.'

He dragged deep on the cigarette and let the tobacco burn his lungs. No, but it had been close. He looked round to smile at her, sitting amidst the rumpled bedclothes in only garter belt and hose.

'I'm glad I didn't.'

He felt guilty that it was this good after all these years. Susan had always been attractive, but she had gained a presence the older she had got. Her figure was still slim, but more rounded these days, and she walked with a poise that made heads turn. At forty, she had become a beautiful woman.

And him? What had he become? Thicker round the waist, more out of condition with each French cigarette, and more cynical about the power games that people played. But at least he made Susan smile, perhaps he made her happy. He hoped so.

He stared out of the window.

'You know, it reminds me of sex,' he said.

'What does?'

'The view.'

'What are you looking at? The pier or the domes on the pavilion?'

He laughed.

'The sea. Crashing waves.'

'Oh.'

'They used to use crashing waves instead of copulation in Hollywood.'

'Then Hollywood would never suit you.'

'That's true.' He finished the cigarette and stubbed it out in the ashtray on the breakfast table. 'Now, how about that walk? It's a lovely day.'

'Do you have the strength?'

'I'll manage, as long as it's only a short walk.'

'And then?'

'A drink or two, a late lunch, and who knows?'

'I do. You'll fall asleep.'

'Before or after?'

'Just as long as it's not during.'

He laughed and went towards the bathroom. The ring of the telephone stopped him.

Susan answered it and then looked at him. Her expression lost its cheerfulness.

'It's for you.'

He took the receiver from her and she climbed off the bed, picked up the items of discarded underwear from the floor, and went back to the bathroom.

'This is Lacey.'

'Have you seen the news?'

It was Rossington-Hall.

'I've seen the morning papers . . .'

'No, I mean *The News*. On television.'

'I haven't been watching television.'

'Franz Haber, the pianist, has been killed. In Vienna.'

Lacey didn't know what was coming, but he knew the weekend was over.

'What circumstances?'

'An assassination.'

'Why? He was famous, but he wasn't John Lennon.'

'I don't know why. But it sounds professional.'

'Coincidence?'

'Possibly. I hope so. But possibly not. We'll have to change our arrangements. The delivery will be this evening.'

'Yes. When?'

'Six o'clock. Same place.'

'Right.'

Rossington-Hall rang off abruptly and Lacey put the phone back in its cradle.

Susan appeared at the door of the bathroom.

'We pack?'

'We pack.'

'Well.' She smiled. 'It was nice while it lasted.'

The Scratchwood Service Area lacked charm even with the sun shining on it from a clear blue sky.

Lacey sat in his car and wondered if there was a special Lego designer school somewhere that all motorway

53

architects attended. He had yet to see any edifying construction related to motorway travel.

Even the people he watched using this one all appeared to be reluctant visitors, driven in by tiredness and lack of choice.

In the old days, before motorways, there had been pubs, roadside teashops, snackbars and transport caffs to pick from. Or was he just remembering it that way from watching too many black and white British films on television?

He stretched and thought about the abandoned weekend. Susan was right. It had been good while it lasted. And at least HRH had shown a sense of timing. An hour earlier would have been most disruptive. He wondered if Rossington Hyphen Hall had a sex life? The man was married, he knew that, but he had never met Mrs Hyphen. Perhaps he should recommend the hotel in Brighton to him, and the lingerie store in Bromley where Susan did her shopping?

The train of thought the idea had started stopped being amusing and became unsavoury. There was no way he could imagine Hector doing it at all.

Now Devere was a different proposition. He imagined that the randy, blond-haired bastard was tomming everything in sight. Another reason to dislike him. No, that was stupid.

He lit a third Gitanes. He didn't know the bloke well enough to dislike him. Blind prejudice had led him to adopt a certain attitude to Devere, he knew that, but his prejudices were comfortable and, he thought, justified. They had been moulded by his experiences of dealing with the ruling class in what was supposed to be a classless society. He would keep his prejudices as protection, until Devere persuaded him otherwise.

Lacey had duplicated the documents Rossington-Hall had given him and presented Devere with a set on Friday night. Duplicating them had been strictly against regulations, but it was one of those small things Lacey liked to do to get his own back on the system. He had also told Devere to set up the safe house and keep himself on stand-by, meaning be available at all times over the weekend.

He had telephoned Devere from Brighton after talking to HRH and they had met at the office in Charing Cross Road. The younger man had given him a set of keys and an address in Twickenham. So far he had done nothing wrong, but this was the first occasion they had worked together. There was plenty of time.

Lacey had also established access to all traffic relating to Haber, using Rossington-Hall's name as authorization, and Natalie had come in to monitor the teleprinters and computers in the absence of Harry Ryburn, who was still waiting for fatherhood for the third time.

It had taken Lacey only a few minutes to scan the first reports on the assassination. They contained the bare facts of the fatal encounter in the park, as related by Haber's personal assistant, but little else. They inferred that it had been a premeditated and professional hit without saying why, although if this was all the Austrian police really had, it could have been a random killing by some bored rich kid. Perhaps at this early stage, and under pressure from the world's Press, they were being cagey.

At quarter to six he left his car and went into the service station coffee shop. He bought a black coffee and took it to the smoking section, even though his throat was too sore for another cigarette.

Rossington-Hall and Sarah Mathieson arrived at five minutes past six. In high heels, she was three or four inches taller than HRH, and led the way into the coffee shop. He waited at the counter to be served, a large brown leather satchel hanging from one shoulder, but she gazed boldly around at the people seated at the tables.

Lacey caught her eye and raised a hand in greeting and she left her small companion and came across. She slid into the plastic seat opposite and stared him in the face. She did not look pleased.

'Are you the person we're supposed to meet?'

'Yes.'

55

'Then shall we go?'

'What about . . . ?' Lacey nodded towards a flustered Rossington-Hall, who now stared about him clutching two cups.

'I've had enough of *him* to last a lifetime. Disgusting little creep.'

'Why?'

'Why what?'

'Why does he disgust you?'

'He gets on my nerves. He's so bloody neat. Do you have a cigarette?'

Lacey produced his Gitanes and she shuddered, but took one. He lit it for her with a match.

'I'm out of cigarettes,' she said.

'There's a shop outside.'

'I've no money and he wouldn't give me any. Do you know, there's a sign in his car that says No Smoking?'

'Why don't you have any money?'

'I don't use it. I use plastic.'

'You can use plastic in the shop.'

'That's not the point. Gentlemen usually offer.' She glared at Rossington-Hall as he finally found them. 'At least, most gentlemen do.'

Rossington-Hall placed two cups of coffee on the table and sat down. He placed the satchel against Lacey's chair.

'I see you two have met.'

'Not formally,' she said. 'You might introduce me to my gaoler.'

'He's hardly that, Sarah. You offered to come.'

She glared at him.

'You left me little choice.'

Rossington-Hall was unfazed by her attitude.

'Quite.' He smiled, a smug stretching of the lips that indicated he was used to leaving people little choice. He made the introduction with a nod of his head. 'This is Peter Lacey. He's the chap who will be asking the questions. We would be obliged if you give him your fullest co-operation.'

Now she had been introduced, she treated Lacey to a full

56

scrutiny. She did not appear to be impressed by his lived-in looks and favourite well-worn leather jacket.

'Can we go now?' she asked him.

'Whenever you like,' Lacey said.

He passed a piece of paper to Rossington-Hall containing the telephone number of the safe house.

'That's where we'll be.'

Sarah Mathieson got up and Lacey followed suit. Rossington-Hall remained seated.

'Don't forget her bag,' he said.

Lacey picked it up as Sarah began striding away and he followed her. She was as tall as him and her long legs covered the ground quickly.

She stopped by the shop and he caught up with her.

'Cigarettes,' she said.

'Plastic,' he said, and as she turned to continue walking to make her point, he added: 'It's going to be a long night. You might need them.'

She stopped again, considered what he had said, and went into the shop.

Lacey went with her and waited while she rowed with the till assistant because they didn't have Black Russian cigarettes. Eventually she settled for a carton of 200 Benson and Hedges and paid with an American Express gold card.

'It's not your day, is it,' Lacey said, as they left the shop and walked to his car. She remained silent until they were on the motorway and heading towards London.

'Where are we going?'

'Somewhere we can talk.'

'How about Le Caprice?'

'How about shutting up until you've got something sensible to say.'

'Oh God, another one.'

'If by that, you mean I'm a disgusting little creep, let me warn you. You don't know yet just how disgusting I can be.'

'Oh dear, you do frighten me. Are you the nasty one

who is going to beat me with a rubber truncheon until I confess?'

'Confess to what?'

'God knows. A bit on the side, I suppose it's called.' She looked round into the back seat, as if searching. 'Anyway, if you're the nasty, where's the nice one?'

Lacey began to wish he'd bought some extra cigarettes himself. It really was going to be a long night.

They reached the end of the motorway and he negotiated the roundabout and headed west on the North Circular.

'Let's start by laying out a few guide-lines.' He tried not to sound antagonistic. 'Like it or not, we're going to be together for some time. Like me or not, it will help us both if we at least try to get on. OK?'

She sighed and looked out of the passenger window. After a few seconds she turned her head forward again and nodded.

'OK.'

'Good. Now, do you want me to call you Sarah or Mrs Mathieson?'

'Christ, I haven't been Mrs Mathieson since my wedding day. Call me Sarah.' She looked at him. 'And I've forgotten your name.'

'It's Peter Lacey.'

'Then I shall call you Lacey.'

'What did Rossington-Hall tell you?'

'Not much. He looked stern and said I'd been associating with the wrong people. Well, wrong person, actually. Aldo Fagioli. He said he was some sort of criminal and asked if I would mind undergoing a debriefing.' She shrugged. 'I may have a reputation – God, I should have, I work hard enough at it – but I'm not thick. I understand people can get compromised in situations like this. Daddy, for instance, being who he is. So I said, yes, of course.' She chuckled spontaneously. 'I told him he could debrief me.'

Lacey wondered if HRH had managed to maintain his pomposity on the journey from the country with Sarah

Mathieson aboard. Anyway, for the time being, he would continue the line the Deputy Director had suggested and see how far it got him before he had to apply pressure.

'You're right. People can, and do, get compromised. Our job is to assess the extent of a possible compromise. You might also be able to help us with background on Aldo. His real name, by the way, is Capaldi, not Fagioli.'

'I'm surprised his real name is Aldo.' She began to open the carton of cigarettes. 'I suspected he was a bit on the shady side, but no more a criminal than many of the men I have met in business. My husband is a merchant banker. After high finance, all the rest is petty thieving.'

Traffic was light and he kept an eye, in the rear-view mirror, on the car that was tailing them two vehicles back. He let the conversation lapse and concentrated on driving, turning left into side streets without signalling, and making his way by a devious route to Shepherd's Bush, before turning back towards Twickenham.

Sarah Mathieson smoked a cigarette and accepted the manoeuvres without comment until curiosity finally got the better of her.

'Your sense of direction seems to be letting you down. Do you know where you're going?'

'We were being followed.'

'What?'

She turned in her seat to stare through the rear window. It was the first time her composure had cracked.

'Not to worry. We've lost him.'

He let her brood in silence for the rest of the journey.

Their destination was a flat above the office of an estate agent in a row of shops on a main road. They parked at the rear of the premises on a patch of waste ground shielded from other nearby houses by garages, shrubs and a fence. They got out and he pulled the overnight satchel bag from the back seat.

'Have a care,' she said. 'It's a Mulberry.'

Another car pulled in behind them and braked fiercely, making Sarah look round in alarm.

'And this is the bloke who was tailing us.'

'What?'

She stepped back as a tall blond-haired man got out of the car and came towards them.

'Let me introduce you. Sarah, this is Roland Devere. He's the nice one.'

Devere smiled and held out his hand and she took it with relief. They didn't shake hands, but held them as if they were in love or at a royal garden party. Sarah Mathieson swiftly had regained her composure and, for the first time, she was showing real interest.

'Devere,' she said. 'Hampshire?'

'My uncle. I'm from the military branch of the family. Gloucestershire.'

She nodded, appraising him as she had appraised Lacey a short time before, and obviously finding a great deal more to appreciate.

'Shall we get inside?' Lacey said. 'Just in case Devere didn't do his job properly and we really were tailed.'

Sarah didn't move immediately, presumably to make a point. When she did, she allowed Devere to take her arm and guide her to a high gate into an enclosed yard. He opened it and stood back to allow her to precede him, and she gave him a gracious smile for the courtesy.

'I shall call you Roland,' she said, ensuring Lacey heard, and making another point.

Lacey followed them, dragging the Mulberry through a cinder patch. He had his own way of making points.

Chapter 8

Everything about the flat was tasteless, second-hand and cheap, apart from the electronics. There were two bedrooms, a living-room, kitchen-diner and bathroom. All were bugged and the recording equipment was controlled from a concealed console in the second bedroom.

Sarah Mathieson was less than impressed and the way she looked at Lacey she seemed to think the flat was his. She took her bag from him and went into the bathroom.

'Switch on,' Lacey told Devere. 'And then put the kettle on.'

The three-piece suite was brown, lumpy and overcrowded the room. He drew the curtains to make the atmosphere even more claustrophobic, and switched on a standard lamp that stood to the side of one of the armchairs. The lamp had a powerful bulb. He switched on a table lamp on the opposite side of the room, and plugged in an electric fire, experimenting with the controls until one bar was lit.

Devere came back into the room and he directed him to sit in one of the armchairs while he sat on the settee. The lavatory flushed and, a minute later, Sarah re-entered the room.

'Good God. What happened to Sunday?'

Devere had got to his feet, but Lacey remained seated. If she wanted nasty and nice, he was quite willing to play. It might also bring results.

'Please,' he said. 'Sit down.'

Her choice was limited to the armchair that sat in the pool of light from the standard lamp.

'How terribly devious.'

She took her place with a look of amusement.

Lacey lit a Gitanes and Devere answered the call of the kettle in the kitchen. Sarah lit a Benson and Hedges and crossed her legs. She seemed totally at ease. Lacey waited until Devere returned carrying a tray containing two mugs of coffee, which he placed on a low table.

'It's powdered milk, I'm afraid,' he said, before leaving the room again.

Lacey took his coffee neat, but Sarah Mathieson tore open four sachets of powdered milk and four of sugar and poured them into her mug.

He opened formally.

'Do you know how the security services work? Which section is responsible for which area?'

'You mean Special Branch, MI5 and MI6 and all that?'

'Yes.'

'I think so.' She blew a smoke ring. 'Five is responsible for internal security, Six for external. Special Branch are used to make it legal.'

He nodded. She had summed it up quite neatly.

'And you understand your father's position?'

'MI5 is answerable to the Home Office, and as Daddy is Home Secretary . . .'

'Good. You understand.'

'Of course I understand. I also understand that this . . .' she smiled at him, '. . . debriefing is being undertaken by MI6 and without the knowledge of my father.' She shrugged. 'That suits me. Believe it or not, I wouldn't want Daddy to get hurt.'

He nodded again. She was not as dumb as Rossington-Hall had said.

'One more thing. We need to tap your telephone.'

'Is that necessary?'

'Probably not. Do you have any objections?'

'None, apart from the invasion of my privacy.'

'Your rights to privacy lapsed with your indiscretion. Any real objection?'

She shrugged.

'I suppose not.'

'Good. Then if you'd sign this.' He placed a two-page closely-printed document in front of her. 'On both pages.'

She signed without reading it. It meant the tap could go on immediately and, at a later stage, her home could be legally bugged and her mail legally intercepted.

'Right,' he said. 'Then we can begin. Aldo Capaldi.'

'Yes.'

'How long have you known him?'

'Eleven weeks.'

'You're very precise.'

'I've had time to think about it.'

'Where did you meet him?'

'Paris. The Cambon bar in the Ritz. I was with friends who had begun to bore me.'

'Who made the introduction?'

'He did.'

'And?'

'And I liked him. He was handsome, amusing, sophisticated.'

She smiled as she listed his qualities, her look suggesting that Capaldi was everything that Lacey was not.

'How did that first meeting develop?'

'We left the Ritz . . .'

'We?'

'Aldo and I. We left the Ritz and went to La Calavados for the music. Aldo likes jazz piano. From there, we went to my hotel. The Bristol. We spent the night together.' She pulled at the cigarette and blew out smoke. 'He was very good.'

'How long did you and Capaldi stay together, that first time?'

'Just overnight. He left in the morning. Said he had a business lunch.'

'Did you see him again in Paris?'

'Yes. He called me the next day and took me to dinner. A Vietnamese restaurant on the Left Bank. I don't know

63

its name. We went to a couple of amusing bars and then back to the hotel. He was just as good.'

'When did he leave?'

'In the morning.' She smiled. 'Late morning.'

'And the next time you saw him?'

'Was in Vienna.'

'Did you discuss politics at all, during your time with him in Paris?'

She laughed.

'Good God, no.'

'Or matters that could have any bearing on national security?'

She was chuckling so much she had to put down the coffee mug. She shook her head.

'Did he mention your father, or intimate that he knew who your father was?'

'No. He did not. Our relationship was purely pleasurable. We pleasured each other.'

'After he had left, was anything missing?'

'Do you mean, did he steal anything?'

'If you like.'

'No. Nothing was missing.'

Lacey stubbed out his cigarette in an ashtray on the table.

'How did you meet again in Vienna? Was it arranged or by accident?'

'It was arranged. He telephoned me in London and was . . . very flattering. He suggested it would be pleasant to meet again, and I agreed. I suggested he come to London, but he said that wasn't possible. Instead, he suggested I go to Vienna. So I did. I stayed two nights at the Marriott Hotel, where Aldo was also staying. We spent the two nights together and then I returned to London. I haven't seen him since.'

'And again, there was nothing in the conversations that suggested his motives were other than sexual?'

'I wouldn't put it as crudely as that. We pleased each other. We enjoyed each other. But, yes, of course, we went to bed together.'

'And, again, none of your belongings went missing?'

'Nothing was stolen.'

'Did you make arrangements to see each other again?'

'Nothing formal.'

'What does that mean?'

'He said he'd call me.'

'When?'

'Two weeks, maybe three.' She shrugged. 'Maybe never.'

'And you accepted that?'

She laughed. 'Why not?'

'Did he give you a number, where you can get in touch with him?'

'No.'

'Are you sure?'

'Quite sure.'

He picked up his cigarettes and tapped the packet with a box of matches.

'Do you often fly halfway across Europe to go to bed with someone you hardly know?'

Sarah Mathieson took a final pull on her cigarette before also leaning forward to stub it out.

'Not often. But it is not unknown.' She sipped the coffee. 'Now. I think I've delivered my part of the bargain, perhaps you can be as obliging? What exactly is it that Aldo is supposed to have done?'

Lacey stared at her, wondering how deep her poise and self-possession went. He didn't answer, but abruptly got to his feet and left the room.

He knocked on the door of the second bedroom. Devere opened it and Lacey went inside. The outline of Devere's head could be seen on the pillow on the bed. Lying on the mattress was a pair of headphones whose cable was attached to the console in the bedside table.

'Your turn,' Lacey said. 'Take as long as you want. Talk about her childhood; talk about your childhood. Maybe she'll relax for you. Talk about national security, responsibility. Then talk about her screwing Aldo Capaldi.'

Devere left the room and Lacey buffed up the pillow and lay on the bed.

According to her, Sarah had spent four nights of passion with Capaldi in the rooms of highly respectable hotels. That made it unlikely that video recordings or photographs could have been made or taken of their sexual activities. Audio tapes were obviously still possible, but would be a lot less damaging and could be denied. There, of course, could be film of them together in Paris and Vienna doing nothing more than strolling in the street, which, on its own, would forge a link between a known terrorist and the daughter of the Home Secretary.

If she was to be believed, Capaldi had made no political demands upon her and she had offered none. If she was to be believed, there was no danger to the state, her father or her father's political party.

Maybe Capaldi had killed the photographer, Jim Brady, to protect his own anonymity. Maybe Capaldi hadn't killed Brady, maybe Brady had been the victim of a fatal mugging. And there was still nothing to connect Capaldi with the death of Franz Haber.

Lacey put on the headphones and listened to Sarah flirting with Devere.

At the moment, it looked as if HRH was going to be well satisfied. He might even still make Sarah Mathieson a tabloid heroine, to ensure security from loose ends. But the interrogation hadn't finished yet. It had all night to go.

Chapter 9

The most Devere discovered was that Sarah Mathieson's favourite book was *Alice in Wonderland*. In a conversation that ranged far and wide, she talked about prep school, an uncle who attempted to seduce her when she was thirteen, an assistant gardener she seduced when she was fourteen, how she married her first husband to prove her independence, and how she married her second husband to clear her debts.

She said that she and her second husband hadn't lived together for three years. It was an arrangement that suited her admirably and allowed her to indulge her whims for travel, amusement and men.

Lacey decided she thought she *was* Alice in Wonderland.

When Devere brought the talk around to Capaldi, she told him the same story she had told Lacey. The affair had been brief and uncomplicated. They had enjoyed each other's company, both in and out of bed. He had a ruthlessness she had not experienced in other men that had attracted her. The only mildly unlawful act they had committed together had been to smoke a little dope and snort a little cocaine, she said.

They had been talking for ninety minutes and Lacey was getting bored. He abandoned the headphones, lit a cigarette and walked to the window. It had gone dark while Devere had been prodding Sarah into explaining the meaning of life.

The secure phone next to the bed rang softly and Lacey walked back and answered it.

'Yes?'

'Something just came in.' It was Natalie at Charing Cross Road. 'It's been claimed by Red Dawn. I've got the text if you want.'

'Not now. Have Vienna accepted it?'

'Yes. They say it fits.'

'Right. I'll call you later.'

If the killing of Franz Haber was the work of Red Dawn, it was unlikely that Capaldi had been involved, and the presence in Vienna of him, and the Mathieson woman, was probably no more than coincidence. At least she couldn't be smeared with the blood of the concert pianist. But that still left Jim Brady.

Lacey picked up a folder, unlocked the door and called Devere. He waited until the other man had come out of the living-room and closed the door behind him, before he spoke again.

'My turn,' he said. 'Don't come in unless I call you.'

Devere went into the bedroom and Lacey into the living-room. It was hot and Sarah Mathieson had flopped in the chair. She looked uncomfortable, but still composed.

'Oh, it's you.' She changed position. 'Get me a drink, will you? Water will do. I've been smoking too much.'

Lacey ignored her and walked into the centre of the room. He held the folder behind his back in both hands and stared at her.

'Look, I asked for a drink. I have a dry throat.'

'You didn't ask. You ordered. Like you do most things.'

'All right.' She crossed her legs and sighed. 'I'm asking. Can I have a glass of water, please?'

'No.'

'What?'

'No. You can't have a glass of water.'

'For God's sake, you jumped-up little prick, I want a glass of water. I'm thirsty. Now get me one.'

'No. You can't have one.'

She began to get up.

'Then I'll get it myself.'

'No, you won't.' He pushed her back into the armchair. 'I'm stronger than you. I won't let you.'

Her mouth dropped open in surprise and she looked round at the closed door into the corridor.

'Roland! Come here at once. Roland!'

'Roland can't hear you. He's gone out.'

She looked back at Lacey, disgust twisting her lips.

'I came here of my own free will. I was given guarantees by Hector Rossington-Hall, who has been a family friend for many years.'

'Is that the same Hector Rossington-Hall who is a disgusting little creep?'

Her eyes flashed in anger.

'He is your superior and a friend of my family. He will not take kindly to your attitude.'

'Dear Mrs Mathieson. I couldn't give a shit. He's not here. There's nobody here except you and me. And I can be as obnoxious as I like.'

She sat back, folded her arms and stared at the wall. Her face was stern.

'All right. Play God. Play your silly little games. But you can't play them for ever.'

'Neither can you. Your silly little games are catching you out, Sarah.'

He opened the folder and took from it an eight-by-ten head and shoulders photograph which he placed on the coffee table in front of her. She glanced at it, despite her pose of non-co-operation.

'Aldo Capaldi,' he said. 'Aldo is not a shady character and he's not involved in business. He is a professional killer.' She looked at him sharply, then looked away again. Lacey began to read from a document. 'Aged thirty-three, Aldo is Italian by birth, his father was a lawyer in Rome. He joined the Revolutionary Cells in West Germany in the late 1970s. They taught him how to be a terrorist.

'He worked for the Red Brigades and the Wadi Haddad network. His motivation was not political, but psychopathic

69

and emulatory. He wanted to become the next Ilich Ramirez Sanchez, the next Carlos the Jackal.'

Lacey stopped reading and glared at Sarah.

'Do you remember the Jackal? He became famous by killing people. By shooting them, blowing them up, kidnapping them. Beautiful women helped him. Sometimes they didn't know who he was or what he was doing. Sometimes they did. But they helped hide him, protect him, carry his guns and explosives. Stored arms until he needed them. Acted as his couriers.'

He paused, his breathing deliberately ragged, and he took his time to take out and light a cigarette, as if he needed it to calm down. When he continued, his voice was softer, but no less deadly.

'Is that what you are, Sarah? Have you been helping Aldo Capaldi to kill people?'

'No.' Her eyes were still angry, but there were other emotions there as well. 'I haven't helped him. I didn't know who he was.' She shook her head. 'He didn't seem . . . are you sure this is the same man?'

'Oh yes. We're sure. Capaldi is well known. He's not as good as Carlos was, but he's effective. He works mostly for Abu Nidal. He's used because he's European and he can go places an Arab can't. He kills people for money and he earns a great deal.'

She looked away from him, shaking her head.

'I think you're mistaken. I think you've got the wrong man. Aldo isn't a killer.'

Lacey took a second photograph from the folder and put it on the table, but she didn't turn her head.

'Look at it.'

She turned and looked first at him and then down at the photograph. It was another head and shoulders.

'James Brady,' Lacey said. 'Aged fifty-three, home address in Ealing.' He placed another photograph alongside it, this time of a couple. 'Here he is on his wedding day. His bride is Sheila Watkins. He was thirty-three and she was twenty-seven when they got married.'

Sarah Mathieson looked more closely.

The wedding picture showed a slimmer Brady. He had never been handsome, but he had been more presentable twenty years before. His bride was slim, dark-haired and sharp-featured. She clung to his arm as if she would never let go.

'Jim and Sheila Brady got married for love. They took wedding vows that they meant. Five years ago, Sheila died of cancer, but Jim Brady's feelings didn't change. When she was alive, they went on holiday to Vienna every year. When she died, Brady still went, on his own. But he took his memories with him, and each day he wrote a diary to Sheila.'

He took typed pages from the folder, glanced down them, and began to read.

'Sunday. Went to Mass in the Hofburg Chapel. I was lucky to get a ticket – do you remember the trouble we had the first time we went? Anyway, as always, it was lovely. The Mass was Schubert and the Boys' Choir was perfect. It brought tears to my eyes, I don't mind telling you, but don't tell anybody else. You would have enjoyed it, Sheila, but perhaps you did. Perhaps you were there? I like to think you were. At times like that, I get the feeling you're still close. Anyway, I'd better close now. Love, as always, Jim.'

Lacey put the pages back in the folder and stubbed his cigarette out in an ashtray on the table.

'Love stories deserve a happy ending. This doesn't have one. Aldo Capaldi killed Jim Brady in Vienna. He stuck a knife in his back.'

He produced more photographs, this time in colour, and threw them one at a time on the table.

'These are police pictures of the corpse. Death doesn't suit Brady. It makes his eyes stare.'

For a second, she had kept looking at the pictures, perhaps expecting more wedding snaps. Now she gasped and looked away.

'Mind you, your eyes would stare if you had a wound like this in your back.' He paused. 'What's the matter,

71

Sarah? I thought you were used to business. Well, this is Aldo's business. This is what he's good at. Is this what you helped him do?'

'No. Of course not.' She began to cry. 'You bastard.'

'Not me. Aldo's the bastard. You remember Aldo? Handsome, amusing, sophisticated. Gave you a good time. Do you know, I'll bet that after sticking the knife into poor old Mr Brady here, Aldo came straight back to the hotel and stuck something in you?'

Sarah Mathieson's eyes were blazing with anger and confusion. She tried again to get out of the chair and again Lacey pushed her back. But this time, she grabbed at his hand and tried to bite it. He dropped the folder and held her off by pulling hard on her hair until she gave up and slumped back.

'You bastard.'

'You bitch.'

'I'll make you pay . . .'

'Like Jim Brady paid?'

She kicked out at him, but he moved out of the way and her feet hit the coffee table, knocking it over on its side and spilling the photographs on the carpet.

'I had nothing to do with it,' she screamed. 'I don't know the man. I don't know how he died.' Her face became set again, the tears of a moment ago freezing over. 'Maybe you're making the whole bloody lot up. Maybe you like hitting women.'

'In your case, yes. It would give me great pleasure.'

'Then why don't you.'

'Because it would probably give you great pleasure, as well.'

'You're sick.'

'Not as sick as you, lady. Screwing a murderer while the victim's still warm. Or maybe you were there? Did you watch? Did it turn you on?'

'For God's sake, I know nothing about it. I had nothing to do with it.'

'No?'

Lacey picked up the folder and took from it another photograph. He set the coffee table upright and dropped the folder and the photograph on top of it. It was a street shot of Aldo Capaldi and Sarah Mathieson. He leaned forward, resting his hands on the coffee table to get closer to her.

'Brady was a photographer. He took this picture. Remember?'

She stared at the photograph and shook her head.

'No. I don't.'

'Try.'

It was obvious from her face that she did.

'We'd been for a meal . . .'

'And afterwards?'

'Aldo had business. He was away about an hour. He . . .'

She looked up at Lacey and then looked away from both him and the photograph.

'What did you do while he attended to business?'

She shook her head but didn't speak.

'Answer me, Sarah. What did you do?'

'I went back to the hotel.'

'And Aldo joined you later?'

'Yes.'

Lacey straightened up.

'And you spent the night together.'

'Yes.'

'Making love?'

'Yes.'

'Is that what you call it? Making love? The same word Jim and Sheila Brady used. It doesn't sound quite the same thing, does it?'

'You bastard. You know what I mean. I didn't know . . .'

She turned in the chair to face him, once again aggressive. 'Aldo was just a fuck. A good-looking fuck. All right? Are you satisfied now?'

'No, Mrs Mathieson. I am not satisfied. And I won't be satisfied until your attitude changes and you realize the sort of deep shit you're in. I want everything from you,

Mrs Mathieson, from flight times and room numbers to Capaldi's cock size. And I want the information freely given, and not dragged out of you. All right?'

He left the folder with its selected typed reports, and the photographs that were spread on the floor and the table, and went out of the living-room.

Devere opened the bedroom door before he knocked. His expression suggested he had not liked what he had heard.

Lacey told him: 'Go back to the office and pick up Natalie's reports. Take the clearance for the plumbers.'

'What are you going to do?'

'I'm going to have a lie down.'

'What about Sarah?'

'She can have an hour alone with her thoughts and the pictures of Jim Brady's corpse.' He smiled. 'By then she'll be all ready for Mr Nice Guy.'

Devere stared hard at him, as if trying to work out whether Lacey was enjoying himself.

'You know, I think Sarah's right. You are a bastard.'

'I do my best.'

Chapter 10

Roland Devere drove into London with the precise bravado that had made him a good officer.

He evaluated traffic risks swiftly, accelerated into gaps, saw tailbacks before they happened and took avoiding action that invariably left him ahead of the field.

It was the sort of skill that provoked envy and abuse from fellow motorists, but to Devere it was second nature. He had been born with the skill to side-step trouble and had done so all his life. Almost all his life.

At Marlborough it had made him a popular hero. He had been a leading rackets player, first rate at cricket and highly successful with the sixth-form girls. Academically he was bright too, although, again, in a precise fashion. He had set his targets and achieved them.

His father had died when he was ten and his education was Roland's only legacy, for he was the second son and the farm-estate went to his older brother, Ranulf.

Roland and his father had discussed it before the old man died and he had grown up aware that he would have to make his own way in life.

'It's the Army or the Church,' the old man had said, half jokingly, for there was a strong military tradition running through the family. 'You don't even have the alternative of Empire. All the pink bits have changed colour.'

But for Roland there had never been a serious choice to make. He enjoyed the tradition of his family and school and it had always been in his mind that he would make a career in the Army. He had gone to Sandhurst, been commissioned and sent to the dragoon regiment in which his father and grandfather had served. He discovered, without surprise, that he was good at soldiering.

Military service, he believed, was much maligned and misunderstood. It could serve a useful purpose, teach an aimless generation pride, the natural order of things, and national identity. Even Lacey could have done with it.

He felt he understood Lacey, but realized that Lacey did not understand him. He guessed his background as red-brick university and imagined him as a bolshie agitator of the 1960s. In the office, Lacey still mouthed off against the Government and corporate business, but Devere suspected it was by now partly an act and partly habit. After all, becoming a civil servant had made him a rebel without a cause. To a large extent, Lacey seemed out of time and out of place, like a kitchen-sink character from a John Osborne play, who suddenly arrives unannounced in the middle of a Nöel Coward revival.

Not for the first time, he wondered how the man could have been recruited into the Service. He was obviously good at his job, but surely he would be even better if he spent less time fighting imagined slights and injustices.

Devere hoped he and Lacey would be able to develop a professional relationship, but the major drawbacks to that happening were Lacey's wariness and suspicion. They were strong enough to be an inferiority complex. That, too, was something Devere felt he understood. He had had a sergeant as good as Lacey, once, and they had both been happy with their relative positions as officer and sergeant. Perhaps Lacey saw Devere as a threat. Perhaps the sergeant felt awkward telling an officer what to do.

Again, not for the first time, Devere pondered on how he himself had got involved in all this cloak-and-dagger stuff. The offer to join military intelligence had come as a surprise, after three years as a soldier. He had trained at the Joint Services of Intelligence at Ashford in Kent and subsequently served in Cyprus. Later, he received further and more specific training from the SAS at a camp near their headquarters in Hereford, before joining the undercover 14th Intelligence unit in Ireland.

The work gave him the mental scope to be dissatisfied. He had always been direct and able to categorize into black and white, friend and foe. In Northern Ireland, it frustrated him that known foes were operating from safe bases a few miles away in the Republic. It was common knowledge that the SAS frequently disregarded the border and he decided to do the same.

He undertook a totally unofficial raid into the South to bring back a known terrorist of the Provisional IRA. His intention was to interrogate him at leisure and eventually hand him over to the RUC, claiming he had been arrested in Armagh bandit country. A sergeant and a corporal volunteered to go with him. They all wore civilian clothes.

Their plan was to intercept the man as he drove from Dundalk to Monaghan, take him as close to the border as possible in his own car, and then take him cross-country into the North towards Armagh. The man was married, but also had a mistress and was known to break his journey to spend an hour in her company.

The house was at the far end of a terrace of cottages off the main road. There were no street lights. The man had been observed before and it was his practice to park his car near the road and walk to the cottage. He followed the same practice while Devere and his men waited and watched. When he was almost at the gate, Devere stepped from the shadows and pressed a silenced Browning into his back, and everything began to go wrong.

Light suddenly spilled out as the front door of the cottage opened. The mistress saw what was happening and began to yell. Two more men came to the door of the house, carrying guns, and the lights of the parked car came on to catch Devere in their beams.

Their intelligence had been wrong. They had interrupted not an evening of snatched passion, but a planning meeting of an active service unit.

Devere's men had opened up, putting out the car lights

and causing the people in the cottage to duck for cover. He had had a split second to decide what to do with his prisoner, a man he knew was directly responsible for more than a dozen murders and whom he had no hope now of taking back across the border.

He remembered the frustration boiling. He remembered the smell of sweat that came from them both. A pragmatic solution would be to kill him, but the discipline of the Army and his code of fair play told him to retreat. He had stepped away and was about to run for cover when the man looked into his face and grinned.

If he hadn't grinned, Devere wouldn't have shot him. Perhaps he had grinned out of bravado, perhaps because he sensed Devere was letting him go. But the grin had tipped the balance of fair play and Devere had removed it with two bullets in the chest. A figure had run from the house and he had fired again, only afterwards realizing it was the woman.

The journey back had been a disjointed fire-fight, during which the sergeant had been wounded. They heard later that two other Provos had been hit, and the woman had died.

They had counted themselves lucky to get across the border to the North in one piece only to run into an SAS patrol which had fired first before asking questions. Before they could identify themselves, the corporal was wounded. When the shooting finally stopped, they were evacuated to secure barracks, away from ordinary squaddies or curious reporters. The Army subsequently attributed the raid to an extremist Ulster terrorist group.

Devere's career in Military Intelligence was over, but his role in the fiasco couldn't be made public. His foolhardiness had caused two subordinates to be wounded and come close to causing a major political row, but his departure had to be handled in a way that caused no scandal. He discovered he still had some friends in the right places, and he was recommended for special duties with the SIS. He was interviewed, assessed and assigned to Charing Cross Road.

The move hadn't disappointed him; he had known the

consequences of his actions and, after all, he was still in the service of his country. The episode hadn't bothered him, either, and he had no regret at killing their target in cold blood. It had been an execution and all that had been missing were the judicial niceties. The terrorist had deserved to die. As for the woman, she had been a victim of a war that had claimed many women, most of them far more innocent than she had been.

He had also been involved in interrogations in Ireland, but the Provos were so well trained in what to expect it had often been a formality. What Lacey was doing with Sarah Mathieson was something else entirely.

Lacey was being a bastard as if he enjoyed it. He had bullied, threatened and denegrated Sarah. As she was neither a terrorist nor a potential terrorist, Devere wondered why Lacey had been so vitriolic. Was he simply being a professional bastard or was it because of her class?

It also occurred to Devere that his own opinions might be coloured by exactly the same reason. After all, he and Sarah had mutual friends. But it also went against his sense of natural courtesy to treat a lady in such a way. In the sweet and nasty routine Lacey had instigated, Devere was glad he was able to be himself.

It took Devere an hour and thirty minutes to make the journey to the office and return to Twickenham. Lacey was still in the bedroom and Sarah Mathieson was still alone with her thoughts in the living-room.

Lacey read the computer print-outs, passing them on to Devere as he finished a page. They told them little they didn't already know and covered media reaction to the assassination. Haber was said to have made his music accessible to a mass audience by breaking down classical barriers. In the process he became a superstar.

It was for that very reason, although it was couched in different terms, that Red Dawn had decided he had to die.

Their statement claiming the killing was full of the usual hackneyed phrases and clichés. In essence it accused

Franz Haber of being the worst kind of capitalist who would do anything for money. The fact that he was also very famous ensured headlines. In death, the left-wing group claimed, he was useful at least in focusing world attention on the evils of capitalism and exploitation.

Long live the people's revolution, they said.

'And so say all of us,' Lacey said. He flopped back on the bed and put his hands behind his head. 'Go on. The lady's waiting for you. Get everything, from start to finish. We still need a line to follow.'

'It's going to take all night.'

'Very probably.'

'Will we switch?'

'Possibly. But at the moment let's stick to what we're good at. I'll use my brain power, you use your charm.'

Devere was right. It did take all night. He did the bulk of the work, taking notes on a foolscap pad despite the tape recordings. Lacey relieved him for two brief spells, using the notes to go back over Sarah Mathieson's story to check details.

Outside it was dawn, but Lacey kept the curtains closed, kept the atmosphere tense. By nine o'clock, he was satisfied they had as much as they were likely to get, at least in this session, and he said so.

'Thank God.' Sarah Mathieson looked drained, her eye make-up was a mess from the tears Lacey had bullied out of her, and her face sagged in exhaustion. 'Does this mean I can go home?'

Lacey hesitated.

'We've not finished. We've just got to first base. We have to find Capaldi and we have to arrange your cover story.'

'Cover story? What are you talking about?'

'Maybe you're wrong. Maybe Capaldi, or whoever he's working for, does have something on you. If they try blackmail or scandal, we have to have an answer.'

She looked puzzled.

80

'Such as what?'

'Such as you being a member of Her Majesty's Secret Intelligence Service.'

Her jaw sagged and then she laughed.

'Are you serious?'

'My reaction, entirely. But yes, I'm serious. The idea comes from HRH.'

'Good God.'

Her eyes glazed into middle distance as the implications began to sink in.

Lacey said, 'If we take care of things properly, we won't need to use it. But if there are complications, your role as an agent will be given to the Press.'

'How marvellous.'

'Yes, isn't it.'

Lacey felt suddenly very tired. She'd screwed around with a terrorist, been responsible for the death of Brady, and was now looking forward to front-page fame as a glamorous spy. She was shedding the discomfort of the night she had just passed, as easily as she changed her fur coat.

'Little old Mata Hari me,' she said, wistfully.

Lacey turned away and lit his last cigarette. The smoke made him cough because his throat was so sore and he went to the kitchen for a drink of water. When he came back, Sarah Mathieson and Devere were in the middle of a conversation. They stopped as he entered the room and looked at him as if he were an intruder.

'So when can I go home?' she said. 'Surely you can give me a call when you need me again?'

He nodded.

'All right. But on conditions. We want your passport, and we want permission to search your apartment. It's insurance for both of us and, who knows, we may come up with something you forgot.'

She pulled a face.

'Who will be doing the searching?'

'Devere. Give him the passport, too. I'd like him to stay close to you over the next few days, if you don't mind.'

'No.' She smiled at Devere. 'I don't mind.'

'When do you want me back at the office?' Devere said.

'Phone in at six. Maybe you should try and get some rest before then. Both of you.'

As he turned to go back to the kitchen he caught a glimpse of the look Sarah Mathieson was giving his subordinate. It appeared as though Devere would be lucky to get any rest in the immediate future. And afterwards . . . ?

Maybe afterwards Sarah Mathieson would talk in her sleep.

Chapter 11

Lacey was knackered and the bed at the safe house looked inviting. But he preferred the thought of his own bed that would still be rumpled with Susan's sleep and impregnated with her smell.

After Devere and Sarah Mathieson had left, he got a briefcase from the car and put in it the folder, photographs and reports, as well as the tapes that had run all night. Eventually, the tapes would be transcribed, but there was no urgency. Tomorrow would be soon enough.

He called Natalie to tell her he was going home, locked up the house and headed into the traffic. It would be a battle all the way to Beckenham.

One day, he was sure, traffic lights at Westminster Bridge would go on the blink, the cars and buses would jam and the tailback would stretch in all directions to the orbital M25. London would seize up and be declared a disaster area. Large parts of it already were.

He played dare at a junction and made a Rolls-Royce brake to let him in. The driver had to; he had more to lose. The car reminded him of Sarah Mathieson; not her shape, but her affluent arrogance. He didn't like Sarah one little bit. On the outside, she was as sleek as the Roller that purred in his rear-view mirror, but on the inside she was hard and bitter, as if life had dealt her a raw deal.

Maybe it had. Maybe the silver spoon she had been born with had stuck in her throat when mummy and daddy abandoned her to nannies while they had a good time. That was the way it was done in her circles, wasn't it? And then boarding school and Benenden and finishing school in Switzerland. Maybe Sarah had been scarred by emotional deprivation as a child and subsequently had chased affection in one-night stands. And maybe she was just a spoiled brat. He knew which option he favoured.

Brady's death had appeared to shock her, but she had soon got over it, and by the time he told her she was going to become a secret agent she was looking forward to the headlines. All in all, he decided, she was an unremitting bitch, but a shrewd one.

It was the shrewd part that interested him, for it meant she would be difficult to take advantage of, particularly by a hit man of Capaldi's reputation. Capaldi was excellent at killing and the mechanics of assassination, but he was not in the same league as Carlos.

Ilich Ramirez had been capable of running a terror network and a string of girlfriends without one getting in the way of the other and without one knowing about the other. His powers of persuasion and manipulation with the opposite sex were legendary; his acts of terrorism spoke for themselves.

If Capaldi was involved in a black operation against Sarah Mathieson, he was not running it; someone else was in control. But so far, whoever it was didn't seem to have gathered a great deal of material. Perhaps they were taking it slowly and perhaps the sting was planned for the next meeting. If HRH was patient, that would be the time to do the cleaning up he wanted.

There was also always the chance that Capaldi and Sarah Mathieson had met by chance and succumbed to a mutual sexual attraction. She had said he was a good-looking fuck. He probably thought the same about her. But that was stretching coincidence too far and Lacey didn't believe in coincidence when it came to terrorists and ministers' daughters. Lacey accepted the necessity of expending a lot of energy looking for, checking out and disposing of Aldo Capaldi, despite his apathy towards most of the people involved.

But he could always console himself with Brady: the silent, small-time, unimportant witness to the plot. When

84

the time came, Lacey would be happy to speak up for Brady. It wouldn't be revenge, because revenge wasn't in the manual. It would be redressing the balance.

The dream had been threatening, but he couldn't remember why. The noise woke him and for a moment he couldn't work out which was reality.

He lay silent and tense, and listened to the sounds until he recognized them and he remembered.

Lacey opened his eyes and rolled his head on the pillow. Susan was half undressed by the dressing-table, watching him.

'Sorry,' she said. 'I didn't mean to wake you up.'

'That's all right.'

He stretched, and eyed her speculatively. She laughed and picked up a dressing-gown.

'It's been a hard day. I need a shower.'

'What is this? Rejection?'

She continued laughing as she walked towards the door.

'Later,' she said.

He relaxed, and, without the distraction of his wife, his thoughts returned to Sarah Mathieson. Later could be too late. He checked his watch, saw it was six-thirty and reached for the telephone on the bedside table to call the office.

Natalie had gone home, but Malcolm was still there.

'You just caught me. I was dashing off to catch Mr Ashraf before he closed.' Ashraf was the owner of a delicatessen and video store on the corner of Malcolm's road. 'It's bouillabaisse and Dr Zhivago tonight.'

'I won't keep you, Malcolm. Just checking in. Anything?'

'Harry's had his baby. It's a boy. He sounded distinctly underwhelmed when he phoned. I think he was hoping for a Tandy portable.'

Lacey laughed.

'What about Vienna?'

'Nothing. You'll discover more by watching television

85

than reading these reports. And nobody's come up with a Capaldi sighting yet.'

'What about Devere?'

'He called in at six.'

'Where from?'

Malcolm gave him the number and Lacey smiled. He was still with Sarah Mathieson.

'OK. Tell the duty man I'm at home. Don't keep Omar Sheriff waiting.'

'I've told you before, I'm strictly a cat person. Mind you, couldn't you just melt into those eyes . . .'

'Bye Malcolm.'

'Bye Peter.'

Lacey put the phone down and wondered whether to call Devere and decided against it. The bloke was supposed to be a professional; he should trust him.

He got out of bed naked and walked towards the bathroom, his interest in Susan returning. She was still in the shower and he poked his head round the curtain. Her eyes were closed as she rinsed shampoo from her hair.

'Room for one more?'

'What?' She jumped at the sound of his voice. 'Grief, Peter, you could have given me a heart attack.'

He stepped into the shower with her.

'We're at a vulnerable age,' he said. 'We should make the most of it.'

She stopped rubbing her hair as he stepped close against her from behind.

'You know, I hate to say this but your timing is lousy.'

'What do you mean?' he said, enjoying the heat, the water and the contact.

'I have precisely twenty-five minutes to get ready. Lucy is picking me up at seven.'

His growing erection went on to hold.

'You're going out?'

She turned to face him, one hand touching his face, the other between his legs as if she were stroking a pet mouse.

'I'm sorry, darling. I didn't think you'd be back, and

86

Lucy, well, you know the trouble she's having.' She kissed him on the lips. A sisterly kiss. 'I said I'd go out with her.'

He didn't know now what to do with his hands that a few moments before had been filled with soft flesh. They hung by his side and felt clumsy and out of place.

'Where are you going?'

'The Italian place. We won't be long. I'll be home by ten.' She smiled and squeezed him gently between his legs, and this time she wasn't playing with a mouse. 'Have a shower yourself and wait up for me.'

The good humour returned and he smiled.

'I'll be waiting.'

'Good.'

She kissed him again and left the shower. He stayed and let the water engulf him.

Sex turned men into little boys. His desire had made him vulnerable and rejection had made him embarrassed as well as disappointed. No wonder sex was an important weapon, in private lives and public scandals. He wondered again about Sarah Mathieson and wondered whether she was simply a hedonist, as Rossington-Hall had said, or whether she was something more.

Maybe Devere would find the answer. At least, he would give it his best shot. Lacey smiled, and hoped he didn't run out of ammunition.

A microwave dinner for one was enough to turn anybody to drink so Lacey had a Beck's. It was so good he had another, and became reflective about the case, Devere, the job, life, every-bloody-thing.

It was a long time since he had suffered depression and he panicked momentarily in case this was a relapse. He had another beer to fight off the feeling of pending emptiness, even though he knew it wasn't the answer.

Depression was like alcoholism; you never fully recovered from it. The bastard kept giving you a nudge when you weren't expecting it, just to remind you of your vulnerability.

He couldn't understand what had provoked this latest nudge. Maybe it was the loneliness of the house after his unfulfilled anticipation. No, it had to be more than that. Career crisis? He'd been through that before and rationalized himself to a standstill. Career was the wrong word for what he did. He was a specialist whose job satisfaction always left him with a sense of guilt. He worked for a government he didn't particularly like and for an establishment he despised. He worked for a department that officially didn't exist and for a country that seemed to have changed out of recognition in his lifetime. Or maybe the country he preferred to remember existed only in Ealing comedies.

Christ, but he sounded a sorry bastard. Everybody could list life's deficiencies and claim they'd been sold short. Everybody, at some stage, discovered they couldn't fly. But at least his job was a better diversion than most, so what right did he have to wallow in melancholy?

He laughed at himself and switched to whisky. He was beginning to count his blessings like Julie Andrews. At least he had blessings to count. At least. Why did he need to keep qualifying life with at least?

Jim Brady. Now Jim Brady didn't need to qualify life at all, any more. Was he to be envied?

Lacey raised the glass of Bell's and decided he was not to be envied. At least not until the bottle was gone.

What about Sarah Mathieson? Still a sad wild child in her late thirties. He doubted if she had qualified in anything. Life had probably confronted her once, and ever since she had been running to avoid answering its questions.

And Roland Devere? The poor sod had been regimented from birth. If life ever confronted him he'd probably shoot it.

Jesus Christ. What a deep, philosophical bastard he was. What a clever, all-knowing sod, sitting in an armchair, swilling Scotch and dispensing philosophies when he didn't have one himself.

The best he could do was shadow box, dance on the fringes and not let the questions get too close and, if they did, drown them.

He poured another Scotch. The depression had gone, if it ever had been there to start with. The twinge that had set him off worrying had probably been tension. Even an afternoon's sleep hadn't been enough to get the all-night interrogation out of his system. It remained with him like a hangover because it had been routine and boring with little challenge and no real end result.

The transcripts would need assessment, reports would have to be written, and Sarah Mathieson would have to be courted until they were sure there was no danger to government or state. What had he said about counting his blessings?

Susan had said she would be home by ten, but she was late. It was closer to eleven when she got in. She was full of apologies and red wine. It made her eyes twinkle with wickedness.

'Lucy's in a state. You have to feel sorry for her,' she said.

'Not tonight.'

Lacey sat in his armchair and watched her standing at the drinks' cabinet, trying to decide what to have. His earlier anticipation had waned, but her legs looked very slim and attractive in high heels and he wondered if he could revive his interest.

She poured a whisky and dry ginger and sat in the armchair opposite.

'You look as if you've had a few,' she said.

'You're late.'

'You look as if you'd started before I was late.'

He shrugged.

'I suppose I did.'

She smiled and sipped the whisky.

'Are you OK?'

He'd had more to drink than he'd intended and perhaps

it was showing, but he knew her enquiry wasn't about how tipsy he was. She, too, was sensitive about his emotional state.

He smiled back and toasted her with his glass.

'I'm fine. I just fell into bad company.' He sipped. 'Mine.'

They held each other's gaze and he felt better at the understanding in her eyes. He grinned sheepishly.

'And I was looking forward to it.'

She laughed.

'So was I. Bloody Lucy.'

'Bloody Lucy.'

Susan finished the drink, got up and put the glass back on the cabinet. She came across the room and stood in front of him.

'You could always try,' she said. 'I mean, I wouldn't hold you to anything.'

He sat forward and ran his hands up the back of her legs and beneath her skirt.

'Very nice,' he said, and smiled apologetically.

She smiled back.

'All right. Let's just go to bed.'

He removed his hands and got to his feet. She remained in front of him and they put their arms round each other in affection.

'There's always the morning,' he said.

She mumbled suspiciously.

'As long as you wake me up first.'

Lacey woke early after sleeping off the alcohol. He slipped out of bed and had a shower, and smoked his first cigarette of the day while making coffee. The combined smell of Gitanes and the percolator always put him in a good mood.

He took a tray with coffee and orange juice back to the bedroom, placed it on Susan's bedside table, took off his dressing-gown and slipped back into bed.

She lay on her side, facing away from him. She was warm, soft and exquisitely vulnerable. He fitted himself against her, moved his hands over her and nibbled her ear. She groaned.

'You told me not to start without you,' he whispered.

Her breathing stopped as she came awake, and then it eased back into a relaxed pattern. She licked sleep's dryness from her lips.

'You've started.'

He stopped what he was doing and kissed her neck.

'I'll wait for you to catch up. There's coffee and juice.'

Susan rolled on to her back and reached for him under the bedclothes.

'No. You've started. You should finish.'

He rested on one arm and brushed hair from her forehead. The phone rang and froze their expressions. It rang again and Susan pulled a face.

'Answer it,' she said.

She moved away and reached for the orange juice.

Lacey swore under his breath, sat up in bed and picked up the receiver. It was Natalie and the tension in her voice alerted him that it was something major.

He listened in silence, trying to make sense of it, but none of it made sense. Without looking, he felt on the bedside table for his cigarettes and shook one out of the packet. He put it in his mouth, but didn't light it. Only when Natalie had finished did he strike a match and hold the flame to it. Alongside him, he could sense Susan watching and waiting, but it still didn't make sense.

Lacey took a deep drag of the cigarette and said to Natalie: 'Tell me again. From the beginning.'

Chapter 12

Sarah Mathieson had moved into Wapping ten years before the developers had transformed it. They had converted the warehouses along the docks into expensive apartment blocks with electric and human security systems and disenfranchised the local population in the process. She had bought a tall thin house in the middle of a terrace that had been there when Jack the Ripper had stalked nearby Whitechapel a century before.

At one time, the ground floor had accommodated shops, stables or small warehouses. Now they were mostly garages with the occupiers preferring to live above street level. The properties had exterior charm and luxury interiors and were worth a fortune. Her neighbours included a gossip columnist and a politician, but the residents were not the neighbourly type. They preferred privacy and were rich enough to expect and get it.

The street door, that she opened with two keys, led directly on to a flight of stairs. At the top, was another door of solid wood, but instead of unlocking it, she first used another key to open a panel in the wall that revealed a digital display and a flashing orange light. She keyed in a four-figure number and the light went out.

'Fort Knox,' she said. 'Alarms are *de rigueur*. The natives have become distinctly less than friendly since civilization came to the East End.' She closed the panel and pushed open the second door. 'Electrically operated,' she explained. 'As long as you know the code.'

They stepped into a large open-plan room that was richly carpeted in cream. There was a leather settee, fur rugs, a four feet high statue of a naked Aztec and a picture-window view of the Thames.

'God, but I'm wrecked.' She dropped her coat on the carpet and headed for a pine staircase that led to the third floor. Halfway up the stairs she paused, as if remembering Devere was with her. 'Oh. Find yourself a drink, or something.'

Devere was tired, too. He put down Sarah's satchel and explored. He found a lavatory, a cloakroom, a study that was used for storage and, finally, a kitchen. He filled a kettle and plugged it in to boil and put Nescafé into two mugs, counting himself lucky that he had wanted coffee. The major items in the refrigerator were six bottles of Bollinger champagne.

While he waited for the water to boil, he wandered the room with the view, admiring the Bang and Olufson hi-fi system and the casual way the compact discs lay scattered on the floor. Sarah's taste in music went from Al Green to Julio Iglesias. There were no female singers at all.

The light on an answerphone flashed to denote it had messages to play.

He went back to the kitchen, made the coffee and carried the two mugs into the living-room. As he re-entered, Sarah came down the stairs. She was wearing a full-length, black silk *peignoir* that covered everything and hid nothing. Her eyes sparkled and her features were mobile again. She was revitalized.

'Your answerphone wants you,' he said, for something to say.

Her response was to unplug it.

'I'm not in the mood to talk to anybody.' She noticed the mugs in his hands. 'Good God, not the cleaner's coffee! We can do better than that.'

She swept past him into the kitchen and he turned and followed her, wondering where she got her energy from. He put one of the mugs down on the sink, but sipped from the other and watched as she took a bottle of Bollinger and a carton of orange juice from the refrigerator. She opened

93

both as if she had had a lot of practice, and poured two tumblerfuls of champagne and juice.

'It's the only way to start the day,' she said, pushing a glass at him.

He put down the coffee and accepted the glass. Why not, after what they had both been through? He raised it in a toast.

'To a remarkable lady.'

She raised her's in return.

'To an officer and a gentleman.'

They drank and she picked up the champagne to top up the glasses. For a moment, Devere attempted to refuse, but relented.

'I'm not sure we should be doing this.'

'I am. I need to regain my sanity after a night with that awful man.'

'Yes. I'm terribly sorry about that.'

'It's all right.' She wrinkled her nose dismissively. 'All in the past. We're here and now.'

She turned back to the refrigerator and took out two more bottles which she handed to him, before picking up the one that was already open.

'Come on.'

She walked out of the kitchen and he followed hesitantly. Sarah began to climb the stairs and he stopped at the bottom.

'Where do you want these?' he said.

'Up here, of course.' She smiled down at him. 'In the bathroom. The jacuzzi should be just about ready.'

Later, Roland Devere had a twinge of conscience. Much later. After the jacuzzi, after watching Sarah inhale more cocaine and after they had gone to bed.

He had refused the drug, but he hadn't refused anything else. It had been a memorable experience, half-wild because of Sarah's lack of inhibition, and half-languid because of the tiredness that came in waves. Eventually they slept.

94

Devere woke at six in the evening and lay listening to Sarah's snores. He wondered if Lacey had planned it this way. Incredibly, Devere himself hadn't, although in retrospect he supposed he should have seen the possibility. He probably had, but had kept the thought at the back of his mind because it had been too complicated to deal with until the situation arose. When it had arose it had been very easy to deal with: he had undressed and climbed into the jacuzzi with her. He had always found it easy to undress and climb into situations with women.

It had started at school, that memorable term he had notched up three conquests. Once he had unlocked the mystery of sex there didn't seem any reason to hold back and wait for marriage or meaningful relationships. He was seventeen, virile, good-looking and, more importantly, he knew how to do it. So while contemporaries who had still to break their duck were reticent when faced with the challenge of the opposite sex, he took every opportunity to exploit his knowledge and practise his technique.

Oxford, where he had studied modern languages, had been an even richer hunting ground until he had fallen in love for the first time. The experience had brought his rampant chauvinism to heel and had caused his close friend from school to claim that he had changed from being ruled by his tool, to being ruled like a fool.

When she had finished with him, it seemed that his friend had been right all along. Devere had gone to Sandhurst in a determined frame of mind.

The second time he had fallen heavily was for a girl called Carol, whom he had known as a child. She had been three years younger than him, and on the occasions he had seen her in his youth, she had been too young to notice. When he saw her again he was a new subaltern and she was a young woman. They had a liaison that lasted six months and which was complicated by his career. His regiment went to Germany and by the time he returned, she had gone to America.

Since then he had grown sceptical about love and had

watched fellow officers marry, grow apart from their wives, and sometimes divorce. He felt he was better off with a career and several girlfriends rather than one in particular. Except that Carol had returned on the scene.

They had bumped into each other three months before, in the village near Stroud where they had both grown up. The meeting had led to lunch at the George for old times' sake, the discovery that both were unattached, and clumsy courtship manoeuvres to revive their friendship.

This time, they had agreed, they would approach any relationship that might develop with more maturity and freedom, make allowances for career demands, and respect each other's rights as individuals.

Carol had been extremely understanding about the weekend when he had to cancel at short notice, but he didn't know how she would react if she ever found out about Sarah, even though going to bed with another woman was within his rights as an individual.

She would, of course, never find out, and what she didn't know wouldn't harm her, or the relationship that was quietly growing, through a combination of his lethargy and her attentiveness. In the three months since they had bumped into each other, this was the first time he had been with anyone else, and this, strictly speaking, was in the line of duty. Besides, bedding Sarah Mathieson was an experience he wouldn't have wanted to miss.

To an extent, he recognized a kindred spirit in Sarah. They came from similar backgrounds and he didn't blame her for enjoying herself while she could. Happiness was one of those weird concepts that only equated successfully for poor people. They saw happiness in wealth and aspired to its achievement by lotteries and football pools. But wealth and privilege did not bring happiness. Instead it brought the perspective to see beyond the obvious. There was no such thing as happiness, but there was enjoyment.

It came in many ways: physical, emotional, cerebral. He enjoyed, for instance, the sense of superiority that had been nurtured at school and that he had accepted as a right along with his academic success. He enjoyed being detached from life and participating when he chose to. The troughs of emptiness in between were simply there to be endured and give purpose to the peaks.

He never felt sorry for himself, never had done, even when he had been reprimanded and moved from the Army. To feel sorry for oneself would be to admit a different element entirely into existence. But, oddly, he felt sorry for Sarah. The reason she behaved the way she did was because she was trapped within the confines of her sex. She should have been a man. He chuckled. If she had been, he wouldn't have been lying here, now.

'What time is it?'

She had woken up.

'Just after six.'

'Morning or evening?'

'Evening.'

She stretched and rolled on to her stomach.

'It's Roland, isn't it?'

'Yes.'

He smiled at her directness.

'Yes,' she said. 'You were rather good.'

'Thank you.'

He rolled towards her, but she moved quickly out of the bed and sat on its edge with her back towards him. She held her hands out and moved her fingers as if weaving a spell.

'Don't touch unless invited.' She stood up, unperturbed at being naked, and found her balance. 'First I have to work magic in the bathroom.'

She walked away unsteadily and he admired the length of her legs and the quiver of her buttocks. He looked at his watch again and realized he should phone the office.

Sarah Mathieson spent an hour in the bathroom and boudoir, but emerged looking marvellous in a white silk dress and high heels, and this time it was without the aid of cocaine.

97

Devere told her how good she looked and she accepted the compliment as a matter of course.

'I'll organize dinner,' she said. 'You'll find various male things in that wardrobe.'

She went downstairs and he went to the wardrobe. It contained men's clothing, mainly casual wear, and underwear. Most of it was in the same size, but not all.

He showered, surprised that she was able and willing to cook and at the same time wondering what she would be preparing as the kitchen had seemed short on food. He was hungry, but he didn't set his hopes too high as it would probably be freezer food cooked in a microwave oven.

Devere was wrong on all counts. The food was delicious. It was Chinese and was delivered. With it they drank saki and, afterwards, Sarah reverted to champagne although Devere chose brandy. She sprawled on a rug while he sat on the sofa. An old Commodores album played on the hi-fi.

'How long are you supposed to stay?' she asked.

'Why? Getting bored?'

She smiled at him.

'Not yet. I'll tell you when I'm bored. But how long?'

'There's no time limit. I'm not sure I should be keeping you under such close observation, anyway.'

'It's probably what your associate wanted.'

'Lacey?'

'Yes. Him.'

'I wondered about that, too.'

She stubbed out a cigarette and fixed Devere with a look. So far they hadn't talked about anything substantial. It had been butterfly conversation to pass the time.

'What's the purpose? Am I supposed to open my heart and divulge all?'

He smiled and shrugged.

'I don't know. Is there anything to divulge?'

She continued to stare at him for a long time before picking up her glass and having a drink. Finally she said: 'Why do it?'

'What?'

'The job.'

He shrugged again.

'It has its advantages. I met you.'

She didn't smile.

'Was it worth it?'

'Yes. I think it was.'

She shook her head and held out her empty glass and Devere filled it with more champagne.

'We're both orphans of the storm, Roland. It's people like Lacey and—' she shook her head again '—they're the ones who pull strings. We're the ones who dance.'

'I'm a terrible dancer. I prefer to watch.'

Now she smiled and took another gulp of her champagne.

'I love your arrogance. It's so . . . reassuring.'

'It's not arrogance. It's self-belief.'

This time she laughed.

'You are a marvellously serious young man, Roland.'

She put down the glass and came to him on hands and knees. Her dress gaped and he could see her breasts. Kneeling before him, she pulled his head forward and kissed him, lips open and with her tongue digging deep into his mouth. He moved forward so that his groin pressed against her and she laughed at the reaction of his body.

'Marvellously serious,' she said, 'and deliciously intense.'

She moved against him and he joined her on the rug, aroused by her wantoness and angered by her laughter. He pulled at her clothes, tearing the dress, pushing up the skirt. He lay on top of her, pressing himself hard on to her body to push the air out of her, but could only stop the laughter by covering her mouth with his own. Sarah still made noises, but they were no longer provoked by mirth. Devere no longer felt sorry for her; he felt threatened by her and he was determined to beat her. Their battle lasted all night.

*

Six o'clock again, but this time it was morning. Devere lay awake and confused. It was the first time he had met a member of the opposite sex whom he felt was an equal. There was more to Sarah than he had thought, and much more than Lacey had given her credit for.

Perhaps the age difference counted for more than he had imagined. He had been to bed with older women before, but it had only ever been on a darling basis. Sarah had a self-possession that rivalled his own and an ability for detachment that was enviable and annoying.

There was no after-the-act tenderness, no soft caresses that spoke of something more than a physical coupling. When she had finally had enough, she had shut him out of her mind with a completeness that bruised his ego.

He got out of bed and went to the bathroom. When he came back she was awake and watched him cross the room. He was naked and felt like a stud under appraisal before auction.

'How about coffee?' she said.

He nodded and went downstairs, past the debris of the Chinese meal and into the kitchen to boil the kettle and dispense Nescafé into two mugs. He was surprised when she joined him, wearing the black silk *peignoir* and her face still puffy with sleep. He found it reassuring that this time she hadn't felt the need to disappear into the bathroom for an hour to work magic.

'It's ready,' he said, pouring the water.

Sarah found a tin of powdered milk and a bag of sugar in a cupboard and spooned large quantities of both into her coffee. Devere had his black.

As she finished stirring it, he stroked her shoulder, but she raised one finger in admonishment.

'That's my choice,' she said. 'When and where. And it's not in the kitchen at this ungodly hour.'

Devere again felt uncomfortable at being put in his place and again the stud image filled his mind. Is that what he was being used as?

Sarah left the kitchen and went into the living-room and

he had a quick look at his equipment. As studs go, he wasn't particularly impressive this morning. It was amazing what a few little words could do. Words such as, that's my choice.

He followed her into the living-room and stopped abruptly.

Sarah was immobile two yards away, staring at a tall man who was standing by the front door. The man wore jeans and a blue wind-cheater and held a silenced revolver which was pointing at Devere.

Sarah spoke to the man.

'I haven't told him anything. You don't have to . . .'

The man turned the gun at her and fired.

Devere dropped the mug of coffee in shock as Sarah's body slammed back into the wall. He felt the hot liquid splash on to his leg and regretted not having thrown it at the gunman as he hurled himself back at the kitchen door.

His shoulder caught fire as a bullet hit it, but he slammed the door shut. The next two bullets came through the door panels, one sending wood splinters into his face, the other taking him in the chest.

He fell backwards on to the floor, banging into the fridge, looking for something, anything, to throw as the man kicked open the door.

God, but he looked tall from down here, Devere thought, as his hand found a bottle in the open fridge. It was the last bottle of Bollinger and he didn't have the strength to throw it.

They exchanged looks and Devere remembered Ireland and the Provo he had shot. He smiled at the gunman; it was the only gesture of defiance he could manage.

The man did not smile back. He pointed the gun at Devere's head and fired.

Chapter 13

He could have taken a train to Dover and gone by boat, but catching aeroplanes was now a way of testing himself.

Amos Fowler found a seat in the departure lounge at Heathrow between a good-looking woman in her forties who smelled of expensive perfume and a man in a crumpled suit who smelled of onions.

Vienna had been full of elegant women who had had the time to enjoy being elegant, unlike London where the traffic and pace was getting as bad as New York and elegant women dashed from one location to another as if they were making a thirty-second commercial.

He didn't like London and came only when it was necessary. It gave the impression of being vibrant, but it was a neon-lit, all-electric vibrancy that had nothing to do with the soul and everything to do with making money. Pull the plug and the office blocks would haemorrhage and the Thames would overflow with suicides. Life might never be the same again. It was a beautiful thought.

The lead story on the front page of all three of the morning newspapers he had bought, were about the killing of socialite Sarah Mathieson. The papers were chasing each other's tales in making her the greatest heroine since Odette Churchill. Who was Odette Churchill? Shit. Everybody was playing games: reporters, assassins, the secret services of the world, even Joe Doakes who read this crap and went along with it because it was better than real life.

On an inside page of the *Daily Mail* were two paragraphs about an old woman of eighty-nine who had been battered to death in her home in Accrington, Lancashire. The thieves had stolen four pounds.

Fowler laughed out loud, and, when the woman looked at him, he smiled at her.

'Excuse me,' he said. 'I just read something very funny.'

News values had always amused him. If the news was hot there was nothing reporters wouldn't dig up and use, nail their morality to their Press cards and justify their actions in the name of freedom and the inalienable right of the public to know.

Where had they been during Operation Blue Skies when the American Air Force had sprayed Agent Orange over half Vietnam and dioxin had killed the crops and maimed the generations to come? Where had they been when the Air-America planes of the CIA had run similar runs into Laos and Cambodia?

Maybe the public hadn't wanted to know that My Lai wasn't an atrocity but a common practice, or hear about the overfull orphanages, or the business cards dropped by helicopter gunships that said, 'Killing is our business and business is good.' But hell, why should he care? He didn't. What angered him was people's innate dishonesty.

Who said you couldn't fool most of the people most of the time? They wanted to be fooled, wanted to be reassured. Conflict was upsetting, dead babies were upsetting. Shit, dead babies weren't news, dead babies put you off dinner.

Babies had always died in Africa and Asia, but no-one took any notice unless a rock star sang a song about them and gave the public the opportunity to salve its conscience for the price of a record.

They wanted easy answers, easy options. They wanted easy wars, clean-cut heroes and beautiful heroines. The world was a crock of shit and the people deserved to live in it.

He turned to the back of the paper and found a cartoon strip of Garfield the cat. Garfield was having trouble with a plate of spaghetti, but he triumphed in the end. It made him smile. He admired the cat's laid-back philosophy. In his own quiet way, Fowler had the same philosophy. He had always got the spaghetti.

Nam had provided opportunities to make fortunes. The black market at Qui Nhon alone had an eleven million dollar a month turnover. But it had been something others did, not him. Until he lost belief.

He didn't know when that had been, but it had probably started one day in the Mekong Delta. He was on a chopper that made an unscheduled stop to pick up the body of an American who had died in action when his infantry company pacified a village.

Fowler had watched his fellow countrymen cut off the ears of dead civilians they said were Charlie Cong, but who looked like women and old men, and thread them on a string. A sergeant said the American had been shot in error by his own side and gave him the guy's Zippo as a keepsake.

He had climbed aboard the chopper that was taking him and the body out of there, and read the inscription on the back of the lighter. It said, 'I pass through the valley of death unafraid – for I'm the meanest bastard in the valley.' The guy was called Oaksie, he was from Maryland and he was nineteen.

It was one of a hundred incidents, but for some reason it had more impact than most. Oaksie hadn't been a mean bastard until someone had put an MI6 in his hand and told him it was OK to shoot gooks. He would have taken part in ear-cutting, mutilation and occasional rape, in much the same way he would have taken part in high-school pranks back home. Even then, he probably hadn't been a mean bastard, just a kid trying to make it with his peers.

Out here, his buddies were the same age, fighting a cowboy and indian war they didn't understand. Shit, they might as well enjoy themselves when they could.

Fowler had sat next to Oaksie in the helicopter. The kid had red hair and freckles. His face was unmarked and he looked younger than nineteen. He was on the first stage of a journey Stateside to a military funeral to make his mom and dad proud, but his right boot tapped out a constant message against a metal strut with the vibration of the chopper. It seemed as if he wasn't as peaceful as he looked and had a lot to say in bad morse. Fowler understood his impatience and his message. Oaksie was saying there's no fun being dead and there's no glory in dying. Fowler had patted the kid's knee to let him know he'd heard.

Soon after that, Fowler began ferrying opium across borders that, for him, didn't exist.

He knew guys who had traded in gold and jewellery and who had sold exit visas to rich Vietnamese as the war rolled to an end, but who had steered clear of drugs because they believed it would tarnish some weird set of values. Drugs killed people, man, it messed up the minds of the youth of America, it was bad stuff.

The war had killed more than a million people, including fifty-eight thousand youthful Americans. It had messed up the minds of so many others that another fifty-eight thousand committed suicide when they returned home because they couldn't readjust to their mom's apple pie.

He had run drugs and it had not offended his values because, by then, he had none that would have been acceptable to anyone but himself. War was good for only two things, killing and making money, and he had perfected both. And when Vietnam was finally falling, he had remained a laid-back Garfield the cat and accepted the increased opportunities, including the liberation of a $50,000 CIA payroll from the Air America offices at Tan Son Nhut.

Fowler had left Saigon two days before the end and headed for Hong Kong. Over dinner at the San Francisco Steak House he had worked out his investments and discovered he was a millionaire. He had laughed then, too, before going out and buying an apartment.

He still lived there, and he trusted the Chinese more than he trusted anybody else because they were more interested in devils than gods, but he still didn't trust them very much. He also had a house in Sydney and a villa in Minorca.

Now he worked only when he wanted to, at a negotiable fee that got higher every time, to see if he could, eventually, break somebody's bank. So far, he had always got his price, which was as it should be, because he was the best.

The Air France flight was called and he helped the good-looking woman when she dropped her Gucci briefcase. She smiled her thanks and her eyes suggested something else, maybe, for when they got to Paris. His smile flirted, but he had no intention of following through because he was on a job, he worked alone and even a one-night stand could cause complications.

He left the newspapers on the seat and looked again at the photograph of Sarah Mathieson on the front pages. Sex and complications.

Benjamin Franklin had a line that was apposite. 'Three may keep a secret . . . if two of them are dead.'

One was dead in a London apartment and he was on his way to see the second in Arras, France.

Chapter 14

The crematorium had the transient flavour of an airport departure lounge. Lacey thought it entirely appropriate for Sarah Mathieson's last trip.

He had been instructed to attend by Hector Rossington-Hall, even though it was obviously going to be a very public occasion. The police hadn't allowed Press photographers into the grounds, but they lobbied the entrance drive and used zoom lenses from a distance.

Lacey slipped into a row three or four from the back, in the hope of avoiding any of the political and gossip column celebrities who were present. Bland church muzak murmured in the background as the room filled with people in solemn colours. Rossington-Hall entered and joined him.

'There's someone I want you to meet,' he said. 'Later.'

The coffin arrived and was followed down the aisle by the family mourners, led by the well-known figure of the Home Secretary. Lacey assumed the tall middle-aged man with him must be Sarah's husband.

Those who had waited outside for the arrival of the cortège found there were no seats left. They lined the sides and stood two or three deep at the rear, with the overspill filling the entrance vestibule. A Right Reverend clergyman nodded approval at the size of the congregation and began the service. His words were as meaningful as the muzak.

Funerals had never thrilled Lacey, but at least Roland Devere's had had more style.

A lot had happened in the last week. Two funerals, a row with Rossington-Hall, recurring self-recriminations and nothing new to chase.

The police who had investigated the double murder had behaved with care as soon as they realized Sarah's identity. Special Branch had been informed and when Devere's name rang alarm bells on their computer screens, they moved to contain the Press.

All that was released initially was that two people had died in a shooting incident. There were no details, and nor would there be, of the state of dress or undress of the victims. Reporters found out for themselves that the shooting had been at the home of a minister's daughter and had smelled a major story.

HRH had moved swiftly to smother unsavoury and unsafe speculation. An exclusive in the *Daily Express*, written by a tame journalist who specialized in security matters, ensured every other newspaper followed the lead the Deputy Director wanted them to follow.

Unattributed facts from informed sources had hinted at Sarah's involvement in the infiltration of European terror networks on behalf of Britain's secret services. Devere's military record revealed he had undergone training with the SAS and he was cast in the role of bodyguard.

There had been, and could be, no direct statement on the deaths, as MI6 officially did not exist, but an early ruling from the coroner at the opening of the inquest stipulated that when the hearing resumed, it would be conducted, on the grounds of national security, purely into the cause of death and not the reasons why.

It was the sort of story the tabloids loved. They had been provided with a patriotic hero and heroine and a loose scenario around which they could weave whatever fantasy they chose.

The police investigation into what had happened had revealed only that a male person in jeans and a short jacket had been seen leaving the premises by a milkman. There was no description as the witness had been a hundred yards away.

Lacey had read the reports, spoken to the first officers on the scene and been to the house with Malcolm. They had searched it while Special Branch had held off local detectives, but had found nothing of significance apart from an address book, which Lacey pocketed.

An answerphone yielded nine messages that related to social engagements, and the bedroom telephone had a memory that logged ten numbers. It allowed a caller to dial numbers that were frequently used simply by pressing a single digit. They retrieved the numbers before wiping the memory clean. This was a murder that would not be solved by conventional police methods and might very well be hindered by them.

Two things were apparent. The killer had known Sarah Mathieson well enough either to be let into the house or to have had his own key and knowledge of the alarm system. It was also clear that her relationship with Aldo Capaldi had been far more meaningful than she had said. She might still be an innocent, but she had known more than she had been willing to admit. Lacey had warned HRH against releasing the cover story on the grounds that they still didn't know what she had been involved in. It could all backfire if it was ultimately revealed she really had been recruited into a terrorist group.

HRH's response had been unequivocal. It was Lacey's job to make sure the cover story stuck, no matter what she had done.

To reinforce the pretence, Lacey had been ordered to attend the funeral so he could be introduced to the Home Secretary. If the Home Secretary believed, those close to him would believe. The ripples of credibility would spread.

Lacey hadn't intended going to either funeral, but after being told to be at Sarah's he had decided to go to Devere's as well. Another gesture, maybe, but it made him feel better.

The Foreign Office always sent a faceless individual, as a matter of course, to represent a department he had never seen and to mourn a man he had never known. Lacey hadn't known Devere very well, but he had shared office space with him, had glared face to face with him, had started an operation with him.

Devere had been buried in the family plot in a church-yard on a hillside near Stroud in Gloucestershire. It had rained, which allowed Lacey to turn up the collar of his raincoat. The Press had attended, but in smaller numbers than had turned out for Sarah, and had been kept from the church grounds.

The church was old and its walls smelled of history and damp. Ancient flags hung in its rafters and a stone knight lay on a tomb in a side chapel. Those who attended were family, personal friends, villagers, two officers from his old regiment, and a very pretty girl whose eyes were red with crying. It had been exactly right.

Afterwards, they had all stood around in the drizzle and watched the coffin slide into the muddy hole. Lacey had felt empty. Maybe it wasn't a gesture that had brought him there. Maybe it was guilt at not foreseeing what might have happened, at setting Devere up for a hit. After all, Lacey had been running the operation; it had been his responsibility.

His intention had been to slip away unnoticed, but in such an intimate group he stood out. Devere's elder brother, Ranulf, came across and introduced himself with a handshake.

'You must be Lacey,' he said.

'Yes.'

Lacey was a little surprised at being identified. The elder Devere smiled.

'You had to be. I know everybody else and the chappie from the FO called at the house. Roland mentioned you. It had to be you.'

Lacey nodded.

'I'm very sorry.'

'Yes. We all are.'

He looked back at the family group.

A tall lady with iron hair and straight back remained by the open grave, leaning on a walking-stick. The young woman with the red eyes held her other arm. Around them, generations of gravestones declared themselves to be

110

Deveres. There was nothing Lacey could say or do.

'I'm sorry,' he repeated.

Ranulf Devere shook his hand again.

'Thank you for coming. I know it must be difficult for you.'

He had walked back to the two women and Lacey had moved away across the grass, stepping on the uncomplaining dead of two centuries to make his escape.

Devere's death might have been premature, but his funeral had had a continuity with nature and history. It made a sort of sense of his short life and Lacey was glad he had been. In contrast, Sarah Mathieson's departure had all the dignity of the morning after an end of term ball. Genuine grief was probably restricted to immediate family; the rest, who had come out of duty and the need to be seen, maintained expressions they appeared to have saved from their last hangovers.

Finally, the cleric finished and the coffin slid tastefully out of sight through red velvet curtains, while a piece of classical music climbed to a gentle crescendo. Lacey wondered if it was by Franz Haber.

The entrance had been locked and they waited to file out of a door at the front. Once there, Lacey saw that the queue crocodiled along a glass corridor to the exit where the Home Secretary and Sarah Mathieson's husband were shaking hands with everyone present. Some held up the proceedings by clinging to a hand and murmuring extended condolences, as if they were begging favours at a medieval court; and perhaps they thought they were. Others went through the vaguely embarrassing formula of sad smile and handshake with a minimum of fuss.

Lacey looked at his watch and prepared to be party to Rossington-Hall's lie. Afterwards, he would find a pub that was still open and swallow the bile in his throat with the aid of two or five drinks.

He had felt guilty at the death of Roland Devere, but he still felt only anger at Sarah Mathieson. If the stupid bitch had been honest with them, neither she nor Devere would have been dead. To an extent, his anger off-loaded the guilt on to her. Having to meet the Home Secretary was, in the circumstances, distasteful, but, because of the rules laid out by HRH, it was necessary. It was another part of the job.

The closer he got, the more agitated he became. He checked the alignment of the ceiling tiles and counted the hairs in the left ear of the man in front. He even attempted conversation with Hector Rossington-Hall.

'Who do you want me to meet?'

'Later.'

'When, later?'

'Patience, Lacey. We're almost there.'

Their turn came. Rossington-Hall took the Home Secretary's hand in both his own.

'Reginald,' he said, in tones of familiarity. 'Deepest, deepest condolences.'

'Thank you, Hector. Thank you for coming.' But his eyes had already passed on to Lacey, as if he had been waiting for him. 'And is this . . . ?'

'Yes. This is Peter Lacey. He's the chap who was working with Sarah.'

The Home Secretary took Lacey's hand as if he was seeking a benediction. Lacey looked into the man's face and saw the same red-rimmed eyes he had seen on the girl in the church near Stroud. This was Reginald Mottram, father, not Reginald Mottram, Home Secretary.

'Thank you for coming, Mr Lacey. I hope . . .'

The man's mouth worked around words that refused to form. Lacey found himself speaking out of compassion.

'It was a tragedy, sir. It shouldn't have happened.'

'No, no.' The Home Secretary still held his hand, but the grip felt recharged. 'It shouldn't have happened. But . . . I understand. Thank you, Mr Lacey. Thank you for coming. And God be with you. Thank you, Hector.'

Lacey nodded, unsure of his emotions, and moved on to Sarah Mathieson's husband, a tall cold man who offered only fingertips for their formal, wordless, handshake.

Outside, he took deep breaths to reassure himself he was still alive. It was as if he'd spent the last hour in limbo.

'Well done, Lacey. Exactly right. Taciturn, stiff upper lip stuff. Just the job. This way.'

Lacey watched Rossington-Hall march briskly across the car park to a black Jaguar XJ6 with smoked-glass windows. The insensitivity of the little prick never failed to amaze him. He wondered if he realized just how close he had come to a kick up the arse. But the moment passed. Lacey followed him.

Rossington-Hall opened the driver's door and motioned for Lacey to get in the back. He did so, and found himself sharing the leather seats with a tall, rangy man with blond hair and piercing blue eyes. They swopped stares.

The Deputy Director leaned over the front seat to make the introductions.

'Lacey, meet Dan Beckindale. He's going to help you clear up this whole mess.'

The prospect of outside help did not fill Lacey with immediate enthusiasm. Beckindale appeared to be equally unmoved. They sized each other up and neither offered to shake hands.

He was unmistakably American. That was obvious from the name, haircut and clothes. In itself, that was not necessarily a minus factor. Lacey had worked well with Americans in the past but, like anybody else, they came in all varieties, from king-sized prats to efficient professionals. What irked him more than anything was the way Rossington-Hall had staged the meeting without prior warning. Judging from the leer on his face, the deputy director had enjoyed it.

Lacey looked at HRH without expression and then back to the American. When he spoke, he was polite.

'Excuse me asking, Mr Beckindale, but why do I need your help?'

Beckindale was equally as civil.

'Because, Mr Lacey, I have information you don't

have, because I know where Aldo Capaldi is, and because Sarah Mathieson was working for me.'

Lacey continued to keep a tight control on his emotions. He nodded.

'As reasons go,' he said, 'they appear to be pretty conclusive.'

Chapter 15

Lacey took out a packet of Gitanes and a box of matches.

'I'd prefer it if you didn't, Lacey.'

HRH's leer changed to a stern glare. As he was so small, it didn't travel well over the expansive upholstery of the front seats. Lacey pretended not to have heard him.

'May I join you?'

Beckindale nodded at the cigarettes and Lacey offered them in surprise at his forwardness. They both lit up and Rossington-Hall remained silent.

The American said, 'I think you two gentlemen may have some things to discuss. How about if I wait in Mr Lacey's car?'

'An excellent idea. Lacey, give Dan your keys.'

Lacey wondered what percentage of his pension rights he might lose for sticking the cigarette up Rossington-Hall's nose. The pension didn't really matter, but he might also lose his job. He compromised by exhaling smoke over him as he handed over the keys.

'It's a blue Sierra. Registration . . .'

'I know the registration.'

Beckindale climbed out of the car and closed the door.

Lacey glared at Rossington-Hall.

'Who is he?'

'About that cigarette . . .'

'Stuff the cigarette. You owe me explanations. Who is he?'

The small man's mouth opened and closed twice in vexation at the tone of Lacey's voice and his refusal to do anything about the cigarette apart from smoke it.

'He's from Washington. He's a trouble-shooter for

Command Group Alpha. That's the control group for the National Security Council's Anti-Terrorism Unit.'

Lacey had heard of the Anti-Terrorism Unit, but not of the command group, but that was not surprising. The Americans had a way of proliferating committees that made Whitehall's mandarins look like amateurs.

'He said Sarah was working for him. How?'

'She was undercover. That's why she was with Capaldi.'

Lacey restrained himself from grabbing the deputy director by the lapels and breaking the man's nose with his head.

'How long have you known?'

The tone of Lacey's voice warned Rossington-Hall and his abrasiveness softened.

'Two days ago. But it was only yesterday we decided you had to know. I couldn't reach you yesterday. You were at a funeral.'

If he had wanted to, Rossington-Hall could have reached him and they both knew it, but it wasn't a point worth labouring.

'Who decided I had to know? You or him?'

'It was a joint decision. I had to assure Beckindale that you were secure. His operation is extremely delicate. It's NODIS scale. Only a handful of very top people know about it.'

NODIS was an American classification that meant no distribution beyond a select few. Its messages were eyes only. Lacey wondered how select the few were, but knew the National Security Council was plugged directly into the President, closer even than the CIA, being quartered in the Old Executive Office building next to the White House. Beckindale was major league.

While he thought, he stubbed the cigarette out in a pristine ashtray. Finally he looked up.

'Who helps who?'

'You help each other.'

'Who has seniority?'

'That shouldn't arise.'

'It will. It always does.'

116

Rossington-Hall became exasperated at Lacey's persistence.

'Beckindale has volunteered to help clear up the Capaldi affair so that his own operation will not be jeopardized. Therefore you are, technically, in control. But I wouldn't advise you to push it.'

'What does he know about our operation?'

'He's had access to the file.'

'So he knows the lot?'

'Yes.'

'What do we know about his operation?'

Rossington-Hall hesitated before answering.

'It involves infiltrating terror groups in Europe and the Middle East.'

'Is that all you know?'

He hesitated again.

'It's all either you or I need to know.'

'Whatever happened to the special relationship?'

Rossington-Hall felt it safe to re-assert himself.

'I suggest that the way forward now lies in your obtaining the aid and assistance of Dan Beckindale. Form your own special relationship. Perhaps he'll tell you.'

Lacey pushed open the door and got out. He slammed it shut with enough force to atomize the ash in the squeaky clean ashtray.

He put another cigarette in his mouth as he walked across a parking area that was now half empty. He climbed into the driving seat of his own car before he lit up. Beckindale sat passively in the passenger seat and, remembering his manners, Lacey offered the Gitanes again.

'No thanks.' The American smiled. 'I don't smoke.'

The pantomime in the Jaguar had been an attempt at an early alliance. Maybe he would be all right.

Lacey said, 'How do you suggest we sort this out?'

'How about over a drink?'

Lacey wouldn't be persuaded to be friends easily, but the bloke certainly was making all the right moves.

They drove past the first two or three pubs on the way back to London, to avoid fellow mourners and journalists. The one they chose was on the edge of an unfashionable urban sprawl. It claimed it sold real ale so Lacey ordered a pint of bitter that was warm from the wood. Beckindale had a can of Budweiser that was cold from the fridge. They still had a long way to go to bridge their differences.

In the car they had talked little and Lacey had been impressed by the American's ability to remain comfortably silent. He also had noticed the way he walked when they had reached the pub. The man was fluid, relaxed and didn't waste movement. He made Lacey feel more flabby than normal.

The bar was mock Victorian and the legend that ran along the top said: work is the curse of the drinking classes. The position and demeanour of three building workers appeared to prove the point. They had been leaning on the bar long enough for the mud to dry on their boots and were debating whether to return to the site at all that afternoon.

Lacey and Beckindale moved to the far side of the room, past two pensioners playing dominoes, and sat at a table in the corner. They had a drink of their beers and looked at each other.

'Let me lay one thing down at the start,' Beckindale said. 'If I was in your position, I'd be pissed off.' He shrugged. 'I'm sorry about this whole thing, about Sarah and your guy and the whole damn thing. But it has happened, we're both involved, and the only way to straighten it out is to go get the son of a bitch who did it. To do that, we have to work together. End of speech.'

Lacey lit a cigarette.

'I'm told you've seen our file on Sarah Mathieson.'

'That's right.'

'I'm also told I don't need to know what you're doing.'

'Not strictly true. I can't give you specifics, in any

case, there's no need to, but I can give you a general outline.'

'I'd appreciate that.'

'Well, as you know, we haven't got the sort of penetration we'd like to have among the Jihad and freedom groups. We've pretty few skins on the wall in the Middle East. Mainly we rely on Mossad. I'm trying to make contacts in Europe. Mercenaries, professionals for hire, arms dealers, what's left of the Red Brigade networks. The sort of contacts that could lead East. Maybe turn one or two people, insert the right agent at the right time and place.' He shrugged. 'We're not looking for overnight results. It's a slow business.'

Lacey was well aware of the shortcomings of American intelligence in that very sensitive part of the world. The CIA had relied on the Shah and the Savak secret police and, quite often, on MI6. It was the revolution and the embassy hostage taking in Iran that had illustrated how few real agents they had and how little they knew. When William Casey had tried to increase his operatives on the ground, Mossad had dismissed them as the players who couldn't play.

'What was Sarah doing?'

'She was getting close to Capaldi. The plan was that eventually she would arrange a meeting for me. Then it would be up to me to persuade him to work for us.'

Lacey watched Beckindale intently, but the American wasn't joking.

'Why should he?'

Beckindale smiled at Lacey's obvious scepticism.

'We believed there was a chance. He'd been profiled and his character suggested he might respond to a new challenge. Capaldi is one of those who's in it for the kicks, not the politics. Besides, we were prepared to pay well, and he hasn't been too choosy who he's worked for in the past.'

'But your profile was faulty. Sarah got killed.'

'We didn't get a chance to find out if it was faulty.

Maybe he suspected Sarah all along, and maybe the photographer spooked him.'

'Then why kill her in London? Why not do it in Vienna?'

'I don't know. Except . . . I was at the house party with Sarah the day before your boss took her away. Capaldi was in London and she was supposed to call him. A check call at a set time on Monday morning. Maybe she didn't make it, maybe she didn't think it was that important. Maybe Capaldi did.'

And maybe, thought Lacey, she couldn't because she was in bed with Roland Devere.

'Why use Sarah? Why not a professional?'

'I've known Sarah a long time. She was a friend of my wife's. She had all the right qualifications and she wanted to do it.'

Lacey knew it was not unknown for ladies like Sarah, with the best of backgrounds, to be used by his own Firm, usually as part of a team that was trying to compromise a member of the international opposition. But in this case, Sarah had been used naked, without back-up. He wondered if he should revise his opinion of her, but told himself she had still been the cause of her own death and that of Devere. Intrepid amateurs were like that.

Using her also said something about Beckindale. The man had said he accepted infiltration was a slow business, but maybe he had been pushing for results. And maybe the whole thing had gone sour simply because a fat photographer had got snap happy at the wrong time.

'You've seen the Mathieson file,' Lacey said. 'Have you seen my file, too?'

Beckindale smiled. It was an easy smile that showed even white teeth. His blue eyes were open and friendly; they smiled, too.

'I know about you.'

'That's good. But I don't know about you. I'd like to; particularly if we're going looking for Aldo Capaldi together.'

The American thought about it and then nodded.

'Fair enough.' He considered for a moment. 'I was in Special Forces in Vietnam and I did a stint with the Rangers and was involved in Grenada. I've seen action and I made colonel, before I left the service. For the last three years I've been with the NSC in Washington. Those are the bones. You'll have to make up your own mind about the rest.'

Lacey had no doubt Beckindale was well able to look after himself. Special Forces had built a ruthless reputation in Vietnam and the United States Rangers were a go-anywhere élite, the equivalent of Britain's Paras. But he seemed a little light on experience in covert operations.

'OK. So tell me about Capaldi.'

'He's in Northern France. Near Arras. If you're not doing anything, I thought we could go over there tomorrow.'

'I'm not doing anything.'

'Good. We'll go by car. I'll make the arrangements.'

'And when we get there?'

'We deal with . . . the situation.'

'Meaning?'

'Let's not be coy. Rossington-Hall wants his scam to stick which means we make sure Aldo has nothing nasty stashed away. But, whatever term you use, the guy has to be silenced permanently.'

'Are you prepared to do that? Or is that why you're taking me along?'

Beckindale looked at him, his expression serious.

'Hot blood or cold. It makes no difference. I'll do what has to be done, because it has to be done.'

It was said with total conviction, but Lacey wondered if the man would be as cool if called upon actually to do the deed in circumstances divorced from battle. Executions were a world away from glory and Beckindale had spent three years sitting behind a desk in Washington.

'You could live with it?'

'I can live with it.' He smiled ruefully. 'Don't take this

the wrong way, but I believe in God and my country.
When you have a belief that strong, you find you can do
most things that need to be done.'

Faced with God and country, Lacey couldn't think of a
thing to say. He lit another cigarette. Maybe it was the
man's honesty, or the naïve way he wore his integrity
like a purple heart, but he liked him.

Chapter 16

Any reservations Lacey might have had were put in perspective by the attitude of Rossington-Hall. The deputy director had made it plain he wanted the affair dealt with immediately if not sooner, and without the possibility of any aspect of it coming back to haunt Six, the Government, the Home Secretary or himself.

But Lacey could think of better partners for a cross-Channel killing trip than a cousin who appeared to be more gung-ho than streetwise. He liked Beckindale, but he didn't know if he could trust him when the going got devious.

After dropping the American off at a tube station, Lacey stopped to phone Susan at the shop to tell her he would be home early. It was something he didn't normally do and only realized the abnormality of the act while he was making the call. He joked with himself about nerves, but it was unsettling. It was one thing to react to changing circumstances in the middle of an operation, quite something else to charge head first into an operation without knowing what the circumstances were.

Beckindale had assured him he had everything under control, that they didn't need a team and that he had his own sources close to Capaldi that guaranteed success. But maybe Beckindale thought he was storming another hill in Vietnam.

Susan was surprised at the call, but tried not to show it.

'I'm going away for a couple of days tomorrow.'

'Oh.' She knew better than to ask why or where. 'Do you want to do anything tonight?'

'Mmmm?'

'Go out for dinner?'

'No. No, I've had enough of socializing. I'd rather stay in.'

'Was it awful? The funeral?'

'About average on the futile scale. The only one who enjoyed it was the vicar. Enjoying death must be part of their vocation.'

The words made him feel cold. They were too close to home.

Susan said, 'I'll get away early.' She dropped her voice to a whisper. 'Lucy's beginning to send me mad, anyway. Is there anything special you want for dinner?'

'Mmm? No. Nothing special.'

He just wanted home. Familiar walls, familiar smells, books to touch, a bottle of Scotch, Susan. Most of all Susan. He shook his head. Two funerals in two days were not healthy.

'Peter?'

'Yes. I'm still here.'

'I'll see you soon.'

'Yes. Soon.'

She cooked a spaghetti and he opened a bottle of Valpolicella. They didn't speak much and she was aware of his unease. Each time they passed in the kitchen he touched her or stroked her hair, as if reassuring himself that she was there. They ate at the kitchen table and started with garlic bread and minestrone soup.

'You'll smell delightful in the morning,' she said.

'So will you.'

'Maybe it will keep Lucy at bay.'

'If it doesn't, try a stake through the heart.'

'Not funny.'

'Not meant to be. I always suspected Lucy. She's been wearing boiler suits too long. At first I thought, latent lesbian. But now you've mentioned it, maybe she's a latent vampire.'

'You've got a great line in sexism, Peter. It's a good job I know you.'

He looked at her.

'Yes, it is.'

They ate in silence for a while.

Susan said: 'She can't help it, you know. It's hit her harder than expected.'

'Michael still not made up his mind?'

'No. Well, partly.'

'How do you mean?'

'He's moved into the spare room.'

'I'd have done that years ago.'

She reprimanded him with a look.

'Where's your milk of human kindness?'

'We've just finished it. I'll get another bottle.'

He got up from the table and opened a second bottle of Valpolicella.

He said, 'Has he got another woman?'

'I don't know. Lucy says not, but she'd be the last to know.'

'Mid-life crisis?'

'I don't know. When does it happen in men?'

'When you discover life's a bitch and then you die.' He toasted her with the wine. 'Sorry. I'm that way out tonight.'

They finished eating and surveyed the debris. Lacey got up and began moving plates.

'Leave it,' said Susan. 'I'll do it in the morning.'

'You'll be late for the shop.'

'Bugger the shop.'

'Lucy won't like it.'

'Bugger Lucy.'

At the moment Susan wasn't bothered about anybody or anything but the danger signals coming from her husband. They were close, but he still retained a privacy that bordered on introversion. She accepted it as partly his personality, partly his job and partly the experiences he had survived.

A by-product of his job were the occasional black moods when, as he described it, the gremlins waited to get him.

She didn't know whether it was fear, guilt, premonition or what that caused the moods, but she could sense the gremlins gathering tonight and they had a lot to work on: two deaths and two funerals.

They took the bottle and their glasses into the living-room and he lit a cigarette. He switched on the television although he left the sound off.

'There's a film on in ten minutes. You don't mind?'

'I don't mind.'

She sat next to him on the settee, close enough but not too close. Sometimes he didn't like crowding. They watched a silent nature film that had been shot under-water, somewhere where the sea was a glorious blue. It was like meditating.

'I met an American today,' he said.

His tone implied he had been in contact with a con-tagious disease.

'I thought you liked Americans?'

'I do.'

'So what's wrong with this one?'

'Nothing's wrong with him.'

'But you don't like him?'

'Funnily enough, I do.'

They continued watching exotic fish being languid in paradise.

Susan, her eyes still on the screen, said: 'Be careful when you're away.'

He chuckled and put his hand on her arm.

'There's no danger. It's a straightforward courier run. Two days, three at the most. I'll bring you back some Chanel.'

She used the contact to move closer to him and he seemed to welcome it and put his arm around her shoul-ders. The nature programme ended and the credits for the film began. It was a re-run of the classic, *Casablanca*. He used the remote control to turn up the sound and they relaxed into the celluloid intrigue.

He had said it was a courier run and she wanted to

126

believe him, but she knew it was more than that. Two of his colleagues had been killed and it was likely the trip would be in connection with the same operation. She had witnessed his depressions and together they had groped their way through the uncertainties of their own relationship, but she had never before seen him display self-doubt. Maybe she was wrong. Maybe it wasn't a lack of confidence. Maybe it was just two funerals in two days.

Lacey drank enough to send himself to sleep as soon as they got into bed. He lay on his back and was grateful for the comfort of Susan lying in the crook of his arm.

He woke about three in the morning. He still lay on his back, but Susan was no longer on his arm. She had rolled away to curl up on her side.

For a while he lay still and stared at the darkness of the ceiling. He had been dreaming about drinking Coca Cola and slowly realized it was thirst that had awakened him, not the gremlins. The wine, and a couple of Scotches, had left him dehydrated.

He slipped out of bed and picked up his cigarettes and matches from the bedside table. He didn't bother with a dressing-gown but remained naked. If he disturbed a burglar it would be the burglar's bad luck. The shock might make the man go straight. He stroked his stomach as he padded down the stairs in the darkness. His belly now stuck out further than anything else. He could remember when another part of his anatomy had enjoyed that distinction. Beckindale was about his age, he guessed. He also guessed that with or without clothes, the American was in far better shape. Was that the niggle at the back of his mind? Jealousy?

Lacey used the downstairs lavatory before going into the kitchen. It smelled of last night's food. When he opened the refrigerator it threw a mocking spotlight on to his body. He took a can of Coke and told the refrigerator to piss off. The cold drink cleared the sour dryness from his mouth and throat and made him feel better. He lit a cigarette and let the smoke fill his lungs. If the job didn't get him the tobacco would. But what the hell, there was little to choose between them. They both came with government health warnings.

He went into the living-room and flopped into an armchair. The girl with red eyes at the funeral of Roland Devere came back into his mind. He wondered who she was and why she had been grieving so much. If he had made a greater effort with Devere perhaps he would know the answers; perhaps if he had made a greater effort, he and Devere would have exchanged the personal sort of information that would have given them the chance to form a friendship. Perhaps then, he wouldn't have consigned his colleague to bedroom duties with Sarah Mathieson in such a crude fashion. Perhaps. Shit, what the hell did perhaps mean?

Devere's brother had known Lacey, which meant Roland had talked about him, but what had he said? Lacey knew it didn't matter a toss what Devere had said, the man was dead and could not be brought back, but he still hoped he had spoken well of him. It was stupid and illogical, an emotional desire for posthumous respect. He shook his head. No, it wasn't. It was a desire to be pardoned, to be cleared of blame.

He stubbed out the cigarette and finished the Coke and walked back up the stairs towards the bedroom. The silent house belonged to the night and he had no desire to disturb its occupation. He got back into bed and Susan moved and snorted gently in her sleep and he stroked her arm and pulled the cover over her. For a while he lay on his back with his eyes open and stared again at the darkness of the ceiling.

Roland Devere had been a colleague, not a friend, but the loss had been deeply felt. Now he had Dan Beckindale and he suspected the man could become a friend, rather than a colleague, and the thought frightened him. He had no doubts about the man's abilities in battle, but this was a different kind of war. Shit. He wasn't frightened for himself. He just didn't want to face another funeral.

Chapter 17

Susan didn't leave for the shop until ten. He had forced a cheerful mood to reassure her, but wasn't sure if she believed it. The funny thing was, it worked on him. By mid-morning he was in a much better frame of mind.

When it was time for her to go, he went with her to the front door, but she hesitated before leaving him.

'I'm fine,' he said. 'You get off before Lucy sends out search parties.'

'You sure?'

'I'm sure.' He smiled. 'It's the sunshine. It puts things in perspective.'

'Then stay out of the shadows.'

He kissed her cheek.

'I will.'

She left reluctantly and he watched her drive away in her corrugated Citroën van. He had an hour before Beckindale was due to pick him up. The good humour remained.

Lacey went to the safe in the study and took from it a large brown envelope and a bundle wrapped in soft leather. He went into the kitchen and sat at the kitchen table to unwrap the bundle. It contained a Heckler and Koch 9mm handgun. It had a magazine that could hold eighteen bullets and an additional stock that acted as a holster and also turned it into a sub-machine-gun.

The gun was made mainly from plastic and he took it apart, checked its moving pieces, and put it back together again. When he was satisfied, he took the gun and the envelope upstairs to the bedroom.

He fitted the gun beneath the false bottom of the holdall

129

before packing, on top, enough clothes for a two-day trip. Finally, he emptied his pockets and put anything identifiable into his sock drawer. From the envelope he took another set of documents, including passport, driving licence and credit cards in the name of Peter Eastwood, freelance travel writer.

The gun and change of identity were strictly illegal which was why he kept them in a safe at home rather than at the office. Going through channels to obtain a new name and authorization to carry weapons was a tedious process that would have caused delays.

He took the bag downstairs, put fresh coffee in the percolator and hung around waiting for the aroma. The black mood had gone and been replaced by optimism. He felt good and his senses tingled. He hadn't been joking when he had mentioned the sunshine to Susan. It had given him a charge, a feeling of life. Emotional extremes didn't surprise him; depression had taught him to survive the downswings and welcome the upswings without question.

The smell of coffee began to permeate the air. He breathed it in deeply. This morning, everything seemed possible. Even a short-notice trip to France. Even surviving a friendship.

Beckindale arrived in a Mercedes at ten minutes past eleven.

'I got lost,' he said, as he unlocked the boot so that Lacey could stow his holdall.

Lacey wore his favourite leather jacket, and dark blue slacks and shirt, and he was pleased to see the American was also casually dressed. Instead of the Brooks Brothers suit he wore Levis and a wind-cheater.

They had agreed on the pick-up because Beckindale was living in an embassy apartment at St Katharine's Dock, overlooking Tower Bridge. Lacey's home at Beckenham was not on a direct route to Dover, but it was more sensible for the American to drive out of the city rather than for Lacey to trek in. From Beckenham it was relatively easy to

130

join the M20 and then cut across to pick up the M2 to Dover.

'Nice house,' Beckindale said, as they got in the car.

'Yes.' Lacey looked back at it. A detached Victorian pile with Gothic pretensions. It had been Susan's choice because, at the time, Susan had had the money from her father's will. He wouldn't have described it as nice, but it was impressive. He quite liked it, too. 'It has a certain character,' he said.

'It's sure does. Big, too. Do you have a family?'

'No. Only a wife.'

Beckindale put the car in gear and drove across the gravel and out on to the road.

'Nice car,' Lacey said.

'It's comfortable.'

'Mind if I smoke?'

Lacey didn't think there would be an objection as Beckindale had defended his right to smoke in Rossington-Hall's car, but it was as well to formalize acceptance of his habit.

'Nope. You go ahead.'

Traffic directions and the standard of high-speed British motoring dominated conversation until they hit the M2. Beckindale nodded at the dashboard clock.

'We're on schedule.'

'Have you made this run before?'

'A few times. Going by boat is less formal than flying.'

Lacey knew he meant there was less security and fewer people taking notice. He wondered how many runs Beckindale had made and what sort of a network he had built up. Somehow he couldn't imagine it would be particularly extensive or influential. Maybe it extended no further than Aldo Capaldi.

'How long have you been involved in field work?' Lacey asked.

'Two months.'

'Two months?'

'I've directed covert operations through the NSC, but

131

coming to Europe was the first chance I got to get in there and pitch.'

It was as Lacey had thought. Beckindale was a novice who, in all probability, needed protecting from himself.

'How many contacts do you have in Europe? Apart from Sarah Mathieson.'

'I can't tell you that, Peter. But there are others.' He took his eyes off the road to glance at him and grinned. 'I know what you're thinking. In your position, I'd be thinking the same. This is your turf, you know how things are done. I'm the new boy in town and my pedigree is all wrong. You don't know how I think or how I'll act in a tight spot. You know zip about me and that's not a good basis for going into any operation. Right?'

'That's right.'

'Good. I'd be worried if it was any different. You have a right to be worried. Me? I've read your file. I'm happy to have you along. And I'll be happy for you to direct the whole operation.'

Lacey lit a cigarette. Once again, Beckindale had said all the right things.

'I'm glad you see it that way,' he said.

'It makes sense. Now, if you look in there, you'll see where we're going and I can fill you in on the background.'

From the glove compartment Lacey took a large-scale road-map of Northern France that was already open at an area that covered the southern approaches to Arras, and a folded piece of paper that proved to be a sketch-map of a small house and outbuildings.

Beckindale said, 'The house is between Arras and Bapaume. It's half a mile from the main road and about a mile from its nearest neighbours.'

'Is he alone?'

'Not always. Sometimes a woman stays with him overnight. A loose woman. She's supplied by a friend who runs a bar in Arras. And sometimes Jo-Jo Gervaise is with him. Jo-Jo is an associate, a sort of bodyguard and runner. He's

132

short on brain power, but he's a vicious son of a bitch. He relies on Aldo.'

'That's it?'

'That's it. At the moment, Aldo is unaffiliated. He has worked as part of a group, but these days he prefers solo assignments. When he's not working, he's happy with his own company.'

'Except on those occasions he picks up a loose woman?'

Lacey was amused at the term Beckindale had used and passed it back to see if it provoked any reaction. It didn't.

'That's right,' he said.

'How do we know when he's alone?'

'A phone call. I've a contact who's fairly close.'

Lacey looked at the map and the drawing.

'Does Capaldi go out much?'

'He drinks at the Tropicana Bar in Arras a couple of times a week.'

'How does he get there? Does he drive?'

'He has a car. Sometimes he drives, sometimes Jo-Jo. He never goes alone. Jo-Jo is always with him when he goes out.'

'And the bar is owned by a friend of his?'

'That's right.'

'Your contact. Is he reliable?'

'Very.'

Lacey put the drawing in his pocket and the map back in the glove compartment. So far Beckindale had been thorough and professional.

'I need to see both the house and the town before we work out how to go about it.'

'I figured that. We've got time this afternoon.'

The conditions were a Channel swimmer's delight on the ninety-minute crossing to Calais.

A gentle swell rolled them towards France without a sign of a breaker and the early May sun bounced off the surface of the sea. Lacey reflected on the nature film he had seen the previous evening and how the sun had cut through the clear blue of the water.

133

There was no chance of that in the English Channel. Pollution provided the mirrored surface and, beneath the glare, the water looked like sludge. Maybe a Channel swimmer would not be delighted, after all, when faced with the challenge of twenty-odd miles through a toxic cocktail.

And maybe he was fooling himself into believing that what he did, in some small measure, was important to the safeguard of democracy and a free world. Maybe the real battle had been lost already and the planet was going to the dogs.

He laughed at himself. He was the unlikeliest conservationist he could imagine. The only aspect of species protection in which he would be at all useful, was culling. The humour went from the thought and he lit a cigarette.

They had lunch in the restaurant and shared a bottle of Chablis. Lacey felt comfortable in the American's presence. There was no conflict of egos.

'Where's home, Dan?'

'Home's a long time ago. I grew up in Portland, Maine, an East-Coast boy. But once I entered the service, I never seemed to stop travelling.'

'What about family?'

He took a sip of wine before answering.

'I had a wife and son. They died in an accident.'

He said it evenly and without drama, but Lacey felt he had hit a nerve.

'I'm sorry.'

'That's OK. But it means I don't have what you would call a home. I have an apartment in Georgetown in Washington. Somewhere to hang my hat but that's about all. I'm one of those guys who likes work.' He shrugged. 'It keeps me sane.'

Lacey said, 'I went through something pretty severe myself. When I stopped drinking, I discovered work was the only way back. It didn't provide reasons, but it did provide distractions until I got into the habit of living again. Until I discovered my wife again.'

134

Beckindale shook his head.

'My work is the reason. The only reason. It's more important than . . .' He became aware they had become serious and chuckled. 'I'd better go easy. I sometimes scare the hell out of people by being over-enthusiastic. In Washington, I'm known as Captain America.'

He said it in such a way that although he acknowledged it was meant to be disparaging, he was proud to be nicknamed after a cartoon super-hero. Lacey had to admit it was better than being called Oddjob.

'So far you haven't scared me,' Lacey said. 'I'll tell you when you do.'

After disembarkation, Beckindale drove them out of the dock area and on to the main road inland with a confidence that indicated he had made the journey before. He took the *autoroute* and they went at speed through a flat countryside and past the signs for Arras.

'I've arranged for us to switch cars,' Beckindale explained. 'We can look at the house on the way back.'

About sixty kilometres further on, they turned off the *autoroute* for St Quentin.

On the outskirts of the town, Beckindale left the main road to burrow into the suburbs. He finally eased the Mercedes off the highway and parked between thin trees that lined a quiet grass verge. They had stopped by the brick wall of a factory building. Fifty yards further on were half a dozen houses whose steps fronted the street. Across the road was a railway line.

He nodded towards a black Peugeot in front that had left-hand drive and French licence plates.

'That's ours.'

They got out, took their bags from the boot, and went to the Peugeot, for which Beckindale had the keys. It was another example of the man's thoroughness and Lacey was again impressed. He was also content to remain the passenger on the journey north, this time along straight and featureless roads.

135

'We can get a look at the house from the rear,' Beckindale said.

The afternoon was still sunny and bright and the flat landscape didn't appear to hold much cover. Beckindale seemed to read his thoughts.

'Don't worry. Nobody'll look at us twice. We're pilgrims.'

'Pilgrims?'

He had to wait until they were almost there before it made sense. The American pointed to the left as he slowed the car. Here, for once, the land sloped upwards and near the crest of the gentle hill was a small iron-fenced cemetery, alone in the middle of cultivated fields.

'Two world wars have left Northern France littered with cemeteries,' Beckindale said. 'Small ones, like this, as well as the big ones.'

He turned the car up a grass track and they drove slowly for a quarter of a mile until they reached the enclosure that held a stone monument and less than a dozen gravestones.

'Aldo lives just over the hill,' Beckindale said. They got out of the car and then he leaned back into the rear seat and produced a camera. 'You go have a look, I'll pretend to take pictures.'

Lacey moved slowly past the cemetery, as if it interested him, while Beckindale went inside and began taking photographs of the monument. As hills go, this one wouldn't win any competitions, and he was soon near the top, following an overgrown footpath through the grass. Then it ceased to be the horizon and several miles distant he could see a fringe of trees and the scab of a factory belching smoke. He looked back the fifty yards to the cemetery, but Beckindale was the only person in sight. Cars drove at speed along the road in ones and twos in bursts of distant sound, uncaring and disinterested.

The slope was steeper on the other side. He saw another road and a track that led from it between the fields. He was wary about being seen in case someone below happened to be looking up, and as the outbuildings came into view, he lay down in the grass and moved the last few yards on his stomach.

The house was tucked into a fold in the countryside. Perhaps the original builder had been fed up with the panoramic boredom of the usually flat land and had opted for coziness with skylines within touching distance. Down there he had created an isolated kingdom out of sight of anybody.

He pulled the drawing from his pocket and compared it with the real thing. It was an excellent likeness, with all the doors and windows faithfully reproduced. A grey Citroën saloon was parked at the rear of the house.

Beckindale was suddenly beside him in the grass. His approach had been silent and Lacey tried not to show his surprise.

'Well? What do you think?'

'I think we're in business. Now show me the bar.'

As a city, Arras did not impress Lacey. It looked dingy and tired as if it were a black and white stage set waiting for someone to finish a post-war *flic* movie, the sort where Jean Gabin ended up dying.

'Straight ahead is the railway station,' Beckindale said, and they began to drive round a large traffic island. 'Down there is the Tropicana.'

He indicated the street before turning into it. They drove slowly past the bar. It looked functional but seedy, as if its main business could be something other than serving booze and food.

'Now,' he said, when they were past. 'How about a drink?'

'Why not.'

Beckindale went down a one-way street past hoardings and a tatty mini-market before turning left at some traffic lights. They turned another corner on to a cobbled street and, without warning, they were in a vast square from another time. The buildings were tall and ancient and arcaded at ground level. The contrast with urban Arras was startling.

'Impressive, isn't it?' Beckindale said.

'Very.'

'Place des Héros. The houses are seventeenth century.'

It was a fairy-tale square that housed discreet banks, hotels, restaurants and bars. Lacey felt it was a shame about the sex shop. They drove through a narrow street into another, equally impressive square that was bigger than the first. At the far end was a cathedral and bell tower.

The heart of the city was skilfully hidden. It was a deception of the highest order and one that Lacey applauded. Perhaps that was how it had survived two world wars.

Beckindale parked in the second square and they walked back beneath the colonaded arcades to a bar of a very different kind to the Tropicana. The waitresses wore black skirts and white aprons and the patron stayed behind the bar with his sleeves rolled up, ministered to the till and missed nothing.

They sat at a window table that looked out into the Place des Héros. Both drank black coffee, but Lacey had a cognac with his. For once he didn't feel out of place smoking Gitanes.

'You know, I was worried about this trip,' Lacey said.

'I hope you're not quite so worried now.'

'No, I'm not. I'm reassured. And not just by the logistics.'

'What do you mean?'

'I mean that for this to work, I have to be confident about you. I wasn't. Now I am.'

Lacey said it with sincerity even though he wasn't telling the whole truth. He had a lot more confidence in Beckindale than when they had started out, but it wasn't total. Covert action in urban France was still a lot different to action in a hostile jungle. But it was important Beckindale believed him, because then Beckindale might behave the way he wanted him to.

'Good,' Beckindale smiled. 'The feeling's mutual.'

Lacey smiled back. It hadn't occurred to him that the American might have had reservations about him. He

138

drank some coffee. There were still things he wanted to explain.

'I've lost two people on this operation already. You've seen my file. I have a reputation for collecting corpses. I don't want to collect any more from my own side. I don't want Captain America. I want close control from both of us, no heroics, no chances.'

Beckindale said, 'I saw bodybags filled with heroics in Nam. I've no intention of doing anything stupid. You call it, Peter. I'll play it.'

Lacey wondered if they were both playing games. If they were, he hoped it was the same game.

Chapter 18

The sky was streaked red along the western horizon. It made dusk spectacular, but failed to impress Lacey who was beginning to feel the chill as he lay in the grass above the small cemetery and kept watch on the house on the other side of the hill through binoculars.

There was some sort of rhyme about red sky at night, but Lacey couldn't remember its significance. Maybe the sky meant God had cut himself shaving.

He levelled the binoculars again, but nothing had changed below. The Citroën remained parked at the rear of the house and a lighted window confirmed that the building was occupied.

Beckindale had made a telephone call to his unnamed source and discovered that Capaldi and Jo-Jo Gervaise were expected at the Tropicana at about nine o'clock. Nothing was certain after that, but if their target conformed to his usual behaviour, he would return home some time after midnight, probably with Gervaise.

Lacey's plan was simple. The first stage was to search the house and ensure there was no dirt about Sarah Mathieson. For that purpose he wore black leather gloves to leave no fingerprint evidence of his breaking and entering. The second stage was to wait in the house for Capaldi to return.

The back door opened and the internal light went out. He peered through the binoculars and saw two men leaving the house. The first was large, with sloping shoulders. He walked like a wrestler. Jo-Jo Gervaise. The second man was slim and wore an elegant tan suit. He recognized him as Aldo Capaldi.

a neat finish. Lacey removed the paperback books one at a time, shaking them individually to loosen any document that might be concealed inside. Nothing was. When all the books were stacked on the floor he saw that the bookcase was screwed to the wall with brackets.

He knelt down and tried to get a finger grip on the strip of wood along the base, but the fit was too snug. He got a bread knife from the kitchen and bent it so that two inches at the end curved like an Arabian slipper. He slid it under the strip of wood and tugged again. The strip of wood loosened and came away.

Lacey put the knife on one side, removed the strip completely and found a slim metal case that fitted the dimensions of the cavity exactly. A piece of string hung from each end of the case and he used them to slide it out. Now he could see that rather than a case it was a simple box. He removed the lid.

Inside were a collection of clear plastic bags. They contained a Russian Makarov pistol, two types of ammunition in boxes, a copy of *Time*, and a second gun that was broken down into pieces with two magazines of ammunition.

At first glance, the gun appeared to be an automatic pistol with a heavier than normal barrel, but he recognized the fitments that came with it: skeleton stock, a sound suppressor that screwed on the end and looked like a collapsible umbrella, two sights and the two different-sized magazines. The maker's name could be seen on the side through the clear plastic. It was a 9mm American-made Viking sub-machine-gun with all the extras, including night sight.

Lacey lifted the box on to the table and went first for the copy of *Time*. The plastic bag wasn't sealed and when he slid out the magazine he discovered it contained newspaper cuttings. He pulled out a chair and sat at the table.

The page in *Time*, where the cuttings had been placed, carried a background story about European terrorism. A section of the story that covered the activities of Red Dawn had been marked with red ink. Lacey unfolded and spread the cuttings, which were from French, Italian, German and Austrian newspapers. Each one referred to an assassination that had been carried out in the name of Red Dawn. There were four assassinations, the last one being that of Franz Haber in Vienna. In the middle of each cutting was a neat red tick of approval. Or pride in a job well done?

It looked as if Capaldi was working for Red Dawn, despite Rossington-Hall's theory that the group's ethics wouldn't countenance hiring a professional outsider. But if he was, it provoked other questions. Capaldi didn't come cheap, so how were they paying him?

'*Restez-la!*'

The command telling him to stay where he was made him look up in surprise. Jo-Jo Gervaise was in the doorway, pointing a large automatic pistol at him.

Lacey had been so engrossed he had not heard him enter by the back door into the kitchen. He glanced at the walkie-talkie with its whip antenna that lay on the table. It looked very proficient, but it had provided no warning of Jo-Jo's return. What the hell had happened to Beckindale? The car had been parked well away from the turning so as not to arouse suspicion when Capaldi had left for Arras. But Beckindale had had to move it closer to be able to watch both directions along the road in case they returned a different way. Maybe he had become too obvious. Maybe he had already paid the price.

Jo-Jo pushed the door open fully and put his finger to his lips. The gun remained steady although Jo-Jo's eyes moved about the room and glanced speculatively at the ceiling, as if trying to guess whether or not Lacey was alone.

Lacey was aware that his own gun lay two feet away from his left hand on the table. It was too far and it was the wrong hand. His curiosity had lapsed; it was no longer important why Capaldi had been working for Red Dawn. Inside, his stomach was so light it made him feel nauseous, and his breathing had become shallow so as not to disturb the delicate balance of the situation.

144

They remained in a silent tableau as the seconds became a minute while Jo-Jo watched and listened. The time dragged towards a second minute before Jo-Jo relaxed. He smiled, and Lacey smiled back. Then he raised the gun so that it was held straight out in both hands and pointing at Lacey's head.

Shit! Was this how it ended?

'*Attendez!*' Lacey said, and wondered which way to dive.

Jo-Jo's grin widened . . . and then his head exploded.

Blood splattered across the newspaper cuttings as if a painter had flicked his brush, and Jo-Jo fell sideways on to a wooden serving trolley. It collapsed under the weight and the body hit the floor.

Lacey wondered why his ears tingled and realized through the shock that it was the retort of the gun; not the one that had blown Jo-Jo's head apart, but the one Jo-Jo had been holding. The man's finger had twitched in death and pulled the trigger. The bullet had gone past his left ear and hit the wall behind him.

He remained seated and was aware of his lungs filling with air as he adjusted to still being alive. His senses returned, sharper than ever, and he could smell the sweat under his armpits. He watched the darkened kitchen doorway and into it stepped Beckindale, a revolver in his right hand.

Beckindale looked at the body on the floor and then at Lacey.

'You all right?'

'I'm fine. What happened?'

'Damn radio didn't work. I followed him, but had to leave the car a way back so he didn't spook. Sorry if I was late.'

Survival made Lacey equable.

'You timed it to perfection, old son. What did you use? A howitzer?'

'A forty-five.' He held up the revolver. 'And dum dums. I like stopping power I can be sure of.'

'Well, you made sure of Jo-Jo. His head's redecorated the room.'

Beckindale walked around the table and looked over Lacey's shoulder at the cuttings.

'What have you found?'

'Aldo's scrapbook. It looks very much as if he was working for Red Dawn.'

'What about Sarah?'

'Nothing. I don't think there is anything.'

'What about Aldo?'

'Yes. What about Aldo? And why did Jo-Jo come back?'

'Search me. But he left his car down the track and walked the rest of the way. He knew somebody was here.'

Lacey looked up sharply at Beckindale.

'How secure is your contact?'

'I thought he was pretty secure. Now I'm not so sure.'

'Then we'd better get into Arras fast and get this job done before Aldo susses what's happened.'

'A frontal attack?'

'We've run out of options. We'd better do it like the marines.'

Chapter 19

Aldo Capaldi and Red Dawn didn't match up. It worried Lacey as he drove Jo-Jo's Citroën towards Arras, following the tail lights of Beckindale in the Peugeot.

Other things bothered him as well; Aldo's newspaper cuttings and the return of Jo-Jo Gervaise. But he couldn't work out why they bothered him, apart from the fact he would have died without the arrival of the American.

At least, Beckindale had proved his worth. When it had been necessary, he had shown no compunction about killing. He had done so efficiently and without a show of emotion or elation. Lacey would have felt better if he had arrived sooner, but he was grateful he had arrived at all.

They had stashed the plastic bag of videos, the walkie-talkies and Lacey's binoculars and Heckler and Koch into the boot of the Peugeot. Beside him on the seat, hidden beneath a car rug, Lacey now had the sub-machine-gun he had found beneath the bookcase, fully assembled and with the silencer attached. It was loaded with the larger of the magazines that contained thirty-eight rounds. He had also brought the smaller magazine of twenty rounds. If he needed more than that he should go home now.

The Peugeot signalled, pulled into a darkened side road and stopped. Lacey followed, drove past and pulled in a few yards ahead. He watched in the rear-view mirror as Beckindale got out and went round to the passenger side and opened the rear door. He took out a coat, which he put on, and a long barrelled gun, which he held in the folds of the coat close to his leg. He locked the Peugeot, walked nonchalantly to the Citroën and climbed in.

Lacey had already fixed the interior light so that it didn't

147

come on when a door was opened, but he could see the coat in the dashboard lights. It was a long loose-fitting raincoat, reminiscent of the dust coats of the old West.

'Very tasteful,' he said.

'Very practical.'

Beckindale moved the folds and displayed a pump-action shot-gun.

Lacey drove and Beckindale directed. It took only a few minutes to reach the roundabout by the railway station. They went round it, made the turn and stopped a few yards past the Tropicana where the street was dark.

'You take the door,' Lacey told Beckindale. 'If he's not at the bar, I'll sweep the place.'

They got out of the vehicle, leaving the keys in the ignition and the doors unlocked. At the end of the street, by the roundabout, there was the distant noise of cars and young men shouting as they crossed the road. The street lights and the neon from the cafés and hotels made it look a world away although it was less than a hundred yards. Down here there was little illumination, only shadows in between the glow of two subdued bars and the night-light in a tailor's window.

The air was still warm and Lacey looked across the roof of the car.

'Nice night,' he said.

'Sure is.'

Lacey held the sub-machine-gun in his right hand and let it hang by his side as he walked round to the pavement.

'Let's do it,' he said.

They walked quickly into the light, Lacey going first up the two steps. He pushed open the door and raised the gun as he went inside.

'*Restez-la!*'

He shouted the same order Jo-Jo Gervaise had used and kept walking, his gaze taking in all the occupants of the premises. Behind him he heard the door shut.

The barman was overweight, forty and unshaven. His shirt sleeves were rolled up and Lacey could see the tattoos

148

on his forearms. He recognized him from Beckindale's description as the owner.

He was standing behind the far end of the bar, a cigarette in his hand, and had been talking to two ladies who sat on high stools and who wore enough paint to be either on the stage or on the game. Lacey knew which he'd put his money on.

To Lacey's right, the bench-seating curved in half-moon scoops around low tables. Two middle-aged men sat either side of a blond teenage boy at one table, all three of them too close to be healthy. At another table a drunk watched uncomprehendingly through bleary eyes. He ignored them and stopped at the end of the bar where the room opened up with a small dance floor, more tables and a table-top football game. Two young men in jeans and sleeveless black T-shirts were at the football game. They remained frozen in combat, their hands on the handles of the machine. Behind him, Lacey heard one of the middle-aged men whimper.

'*Tais-toi!*' Beckindale shouted, and the man shut up.

Lacey turned to the owner of the bar and pointed the gun at him. The man's eyes fixed on the end of the barrel before rising to look Lacey in the face. The man was not happy about the situation, but he was not abject with terror. It appeared he had seen the business end of a gun before. He raised his right hand slowly and put his cigarette in his mouth.

'Capaldi?' Lacey said.

'*Qui?*'

The man said it with a shrug. It was a marvellous gesture and in other circumstances Lacey would have admired it, but right now he was pushed for time. He fired a short burst past the man's head into the bottles on the shelf behind. The fast throaty cough of the gun sprayed booze and broken glass.

The two painted ladies fell off their stools and lay cowering on the floor, one showing far too much thigh to be decent. The bar owner stayed on his feet, but the cigarette had dropped from a mouth that had gone slack. An ear had been cut by flying glass and blood dripped on to his shoulder.

'Capaldi,' Lacey repeated.

The man glanced towards a door in the corner beyond the football game. It was painted red and marked private. Lacey went towards it and the two youths in T-shirts got out of his way. The door was unlocked and opened outwards. He stood to one side and pulled it open, but was confronted only by a flight of stairs. Shit. Here he went again. For God, Harry and St George.

He took a deep breath and went up the stairs quickly, pointing the gun ahead of him like a geiger counter. There were a dozen steps and they hurt his legs, but no-one appeared at the top to hurt him more severely. He reached a landing and found three closed doors and felt he was being drawn into a maze that was getting more complicated every second.

Lacey stood with his back against the wall alongside the first door, and turned the handle with his left hand. The thin wood panelling shattered as bullets from a handgun tore through it at chest height. He counted four shots, gave the silence that followed two seconds and ducked back down the stairwell. From floor level, he fired back, the first burst through the bottom panel aiming upwards, the second burst at the door knob and lock.

The door splintered a lot more and jerked partly open. He couldn't hear sound from in the room but he could hear sound from beyond it.

He charged the door, knowing as he did so that it was against all the rules, but for chrissake they were running out of time. It crashed open and he rolled, looking for moving shadows or gun flashes to aim at, but the only thing that moved was a flapping curtain.

The window on the other side of the bed was open and from outside he could hear grunts of exertion. He reached it in time to hear the man drop from the drainpipe and land on all fours in the yard at the back of the bar. Something metallic skittered away across the flag stones. He risked another look but couldn't penetrate the darkness. At least no-one shot at him. Maybe Capaldi had lost his gun.

An engine turned over and died. It turned over again, and again died. Capaldi had some kind of motor cycle down there.

Lacey evaluated quickly. He was not fit enough to scramble down drainpipes in the dark and he was not certain that Capaldi really was unarmed. The engine fired below and made his mind up for him. He ran for the stairs.

He crashed through the door at the bottom yelling at Beckindale. Even though they were in a rush he still used French for the benefit of witnesses.

'*Allez! La voiture!*'

Beckindale didn't hesitate, he opened the door, kept the room covered until Lacey was halfway towards him, then turned and ran for the car. Lacey was seconds behind him, almost stumbling down the steps out of the bar. He got to the passenger door as Beckindale started the engine.

'He's got a motor bike. At the back of the bar.'

As he spoke, a man, crouching low over a motor cycle, came out of an alley fifty yards ahead of them. The machine whined at the speed it was being pushed towards, crossed the road and turned left. Beckindale put the car in gear and set off in pursuit.

Lacey sat back and got his breath and shook his head at another cock-up. They had planned a discreet confrontation in the country and were now involved in a Keystone cop chase across a French city.

'You OK?' Beckindale asked.

'Out of condition. Running up and down stairs is not my forte.'

The motor cycle cut through narrow streets that gave them no chance to overtake and took such a tortuous route that Beckindale was unable to ram him. The American braked for another sharp corner and laughed.

'We've got him. He's heading into the Place des Héros. It's wide open.'

Beckindale was right. They were back in the medieval square, the tall buildings impressively illuminated above street level, leaving the colonaded walkways in darkness. It was deserted apart from a few cars parked near the bars in the far corner, and two lorries that sat in the middle of the cobbles. The motor cycle headed diagonally across the square to cut between them.

Lacey tensed himself for the end of the chase as the lorries got nearer and suddenly sensed what they were.

'It's a set-up!'

He pushed open the door and dived as Beckindale braked. Simultaneously, two sub-machine-guns opened up, smashing the windscreen and riddling the bodywork of the Peugeot. He could hear handguns barking, too, but kept on rolling, despite the pain in his shoulder, until he was off to the right of the ambush. He lay still and watched and listened and heard the motor cycle circling beyond the lorries and heading back. Lacey seemed to be in a blind spot and took advantage of it to limp to the cover of the dark arcades.

The gunfire stopped and two men ran from the lorries towards the wrecked Citroën. The man on the motor bike remained in the rear, content to watch. Lacey judged that when he went it would be through the narrow gap between the squares. He could still get the bastard.

He was about to start running when the battle recommenced. A shot-gun roared and flung one of the two men who were in the open to the ground. The other turned and fired a sub-machine-gun from the hip at a target out of Lacey's sight. The shot-gun fired again and he went down, too. Handgun fire from the second lorry was heavy until a grenade blew up the lorry. The blast knocked the motor cyclist off his machine.

Jesus Christ!

Lacey shook his head. When Beckindale went in like the marines he didn't mess about.

The motor cyclist was pulling his machine upright again and Lacey stopped watching and began running. His shoulder hurt and he felt like he had been knee-capped from where he had hit the cobbles, but he kept going along the arcade, trying to judge the motorcycle by sound rather than lose speed by risking a look. He was heading in a straight line towards the narrow street that linked the squares; the motor cycle was going across the middle of the cobbles. It was a lost race.

Lacey changed direction and ran out from the arcade. He could see the motor cyclist ten yards ahead of him over the top of a parked car. He leapt on to the bonnet of the car and raised the sub-machine-gun over the roof. Shit! People had come out of the bars to see what was happening and were standing on the pavement.

He aimed at the motor cycle and fired a long burst. The bullets threw sparks off the road and he was vaguely aware of screams and the onlookers suddenly diving for cover, but his main attention was on the motor cyclist. The gun stopped, the magazine empty. Had he missed him?

The motor cycle slid one way and then the other, as if the rider had lost control, before its engine was gunned to take the corner.

Lacey cursed at losing him as he went out of sight, but the noise of a crash a second later galvanized him back into action. He leapt off the car and began running again, changing the magazine as he did so. This time the curious stayed out of sight in the bars and behind parked vehicles, their faces wide-eyed and white at the periphery of his vision.

He ran through the linking street into the second square, the one Beckindale had never told him the name of, and saw the motor cycle embedded in the side of a trader's caravan.

The van had been selling hot dogs and *frites* and its canopy was still raised over its counter even though it had been tilted to one side. Light from it shone out on to a gawping crowd of young people. Some had been in the bars, others were in motorcycle leathers and leant against their bikes, many still held bags of chips and hot food.

153

Yelling came from inside the van. A door was kicked open and the yelling man leapt out. Behind him, flames were already getting a hold.

Lacey ran past the caravan and saw Capaldi. He was limping across the square, using the occasional parked car as cover, making for the church. He set off after him.

His legs hurt and his chest burned, but he no longer had to run so fast. He could see his quarry and knew he would catch him. Capaldi stopped and rested against the last car between him and the church and turned to look back. The man's left leg was stiff and his arm hung loosely by his side. But he raised his other arm and Lacey was surprised when he saw and heard the gunshot. He was still armed, but his wounds had affected his aim.

Capaldi heaved himself off the car and staggered on towards the church. What was he looking for? Sanctuary?

Now it was near the end, a jumble of thoughts invaded Lacey's mind. How soon before the police arrived? How would he get away? What had happened to Beckindale? Could he find the parked Peugeot? Did he have time to question Capaldi?

Lacey put a short burst into the ground alongside Capaldi sending up sparks like fireworks from the cobbles, and the man stopped and turned again, only yards from the door to the church. Capaldi raised his right arm and fired two shots and Lacey had no choice. His next burst was on target, taking the assassin in the stomach and chest, and sending him dancing backwards with a sudden and fatal lightness of step. He collapsed against the door of the church.

He wasn't dead when Lacey reached him, but he was near. The revolver he had carried was a yard away and no longer a threat. All the strength he had left he saved to stare into Lacey's face and to say the one word.

'*Pourquoi?*'

A motor bike roared up and Lacey turned with the sub-machine-gun ready. It was Beckindale. His face was dirty and his raincoat was badly ripped, but he was in one piece.

154

Back at the other side of the square, the food caravan exploded as the fire reached the gas cylinders.

Beckindale shouted above the noise.

'Is he dead?'

Lacey glanced back at Capaldi.

'Yes. He's dead.'

'Then let's get out of here.'

Lacey dropped the assassin's sub-machine-gun on to the ground and climbed on the back of the motor cycle. The job had been messy, but he should be feeling good that it was over. He wasn't. Capaldi had asked him why? It was a question that suggested it wasn't over at all.

When it was clear that all the shooting had finished, the bars emptied and people of all ages, who had been enjoying a night of normality, stared curiously at the abnormality of bodies and burning wrecks.

Police cars arrived, their two-tone sirens echoing from the tall buildings, and officers began to try to keep people from getting too close.

The fast food van blazed in medieval glory, as if burning witches was back in fashion, and the crowds formed and fluctuated at each sequence of the drama that had been played out, moving from one to the other, as if making the stations of the cross.

Among them was the drunk from the Tropicana bar who eventually crossed the square towards the church. He no longer looked drunk, but walked quickly towards the small throng and pushed his way to the front to stare down at the body of Capaldi.

Around him the killings were being discussed in excited voices, but he remained quiet. He kept his opinions to himself and complimented Benjamin Franklin on being exactly right.

155

Chapter 20

Lacey hurt too much to analyse what had happened. He was content for Beckindale to drive the Peugeot to a motel near St Quentin and slot it into an end bay next to the Mercedes. The car-park light at this end of the complex was not working, but Lacey could still see the shape of a man in the Merc.

They got out of the Peugeot, leaving the engine running, took their belongings from the boot, and went to the end room of the wing. The light was on and he could hear a television.

The door was unlocked and Beckindale led the way inside. It was empty although there was an open carton of Stella Artois beers and several empty bottles in the waste-bin, as well as a half-empty whisky bottle and a used glass. There were even Gitanes butts in the ashtray.

Lacey heard the car outside go into reverse and then purr away into the night. The exchange had been completed and nothing, it appeared, had been forgotten. They had been here all evening, drinking, smoking and watching television with the sound turned up. He turned the sound down, reached for a beer and flopped on one of the beds. He was tired, but the adrenalin was still pumping and he would need a few drinks before he would be able to sleep.

Beckindale poured himself a whisky and toasted Lacey. 'To a job well done.'

Lacey vaguely waved the bottle and said, 'You don't mess about, do you?'

The American smiled.

'You mean back there?'

'You were Steve McQueen, John Wayne and the Seventh Cavalry all rolled into one.'

'It's what I'm trained for. You don't run from an ambush, you attack it.'

'I didn't.'

'No, you were clever. You got Capaldi.'

Lacey took a long gulp of beer, sat up on the bed and reached for the pack of cigarettes that had been left on the bedside table.

'What the hell happened?' he said.

Beckindale finished the drink before replying.

'He had more friends than I thought.' He shook his head. 'I don't know what happened. He tried to sucker us and it nearly worked.' He poured another whisky, but left the glass on the table. 'But it didn't work. And we got the bastard.'

He went into the bathroom and turned on the shower. When he returned for his bag he had already stripped to the waist and walked across the room unselfconsciously, a soldier at home in the company of men. Lacey had been right. Beckindale's body was in excellent condition. They were paired perfectly to do a before and after ad. Lacey decided that when he took a shower, he would be more discreet.

On the way back into the bathroom, Beckindale paused. 'You don't mind sharing, do you?'

He indicated the room. Lacey wondered whether the question had been prompted by his surreptitious appraisal of Beckindale's body.

'I don't mind.'

'Good. It makes it easier, that's all.'

Lacey nodded and got off the bed to get another bottle of beer. The muscles in his legs had already stiffened and he limped although he tried not to show it.

'You hurt?'

'It's nothing. Just my knees. I banged them on the cobbles.'

'There's a first-aid kit in my bag. I'll look at them after my shower.'

157

'No. Really. I'm all right. Thank you, all the same.'

Beckindale shrugged.

'OK.'

He went into the bathroom and closed the door. Lacey sat back down on the edge of the bed, unfastened his trousers and eased them down to look at his knees. One was red, angry and skinned; the other was turning blue already with a bruise bigger than his handspan. He got dressed again and lay down on the bed, the bottle in one hand and a cigarette in the other. It could have been worse. He could have been dead.

Instead, Aldo Capaldi and Jo-Jo Gervaise were dead and several unidentified opponents were also deceased or injured.

Lacey had killed before and tried not to think about it too much, but every death was unique and evoked different emotions. Capaldi's had been in the heat of battle, a reflex burst of gunfire in self-defence, except that he knew it hadn't been like that. If he had done it right, he should have put the burst in the Italian's back as he ran to the church; he shouldn't have given him the invitation to turn by firing into the ground. No matter what reasons he had given himself at the time, he had wanted to provoke Capaldi into making the shooting self-defence.

Did that mean he was losing his edge? It was a consideration he had to make and was not prompted by paranoia. If he started to lose his edge then next time there would be a much greater chance he wouldn't make it.

Maybe his self-criticism was prompted by comparison with the way Beckindale had behaved. You don't run from an ambush, you attack it, he had said. Bollocks. Lacey would continue to head for the shadows. On this occasion, Captain America had been victorious, but how many times could he buck the odds and get away with it?

He lit a fresh cigarette from the stub of the old and felt guilty at putting the American down.

For Christ's sake, the bloke had saved his life at the farmhouse and destroyed the opposition single-handed in

Arras while he had scuttled for safety. Was jealousy making him sceptical?

The bathroom door opened and Beckindale emerged, face gleaming and short hair damp. He wore fresh blue pyjamas as if they were uniform and looked ready for parade inspection. He grinned at Lacey.

'It's all yours.' He picked up the glass of whisky and drained it. 'God, I feel good.'

Lacey got up slowly and collected his bag. He wouldn't be able to match Beckindale in the pyjama stakes because he didn't wear any, but he did have a bathrobe with him.

'The first-aid kit you mentioned. Could I borrow it?'

'Sure thing.'

Beckindale handed it to him and Lacey retreated into the bathroom to shower gingerly so as not to make his bruised shoulder and knees sting with the hot water. He patted himself dry and covered the knee that was raw with non-stick gauze held in place with a bandage. His legs were far too hairy to use surgical tape. In the past, removing it had proved more painful than original wounds.

He opened the bathroom door to go back into the bedroom and stopped in embarrassment. The television had been switched off and the room was silent. Beckindale was kneeling by the side of his bed, hands clasped in front of him, eyes closed. He was praying.

It seemed so incongruous. Only hours before he had been killing people; only minutes before he had been saying how good he felt. Now he was praying.

Lacey turned round quietly to go back into the bathroom, but Beckindale called to him.

'It's OK, Peter. I'm finished.' He laughed comfortably as he got to his feet. 'Hope I didn't scare you this time?'

'No. You didn't scare me. Surprised me, maybe.'

'A lot of people are surprised by religion. A lot are scared, too. They don't think it sits right on a military man.'

'Well, I have to admit . . .'

'See? You too.' He picked up a small chunky book that

was bound in blue leather and held it up. 'But maybe you'd be more surprised if you read this. The Bible. It's a military book from start to finish, a manual in the war against Satan.'

'I'll take your word for it.'

Beckindale lowered his arm, grinned disarmingly and let the fire ease out of him. He put the Bible on his bedside table. Lacey got himself another beer, unscrewed the top and took a long drink.

'Can I have one of those?' Beckindale said. Lacey passed him a bottle. 'Don't worry. I'm no freak.' He continued smiling, as if he were explaining a joke. 'I'm an old-fashioned boy. I believe in my God and my country.'

Lacey lit another cigarette and lay on the bed.

'That's all right. I believe in West Ham. Trouble is, they don't believe in themselves.'

Beckindale laughed although he obviously didn't fully understand the humour. He took a swig of the beer and sat on the edge of his bed, facing Lacey.

'Do you believe in God, Peter?'

'I've never felt the need.'

'I know what you're saying. I was brought up to go to church every Sunday, but religion didn't mean a whole lot. Not until Vietnam. I got into some tight spots there. A lot of guys who were with me didn't make it, but I did. At the time, I had a feeling about it, that God was looking out for me. That I would be OK, and I was. Then later, I lost my wife and son, and damn near lost my faith. But I was lucky. I had good friends and good counsel and I saw why God had guided me through Nam.'

He paused for a drink of beer.

'We all have a destiny, Peter. What we do is preordained by God.'

'And God is on your side?'

Beckindale gave another disarming grin.

'Shit, Peter. Jesus is my buddy.'

'Doesn't he object to the language?'

'He understands the language of soldiers.'

'Does he understand the killing?'

160

'He understands that the military are the peacemakers and that without us the world would be at war.'

Lacey took a long pull at his cigarette and observed Beckindale through the smoke. Was he the devil or an angel of divine retribution?

'What was God doing during Vietnam?'

'Suffering. Like everybody else.'

'Maybe He wasn't as committed as you were. You lost the war in Vietnam.'

'No. We lost the war in Washington.'

'And if Washington hadn't run scared, you could have won it?'

'Hell, yes.'

Lacey blew a smoke ring at the ceiling. At least he knew where he was with Beckindale.

'You're very certain about things, Dan. Aren't there any doubts?'

'There are always doubts and temptations. But they're minor league. The main thing is that I know where I'm going and minor irritations aren't going to get in my way.' He smiled and picked up the Bible again. 'The good book provides any answer I might need to put doubts in their place.'

'Does it only work for soldiers?'

'It works for anybody. After I lost my family I started on Lamentations. ''He hath turned aside my ways and pulled me in pieces; he hath made me desolate.'' He smiled again, as if he enjoyed scoring points. 'Now I'm on to Revelation. ''Be thou faithful unto death and I will give thee a crown of life.'' '

Lacey sat up to stub out the cigarette.

'I think Revelation suits you better.'

'And I still don't scare you?'

'No. But by Christ I'd be scared if you were the opposition.'

Beckindale laughed with good humour.

'Never forget, Peter, that Jesus was a soldier. He mobilized an army that's still marching. He was a hawk.'

161

'He also got killed for his beliefs.'

'I can't think of a better way to die.'

Lacey looked at him.

'You mean that, don't you?'

Beckindale held his gaze. His expression was neither righteous nor extreme. It was sincere.

'I mean it.'

Lacey got up, dropped the empty bottle in the bin and got another.

Beckindale said, 'I wanted you to know about me. I wanted you to know I'm no holy roller, and I'm no kamikaze. But I go all the way.' The smile broke out again. 'Just like Jesus.'

Lacey smiled back, and then laughed. He toasted the American with the new bottle of beer.

'The next time you say your prayers, say one for me.'

'I already have. You're looking for something, Peter. A reason, a belief. Maybe you're looking too hard. Maybe that prayer will help.' He held up the Bible and smiled that smile that kept the whole conversation low key and half joking. 'It's all in here. From Lamentations to Revelation.'

'Does it have anything for hangovers? Because that's what I believe in. A hangover makes life worth living simply by surviving it.' He took another drink from the bottle. 'Watch me. Philosophy in action. Each to his own, Dan. Only, in the morning, I'd be obliged if you practised yours quietly, while mine gets a chance to mature.'

Chapter 21

The world always looked different the morning after the night before. Which was why Lacey hadn't dwelt on the inconsistencies of Arras and precisely what Capaldi might have meant when he had asked why, until time – and a hangover – provided objectivity.

Beckindale had said he dealt with doubts by reading scripture. Lacey let his develop as a side effect of an excess of alcohol. He found they gained the clarity of a cold lavatory bowl when viewed from post-survival relief.

They had talked little during the return drive to Calais, mainly because Lacey had been in the later stages of recuperation and had preferred to sleep on the back seat. The dramatic events in Arras had happened too late for the morning newspapers, but television had reported them as a shoot-out between underworld rivals in which three people had died and two had been injured. At that time, there had been no mention of Jo-Jo Gervaise in the house in the country. Lacey and Beckindale had listened to the commentary and viewed the scene of their battle without comment.

On the ferry, they sat on deck at Lacey's insistence. The wind made him feel more human and, he believed, gave him a better-than-average chance of keeping down his lunch.

'How's philosophy?' Beckindale said.

'It's working. I feel better now than when I woke up.'

'I thought you were dead when you woke up.'

'So did I. QED.'

Beckindale laughed.

They watched white-tipped waves in a sea that couldn't

make its mind up whether or not it wanted to gallop. Above them was a cathedral sky, a mile high and streaked with clouds like vapour trails.

Before they docked, Lacey would have to make a sortie below decks to the duty-free shop to buy Chanel for Susan but, for the moment, he would stay in the fresh air. He also felt the time was right to confide in Beckindale.

'Capaldi spoke before he died,' Lacey said.

The American stopped smiling. He looked at Lacey curiously.

'Why didn't you tell me?'

'I don't know.' He shrugged. 'It puzzled me. Sometimes I let puzzles lie there. See what they do.'

'What did he say?'

'He asked me why.'

'Why? What do you mean, he asked you why?'

'I mean he said, "*Pourquoi*?" before he died.'

Beckindale looked back at the waves.

'So what's the puzzle?'

'I don't know, it didn't seem to fit. To question your executioner, like that.'

'People say strange things when they die. I read about a gangster in Chicago whose last words were "dog biscuit". Who the hell knows why Capaldi said why? Maybe he wasn't asking you. Maybe he was asking God.'

'And maybe it puzzled him as to why he was the target. Christ, it's not the only thing that doesn't make sense. What about the cuttings? What about Red Dawn?'

They lapsed into silence and Lacey watched three small boats in the distance. Beyond them was another ferry. A normal day on one of the busiest stretches of water in the world. The captain on the bridge had the worry of command and the men on the fishing smacks or tugs or whatever they were, would have their own set of troubles. Everybody had problems, but everybody else's fitted a pattern. His didn't.

Beckindale said, 'You don't think it likely that Capaldi was working for Red Dawn?'

'The cuttings suggest he was. And he was in Vienna with Sarah Mathieson shortly before the last assassination. Before the cuttings I'd have said no. But now . . .' He snorted. 'I don't think this is over, Dan. I think Capaldi is going to come back and haunt us.'

The American got up and walked the deck. Lacey watched him and wondered which part of the Bible was going to help him on this one. When he came back he stood and looked at Lacey as though it were his fault. Then he nodded.

'You may be right. But there's no point provoking anything. Maybe we should just wait and see. I've had a hunch about this all along and maybe now pieces are beginning to fall into place.'

'What sort of a hunch?'

'If the whole thing turns to shit I'll tell you. But there's no point looking for plots that might not be there. Hell, the whole thing might still be legit. Maybe Red Dawn did hire Capaldi, and maybe Capaldi was talking to God. Let's not panic until we have to. And don't forget, I'm still running an operation out there. I don't want it compromised.'

Lacey nodded and lit a cigarette. Physically he was feeling better, but the alarm bells were ringing more persistently now. Beckindale was an action-man whose strength was charging an ambush, but Lacey was still around because he took nothing for granted, dissected every hunch, and invented plots to see if they could fit. He had learned that nothing was unlikely and everything quite probable in his profession. Beckindale could wait upon events, he would do his own probing.

Traffic was bad heading towards London as they drove through one suburban swath and commuter belt after another. It eased as they got closer to the capital and by the time Beckindale dropped Lacey off in Trafalgar Square at seven-thirty, it was almost reasonable.

Lacey walked through the square, past the church of St Martin's-in-the-Fields and up Charing Cross Road. He unlocked the street door into the office block and went up the two flights of stairs. Eddie, the haemorrhoid, let him in.

The department was empty, but there was a note from Malcolm on his desk. It lay on top of a stack of pink computer print-outs and facsimile sheets. It said:

> Thanks for not calling, I could have had your dinner in the oven and it would have been ruined. Poor Susan. Anyway, I've had enough. It's six-thirty and I'm leaving. HRH has been a royal pain. He phoned four times and left an invitation for you to send your head round to Century House on a platter. Apart from that, everything's hunky-dory. All the latest on Capaldi is here and there's a standing order for whatever we can wheedle from the French. Anyway, as I said, I'm off. There's a lot to be said for a warm pussy and I have three waiting for me, dear. Take care, Malcolm.

Lacey dumped his bag, threw his leather jacket on the spare chair and opened the filing cabinet. He looked at Jim Beam and Jim Beam looked back and they both knew the timing was wrong. He closed the cabinet and went into the main office where there was a kettle and a jar of Nescafé and made coffee.

The reports did not take a lot of reading. They ranged from superficial to speculative. Among them were translations and transcripts of the French Press and television coverage, statements from the French police and the internal security service, *La Direction de la Surveillance du Territoire*. There was also background information on Capaldi that Lacey already knew, and an early analysis from someone in the western Europe section at Century House that was about as analytical as Enid Blyton.

Most interesting was the statement from the police. It named Capaldi as a professional assassin, but classed the men who had been involved in the Place des Héros ambush as straightforward criminals with no terrorist connections.

Journalists had worked this into a theory that Capaldi had been hired to eliminate the boss of a rival gang.

The body of Jo-Jo Gervaise had also been found, but very little information had been released about the circumstances or the contents of the house.

He needed complete access to the French reports, but would have to declare an interest if he made the request direct and he was only too aware that that could lead to embarrassment. To get the relevant information he needed to be circumspect, he needed somebody else with a valid reason to ask on his behalf.

The link was terrorism. He needed an assessment of Red Dawn and Capaldi. Western Europe had agreements to co-operate fully on matters of terrorism and a request from an acknowledged expert would be treated as routine.

He picked up the phone that gave him a direct line to Century House. Lacey would place his order for an expert and go home. Tomorrow was time enough to face recriminations, and by then Lacey might have collected enough loose ends to weave a prayer mat. If Rossington-Hall's neatly conceived scam started coming apart, the pretentious prat might find it very useful.

Chapter 22

Those mornings Lacey woke up with a thick head and an afghan tongue he knew things had to improve. But this morning he woke up with a clear head and a blood stream that would have passed a drink-driving test. He had a heavy feeling in his gut that this was as good as the day was going to get.

Last night, he could have stayed in one of the annexe bedrooms at Charing Cross Road, nursed his aches and pains in private, and been at his desk first thing. It would have been a sensible decision. But he had wanted to come home, not for conversation or sex or even a good meal. He had wanted the companionship of his wife, to be in his own home with her, and to lock the doubts and troubles outside.

He and Susan had said very little to each other the night before. She had the propensity to read his moods better than he did himself and to understand his needs. He had wanted reassurance and refuge and she had supplied both.

But she had raised an eyebrow when he undressed and she saw the damage.

'What did you do?' she had said. 'Fall off your bike?'

He had laughed and let her change the dressing on his knee. In bed, she had kept a safe distance. They had gone to sleep holding hands.

Now the dawn had sneaked up and brought reality back. He had an office to go to, a superior to soothe, problems to foresee before they occurred, and a limp.

Susan had brought him coffee and toast in bed, run him a bath and left for the shop and round nine of Lucy.

168

She had let him smell the Chanel in her cleavage before leaving, but hadn't let him touch. He had promised to be home at a reasonable time. But now he had the day to survive. He lit a Gitanes and wondered why the first always hurt.

He telephoned the office and Malcolm chastised him.

'He's been on again this morning. Twice. I told him you were incommunicado. He probably thinks that's somewhere in Italy. But if you deign to tell me when you *are* coming back, I could lie a little more convincingly.'

'I'll be there by lunchtime. Is there anything new?'

'Nothing. But there was a call from someone with the anti-terror mob. About the briefing you requested. He said he could see you this afternoon across the river.'

'Call him back and confirm a time, early afternoon, but I'm not going to Century House. Tell him it has to be in my office.'

'I'll tell him, but I don't think he'll like it.'

'I don't care if he likes it, just as long as he's there.'

'Mmm. Very forceful. You should have been a leader of men, Peter. But it's me who has to tell him.'

Lacey laughed.

'You'll do it, Malcolm. With charm, wit and diplomacy. I have confidence in you.'

'I wish it were mutual. What about HRH?'

'You can tell him I'm expected back at four. That'll present him with the perfect dilemma.'

'How do you mean?'

'What do civil servants do at four o'clock on a Friday afternoon?'

'They go home.'

'Exactly. With luck, I might not have to see the little shit until Monday.'

Lacey's tame expect was Ashley Ballantyne. Malcolm had written his particulars on a sheet of paper. They said that Ballantyne had been to public school and Oxford, that he had studied the psychology of terrorism and the

169

urban guerrilla, and was a senior British adviser to the Kilowatt and Trevi groups that co-ordinated anti-terrorist intelligence and international response. The particulars also included the fact that Ballantyne was not just an armchair theorist. He'd had field experience in Europe and the Middle East. He'd reluctantly agreed to visit D14a and the time of the appointment had been fixed for two o'clock. Lacey suspected he wouldn't be very tame.

Ballantyne arrived five minutes early and Lacey was not reassured by first impressions. The man was tall, blond, aware of his good looks, and had eyes that didn't take prisoners.

'I don't usually make house calls,' he said, after sitting in the chair on the visitor's side of the desk. His voice was languid enough to make Lacey want to smack him.

'I don't usually request them,' said Lacey. 'In this case, it's necessary.'

Ballantyne tilted his head as if to suggest that could be open to interpretation, but he said nothing. He opened a briefcase and took from it a large fat brown envelope which he handed to Lacey.

'I understand your department operates outside normal channels, so I thought all communications should be non-attributable.'

'Very thoughtful.'

'I was told you wanted analyses of the organization known as Red Dawn and of the assassin Aldo Capaldi, who was killed in France two days ago, and that you were interested in any possible association between the two.'

'That is correct.'

Ballantyne smiled drily.

'Until two days ago, there was nothing to suggest any association between the two.'

'And now there is?'

'Now there is.' They exchanged bland looks for a few seconds before Ballantyne went on. 'Capaldi's death provided the link. In the envelope are reports relating to the

170

rather dramatic events that occurred in Arras where he was killed. The reports are from both the Police Judiciaire and the DST, along with transcripts of the interrogation of surviving participants.' He smiled. 'I'm afraid they're all in French.'

'That's all right. I read French.'

'I rather thought you would.' He crossed his legs and made himself more comfortable. 'Right. I will provide a verbal briefing that is based on the material now in your possession. I'll answer any questions, and if the questions don't present themselves until after I've gone, I will leave a telephone number where you will be able to reach me over the weekend, although I would prefer not to be disturbed. All right?'

'Super,' said Lacey, and lit a cigarette.

Ballantyne was a superior bastard, but if his briefing was as succinct as his preface, Lacey would be happy. He allowed himself a small smile as the man's nose twitched at the smoke.

'Let us start with Red Dawn,' said Ballantyne. 'Their origins are obscure. Their membership unknown. No individual has been identified as belonging to them. At first it was thought they came from the remnants of *Action Directe* in France. Later that they were Italian-based, another new-wave Red Brigade. Neither now seems likely. Their security is total and their hits are professional. Also, they appear to be of independent means. They haven't committed any bank robberies, kidnappings or extortions, which are the normal terror-group methods of raising funds.

'An alternative is for them to be funded from the Middle East, but there's no evidence to support that. If there were, we would have known from Mossad's Branch 40.'

He smiled condescendingly. Perhaps he didn't think Lacey knew that Branch 40 was the co-ordinator of terrorism intelligence for the Israeli secret service.

'Another theory was that they were being organized by a re-born Japanese Red Army and funded from the Far

171

East. But, apart from anything else, the method of making their point is not in the style of the Red Army. If you recall, those gentlemen went in more for wholesale slaughter at airports.'

Lacey nodded. He recalled them as being one of the bloodiest of the terror groups of the 1970s.

'So. There has been nothing to evaluate except their operations. There have been four and, what witnesses there are, all describe a similar assassin. Slim, medium height, probably European, well dressed.

'The first hit was Jacques le Gall, the former French Social Affairs minister, in Athens four months ago. He was on holiday and was shot by sub-machine-gun from a moving car as he left his hotel. As a first attempt, they couldn't have picked a better location. Athens has been a favourite killing ground for years with one of the most suspect security services in Europe.

'Next was Frederik Hals, a senior Dutch scientist, three months ago. He was shot at close range with a handgun while leaving a restaurant in The Hague. The killer ran to a waiting car. The location was again well chosen. The Netherlands has little experience of dealing with terrorists and the country is liberal, welcomes foreigners and has an abundance of escape routes by sea, air or road.

'Third was Michel Chodron, a Belgian financier. He was shot by handgun as he left the apartment of a high-class prostitute in Stockholm in the early hours of the morning, seven weeks ago. His chauffeur was wounded in the attack and the assailant again escaped by car. Sweden is another country with a low-security awareness. They also have a secret service that is often more concerned with its own internal problems than the death of a foreigner.

'Finally, there was Franz Haber, the West German classical pianist. He was shot while taking an early morning stroll in the Stadt-park in Vienna two weeks ago. The killer rode a motor cycle and used a handgun.

'In the three cases where a handgun was used, the bullets were dum dums. In the three cases where a car was used, the vehicle was driven by a second man. In all four cases, the descriptions, and they are not detailed, suggest the same assassin. None of the targets had been considered high risk although all were high profile.

'Each assassination was claimed in the name of Red Dawn in a telephone call to the police. That was followed by a statement telephoned to the office of an international news agency in the city where each killing occurred. The statements used the same terminology and made the same claims. They said the victims had been executed because they were, and I quote, cancers of capitalist decadence.'

Ballantyne waved his hands.

'The four victims were all wealthy and they moved in influential circles, but they could hardly be described as enemies of the people.'

He uncrossed his legs.

'Any questions so far?'

'No questions.'

'Good. Then let's move on to Aldo Capaldi. Italian, aged thirty-three, born into a wealthy legal family. Psychologists would say that too much of everything led him to rebel and look for the meaning of life in aggressive socialism. Whatever they say, Aldo was a teenage recruit to terror who soon learned to enjoy it. At the beginning, in the late seventies, he operated mainly in West Germany and Italy. Then, for a time, he was with the Wadi Haddad group. He dropped out of sight for two years and when he resurfaced he had gone freelance.

'He had good connections in the Middle East and it's believed he acted as adviser and quartermaster for Arabs undertaking hits in Europe, as well as fulfilling contracts himself. He was suspected of involvement in a bomb attack on American servicemen in Frankfurt a year ago, but he was always careful. He never operated in France, where he frequently stayed, and he never left any hard evidence that could get him extradited or convicted. He was very good at what he did.

'Aldo died two days ago in Arras in rather spectacular circumstances. There was a gun battle in the middle of town that might have been mistaken for a NATO exercise. Machine-guns and grenades. Two other men died, and two were wounded. Aldo's bodyguard was also killed, but he was found some miles away, at the farmhouse where they'd been staying.

'The other four people involved were criminals, not terrorists, and the police thought they had an underworld gang war on their hands, over the control of the ports of Calais, Boulogne and Dunkerke. They accommodated Aldo into the theory, by suggesting he'd been hired to kill one of the gang leaders. It never really stood up, and the DST have provided a more likely explanation of what happened.

'Aldo had been running scared for several days before he died. He'd told a close friend, a bar owner called François Rocard, that his life was in danger. He said he suspected the people he worked for wanted him dead, but that he had to meet with them one last time, for payment and to find out. Rocard is an ex-mercenary and well known throughout criminal circles in Northern France. He helped Aldo recruit four extra guns. The night he died, Aldo was expecting trouble and prepared an ambush. Unfortunately for him, the hired guns came up against greater fire power.

'Until two nights ago, there had been nothing to connect Red Dawn and Aldo Capaldi. But at the farmhouse, the police found a handgun, that ballistics have matched to at least two of the assassinations, as well as newspaper cuttings of all four killings. The cuttings had all been ticked in red. It was also clear that Aldo matched the rather loose description of the killer. The obvious conclusion is that Aldo was working for Red Dawn, but that still leaves the major question – who are Red Dawn?

'They don't fit any recognizable pattern for a terror network. Terror needs a high level of publicity to survive. Its perpetrators need to read it to believe it. The Czech playwright Havel explained the role of language. He said it becomes a creator of reality, a motor of events more real than reality itself. For terrorists, the words that appear in the newspapers and the words that are said on television become the reason for the war they are waging. The words reassure them that they are being effective and are being taken seriously by the public and the authorities. But Red Dawn have shunned exposure, except simply to claim four killings. They also purport to have purist principles, yet they have used a hired assassin throughout, rather than implement their own executions. Finally, they have no visible means of financial support.'

He spread his hands.

'What are you saying?' asked Lacey.

'Well, from an operational sense, Aldo Capaldi *was* Red Dawn. But I have strong reservations that Red Dawn is what it claims to be.

'If this were an Agatha Christie plot, I'd look for criminal motives. Either something that links all four victims, or that killing four hides the fact that only one is the target.' He shrugged. 'But that's too far-fetched and this has been set up with too much international skill.'

'You're saying Red Dawn is a cover?'

'Yes.'

'For who?'

'I wouldn't like to guess.'

'A government? Or government agency?'

'Probably.'

'Shit.'

'Oh. And there's one other thing. This was in Aldo's wallet when he died.'

Ballantyne took a folded sheet of paper from his pocket and handed it across the desk. It was a faxed copy of another newspaper cutting. This one was in French and it reported, in five paragraphs, the murders of Sarah Mathieson and Roland Devere in London.

Across this cutting there was no red tick. Across this cutting was a large question mark.

Chapter 23

The weekend was like a hole in reality. Lacey had climbed through and zipped it shut behind him.

Rossington-Hall had not bothered him Friday afternoon and Lacey suspected he had calmed down after seeing the French had made no connection between the SIS and what had happened in Arras. His attitude might change, however, when the DST asked about the relevance of the newspaper cutting that had been found in Capaldi's wallet.

Lacey had left all the problems behind him in the office. He and Susan had enjoyed a relaxed Friday evening. Saturday had slipped by with television sport, and dinner in the country, and Sunday had been a wallow in indulgence. They had read all the newspapers in bed before walking in warm sunshine to the pub for a traditional roast beef lunch and alcohol, and, in late afternoon, had gone back to bed for a nap. It seemed they had spent most of the day without any clothes on, an experience Susan described as decadent and which Lacey said was highly enjoyable.

He allowed business back into his mind as he settled for sleep late Sunday night. He scrolled it on to his closed eyelids: the events that had happened, reports he had read, background information he had been told, suspicious, speculations, theories, possibilities.

When he had run the lot, he was content to let it lie in his subconscious without attempting to shuffle it into a conclusion. He slept, for some reason confident that the next day would bring answers.

*

Monday started early. Beckindale called at six and asked for a breakfast meeting. Lacey told him he didn't eat breakfast. Beckindale said that was OK, he could slurp coffee and smoke cigarettes for half an hour, just as long as he went to the apartment at St Katharine's Dock and listened.

The weather remained summery and reinforced his positive frame of mind. He transferred from a mainline train to the tube at Charing Cross and walked from Tower Hill. It wasn't yet eight o'clock, but the sunshine had brought a group of American tourists out early from the hotel by Tower Bridge. Their multi-coloured leisure-wear made them look like a protected species as they waited in a brood, presumably for a bus to take them to Windsor or Stratford in search of history and stories to take home.

Lacey was impressed with Beckindale's apartment. It was on the third floor of a converted warehouse and had views of the river and Tower Bridge. On the ground floor were high-class shops and restaurants and out front was a marina packed with boats.

'The apartment belongs to the embassy,' Beckindale said. 'I was lucky to get it. It came vacant just at the right time.'

Either that or somebody at the embassy wanted to stay on the right side of Captain America.

The place had been furnished with elegance and a large cheque book. This was an apartment reserved for the most senior of diplomats and gave another indication of the circles in which Beckindale moved. The neatness of the interior was a reflection of the man. Nothing was out of place. Lacey suspected Beckindale would have court-martialled himself if he'd found crumbs on the floor or a sock hanging from a linen basket.

He showed Lacey into a study.

'I'll get the coffee,' he said. 'Unless you've changed your mind and want something to eat?'

'No, coffee will be fine.'

The room was panelled and furnished with a desk and leather armchairs. Books filled one wall, floor to ceiling, leather-bound standard works of literature. The morning newspapers lay stacked on a coffee table. Lacey walked round the desk to look at the four framed photographs that held pride of place.

In two of them Beckindale was in uniform, in the third, and most recent, he wore a civilian suit, but still looked military. In all three he was shaking hands with a president of the United States. All the photographs were signed by the Presidents and one had the inscription, To an American hero.

The fourth photograph was of an attractive young woman and a tousle-haired youngster.

'That's Jenny and Damien,' Beckindale said from the doorway, as he carried in a tray.

Lacey didn't know how to respond so he said nothing. Instead he made himself useful by moving the newspapers so Beckindale could place the tray on the table.

'Help yourself,' his host said, going to the desk and taking a folder from a drawer. He was full of business, without time for extraneous distractions.

They sat in armchairs and Lacey lit a cigarette.

'Is this important?'

Beckindale shrugged as he shuffled papers.

'I think so. You'll have to make up your own mind.' He put them into a final order, and was ready. 'OK?'

'Go ahead.'

'OK. What you said on Thursday started me thinking. I told you I'd had a hunch things weren't right, and I put a few things together and asked Washington to come up with an intelligence estimate. It came this morning.'

Lacey drank coffee and waited.

'The estimate suggests Red Dawn doesn't exist. That the assassinations were the work of just one man – Aldo Capaldi.'

Beckindale was looking for reaction.

'That's what my experts told me,' Lacey said. 'On Friday.'

The American grinned and suddenly became more human.

'I might have known. What else did they say?' He waved the papers. 'I don't want to waste your time.'

'They said the Red Dawn operation was probably being run by a foreign power.'

'Did they say who?'

'No. They left me to figure it out.'

Beckindale nodded.

'Same reasoning. Only they gave me a possible.'

'Who?'

'You won't like it. The Soviets.'

Lacey didn't like it. It made no sense.

'That's crazy.'

'Not the way I heard it.'

'Then you'd better tell me.'

Beckindale dropped the documents on the floor, as if they were a prop he no longer needed.

'Mikhail Gorbachev is a man in a hurry. Above all, he's a realist. Let's look at the guy, at what he inherited and what he's done.'

Beckindale waited for permission to provide a history lesson and Lacey inclined his head.

'First off, he was an apparatchik of Brezhnev before he manoeuvred his way to power. He knows all about being ruthless. It was a hard fight to get where he got and he made plenty of enemies along the way. A lot of them would like to see him fail.

'What he inherited was a mess. The Soviet Union of Socialist Republics is based on the old empire of the Tsars. It has two hundred and eighty million citizens speaking fifteen different languages and a thousand different dialects. They have a history of not liking each other. Most of them live in poverty. When Gorbachev took over, the standard of living in Moscow itself was that of a third world country. It still is.

'For the empire to survive, he needed to cut defence spending, attract western money and technology, get cash

180

into people's pockets and food and consumer goods into the shops.

'So far, his major success has been abroad. The guy's got charisma and a beautiful wife. He's preached peace, cut the military budget and won conditional help from the West. But he has two major problems. History hijacked his revolution and perestroika isn't happening fast enough.

'Glasnost was a necessity if the economic revival was to work, but no-one could have predicted what's happened in Eastern Europe. It's made the job back in the USSR even tougher. Now everybody wants independence.

'Gorbachev may be a hero abroad making the world safe from nuclear war, but he's not as popular at home where people are more interested in bread and meat and democracy. The guy is on a tightrope and it won't take much to make him fall. He's said it himself, if perestroika fails the Soviet Union will not survive as a great power. They reckon they have another year before the cracks splitting the empire get too big to paper over.'

Lacey stubbed out his cigarette. He agreed with everything Beckindale had said, but couldn't see where it was going.

'Where does Red Dawn come in?' he said.

Beckindale raised his hands as if to apologize for taking too long with his explanations.

'The man has enemies and the KGB has six hundred thousand members. Many have been in the service years and don't accept the new realities. There are still politicians in high places who carry grudges, men of influence all over the empire who would like to see Gorbachev fail for any number of reasons. There's a strong conservative faction openly against him.

'Let's hypothesize. If a secret Soviet operation to assassinate prominent West Europeans was suddenly blown, it wouldn't do Gorbachev's credibility much good. Maybe people in the West would take a second look at the Russian brand of glasnost, maybe they would look long enough to delay the economic miracle he needs. It's a matter of time.

181

If he doesn't work the miracle soon, he'll be yesterday's news. A new regime will move into the Kremlin.'

Lacey lit another cigarette. It was no secret Gorbachev had enemies within the USSR and had survived assassination attempts. Beckindale's theory was more subtle. If it were true, and successful, it would discredit the Soviet leader and his theories, rather than make him a martyr.

'It's an interesting proposition. Is it based on anything other than speculation?'

'Yes. Western Europe division of the CIA have sensed something is happening. There's nothing concrete, hints in radio intercepts, the movement of personnel . . . a senior member of the Executive Action Section visited the Russian embassies in Paris and Vienna in the last two months, and Anton Kindl is in Vienna now. There's enough for it to be taken seriously.'

The Executive Action Section was the department of the KGB that dealt with assassinations. Kindl was a Czechoslovakian freelance who had worked for both East, West and the Middle East. He was a broker, a dealer and one of the most talented fabricators in Europe. He would be an ideal choice to leak enough information to motivate western secret services to find out more, especially if it had been planted with the intention of being found.

'Who visited Paris and Vienna?' Lacey asked.

'Andrei Chebrikov.'

'What are you doing about it?'

'I'm going to Washington today, to get co-operation from other agencies in tracking what's going down. The chief also needs to be told.'

Beckindale was talking as if he had direct access to the President. The photographs suggested he had.

'How long will you be away?'

'As long as it takes. This is still a theory, but if it holds up we get a new set of problems. Can we be sure it is a renegade KGB operation? And do we trust Gorbachev enough to tell him what we suspect? I don't see Gorbachev

182

as a knight in shining armour, but he's still the best hope we've all got for change without chaos. He needs his ass protecting. Whatever happens, the best place for me is Crisis Centre at the NSC.'

'Will it be your operation?'

'I sure hope so.' He grinned. 'You're still not sold on the idea, are you, Peter?'

'You've made a case. It has to be checked out.' He smiled back. 'I'm glad I'm not doing the checking.'

Beckindale laughed.

'You're right. Even if we stop the shit hitting the fan, we could still be left with a bowl of turds.'

Lacey laughed with him.

'You know, for a soldier of God, you have a hell of a way with words.'

Chapter 24

Sam Bryson was back at D14a. Lacey smelt the distinctive pipe tobacco as soon as he arrived in the office. Perhaps that was why he had felt confident the night before?

He stuck his head round the door of the room occupied by his head of department before going to his own office.

'Morning, Sam.'

'Peter! Good to see you. I think.'

'You think?'

'Rossington-Hall's been on the blower. Fortunately Malcolm fielded the call. Perhaps we should talk about it?'

'I'd like that.'

'In ten minutes?'

'Right.'

Bryson was a former Cambridge don who dressed eccentrically in string ties and tweed jackets, wore his grey hair long, and enjoyed the company of attractive young women. His trip had been a three-week lecture tour of American universities. The Foreign Office allowed him two such excursions a year. He said it kept his academic hand in, took him to a country he admired, and allowed him to mingle with beautiful young things without appearing to be a dirty old man.

The establishment across the river avoided Bryson and called him a renegade, which was why he had been given D14a. Lacey couldn't imagine him being suitable for any other of the Firm's departments and suspected he had been specifically recruited to head the section that cleaned up messes made by other people. His unorthodox mind and a Who's Who list of personal contacts made him eminently suited to the role.

In his own office, Lacey stacked the documentation he had acquired, lit a cigarette and jotted main points on a sheet of paper. It would be good to bounce the whole puzzle off Sam's considerable intellect.

When he carried in the bundle of papers, Bryson lifted an eyebrow.

'Are you planning a bonfire?'

Lacey laughed, placed them on the desk and sat down.

'I might just do that.'

'It's that bad?'

'I don't know. Maybe I'm looking too hard. As far as HRH is concerned, the file can be closed. But . . .'

'With you, Peter, there's always a but. Does the fact that you lost young Devere have anything to do with it?'

'I don't think so.' He'd forgotten how important Devere's death had seemed a week ago at the funeral in the rain. 'I felt guilty about it. It was a waste. I wanted revenge, but that was never motivation, and I've got that out of my system.' He sniffed. 'I didn't even like Devere very much. I think it was not liking him that made me feel guilty.'

'Yes. It was a waste. It was also one of the percentages we play. There's no guilt involved. Just luck. Now. Tell me about it. From the beginning.'

Lacey told him. He recounted everything from the first briefing with Rossington-Hall, to the meeting in Beckindale's apartment earlier that morning. He left out nothing, even though his report for HRH would omit certain activities to allow the Deputy Director to retain plausible deniability.

Bryson listened in silence, content to suck on the pipe even after it had gone out. When Lacey finished, he loosened the remnants of his last smoke with a penknife and tapped it into a waste-bin. He settled back in his chair and began to repack the bowl with fresh tobacco.

'Intriguing.'

'I know.'

'You could walk away from it.'

185

'I know that, too.'

'But that would be too easy.'

'I'd like the answers.'

'That's not in the rules of engagement. You've fulfilled your assignment.'

'But there's more to it. And I'm not sold on Dan's theory.'

'You should submit your report and let the relevant section at Century House take care of it. Your job was to discover what Sarah Mathieson was doing. You found out she was working for the Americans. You also had to ensure nothing would spoil the cover story put out by Rossington-Hall. You did that, too, by removing Capaldi. The fact that Miss Mathieson was killed is purely coincidental. She got involved in a much bigger operation than she realized. She was another percentage player who misjudged the odds.'

'I'd like to know who killed her and Devere.'

'You don't think Capaldi was responsible?'

'He didn't do it. That's why he left the newspaper cuttings. It was a way of saying somebody else was involved in case they got him, too.'

'But *you* got him.'

'Yes. But after Sarah Mathieson had been taken out, he was expecting a hit, and not from me. His paymasters were cleaning up and he knew he was on the list.'

'Who they are, and the reasons for their operation, have nothing to do with you, Peter. It's a problem that belongs elsewhere.'

'It feels like it belongs to me.' Lacey lit another cigarette. 'If it goes across the river, nothing may be done about it. They could just wait for Washington to sort it out.'

'Perhaps that might be for the best.'

'I don't think so.'

Bryson moved in his chair, as if the physical shift was to announce the shift in conversation.

'What about Beckindale? How do you rate him?'

'He saved my life. Possibly twice.'

'So could a lifebelt in the right circumstances. It's clear

186

he's effective in action, but what about his mind? Does he have one?'

'He has a mind. I don't know if he'd qualify for Mensa, but he can assimilate facts and put a persuasive case. Perhaps he's too persuasive. It comes from his religion. He believes so much, you believe along with him.'

'Yes, you said.' He sucked on the pipe. 'What do you think of his promulgation concerning the Soviets?'

'He made it sound feasible.'

'But?' Bryson said, and puffed smoke.

'But.' Lacey spread his hands. 'But I don't know.'

Bryson said, 'Gorbachev is in a tight spot. He's tough, of course. No-one becomes General Secretary of the Politburo and Chairman of the Supreme Soviet without those qualifications. But perestroika is taking longer than expected. Beckindale's right. He has about a year to make it work. If he doesn't, there could be unpredictable changes within the Soviet Union, changes that may not be for the better.' He sucked the pipe stem a moment. 'Did you come to an understanding with Beckindale?'

'He suggested the Sarah Mathieson file was closed. He said the same as you. That my part of the job was complete.'

'He's right.'

'But, if Dan's on the wrong track and something major is happening, I'd like to find out what.'

'Do you have any theories of your own?'

'Not really. The targets aren't linked in any obvious way, so the motive remains unclear. Anything's possible. But if it is someone else, and Dan gets carried away with enthusiasm chasing KGB hardliners, the whole thing could get very messy.'

'All right.' Bryson put a box of matches over the pipe bowl and drew on the stem to keep the tobacco alight. 'So find out if the Soviets are involved.'

'How?' Lacey said, and wondered it he had missed something extremely obvious.

'Ask them.'

Bryson smiled and blew smoke. He was enjoying the blank look that Lacey didn't try to hide.

'You should have been in music hall,' Lacey said.

'Thank you. I take that as a compliment.'

'But I don't see any white rabbit. I don't even see a top hat. How do we ask them?'

'The white rabbit is in Vienna. Anton Kindl. Go and ask the man who is supposed to make it work.'

Kindl had been a successful broker for more than a decade, working both sides against the middle. He'd arranged end-user certificates for arms deals, used CIA airlines for illegal shipments, paid Central Americans with United States green cards, acted as private negotiator for Middle East hostages.

He'd also proved to be masterful as an exponent of black propaganda. In American parlance, he was a very talented fabricator.

As far as Lacey was aware, the West hadn't used him for a long time, judging he'd outlived his credibility, but he was still well known around the capitals of Europe.

An approach would make Kindl consider three options. He would offer to sell Lacey information, he would report straight to the KGB, or, he would do both, and he would do so whether he knew anything about Red Dawn or not. After all, this was exactly his sort of deal, evaluating one side's suspicions with another's ignorance and getting a percentage from each. As Bryson had pointed out, percentages were dangerous, but Kindl was no amateur.

Whatever the outcome, an approach to him would let any renegade Soviet element know they were rumbled, if, in fact, they existed and were involved.

'What are you thinking, Sam? That they can be warned off?'

'It might be the simplest solution. If they know we know, their inclination could be to drop it before it blows up in their faces.'

Lacey mulled it over.

'Do you think Dan's theory is likely?'

'I don't know. But if it is, it needs stopping as soon as possible.'

Lacey stubbed out his cigarette in the ashtray on the desk.

'I could have been a teacher, you know,' he said. 'Or a probation officer. Or a bus driver. Some occupation that's so boring you know it's real.'

'You're much better in the music hall, Peter. Make-believe suits you.'

'Yes. I get to tour, as well. What's Vienna like, this time of year?'

Chapter 25

Anton Kindl wasn't hard to find. In his business, it was essential to be available. Vienna station supplied the information that he was staying at the Hotel Ambassador near the Opera House.

Lacey flew to Schwechat Airport the next morning and took the bus to the city terminal near the Hilton. He was armed with a photograph of Kindl from central registry, the name of a former contact from Six, and a reservation in the same hotel where Brady had stayed on Währingerstrasse.

Kindl's choice of hotel provided reason for speculation. When the man had operated at the peak of his success, he had always stayed at the Hotel Bristol. That was when somebody else had usually been paying the bills. If he was working for the Soviets, they could either have him on hold or, knowing his reputation, they could have dictated his budget. There was also the possibility that he wasn't involved at all, and that his personal finances had caused him to drop a notch or two down the luxury scale.

Lacey took a taxi from the terminal to his own hotel. It wouldn't have looked out of place in a remake of *The Third Man*. The marble staircase circled a central cage lift and he felt sure that if he listened carefully he would be able to hear the echoes of jackboots.

His room was on the top floor, two flights above where the lift stopped, and along two corridors. If the place caught fire he didn't fancy his chances, but at least the height gave him a view. To the north, beyond the suburban sprawl, he could see the slopes of the Vienna Woods, while to the south-east he could just make out the top of the big wheel in the Prater.

He did minimal unpacking, took a beer from the fridge

190

mini-bar and lay on the bed, propped up against the pillows, and wondered why he had picked Brady's hotel.

The fat little photographer was still on his mind, even though Lacey had taken care of Capaldi. The whole damn mess had started here because of him. Brady remained a link and, he was surprised to admit, a motivation. He sipped the beer straight from the bottle and tried not to worry. It wasn't like him to play St George.

He got change from reception and went to a telephone kiosk across the road. Kindl wasn't in his room at the Ambassador, so Lacey went back to his own room and had another beer. He made the trip to the kiosk three times before he finally made contact. It was six o'clock. Lacey spoke in English.

'Is that Anton Kindl?'

'*Ja*. Yes. This is Kindl.'

'Hello, Mr Kindl. My name is Peter Eastwood. My firm is in London. A colleague suggested you might be able to help me in a business matter.'

'That is possible, Mr . . . ?'

'Eastwood.'

'Mr Eastwood. What is your business?'

'I'm a travel writer.'

'Ah, yes. And your colleague?'

'Arthur Pimm. He speaks highly of you.'

'Of course. Mr Pimm.'

Kindl had had no problem conversing in English, which he spoke with an American accent. There was no hesitancy in his voice, although it did have an irritatingly gruff edge, as if he needed to clear his throat.

'I wonder if we could meet to discuss my requirements?'

'That is possible.'

'Dinner?'

'Tonight?'

'Yes.'

'No. That is not possible.'

'My business is urgent.'

191

'All business is urgent. If there is no urgency, there is no business.'

'Tomorrow?'

'Tomorrow, perhaps. Where are you staying?'

'How about lunch, tomorrow?'

'Mmm? No. Not lunch. I have arrangements for lunch.'

'When then?'

'Where are you staying? I will call you tomorrow.'

'I would prefer to call you, Mr Kindl.'

Kindl chuckled.

'So urgent. And so . . . to the point.' He paused. 'OK. Tomorrow afternoon at three-thirty.'

'Shall I come to your hotel?'

'No. The Café Hummel. It's in the Josef-stadt district, behind the town hall. Do you know it?'

'No, but I'll find it.'

'Good. Three-thirty.'

'I'll be there.'

'*Gute Nacht, Herr* Eastwood.'

'Good night, Mr Kindl.'

Vienna had never impressed Lacey on the occasions he had been there before. There were too many statues and too many wealthy middle-class people. The city was like an open-plan museum. On the day when the rain was fine enough to be confused with mist from the Danube Canal, it was as if an artist had water-coloured it grey. It gave his mission a B-movie flavour.

He took a taxi to the rendezvous and found it was a large unpretentious café on a busy corner. Its pavement tables beneath the orange awning were empty in the drizzle, but the lights inside were warm and welcoming. He went in.

To his right, where the room expanded, two old men were playing chess. At another table, three students argued in good humour. To his left, a bar faced alcove tables by the window. He saw Kindl halfway along, watching him above a copy of *Die Welt* that he held in a metal reading-frame.

The man's forehead arched into a dome before it met

192

thinning grey hair. As if to compensate, his grey beard was full and bushy. He looked like an academic and wore a tweed suit and a dark blue shirt and tie. He was watching Lacey over the rims of half-frame glasses. His shoulders were rounded and he looked as if he had once been a bigger man who had shrunk with age.

'Mr Kindl,' Lacey said. 'I'm Peter Eastwood.'

Lacey stood by the table and held out his hand.

Kindl's head tilted to look up into his face and Lacey was reminded of a tortoise appraising a piece of lettuce. The man smiled and shook hands, but didn't get up.

'Please. Sit down.'

Lacey slid on to the bench seat opposite and Kindl closed the newspaper and placed it on the table. In front of him was an empty coffee cup.

Kindl said, 'What can I get you, Mr Eastwood?'

'A black coffee would be fine.'

'Nothing to eat? The chocolate cake here is particularly fine.'

'No, thank you. Just coffee.'

A waiter came and Kindl ordered a black coffee for Lacey and another coffee with cream for himself.

'Is this your first visit to Vienna?' Kindl asked.

'No.' Lacey looked out of the window to watch a red and white tram rumble round the corner. 'But it's the first time I've been to this part of the city.'

'If you are staying for a few days, you must explore Josef-stadt.' Kindl nodded across the square and down the hill towards the city centre. 'There are many bars and cafés that have escaped the tourists. It's an artistic quarter. Bohemian.'

Lacey nodded.

'I'll remember that.'

They waited until the waiter brought the coffee before continuing.

Kindl said, 'You work for the same firm as Arthur Pimm?'

'Yes. Different departments, but the same firm.'

193

'I remember Arthur Pimm very well. It was a long time ago, but I remember these things.'

'Arthur sends his regards.'

Kindl accepted them with a nod.

'The business with Mr Pimm was satisfactory,' he said. 'The commission was not generous, but it was . . . satisfactory.'

'Perhaps our business can be a little more satisfying,' Lacey said.

Kindl gave him the hint of a smile.

'Perhaps. I hope so.' He spooned sugar into the coffee. 'But times change. The opportunities are no longer the same.'

'You come highly recommended. I'm sure if anyone can help me, you can.'

The man shrugged and, after a moment, said, 'Vienna, you know, used to be an exciting place. Before its history became history. You know what I mean? It was the crossroads of East and West for two thousand years. The capital of an empire for six centuries. I, myself, am related to the Habsburgs.' He waved a hand. 'Distant, but related. My family was titled but . . .

'People now come to Vienna for the music or the food. It used to be they came for intrigue.' He smiled at Lacey. 'Everything has changed.'

'Not everything. Vienna is still a crossroads. It's curtained on three sides. Czechoslovakia, Hungary, Yugoslavia.'

'But these days the curtain flaps in the breeze. People come and go as they please.'

'Do you?'

Kindl's shrug was so studied, Lacey thought he was going to withdraw his head completely into his body.

'I like to travel and I choose not to notice boundaries. My blood acknowledges no frontiers. Before the war my family had estates in Czechoslavakia. My father was a count.' He shook his head. 'First the Nazis, then the Russians. I was lucky. I escaped.'

194

He smiled at Lacey.

'I was a fifteen-year-old boy with nothing but courage and a tin of plum jam when I set out to walk to the West. It was a walk that taught me many things. It taught me patience, survival and cunning.' He touched Lacey's arm with a finger. 'The tin of jam was a fake. It had a secret bottom. It contained saccharin tablets.'

Lacey lit a cigarette. Maybe the man didn't get many people to talk to, these days. Maybe his jam tin was a Trojan horse.

'Saccharin tablets were worth a fortune after the war. I kept them all the way to Belgium before I made my first deal. That was how I started. Saccharin tablets.'

'A sweet deal,' Lacey said.

Kindl laughed politely, then more robustly as he got the joke.

'Yes. A sweet deal. Very good, Mr Eastwood.'

'The first sweet deal of many. You've had an impressive career.'

'It is kind of you to say so.'

'A long career. I had heard rumours you'd retired.'

'Never believe rumours, Mr Eastwood. Listen to them, use them, but never believe them.'

'If I'd believed them, I wouldn't be here.'

Kindl nodded.

'Ah yes, business. Urgent business. You English are so brisk, even when you are not telling the truth. It makes business so clinical. Business should be about relationships, about people trusting each other. I am a dealer in commodities, but when I accept a client my discretion is the confessional. It has to be this way, or my career would not have been so . . . impressive.' His unblinking eyes held Lacey's gaze. 'I believe in people and I believe in trust. Can we trust each other, Mr Eastwood?'

'I hope so.' Lacey held his stare. 'Discretion is essential.'

'Good.' He nodded. 'Good. Then we can do business.' He leaned forward to rest his elbows on the table. 'Perhaps you will tell me how I can help?'

Lacey also leaned forward and started without preamble. He felt Kindl had preambled enough for the pair of them.

'Franz Haber's assassination two weeks ago. It was claimed by a group calling itself Red Dawn. The same group have claimed three other killings. Jacques le Gall in Athens, Frederik Hals in The Hague and Michel Chodron in Stockholm. Well, we've been listening to rumours. Rumours that say there's no such group as Red Dawn. Rumours that say the assassinations were directed from Dzerzhinsky Square.'

He stubbed out his cigarette in the ashtray on the table.

'We'd like to know if the rumours are rumours, or if they are something else.'

For a while, Kindl didn't say anything. He stroked his beard.

'Interesting. Did the rumours suggest why this action was ordered?'

'There's a theory. It says somebody is playing a dangerous game. That they're hoping to blame someone else.'

'That is dangerous.'

'Especially as the rumours are out. We have interests to protect. Our own, and those of both our cousins and our comrades. I hope you can help, Mr Kindl. We need to know.'

Chapter 26

Lacey spent two days sightseeing before he met Kindl again, but it wasn't ordinary sightseeing. He visited by night the cobbled street where Brady had been stabbed to death, and he went to the Stadt-park early in the morning, to recreate for himself the circumstances in which Franz Haber was killed.

The cobbles told him nothing. The shadowed shops and houses kept their secrets. He could have committed murder himself without anyone noticing. He leaned against a wall, smoked a cigarette and tried to absorb the atmosphere, but there was no blinding flash of inspiration. Not only wasn't he St George, he wasn't St Paul either, and this was not the road to Damascus. It was a street near the Judenplatz that had learned discretion after being witness to genocide fifty years before, following the Anschluss of Austria by Nazi Germany.

The park was equally uncooperative. He had seen the police photographs, but expected he might get something extra by being there. He didn't. The statue of Strauss in its white arbour, of course, had been cleaned. He felt that if he stayed in the same spot long enough, someone might come along and clean him, too.

Vienna was that sort of place. Its citizens waited at empty roads for a green light to give them permission to cross, they were trusted to buy tickets for the trams and underground, without ticket collectors and inspectors to check their honesty. People obeyed orders and minded their own business. Maybe anyone caught disobeying was taken out and shot.

It made Vienna a perfect place for both intrigue and

197

murder. As a matter of policy, the public would notice neither.

He telephoned Kindl at the appointed time the next morning, but the Czechoslovakian broker was not available. It meant Lacey had nothing to do until the next call the following morning.

He went window-shopping along the Graben and Karthner Strasse and regretted being on his own. He was jealous of the elegant couples in the fashionable stores simply because they were couples. If he had known how, he would have bought Susan something extravagant, but it was a long way to go to change a dress if it didn't fit, and he didn't have the nerve to enter the lingerie shops. It would be perfume again from the airport duty-free.

Check out the Josef-stadt district, Kindl had said, so he did, and killed the evening in a bar below ground level whose windows gave him a worm's eye view of people passing. It suited his mood to drink strong draught beer and watch legs without identities go by. The fact that they were anonymous made him anonymous. He was a non-person without destination in a waiting-room licensed to sell oblivion.

The more he drank, the more he missed Susan and wondered whether the time had come to ask for a transfer out of the looking-glass war. But if he did that and lost the danger, and the loneliness of cities like Vienna, would he still think of Susan in the same way? Did he love her because he missed her and if he stopped missing her, would he stop loving her?

He decided he couldn't think straight because he was hungry and ordered what he thought was cheese on toast. It was grilled Gorgonzola with lumps on toast. When he cut into it, he discovered the lumps were half pears. He knew he was drunk when he ate it and enjoyed it.

The sensible way to get back to his hotel would have been by taxi but he had a desire to walk and trusted his innate sense of direction to guide him. He hardly noticed

198

the rain, even though he hadn't brought a top coat, and he headed roughly the right way through side-streets.

An hour later, he wanted a pee and knew he was lost. It was well past midnight and the streets were deserted. He found an alley in which to relieve himself and a shop doorway where he tried to light a cigarette, but they were too wet. Normally he didn't throw litter in the street, but as this was boring bloody Vienna he made an exception and dropped the packet of Gitanes on the pavement. He waited in case a police car came by and he could confess his indiscretions, but instead a taxi came and he hailed it. His hotel was a five-minute ride away.

He hadn't realized how wet he was until he heard himself squelching along the corridor. He could be the first secret agent to die of a bad cold. In his room, he stripped off and climbed into the shower and let hot water put feeling back into his limbs. The effect of the alcohol he had consumed was fast dissipating and, after he had towelled himself dry, he rectified the situation by having a large whisky followed by a beer from the mini-bar. He felt the balance restoring itself, got a fresh pack of Gitanes from the duty-free carton and lit a cigarette. He poured another whisky and opened another beer and got into bed.

Sleep would have to be induced tonight and he wasn't taking any chances. He didn't want to wake up with only a partial hangover and a bad thirst at two-thirty and find he had nothing for company but his own doubts.

Kindl, he told himself. He had to telephone Kindl in the morning. He used the name as a mantra, finished the whisky, and fell asleep with the light on.

The sunshine woke him at seven and he was surprised he had survived the night. Perhaps it was time he took his depressive paranoia to a shrink. If someone told him he was cured, he might be. Hell, he'd had enough of shrinks in the past. They'd put his head back together when he'd wanted it left in pieces. He would tell himself he was cured. Trouble was, he never believed anybody, least of all himself.

He drank a bottle of Coca Cola before going for breakfast. His hangover was light, which was just as well, as the hotel had filled with Italian students overnight. The boys were boisterous and being macho to impress the girls who pretended to ignore them with flirtatious eyes. Lacey liked Italians and was prepared to put up with the bustle. Just as long as they didn't start throwing bread rolls.

At ten o'clock, he made his call to Kindl from the kiosk across the road. This time, Kindl was in.

The message was brief.

'The Café Hummel. Remember?'

'I remember.'

'Be outside at eleven-thirty.'

Lacey worked out the location of the café from a large scale street-map and walked. He allowed himself plenty of time and, once he had it in view, he reverted to window shopping along the main road that ran up the hill from the city centre. He entered the square where the café was at eleven twenty-eight, waited by the taxi rank for a tram to manoeuvre the bend, and walked across to the pavement on the far side.

He stood on the corner and wondered from which direction the pick-up would come. He had been there less than a minute when a Volvo estate car pulled out of a side-street opposite, turned left across the traffic and stopped in front of him. Kindl was driving.

Lacey got in and the car pulled smoothly away, heading out of town.

'We have a nice day for it,' Kindl said, with a smile.

'A nice day for what?'

'A walk in the Vienna Woods.'

Lacey now noticed that Kindl was wearing plus fours, patterned walking socks and sturdy shoes, along with a typical Viennese hacking-jacket. On the back seat was a green felt hat with a feather in it and a leather binocular case.

'You should have told me. I'd have worn my *lederhose*.'
Kindl chuckled.

They drove out of the city, past the last tram terminus and through a village that was distinct from the suburbs. The road curved over a hill with vine fields to the left and the start of the woods beyond. Kindl negotiated the narrow streets of another village, taking a sharp left between houses quaint enough to be a film set.

'Where are we?'

'Sievering. It's well known for its *heurigens*, its inns that sell the heurige white wine.'

The road was very narrow between the houses, but widened when they reached the woods that rose thick and steep on both sides. Half a mile from the village, Kindl pulled off the road into a lay-by.

'From here, we walk.'

Lacey got out and stretched. The sun broke through the trees in splashes of light and warmth, birds sang and the forest felt alive. If you liked walking, the day was perfect, but the only walking Lacey liked was between bars.

Kindl, his hat now perched on his balding head and his binoculars around his neck, opened the back of the estate car. Inside were a pair of rubber overshoes, a pair of wellington boots and a carved walking-stick.

'The paths may still be muddy from yesterday's rain,' Kindl said.

Lacey tried the overshoes and found they were a reasonable fit.

'This way.' Kindl said, pointing with the walking-stick.

They crossed the road and entered the woods along a well-worn path. Their pace was gentle and they didn't talk. After half an hour they came to a clearing on their right where there was a wooden watch-tower, its platform reached by a fixed ladder.

'I shall wait here,' said Kindl. 'You will go that way.' He pointed to a minor tributary to the main path that was signposted *gasthaus*. 'When you reach the inn, you will be

201

contacted.' He smiled. 'Try the dumplings. They are very good.'

Kindl turned and pushed his way through the undergrowth to reach the tower. He climbed the ladder, settled himself on the bench seat at the top and took out the binoculars. Bird song to his left caused him to swivel and focus the glasses. Lacey turned away and took the trail to the *gasthaus*.

It climbed a hill and came out of the tree line, zig-zagging through chest-high grass and bushes. He heard the road ahead before he saw it. Occasional cars went along it at speed, their engine and wind noise whipping by above his head. The path went under the road, beneath a dank stone bridge. The mud was still sticky here, and it nearly took his right overshoe.

The path now climbed steeply in a straight line. There was a car park on his left that was occupied by five vehicles. Above him, he could see the terrace of the inn and the cuckoo clock superstructure of its gabled roof. Out of the trees, the sun was warmer than he had expected. He was panting and looking forward to a rest.

The inn was straight out of a holiday brochure. Its terrace, now set with tables, would have been ideal for summer evening waltzes. A dining-room alongside had picture windows that looked out over the valley. The building itself had painted shutters and ivy covered walls. Potted plants and flowers added technicolor. It was waiting for a remake of *The Sound of Music*.

Lacey kicked off the overshoes in the lane outside and walked on to the terrace. Three tables were occupied, two by groups, one by a single man in sunglasses who wore green slacks and a green sweater over a yellow shirt. His dress co-ordination looked American.

The man raised his hand and Lacey walked towards him, hot and sticky under his leather jacket. The man got to his feet and removed the sunglasses. He smiled wrily and held out his hand. Lacey took it and his sweat went cold.

202

'Hello, Lacey,' the man said.

'Sutherland?'

Lacey was close to shock. He had been expecting Julie Andrews. He had got the top assassin of the KGB.

Chapter 27

The last time Lacey had faced Sutherland had been in an empty warehouse in London's dockland – across the body of Sutherland's wife.

Now they faced each other across a table in the sunshine, Sutherland ordering white wine for an adversary who had become a guest.

Their dockland confrontation had come at the end of a complicated KGB operation that had covered two decades, threatened the life of a United States presidential contender and left a lot of dead bodies spread across two continents. Sutherland had been responsible for most of them.

The Russian with the perfect American accent and the nondescript features that passed anywhere in a crowd, had been operating undercover for more than twenty years. It had been his last operation before heading home, out of the cold, with a new wife. She hadn't made it.

His wife had been no innocent pawn in the gameplan that had had the Governments of the United States and Great Britain on the verge of panic. She had been a queen operator, more ruthless than the male, and she had paid the price when the operation went wrong.

Lacey indirectly had been responsible for her death and Sutherland had had the chance to kill him in return. He hadn't because he was the consumate professional. And, Lacey liked to think, because of mutual respect.

Sutherland had killed frequently but never gratuitously. It was a distinction that mattered, although Lacey accepted that society would never see it that way.

The profession the two of them had chosen to pursue

was, of necessity, governed by a code of ethics far outside the scope of civilized man. Civilized man solved world problems from a bar stool with tipsy wisdom and accepted the right to kill only when his country told him death was licensed by war. In those circumstances, civilized man also had God on his side.

As far as Sutherland and Lacey were concerned, war was continuous and secret and, most of the time, distasteful. For all of these reasons, governments preferred it to be deniable. And God was on nobody's side.

'I thought you'd retired,' Lacey said.

Sutherland shrugged.

'I don't get around much, any more. But I didn't retire.'

The waiter brought two glasses of white wine and they waited until he'd gone.

The Russian picked up his glass and toasted Lacey who, after a moment's hesitation, responded and tasted the wine.

'It's good,' he said.

'It's fresh and young,' Sutherland said. 'I can almost remember when I was the same.'

Lacey put the glass down and stared across the table. Sutherland was relaxed and affable. He was in his mid-fifties, but looked younger, still fit, still showing no signs of excess weight. His short auburn hair was a distinguished grey at the temples. The smile remained on his lips and his eyes were amused. The last time Lacey had seen him, his eyes had been as dead as his wife.

'Why you?'

'Because you know me. Because I know you.'

'Does that mean I'm supposed to believe what you say?'

'No. But you may listen more carefully than to a stranger.'

Lacey took out his cigarettes and lit one.

'Are you delivering a message? Or are you a player?'

'I don't play any more. I'm a boardmaster. A full colonel with the Order of Lenin. I'm with the Foreign

205

Department at the Lubianka.' He grinned. 'My office has a view of the square.'

'I'm impressed. My office doesn't have a window.'

'Come to Moscow. I'll fix it for you.'

Lacey smiled.

'I'm a happily married man.'

He regretted the comment even before he had finished saying it, but Sutherland did not react.

'We can arrange for Susan to come, too. Tickets for the Bolshoi? A dacha in the country? Holidays on the Baltic? You would be celebrities.'

'You make it sound tempting.'

'I'm supposed to.'

'No. I'm a beer drinker and I support West Ham.'

'We import English beer and there's always Moscow Dynamo. Hammers by any other name.'

It was banter to cut the ice, but Lacey was impressed at the depth of the Russian's knowledge of British soccer and the nickname of West Ham United. He imagined he would be just as familiar with American baseball and football teams.

'I think I'll stick with what I've got.'

Sutherland nodded.

'I thought you would.'

Lacey sipped his wine.

'Is Red Dawn a Soviet operation?' he asked.

'No. But we have been aware of it.'

'How aware? Funding, logistics?'

'We haven't been involved at any level. We've monitored it, like you.'

Lacey took a long pull on the cigarette.

'Could Red Dawn be the work of a renegade section of the KGB? A group acting unofficially?'

'No.'

'How can you be so sure?'

Sutherland smiled.

'I know it isn't.'

'As I said. I'm supposed to believe you?'

206

'You'll believe that I took a chance coming here. Your cousins still have an outstanding sanction on me. This is the first time I've been back to the West.'

Lacey nodded an acknowledgement. The Americans took grudges to excess and their order to demote maximally did remain in effect. Sutherland may have only had a ninety-minute drive from Bratislava and the safety of Czechoslovakia, but the whole time he was here, he was in danger.

The Russian said, 'You'll also believe certain facts I give you, because you'll be able to check them from your own sources. You already believe the situation is serious, otherwise you wouldn't have asked for this meeting. You will see that we believe it to be serious, too. But for different reasons.'

The waiter returned with two menus and asked if they liked the wine. They told him they did and again waited until he had gone before continuing.

Lacey stubbed out the cigarette and looked at the view. A burst of laughter from another table caused him to glance at the other occupants of the terrace and wonder briefly if it was a KGB outing. Sutherland seemed to read his thoughts.

'It's just you and me. It's up to us to sort it out.'

'How?'

'An exchange of information to show good faith. You tell me what you know about Red Dawn . . . and Sarah Mathieson. Then I tell you what I know.'

Although there had been no publicity to connect Sarah Mathieson with the assassinations, it didn't surprise Lacey that Sutherland knew there was one. He also recognized that the extent of what Sutherland knew would put his own good faith to the test. Lacey might try to be economical with the truth, but he wouldn't be able to tell untruths because they might be found out.

He had no option but to agree if he wanted to make progress. As far as he was concerned, Sutherland's very presence emphasized how serious the Soviets had taken his approach through Kindl, and if they had taken it this seriously, and arranged a meeting this quickly, his own need to know had become even more urgent. But there were still the formalities to be gone through. Haste would be unseemly.

'All right,' he said, and opened the menu. 'Over lunch.'

In between dumpling in vegetable soup and mouthfuls of peppered steak, Lacey talked about Sarah Mathieson, Aldo Capaldi and Red Dawn. He was circumspect, and dealt in theory and hypothesis rather than describing his own actual involvement, but from time to time, Sutherland would fill in gaps he had purposely left out, to show that he knew more than Lacey was telling.

It was a game in its own right, a cerebral version of poker, and by the time they reached coffee Lacey couldn't decide who had won. Probably the best result would be to declare it a draw.

He lit another cigarette.

'That's the background. When we realized Red Dawn was a hit squad operating to order, we wondered who was giving the orders. The analysts said a section of the KGB may be acting as independents.'

Sutherland poured mineral water into his wine.

'Two questions. One, is there any evidence to connect us with Red Dawn or Capaldi, and two, what reason would renegades have for removing four, rather innocuous, targets?'

'There's evidence. Andrei Chebrikov was in Paris and Vienna in the last two months. And there's Kindl.'

The Russian paused in raising his glass, as if surprised at Lacey mentioning his KGB colleague.

'Chebrikov was promoted. He's no longer with the Executive Action Section. He did go to Paris and Vienna but, if you check the dates, his trips preceded visits to both cities by the Foreign Minister. Chebrikov is now with diplomatic security.'

'And Kindl? He knew who to contact to set up a short notice meeting.'

'Kindl always knows who to contact, whichever side he's dealing with. Answer my second question. Motive?'

'Carry out the hits then blow the operation so that the West believes it was officially sanctioned. Discredit Gorbachev abroad and delay perestroika at home. Result, a change of leadership in Moscow.'

Sutherland smiled.

'It's almost convincing, until you step back and take a good look. Then you see it for what it is: a product of its own making. Take four killings scattered around Europe and invent a plot into which they fit.'

Lacey said, 'Well, that's my theory. Let's hear yours. Who do you think's responsible?'

'There is no doubt who is responsible. The Americans are responsible.'

The response made Lacey smile. But Sutherland wasn't smiling and his eyes said he meant it. Lacey needed to do what the Russian had said. He needed to step back and take a good look. He needed to ensure that his powers of assessment had not been clouded by Dan Beckindale's fervour. He also had to be alert to clever fabrication.

It annoyed him to discover he had come to the meeting with his mind already setting parameters to what could be acceptable theory. It annoyed him even more that he had shown the limit of his parameters to Sutherland.

The smile left his face.

'Tell me,' he said.

'Do you remember General Alexander Haig? He was Reagan's Secretary of State in 1981. A hardliner straight from NATO. He didn't like Reds of any shade or persuasion.'

'I remember.'

'General Haig made headlines at his first Press conference. He stated, quite categorically, that the Soviets supported, fostered and encouraged, international terrorism. He said the Soviets were behind many of the outrages being carried out around the world.

'Newspapers and television everywhere carried the

story. In the United States, about the only people who didn't believe him were his own intelligence advisers. They asked him where he'd got his information from. He told them he'd read it in the galleys of a new book about terrorism. Maybe they should check it out?

'They checked it out. They discovered part of the author's information had come from a story in the foreign Press in Europe. They also found the story had been planted by the CIA.' Sutherland shrugged. 'You know the sort of propaganda operation. We all do it, leaking stories to other countries to score points. To change the balance of goodwill, to cause confusion.'

'Disinformation.'

'Right. Well, this time it went wrong. The disinformation was carried back home, was picked up by the Secretary of State and delivered as fact with the implication that this was what the whole Administration believed. It caused a major embarrassment, internal investigations, and set detente back a mile.

'It's known as a blowback and it happens from time to time.' He sipped from his glass. 'It's happened again.'

Lacey lit a cigarette. Blowbacks did occur and if they weren't identified immediately there was a danger that analysts in one department started inventing theories to fit false intelligence planted by a dissimilator in another department.

'Perhaps you'll explain?' Lacey said.

'Of course. Three years ago, Langley produced a draft proposal for a covert propaganda operation. It was called The VIP List.

'America was having a hard time with its NATO allies about all sorts of things. The European contribution, updating nuclear weapons, first-strike option. They also weren't too pleased with the attitude of most of Western Europe towards the Soviet Union. Mikhail Sergeyevich had been a hit and public opinion was affecting the way national governments could behave. America felt it needed some leverage.

'The VIP List contained names of prominent citizens of NATO countries. They were supposed to be deep penetration agents who had been spying for Russia for years. None of the people on the list had ever betrayed their countries or even been approached to work for us.

'The purpose of the list was to provide a scenario with which America could threaten those allies who were questioning the role of NATO. No government likes a scandal, particularly one with such ramifications. It could also be used to sway public opinion.

'If the list was leaked, the man in the street would believe glasnost was a sham and that Russia was still a threat with agents in high places. The political climate would change and national governments no longer would be restrained by what the people thought. The list could give America the edge if the balance was going against them.'

Lacey said, 'Was it ever used?'

'No. It remained an eyes-only project that never reached the White House.'

'How did it reach you?'

Sutherland smiled but didn't answer.

'The fact is, it's in existence, and four of the names on the list are those of Jacques le Gall, Frederik Hals, Michel Chodron and Franz Haber. There's one other name on the list.'

'Who is it?'

'Unfortunately, I don't know.'

'Shit.'

'Quite.'

The implications didn't bear thinking about, but Lacey had to.

'Why are you telling me? Why aren't you telling the world?'

'It's too messy, it's too dangerous and it can do no-one any good.' He shrugged. 'We considered using it, but the opportunity was never right. Then the killings started. Besides, we don't want another cold war and we don't want to jeopardize what's been achieved. For everybody's sake, this needs shutting down before it becomes public.'

'How?'

Sutherland shook his head.

'I don't know. We're not doing the killing. I don't know who is, but whoever they are, they're using a forged list created by the CIA. What I'm doing is giving you the facts. It's up to you to make sense of them and find out who the next target is. It's up to you to stop it.'

Chapter 28

Sutherland paid the bill.

'I have to go.' He shrugged. 'I would have liked the time to drive you back to Vienna, perhaps do a little shopping, but . . .'

'Kindl is waiting for me.'

'Avoid Kindl. He's a liability. Take a bus back.'

Lacey nodded. He agreed with the sentiments. The fewer who knew anything about all this, the better.

Sutherland got up and Lacey rose with him. They shook hands and there was nothing left to say except the obvious.

'Thanks.'

The Russian nodded, smiled and walked away between the tables. At the exit he turned and raised a hand in farewell, the smile still in place, and then he was gone.

To casual observers, he had made the lunch seem a meeting of two old friends. Even the smile was in keeping with the cover, but Lacey also suspected it was a smile of sympathy for the job ahead.

He sat for a while longer, to give Sutherland time to get in his car and start his journey back to the Czechoslovakian border, and also to let the doubts start.

Sutherland's story could be phoney from start to finish and the best way to test it was by being as sceptical as possible. The walk back through the woods would help.

He left the inn, put on the rubber overshoes, and went down the path that ran under the main road. The weather hadn't even had the decency to cloud over to match his mood but remained clear and sunny and he was sweating

213

again before he reached the trees. It was quicker walking downhill and it was not long before he reached the wooden tower but there was no sign of Kindl.

His absence annoyed Lacey. The man was supposed to be a professional; he shouldn't have let birdwatching divert him from the real purpose of being in the woods.

Lacey pushed through the undergrowth. Perhaps he'd left a message on the tower? There was no message, but there was an explanation.

Anton Kindl's body lay at the foot of the ladder. He lay on his back, one arm trapped behind him, the other stretched towards a scattered packet of sandwiches. One foot rested on the first rung, the other was bent at the knee at an unnatural right angle. His neck was broken and his eyes stared sightlessly at the sun. A fly sat on the bottom lip of his open mouth.

Take a bus back to Vienna, Sutherland had warned. Kindl is a liability.

Lacey had been so wrapped up with his own problems it hadn't occurred to him that the veteran double-dealer might have problems of his own. It appeared that Sutherland hadn't been entirely alone on his excursion into the West. While they had eaten dumplings and steak, the liability in the woods had been taken care of, quietly and efficiently, and in a way that would cause no repercussions.

A coroner would conclude that Kindl had been elderly and no longer agile. His innocent day of pleasure had ended in a tragic accident. But it was an accident to which Lacey did not want to be an inquest witness.

He touched nothing, backed out of the undergrowth and continued down the path. He walked at a normal pace, but lengthened his stride. If there were any other casual walkers in the forest, he did not want to attract their attention by behaving suspiciously. He saw no one and when he reached the road, the Volvo was still the only vehicle in the lay-by.

The path was now tarmaced and ran alongside the road.

214

When it crossed a shallow river, he removed the overshoes and threw them into the water. One sank immediately, but the other floated away on the current, a proud black boat destined for oblivion in the first rough water it came to. Lacey hoped his own chances would be higher.

The death of Kindl had affected him, but not in an emotional way. He neither regretted nor approved of it, although he could see its logic. He also knew he was responsible for it, because he had involved the Czech by telling him enough about the operation to ensure a meeting with the Soviets. He had given Kindl information that had become a death warrant.

But Lacey allowed none of the subtleties of the killing to affect him. He couldn't allow that luxury until he was safely away from the scene, and even then he would avoid thinking about it.

What it had done was clear his mind. He saw the situation now with a strong clarity. For the time being, he had simple targets to achieve. To contact Sam Bryson and to get back to the city without being connected to Kindl's body.

The opportunity to do the first came when he reached Sievering and a telephone kiosk. Fifty yards down the road a bus waited, pointing towards Vienna. Its engine had been shut down and its driver was leaning on the wall nearby, reading a newspaper in the sunshine. If the call was quick, he could catch it.

Malcolm answered.

Lacey said, 'This is your hero calling. Give me Sam. It's a thirty-three.'

He used service-speak that meant it was an emergency.

'He's on another line.'

'Break the connection and put me through.'

Malcolm didn't argue and Lacey listened to a series of clicks and caught the tail end of a Sam Bryson curse.

'Just listen, Sam. I've got a bus to catch.' He was watching it through the glass of the kiosk. 'I met an old friend who gave me an update on the four who left suddenly.

215

They were all on the same list to be head-hunted by the Americans. He says another is due to leave soon, but he doesn't know who. He told me other things, too, things we should talk about.'

'Is this reliable?'

'It's reliable.' Down the road, the driver folded his newspaper and straightened up. 'Look, I've got to go. I'm coming home. Will you be there tonight?'

'I'll be here.'

The driver boarded his vehicle.

'See you then.'

Lacey ran.

He made the bus, checked out of the hotel and got an Austrian Airlines flight to Heathrow. He even had time to visit the duty-free supermarket at the airport and buy a bottle of Nino Cerutti perfume. He called Susan from the departure lounge to tell her he was coming home.

Two hours confined in an aeroplane seat gave him time to run events through his mind. It was a cataloguing operation, listing and evaluating the assassinations, the involvement of his own department and the deaths in Arras, Dan Beckindale's theory, The VIP List and Sutherland's counter-theory of an American blowback, and the possibility that Sutherland himself might be a renegade.

All he wanted was to give them all an airing so that nothing would slip into the background and get overlooked. The only way to play it at the moment was the way Sutherland had suggested. If Sutherland had been lying, the lies would be uncovered. If he had been using the truth with selective emphasis, then it would take a little longer, but would still be uncovered.

Lacey retained an open mind, but he wished Sutherland had had a complete list. It would have eased the worry if he had known the identity of the fifth target.

From Heathrow, Lacey took the tube into London and

arrived at Charing Cross Road early evening. Sam Bryson was waiting for him.

The department chief boiled a kettle in his office and made a pot of tea. He used a spoon to squeeze the flavour out of the teabags, gave the pot a swirl and poured the brew into two mugs. He gave one to Lacey and didn't speak again until they were settled on either side of his desk.

'Now. Tell me everything.'

Lacey told him.

Bryson listened intently, saving his questions until the end. Lacey smoked cigarettes and Bryson smoked his pipe. Between them they recreated the good old days of London smog. When they had finished, they lapsed into silence. Bryson eventually broke it.

'The VIP List,' he said. 'It's conceivable. West Germany, the Netherlands and Belgium were among the renegades of NATO. Still are. They wanted a standstill on short-range nuclear forces, no modernization. Some of them wanted a complete ban. The cousins would have liked to have been able to lean on them a couple of years ago. Threatening them with a spy scandal could have worked.'

'What about France? One of the targets was a former French minister.'

'A serving minister at the time the list was supposed to have been created. But why not? France has always had her own mind. She's quite often been a stroppy ally.'

'So you think there could be a list that was devised by the cousins?'

'On the face of it, yes.'

'Could it have worked?'

'Of course. We've suffered it ourselves. The renegade group at Five who tried to destabilize the Wilson government. The only winner out of that was Peter Wright.'

'Maybe I should write a book.'

'Maybe you should. Maybe we should also consider the repercussions if this is true. If the countries concerned find out their citizens are being killed because of an American

217

blackmail list, NATO could break up quicker than predicted.'

Lacey nodded. He'd already realized the implications, but preferred to concentrate on his own role: stopping them happening.

'We've had French, Belgian, Dutch and West German. Any ideas about which nationality could be next?'

'The choice is too wide. Maybe Scandinavia.'

Lacey said, 'That's part one. What about part two? Could it be the cause of a blowback? Could somebody be killing these people because they believe they are spies?'

'If we accept the existence of The VIP List, we have to accept the possibility of a blowback.' He shook his head. 'If the document wasn't circulated, the number of people who know about it might be very few. Now the list has been activated, those few could be keeping quiet, too frightened about their careers to say anything.'

'If it is a blowback, who's responsible for the hits?'

'Someone with a motive.'

'The CIA?'

Bryson shrugged.

'If it's the cousins, it's unlikely to be official. It's more beneficial to compromise than to kill. But it could be one man or one section that's gone freelance. Maybe someone left the Company with a copy of the file and a burning desire to give the Soviets a warning about agents of influence.'

'Aren't we closing down our options?'

'Who else is possible?'

'The Chinese?'

'Why?'

'China aims to be the third most powerful country in the world within ten years. The Beijing massacre screwed their timetable and the cosiness between Moscow and Washington isn't helping. If the KGB got a copy of the list, maybe they did, too. Maybe they've activated it as a spoiler. Get both sides blaming each other, change the climate. They could only benefit if Russian glasnost was put on a back-burner or the empire cracked up. They'd benefit if America was isolated, too. It would give them more options for trade, a way back in.'

Bryson puffed his pipe. He didn't seem impressed.

He said, 'Of course, anything is possible. But before pursuing it, how about getting back to basics.'

'OK,' Lacey lit another cigarette. 'What about the source? Can we trust the KGB?'

'Certainly not. But in this case, I can't see what they might gain from spinning fairy-tales.' He puffed out more smoke. 'I can understand Sutherland's concern. It is messy and it could backfire on them. They can't afford these sort of risks.' He paused to thicken the smog. 'On the other hand . . .'

'You're going in circles, Sam.'

Bryson smiled.

'It's part of the charm of the game. But before we get more deeply involved, we need to find out whether the list actually exists. How do you propose to do it?'

'The most direct way. Through Dan Beckindale. He has access at the highest level. If I can convince him to help, I'll have God and the President on my side.'

'You might have problems with Beckindale. If he's convinced the Soviets are behind it, this could just confirm it for him.'

'He doesn't like Russia, but he's no fool. He'll listen.'

Bryson put his pipe down in an ashtray, stretched and looked at his watch.

'It's four in the afternoon in Washington. Call him now and take a morning flight out.'

'Right.'

Lacey went into his own office and collapsed in his chair. He was beginning to feel tired and his throat was wire wool. Another half an hour and he could go home. The thought of Susan and his own bed made him smile. He reached into a drawer and took out an address book and looked up the number Beckindale had given him.

219

He got the White House switchboard and asked for the extension.

'Colonel Beckindale's secretary.'

She sounded nice. Lacey imagined blond hair, long legs and perfect teeth.

'My name is Peter Lacey. I'd like to speak to Colonel Beckindale.'

'Oh, Mr Lacey. My name is Cherise. Dan mentioned you. I'm sorry, but he's not available right now.'

'I need to speak to him urgently. Can you get to him?'

There was a pause longer than the normal transatlantic time-gap while she prepared a response. She was being the protective mother hen.

'Yes, I think I can get to him. Can he call you back?'

'I'll be at my office for the next fifteen minutes. After that, I'm going home. He can get me there and he has both numbers. Tell him there have been developments. I'm flying to Washington tomorrow.'

'I'll tell him. I'll get him to call you back, Mr Lacey.'

Beckindale called back within ten minutes.

'I hear you're coming to Washington?'

'That's right. More developments. We need to talk. I think your theory just fell flat on its face.'

'You never did like it.'

Lacey laughed.

'This isn't prejudice, Dan. When you hear me out, I think you'll agree.'

'OK. I'll hear you out. But you don't have to cross the pond. I'm coming back to London.'

'So soon? But what about . . . ?'

'You're not the only sceptic in the service, Peter. I had a hard time convincing people here, too. They're looking at it, but it's a long way short of top priority. Maybe we need more developments. Maybe you've got them. I'll be back tomorrow. Where?'

'Come to the house.'

'OK. I'll be there in the afternoon.'

Lacey felt better now that a course of action had been

220

decided and he shelved any further thoughts about the case. It was also a bonus that he didn't have to go away again. He thought of Susan and began to look forward to the night ahead and his desire made him feel guilty.

Was it normal for a middle-aged man to miss his wife like this, to desire his wife like this? Maybe not, but since when had he been normal?

Chapter 29

Susan talked while she got ready for work the next morning and Lacey wondered where his passion and deep affection had gone. She talked about Lucy and corduroy Michael and the possibility that they might get back together again. He didn't care whether they got back together again and all Susan was doing was irritating him. He lay in bed and feigned sleep, but she knew him well enough to know he was awake.

'Look, you may not have a great deal of sympathy for them, but, well, they are trying to save a relationship.'

She waited but there was no response.

'And I just feel obliged to help, if I can.'

Lacey remained silent.

'So I said I would go out with Michael and talk things over.'

'Go out with Michael?'

'Yes.'

He pushed the sheet back and looked over the top.

'Why?'

'To lend a sympathetic ear, be a samaritan.'

'That's no answer.'

He opened his eyes wide to stretch the sleep away and she waved her hands, but was unable to conjure anything more illuminating.

'Because Lucy asked me to,' she said.

He sat up in bed and pushed the pillows behind him.

'Why should you see Michael? Lucy should see Michael.'

'Yes, well, she's seen him and they had a long talk but—' she shrugged '—she feels that if he heard the

222

woman's point of view from another woman, it might help solve their problem.'

'You'd be better off talking to Lucy.'

'What do you mean?'

'One of the main problems in their relationship is her bloody boilersuit. Man cannot live by middle-class pretensions alone. He also likes a bit of the other, even Michael. I'll bet he's been getting the other somewhere else and found he likes it. If Lucy's serious, she needs to compete, not mope in a corner.'

'A typical chauvinist interpretation.'

'Probably because I am a chauvinist. But don't forget, under all that corduroy that Michael wears, is a chauvinist waiting to break out. Lucy should change her tactics.'

Susan's defensive pose cracked and she laughed.

'If she could hear us discussing it, she'd die.'

She turned back to the dressing-table to dab her new perfume on to strategic areas of her skin. It made Lacey remember the previous night. When he had come out of the shower and gone into the bedroom, he had found her lying on the bed almost naked.

'I thought you were going to wear something special,' he had said.

'I am.' She had smiled and offered her breasts. 'It's called Nino Cerutti. Do you like it?'

He had liked it.

The memory of their intimacy prompted a secondary reaction: jealousy. He didn't want her meeting corduroy Michael, but didn't know how to say so without sounding stupid.

'When are you supposed to be seeing him?'

'It depends. Sunday, Monday. I didn't make any definite arrangement. I wanted to talk to you first. I didn't want to make arrangements that might clash with anything you had planned.'

Lacey was angry that she was being so reasonable. It gave him no excuse to start a row in which he could provoke her into saying she wouldn't meet Michael.

'I don't want you to see him,' he said lamely.

Susan turned and looked at him and a smile spread across her face.

'You're jealous.'

He could feel himself going red.

'Yes. I'm jealous. All right?'

She came round the bed and kissed him gently on the forehead and he tried to slip his hand up the back of her skirt, but she moved away smartly.

'I haven't time. It's a busy day. Bank holiday weekend.'

He'd forgotten Monday was a public holiday, probably because he rarely took them. This one was to celebrate the end of May, or something. Perhaps to placate the workforce at the start of warm weather that always took Britons by surprise.

'Make lots of money so I can retire and keep you in the underwear to which I've grown accustomed,' he said, to retrieve his lost macho image.

Christ, he would never understand how this thing between men and women worked. When he had woken up, she had annoyed him with her chatter and now here he was lusting after her again.

'Jealousy. That's made my day,' she said, and blew him another kiss from the safety of the doorway.

'Are you going to see him?'

'Now don't be silly, Peter. Remember who we're talking about. This is Lucy's Michael. He's harmless. Boring and harmless. And I promised Lucy.'

'We'll talk about it later.'

'If you like. But I'll still have to see him.' She blew him another kiss. 'See you later.'

Lacey lay in bed and did what he had been trained to do – he analyzed himself and was amazed at the result. He could stay cool under the pressure of world politics or the threat of death, but his wife could reduce him to an idiot.

He shouldn't be surprised. Love, sex and infatuation were well recognized for their power-potential by every secret service in the world. They all had stables of ladies

224

and sisters, of male ravens to seduce female targets, and increasing numbers of homosexuals.

Maybe he had been wrong in declaring that Michael was a chauvinist unleashed. Maybe Michael had found himself a nice chap in matching corduroy?

Dan Beckindale arrived by taxi at three o'clock and they settled in the study with a pot of coffee.

He was less ebullient than the last time Lacey had seen him, and it looked as though he had not had great success in Washington.

'They didn't buy it?' Lacey said.

'Not completely. They've accepted it as a possibility, but the NSC has passed it to Langley for an estimate. Shit, those CIA bastards are likely to give it a negative response simply because of where it came from.'

'You and Langley don't get on?'

'They're pussyfooters. Too much college, not enough street.' He shrugged. 'We've crossed, from time to time.'

Lacey couldn't decide whether Beckindale's antagonism towards the CIA would help or hinder his own case. There was only one way to find out. He told him the story of his trip to Vienna.

Beckindale had trouble keeping himself under control at what he obviously saw as a breach of security on Lacey's part by making an approach to the Russians.

'Sweet Jesus, Peter. How could you?'

'Hear me out. It's worth it.'

The American shut up, but got to his feet, went to the drinks and poured himself a Scotch without asking. He listened in stone-faced silence as Lacey gave him the reasons why he had gone solo, how he had made contact, and enough of Sutherland's history to put the KGB Colonel's importance in no doubt.

When the existence of the VIP List was mentioned and its supposed creation at Langley, he was momentarily startled, before shaking his head in disbelief.

Lacey went on to expound all that he and Bryson had

225

discussed the previous day and the possibility of a rogue American operation. When he had finished, Beckindale was smiling to himself.

'What's the joke?' Lacey asked.

'No joke. I'm just amused that you thought my hypothesis was far-fetched.'

'I didn't think it was far-fetched. I took it seriously enough to go to Vienna.'

'And you came back with it tied in a knot and pointing two ways at once.'

'I came back with additional information. The fact that you might not believe it does not invalidate it. If it's a lie, it's a lie that's been told for a purpose. True or not, everything that Sutherland said needs to be evaluated, and we need to go looking for this bloody list.'

Beckindale smiled again, but this time without irony.

'True. And I'm going to surprise you, Peter. I believe we have a lot of common ground. You're right, we have to look for this . . . list. If that doesn't exist, your Russian friend's whole line is lost. But he knows that, too, so it's reasonable to suppose we'll find it.

'If it does exist, we're faced with more questions. Is it what the Russians say it is, has it been planted by the Russians, or, is it genuine?'

'Christ, Dan, the fantasy has to stop somewhere . . .'

Beckindale grinned and held up his hand for Lacey to let him continue. Lacey went and got himself a Scotch and water.

'No matter who's responsible for the list, the fact remains that someone is killing the people on it. We need to know who that is, who the next target is, and we need to stop them. Right?'

'Right.'

'We also agree that if this leaks out we'll all end up covered in shit. Right?'

'Right.'

'Then it doesn't matter what theories you and I have. We just need to work together to stop it.'

226

'I'll go along with that.'

'OK. I have an encrypter at my apartment. As soon as I get back, I'll contact the NSC and get them to search for any file relating to a VIP List. We don't have access to CIA files so that'll mean an official request to Langley.' He pulled a face. 'Of course, it's Saturday and Washington'll be empty for the weekend. It's likely to be Monday before we get a reply.' Beckindale got up and went to freshen his drink. 'Just out of curiosity, who do you suspect?'

Lacey shrugged.

'I don't want to speculate. I just want to find out.'

Beckindale laughed.

'What the hell, whoever it is, they're not going to make it. Right, Peter?'

Lacey raised his eyebrows in acknowledgement but didn't answer. Sutherland was beginning to make him feel like a sidekick in a movie, playing Tonto to the Lone Ranger.

The All-American hero had his defects but, he reflected, he could live with them. He remembered him in action.

Chapter 30

Martin Goodman walked the banks of Loch Lomond, along the path from Inversnaid Hotel to Rob Roy's Cave, and reflected he was a long way from home. Except he didn't know where home was any more. The United States, he supposed, the land of immigrants.

He had been born in Appleton, Wisconsin. His father had been the son of a lapsed Jew who had changed the family name from Guttman, and his mother had come from a mixed background which featured Scandinavians, Hungarians and Scots. They had both died when he was a teenager. He had been an only child and had broken any lingering family ties when he had gone to college and never returned.

From an early age, he had thought of himself as a loner, because it was a more romantic concept than admitting to being just plain lonely.

He was alone now, in the rain that mottled the loch and ensured the emptiness of the trail. The canopy of the trees kept the worst of the weather from him but, in any case, he was dressed for it, in blue waterproofs and walking boots.

Like a boy scout, he was always prepared, always had been, ever since his parents had proved their unreliability by dying on him.

Goodman was of medium height and medium fat. His features were thick, his limbs heavy and his hair dark and wavy with a natural grease content he tried unsuccessfully to wash away with a special shampoo. He had flat feet, wore glasses and his dress sense was mediocre verging on bad. He had no illusions about himself, rather the reverse, and was three weeks from his fortieth birthday and halfway through the first sabbatical in his career.

Reaching twenty hadn't bothered him, but thirty had. The imminence of forty had built into a major depression partly because the sabbatical had given him time to consider its significance, along with all his other problems.

Forty was halfway to death, a time to look back at what he had done with his life. What he had done might look good in a curriculum vitae, but it was not the stuff of which dreams were made. The sad thing was, his dreams had never been that outrageous.

At college, his contemporaries had planned to travel the Pan-American Highway to Cape Horn, to become novelists, to follow the bulls in Spain. His dreams had revolved around meeting the right girl, settling down and having a family.

An unconsummated and broken love affair at twenty-one had robbed him of self-confidence and confirmed what he had already suspected: he was not much of a catch. To compensate, he had concentrated on his studies and been an exceptional student.

He had followed his career with the same single-mindedness and had done well, despite another romantic hiccup when he was twenty-seven. She had been the daughter of a Hungarian refugee and she had responded to his sympathy and his ability to speak the language of her homeland. Bekki had been a dumpy girl, but her laugh had been spontaneous and she had taken him to bed and helped him shed his virginity. The affair had lasted three months before she met someone else.

At least he was no longer a virgin, but being introduced to sex had been a good news – bad news joke. Bekki had revealed its delights but, after she had moved on, there had been no one else with whom to enjoy them. He, once again, had submerged his desires and hopes in his work and had become highly proficient, and an acknowledged expert in his field.

Goodman kicked a piece of wood from the path. With all that expertise, what the hell was he doing here, avoiding people by walking in the rain? The answer, he kept telling himself, was another woman. He had fled to Scotland to avoid the Jane-drain.

Maybe he should have seen it wouldn't work from the start. They had been of a certain age where wariness was second nature, Jane had still been nursing emotional bruises from a marriage that had ended seven years before and he had been wracked with self-doubt.

The affair had been conducted slowly and with such gentility that Goodman had found it impossible to develop it. They had held hands and exchanged chaste kisses that had made him both quiver with anticipation and frightened him, in case any carnal moves he made might be rejected with horror. In the end, he had made no moves at all and the affair had stultified.

He reached the hole in the rocky bank that could, conceivably, have been Rob Roy's Cave. He'd been here many times before and it had always provoked the same sentiments. It looked one helluva place to spend winter, even for a hero on the run.

Shit.

He thought the curse and gave the grey sky a hard look. 'Shit!'

He said it out loud but didn't feel any better.

This was the first time in years Goodman had had the time to indulge his dissatisfaction with life and the experience was confusing.

Jane worked for the same organization and after their affair dried up they had still bumped into each other, causing them both distress. The coincidences had started to occur by then, as well, and he had been unable to concentrate. To colleagues, he blamed his distraction on what he termed the Jane-drain syndrome, but when the coincidences got too frightening he looked for a way out. A sabbatical had seemed ideal.

The advertisement in the *Washington Post* had offered a modernized farmhouse at the foot of the Trossachs at a peppercorn rent. It was perfect, he had told himself. He

230

hadn't taken into account the climate in February.

The weather had been a bitch for the first two months. It shouldn't have been a problem, as he had come loaded with excuses as to why he was in Scotland, and sightseeing hadn't been one of them. He had needed a break in complete isolation, somewhere he could avoid newspapers and television and people, somewhere the hallucinations and disappointments didn't reach.

Shit, after a while of doing what he did, it got so you couldn't trust your own imagination.

He hadn't come to look at the sights, but to immerse himself in a lifestyle completely different to what he was used to and, maybe, research the ancestry of his great grandmother McGregor. But the short days and the damp cold had been claustrophobic.

Time had slipped by and he had done nothing but avoid thinking about his job. In the process he had acquired an encyclopedic knowledge of malt whisky and the collected works of Charles Dickens and Robert Louis Stevenson.

Goodman had spent three months hiding out, much the same as Rob Roy had hidden out. But Goodman hadn't been hiding from an enemy, he'd been hiding from himself.

Jesus H Christ.

He wondered if Rob Roy had ever got as pissed at being as lonely as he was?

The rain stopped and he headed back towards the hotel before Sunday strollers were tempted out of their cars and on to the path.

In the public car park, he got in the 4 × 4 Suzuki that had come with the farmhouse, and headed back towards Aberfoyle. The road ran by smaller lakes on his right, and the beauty of the haze across Loch Ard made him long for someone to share it with.

Aberfoyle was busy with ramblers and trippers from Glasgow and he resented their intrusion into his melancholy. He negotiated the traffic through the small town until he was back in the country, eventually turning on to a side road.

He turned again, into the woods, glanced in his wing mirror and saw an estate car turn to follow him, thirty yards behind. The manoeuvre did not strike him as anything out of the normal. The land was National Forest Park and most of its trails were open to the public. Dog owners frequently parked along here before taking their pets for walks.

He took the private road to the farmhouse, looked in his mirror again and noted that the vehicle was no longer in sight.

A small animal scurried in the trees and he remembered the first time he had travelled along here. Donald Donaldson, the owner of the farmhouse, had picked him up from the Holiday Inn in Glasgow. It had been early evening and it was dark when they reached the forest. Snow had been on the ground. The headlights had become searchlights as the car had bounced across the frozen ruts of the track. The snowclad forest could have been copied from a Disney fantasy. And then it had happened.

A stag had bounded from the trees to the left, crossed in front of them in two strides, and disappeared into the trees on the right. Its sudden appearance and disappearance and the elegance of its leap had been breathtaking. He had accused Donaldson of stage managing the scene to confirm the letting of his home, but it had impressed him. So had the farm.

He came out of the tree-line and the white-walled building was in front of him, roses round the door and a white-fenced garden at the front. There was a barn and paddock at the end of the house, although Donaldson had found other accommodation for his two horses for the duration of Goodman's let.

The land fell away beyond the house. The forest rose again from the bottom of the hill. To the left, it climbed toward the heights of Ben Lomond. To the right was the peak of Ben Venue and the start of the Highlands.

He let himself into the house, took his boots and

232

waterproofs off in the kitchen, and went into the living-room. When the house had been modernized, the architect had sensibly replaced the far wall with floor-to-ceiling double-glazing. How could anyone improve on nature? The view was breathtaking.

Goodman picked up the bottle of Glenmorangie he had started that morning after breakfast, and poured himself a large one. He sat in the armchair facing the window and continued to remember his arrival, when he had been embarrassed at being a guest-in-waiting.

Donaldson and his wife had stayed in the house with him for the first three nights, introduced him to the tradespeople in Aberfoyle and explained the peculiarities of the premises. They were in their early thirties, vibrant and about to set off for Australia via Phuket, Bangkok and Singapore. They were chasing their dreams.

They had gone and left him in possession of a sanctuary that had gone sour. He had felt deprived, not just because of the journey they had embarked upon, but because Donaldson was making it in the company of a beautiful wife.

Goodman sipped the whisky. Maybe he *was* a loner. He felt safe on his own, even out here in the middle of nowhere, in the middle of lethargy. He hadn't done anything, except drink and read. He hadn't attempted to trace his roots. It had been enough to know that, generations ago, this was where he had come from.

America was a new world still. This was the land of his fathers. Him and Rob Roy McGregor. Where was home? As long as the whisky lasted it was right here. And his dreams? He might stay and make this a dream fulfilled.

The solitude had helped him bury his fears beneath days of boredom and he had always been able to cope with loneliness. It was an old friend, even it if did sometimes get on his nerves.

The whisky was smooth on his tongue. Donaldson had described malt as sipping-whisky. One glass should last a long time, he had said. That depended on the size of the glass. He finished the drink and poured himself another large one.

Hell. The chances had been there to grab the dream, but his temerity had stopped him. He wondered, as he had more and more frequently in the last few weeks, as the apprehension had receded, whether it was still worth taking a chance on calling Jane? Maybe he could still achieve something apart from success?

The malt and the thought both warmed him, and he admired the colour of the liquid in the cut-glass tumbler by holding it against the sky. On cue, the clouds moved and a laser-beam blazed across the valley. He caught the sun in his glass and diamond bursts of light sparked around his hand.

It was a sign that now was the time for decision. He had to make the call. If he waited, he might never make it. He got out of the chair, raised his glass once more to the mountains in a toast, and sipped the whisky.

To success. And if not . . . ? Hell, he might just as well stay here for ever.

The telephone was in the kitchen and he took his drink with him. He opened the door and stopped in shock at the sight of the stranger standing in the other room.

'Jesus!'

He dropped the glass in which he'd caught the sun, and it shattered on the stone floor. The man smiled and pointed a handgun at him.

'Mr Goodman? I'd very much like to talk with you.'

The man's American accent did not reassure him. The apprehension he had attempted to bury beneath three months of indolence, surfaced and mingled with the instant fear of being threatened with a gun.

'Who are you?'

'No, Mr Goodman. I'm the one with the questions. Will you come with me, please?'

'Where?'

'Not far.'

He had no choice. American accent or not, the man

did not seem the type with whom you argued.

'I'll just . . .'

Goodman put on a pair of wellington boots and the man opened the door and backed outside, still keeping him covered with the gun.

'This way.'

He pointed him towards the barn and the balance of Goodman's fear shifted several degrees from the possibility of ruin to the possibility of being hurt. Barns did not fit any logical pattern. He had expected to be put into a car and driven away, except that the stranger didn't have a car there. The Suzuki was the only vehicle parked outside the house.

'What's all this about?'

The man ignored him, but pointed to the side door of the barn with the gun. Goodman hesitated a moment. This was all happening too fast and made no sense. His initial panic had receded and his professionalism had taken over to interpret what was happening, but his training hadn't prepared him for anything like this.

He shrugged, and stepped through the door.

'Look. I think you've got the wrong . . .'

The noose hanging from a hook in the crossbeam of the barn silenced him. He felt numb and his analysis dried up.

Positioned below the noose was a metal milk-crate standing on its side.

'Let me explain,' the man said.

Goodman licked his lips, but said nothing.

'I have questions to ask that you might not want to answer.'

'I'll answer them.'

The man smiled.

'Maybe you will, maybe you won't. This way saves a lot of time. Please. Climb up there, and put the rope around your neck.'

'No. Look. I'll talk. I'll tell you anything you want to know. But I'm not responsible. I'm Martin Goodman. I'm a nobody.'

'Mr Goodman, I know who you are. You shouldn't underestimate your importance. Now, please. Get on the crate.'

Goodman climbed nervously on to the crate. Its balance was precarious and it was the most dangerous act he had performed in years. He stood on it, half-bent and arms extended and felt foolish, as if he was the butt of a company joke.

'Look . . .' His bluster was closer to a blubber. 'This has gone far enough. Let me . . .'

'Now the rope.'

Goodman looked up at the noose that was hanging above his head.

'Hold on. Hold on just a minute. This isn't funny any more.'

'It isn't supposed to be, Mr Goodman. It's supposed to make you talkative.'

'It has, it has. I'll tell you everything.'

'Maybe, maybe not. Indulge me a little longer. Put the rope around your neck. I want you to get the feel of it, so we don't have to go through all this again.' The smile left his face and he pointed the gun at Goodman's genitals. 'Do it.'

Goodman straightened and raised his hands to the rope. He had to lift his chin to fit the noose underneath. He gingerly tucked the rope behind his ears.

'Fit it properly or I'm going to lose patience.'

Goodman pushed the noose completely over his head and the knot slipped down at the back. It fitted snugly around his neck and he no longer had to stretch, but the pressure at his Adam's apple was already making his breathing irregular.

He was at the total mercy of this man and the panic returned and made his legs shake. Dear God, he couldn't afford to shake in case he fell. He was holding the rope above his head with one hand, but his arm was already aching. His other arm was held out for balance. Jesus, but the man was right. Having the noose round his neck put everything in perspective. He'd tell him anything to get out of this position.

Goodman licked his lips again and looked down. The man stared back at him impassively.

'What do you want to know?' Goodman asked.

'Nothing.'

The man stepped forward and kicked the milk-crate away.

Chapter 31

Lacey met Beckindale at Heathrow for a Monday morning shuttle to Glasgow. The aeroplane left behind a grey day and climbed into the sunshine above a solid white blanket of cloud. On the flight, the American briefed him on the man they were going to see.

'The VIP List rang a bell when it was run through the CIA's code-word records. It showed the name had been used three years ago and had been logged to a political analyst specializing in Western Europe.' He handed Lacey a photograph. 'Martin Goodman.

'Goodman is thirty-nine, white and single. He is believed to be heterosexual and his colleagues say he took a sabbatical because an office romance didn't work out. The woman involved confirms he was a friend, but denies any romantic relationship. Reading the small print suggests she wishes there had been. He's been in Scotland three months.

'He's an egg-head, went to Langley from Columbia University as scholar-in-residence.' Beckindale read from a faxed report. 'He specialized in spotting misperceptions in intelligence gathering and decision-making.'

He stopped reading to look at Lacey.

'He had total access to the most sensitive traffic, including eyes-only. There are no other records about the VIP List except that it was BIGOT listed – that means restriction to the President and Secretaries of State and Defence.

'There's nothing on paper or computer and no reference to anybody else and, right at this moment, I don't feel like asking the President, or the Secretaries of State and

Defence, whether they or their predecessors remember anything about it. Not until we get something we can hang a reason on.'

Lacey nodded.

'Why's Goodman in Scotland?'

'Don't know. He rented a property near Loch Lomond at short notice and took off. Maybe he'll tell us.'

'I hope to God he'll tell us a lot more besides.'

They left the cloud behind in the Midlands and by the time they reached Glasgow the weather was sunny and warm. They hired a car and Lacey drove. Beckindale, being Captain America, had anticipated and brought a large-scale map with him. He had already plotted a route to Aberfoyle, the nearest town to where Goodman was staying.

The grey urban streets and factories were quickly left behind after they crossed the Clyde. Suburbia on this side of the city was pleasant, then that, too, thinned, and they were in the country, driving along winding roads towards the distant hills.

Aberfoyle was busy with people making the most of the weather and the bank holiday, the streets thronged with armies of back-packed walkers clutching maps. Lacey could think of less strenuous ways of enjoying himself.

Beckindale asked at the garage how to get to the village they wanted and both listened patiently to a helpful mechanic with a strong accent.

'Did you understand him?' Lacey asked, when they were back in the car.

'Some.'

'Me, too. Let's give it a try.'

After they had turned off the main road, they stopped by a humped-back bridge and asked again, this time from a woman in jodhpurs and green wellies who was walking a red setter. Her accent was English and she gave them further directions that were clear to follow, although Lacey began to doubt them when they bumped up a long and rutted private road through a forest.

239

'Christ, this bloke really wants to be alone, doesn't he?'

'He has that reputation.'

They emerged from the trees and saw the farmhouse.

'That is some holiday cottage,' Lacey said.

'That I'd like to buy and ship home,' Beckindale said.

'You'd have a hell of a job moving the mountains,' Lacey said, referring to the Trossachs beyond. 'Even in numbered sacks.'

Beckindale laughed and Lacey parked next to the Suzuki jeep.

'Well, the car's here.' Lacey switched off the engine. 'With luck, he's at home.'

They walked down the path, Beckindale taking care to shut the garden gate behind him, and Lacey banged on the door. After a while, he banged again.

'Shit.'

He tried the handle and the door opened.

'Hello?' He stepped inside a kitchen and pushed open an inner door. 'Mr Goodman?'

The house greeted them with silence.

'Maybe he's out walking,' Beckindale said.

Lacey took a step forward and his shoe crunched glass. They both looked down at the floor.

'Maybe not.'

His hand automatically reached into the small of his back, but there was no gun there. He hadn't thought he'd need a gun on a trip to see a political analyst in rural Scotland.

'It's just a broken glass,' Beckindale said, as if to calm him down.

It was true. An accidental breakage that was not necessarily sinister. But why hadn't it been cleared up? Everything else in the kitchen was tidy. Perhaps a cat had knocked the glass off a shelf and Goodman hadn't seen it yet. Perhaps. Nonetheless, Lacey went into the house cautiously.

The kitchen entered directly into the living-room. Opposite was another door that led from the living-room

240

into a corridor that ran the full length of the house. The rooms, and a staircase, were located off the corridor to the right.

'I'll take upstairs,' said Beckindale.

They separated, but the deeper into the house Lacey went, the more convinced he was that it was empty. He checked a study, two ground-floor bedrooms and a bathroom.

Goodman's clothes were in the wardrobes and drawers of one of the bedrooms and male toiletries were in the bathroom, but there was nothing of interest or out of place. In fact, everything indicated that Goodman was a very tidy man, which made Lacey wonder again about the significance of the broken glass.

'Yo?'

Beckindale was calling from the bottom of the stairs and Lacey went and joined him.

'Anything?' he asked.

'Zilch. You?'

'Clothes. He's using one of the bedrooms.'

'He'll be out walking. It's a nice day.'

'The door was unlocked.'

'Hell, we're in the middle of nowhere. If somebody wanted to break in they could do it with a sledge-hammer and no one would hear. Why risk the damage? Besides, this is the country. Different rules apply.'

'In America, too?'

'In America too.'

Lacey led the way back into the living-room and looked out of the full-length window at the view. He lit a cigarette and, as he turned, noticed the collection of malt whiskies.

'I suppose we could wait.'

Beckindale laughed.

'Let's check the jeep and the out-buildings first.'

The American went across the garden towards the Suzuki. Lacey took the path along the front of the house towards the barn.

It was a beautiful place in a beautiful location and

241

Beckindale was probably right about different rules. But they were rules that could also be perfect for someone with criminal intent.

He dropped the cigarette and stubbed it out on the cobbles before pulling open the door of the barn. The light spilled in and something scurried in a corner. His eyes adjusted and he saw the body on the floor and an upturned milk-crate.

'Dan!'

Lacey didn't move, but waited until the American came running, all the time assessing the interior to make sure that, apart from the body, it was empty.

Beckindale said, 'Shit.'

They went inside, still moving cautiously and watching for sudden movements in the shadows, but there were none. Tools were hanging from hooks on one wall, beyond a work bench, and two bales of hay were stacked against the other. They knelt by the body and saw the rope around its neck. The man's weight had pulled the hook out of the beam from which he had been suspended.

'Suicide?' Beckindale said.

The man was lying face down. His trousers were stained and there was a lingering smell from a bowel movement.

Lacey leaned closer and moved the man's head for identification.

'Goodman,' he said. His finger flickered on his neck. 'And he's alive.' He looked up in surprise. 'Jesus Christ, he's alive!'

'Ambulance!'

Beckindale pushed him.

Lacey got to his feet and ran for the house. He was out of breath when he reached the telephone in the kitchen, but it didn't matter. The telephone line was dead. One of them would have to go and get help.

He ran back and stopped abruptly inside the doorway of the barn. Beckindale and Goodman were no longer alone. A third man was standing in the shadows by the hay bales. He was holding a handgun.

242

'Come in, Mr Lacey,' the man said, in an American accent. 'We need your help.'

Beckindale was still kneeling by Goodman, whom he had rolled on to his back. Lacey exchanged looks with him but obeyed.

'Now, first things first. Colonel, I'd be obliged if you would lie face down and stretch your arms and legs.' He waited until Beckindale had done so. 'You, Mr Lacey, will face the wall and assume the position. I trust you watch TV?'

Lacey faced the wall and leaned against it with his arms outstretched and his legs spread in the classic cops and robbers position. The man pressed the barrel of the gun into the base of his spine so hard that it hurt.

'It's a .357 Magnum,' he said quietly.

He didn't need to elaborate. If it went off, Lacey would be carried out in a plastic bag. Maybe two plastic bags. He co-operated with the body search.

'Now if you gentlemen will exchange places?'

Lacey lay on the floor and Beckindale leaned against the wall. The man was so expert that not even Captain America could take one leap and be free. When he was satisfied, the man stepped back.

'Let me explain what we're going to do. You two gentlemen are going to pick up Mr Goodman here, and carry him into the house. Then we'll sit down and have a civilized discussion. OK? So let's do it.'

Lacey took the feet of the unconscious Goodman, and Beckindale removed the noose from around his neck, and took his arms. He was a heavy sod, and Lacey was thankful he hadn't got the weightier end. They carried him along the path to the kitchen door and manoeuvred him into the living-room. The stranger with the gun followed.

'Put him on the floor.'

They did so and straightened up. The man was in the kitchen doorway, the gun still covering them. He was a similar height and build to Beckindale, but maybe ten years older, his hair grey at the temples, his face square-jawed and his eyes dull brown. Lacey believed in eyes and these were dispassionate. He judged that if the man had to, he wouldn't hesitate to use the gun.

'Mr Lacey, I'd be obliged if you would put your hands in the pockets of your pants and sit down.' The man indicated the floor by the window, and Lacey went and sat down. 'Colonel, it would also be good if you were to put your hands in your pockets and stand over there.' He indicated a place several feet away from Lacey. When they had done as he asked, he smiled. 'Thank you.'

He leaned against the table where the bottles of malt were lined up and scratched the back of an ear with the gun.

'You were too easy.' He shook his head. 'It worries me.'

Beckindale said, 'Who the hell are you?'

The man smiled, but didn't answer the question.

'You need an ambulance,' he said. 'I'll give—' he stared from one to the other before picking on Beckindale. '—you a lift.'

Lacey said, 'What about me?'

'You stay and keep Mr Goodman company.'

'Alive or dead?'

The man laughed.

'I have no need to kill you, Mr Lacey. You are of no consequence, alive or dead.'

Being told he was of no consequence stung Lacey, even though it appeared to be the major reason he was not going to be shot.

'What about Dan?'

'Don't be tedious. If I wanted to kill either of you I could do it now, without any games. Come on, Colonel. Let's go.'

Beckindale walked outside, hands still in his pockets, the man holding the gun in his back. Lacey got up and watched through the window as they climbed into the hire car, Beckindale in the driving seat and the stranger sitting behind him, the barrel of the gun pressed into his neck.

Lacey was angry, worried and confused. He'd been

244

dismissed as a nonentity, he was worried about Dan Beckindale's safety despite the assurances, and he didn't know what the hell was going on.

He felt as if he was on the Yellow Brick Road to nowhere with the Wicked Witch changing the rules and the signposts every hundred yards. He kicked the table and knocked over a bottle of malt whisky. But which bloody witch was it.

The Wicked Witch of the East . . . or the West?

Chapter 32

Lacey was sipping whisky and admiring the mountains from the armchair when he heard the ambulance arrive. Taking it easy had seemed the most sensible course of action, under the circumstances.

He had changed Goodman's position from lying on his back and had rolled him on to his side in case he vomited on waking and choked to death. The man's breathing was shallow but it was regular and he hadn't wanted to leave him. He had decided to allow an hour for help of some kind to turn up before going himself. The ambulance came after forty minutes.

The onus of action had been taken from him and the enforced wait had eased his nerves. The American had made sense when he had said he could have killed either of them there and then, if he had wanted to. Lacey was reasonably sure Beckindale would be back. Either way, there was nothing he could do about it.

An ambulanceman pushed open the outside door and leaned in.

'Halloo?'

He sounded as if he were calling sheep.

'In here.'

Lacey pulled the connecting door open and stepped back to allow the man to see the body.

'Oh, yes.'

The man was of indeterminate age, his face worn thin and full of sharp angles. His legs were crooked, as if he'd had rickets, and he put his hands on his hips and gave the body a good look before eventually crouching beside it and lifting an eyelid.

'And what's the laddie been doing?'

'He's been trying to hang himself.'

The man turned and gave Lacey a doleful look.

'Has he now?' He looked back at the body and touched Goodman's neck before finally standing up. 'He didna make a good job of it, did he?'

'The rope broke.'

The man's expression didn't change, but he nodded sagely.

'Aye, well. There's an art to everything.'

His companion arrived at the kitchen door. He was a younger man with red hair as thick and shapeless as a thicket.

'Will we be needing it, Andrew?'

'Aye, we'll be needing it.'

His companion went back towards the ambulance.

Lacey said, 'My colleague rang for you. Have you seen him?'

'An American gentleman?'

'That's him.'

'Aye. He met us by the river and we dropped him at the end of the track. That's where his car was. He should be here any time.'

Lacey nodded and the man began to leave the room, but hesitated and looked back.

'You're no the police?'

'No.'

'Aye, I thought not. They'll have to be told.'

'I know. I'll tell them.'

'No. I'll tell them. On the radio. They'll want to talk to you.'

'Yes.'

The man looked at Goodman and then back at Lacey.

'Aye. They'll be interested.'

He finally left the house to help the lad with red hair unload a stretcher and a collapsible trolley and Lacey finished the whisky. He had to admit the situation must look odd. An Englishman, an American and a failed suicide.

Perhaps the ambulanceman thought it had been provoked by a complicated homosexual love-triangle. He poured another whisky.

Goodman was placed on the stretcher and covered with a blanket. The two men picked him up and carried him outside where they put him on the trolley and wheeled him down the path. Lacey put down the glass and went with them.

As they put Goodman into the ambulance, Beckindale drove out of the forest in the hire car. Lacey went to him.

'What happened?'

'Apart from getting my scalp creased, not a lot.'

'He hit you?'

Beckindale shrugged.

'My own fault. I tried to jump him.'

'Jesus, Dan.'

'I know. Stupid.'

'He's not the type to try tricks on, especially when he's got a gun at your head.'

'What about Goodman?'

'He's still unconscious.'

The senior ambulanceman with the legs came across to them.

'You'll be coming with us, then?' he said to Lacey.

'Yes.'

'And your . . . friend?'

He nodded at Beckindale.

'He'll follow in the car.'

'Aye. That's just as well.'

'Where are we going?'

'Stirling Royal Infirmary. It's no far. The police'll meet us there.'

It may have been the cut of the tunic, but Lacey got the impression the uniformed police sergeant who was waiting for them at the hospital, was a tree trunk on legs. He had no neck, but he did have a healthy black moustache that turned down at the edges in the hint of a zapata. Maybe at

248

one time he had been a hippy. It was hard to imagine.

Beckindale, Lacey and the sergeant went into a borrowed office and sat around a table upon which were only a telephone and the sergeant's notebook. The officer was sceptical when Lacey told him he worked for the Foreign Office, but he agreed to let him make a telephone call. Lacey called Bryson and prevailed upon the sergeant to await the outcome.

The officer was not happy but, within ten minutes, he received a telephone call that made his eyes widen in surprise. He put away the notebook.

'If you want me to stay, I'm to stay,' he said, with obvious irritation. 'If not, I've got other things to occupy my time.'

'You don't have to stay, sergeant.'

'Then I'll be off.'

They all got to their feet.

'There is one thing you can do before you go. Tell the hospital authorities we are to be given access to the patient and every other possible help.'

The policeman nodded.

'I'll tell them. I'll get the administrator.'

He left the room and they sat down again. Beckindale felt his scalp tenderly.

'I have one helluva headache.'

'Get a nurse to look at it.'

'No. Hell, he didn't even break the skin. Just raised a lump.'

They sat in silence.

'Why did Goodman try to kill himself?' Lacey said.

'Who the hell knows. Maybe he was upset about his love life.'

Lacey laughed.

'The ambulanceman thought we were his love life.'

'What?'

Captain America was not amused. Lacey guessed he had strong moral principles against sexual acts that didn't propagate the species.

A few minutes later, the sergeant returned with an elderly man in a grey business suit who was carrying a clipboard. He introduced him as Mr Craigmore, the hospital administrator.

Craigmore's opening words were, 'This is most unusual.'

'Of course it is,' Lacey said. 'It's also a matter of national security. As well as your co-operation, I hope we can rely on your discretion?'

'Of course.'

'We don't want stories leaking to the Press, do we?'

'Mr Lacey, there will be no leaks from me.'

'Do we, sergeant?'

'There'll be no leaks.'

Lacey smiled.

'Good. Sergeant, you've been a great help. I'll say so.' Lacey opened the door for him and the policeman nodded and left, still unhappy and irritated. 'Now,' Lacey turned to the administrator, 'how's our patient?'

'He's in no immediate danger, but it will be a little time yet before you can see him.'

'When is he likely to regain consciousness?'

'Oh, he's conscious. Not saying a great deal, but conscious.'

'Mr Craigmore, it's very important that we speak to him as soon as possible.'

'I understand that, but not yet. He has to be X-rayed and we are aiding his breathing at the moment, as a precaution. Apart from physical damage he is suffering from shock.'

'When can we see him?'

'Well, in normal circumstances . . .'

'These aren't.'

Craigmore shut his mouth and preened his lips to regain composure.

'An hour. Maybe less.'

Lacey smiled his most charming smile.

'Thank you.'

Craigmore inclined his head in response.

'If you wait here, I'll have some tea sent. I'll call you as soon as is practicable.'

When he had gone, Beckindale sat in his chair and massaged the back of his neck.

'My head hurts. Look, do you mind waiting for Goodman alone?'

'I don't mind. What are you going to do?'

'Find a hotel, take a pill and lie down.'

'Sure you don't want a nurse?'

Beckindale laughed.

'I'm a clean-living Christian. I'll settle for a bed and a sleep. Wake me when it's over.'

Craigmore returned an hour and ten minutes later and told Lacey Goodman wouldn't be able to talk to him.

'His windpipe has been damaged. We had to do a tracheotomy.'

'Shit!'

Craigmore ignored the sentiment and looked at his clipboard.

'He's a very lucky man. It is, of course, rare for anyone to die immediately by hanging. Unless the act is supervised by an expert.' He said it as if you could send for a hangman like you could send for a plumber. 'I understand the rope broke? It's impossible to say how long he was suspended, but the thickness of his neck saved him. He was in that barn overnight, you know?'

'When can I . . . communicate with him?'

'A few hours.'

Lacey turned away in frustration.

Craigmore said, 'There's an empty room next to Mr Goodman's. You could wait there. There's a television . . . a bed . . .'

There was no point being moody about it. Lacey turned back and gave Craigmore a smile of resignation.

'Thank you. That would be good. Thank you for all your help, Mr Craigmore, and I apologize if I appear

251

rude.' He shrugged. 'I really do need to talk to the man.'

'I understand. If you'll come this way?'

The room had fitted carpet and pictures on the wall, as well as a television. It was definitely not National Health. He phoned the office and told Bryson the state of play.

'So you don't know when you'll get to see this chap?'

'I'm afraid not.'

'What a bind. However, I know you'll stick with it, Peter. I'll be going out later. Dinner at the Reform, but do call if you get something interesting. There'll be somebody here.'

'I will. Have a nice dinner.'

Lacey lay on the bed and watched an old film and wished Bryson hadn't mentioned dinner. He'd missed lunch and was even low on cigarettes. He had to ration himself, despite the hunger pains.

He'd resigned himself to starvation when a plump nurse with fat legs knocked on his door and brought in afternoon tea. Perhaps it was the way he eyed the neat triangles of cucumber, tomato and egg sandwiches she placed on the bedside table that made her hesitate at the door.

'Do you fancy some more?' she said.

He nodded as he couldn't speak because his mouth was full of sandwich.

'They didn't tell me the condition of the gentleman next door. I don't suppose he'll mind you having his.'

She brought him a second plate.

'You're an angel.'

'That's what they all say.'

'I mean it. Marry me.'

The sandwiches were the highlight of the day because they were unexpected. Finding Goodman's body had been unexpected and being held at the point of a gun even more unexpected, but the sandwiches had been the one extremely welcome surprise in a day that seemed to have gone on too long without achievement. Even the egg sandwiches had been delicious, and he didn't like egg sandwiches.

Tedium and a crossword gameshow on television that had been designed to appeal to the intellect of lemmings eventually made him fall asleep. A young English doctor woke him up.

Lacey looked at his watch. It was eight o'clock.

'I understand you want to question Mr Goodman?' the doctor said.

His voice was thick with a cold and he blew his nose into a handkerchief that was a health hazard. Lacey got off the bed on the side away from the doctor. Now the man had removed the handkerchief he could see his nose. It was a snout with nostrils black enough to swallow spaceships. This was a doctor who did not inspire confidence.

'It's imperative I question him.'

'Under normal circumstances . . .'

'I've been through this before.'

'Yes. So I believe. Well, you can see him now, but he's still suffering from shock and, of course, he can't talk. He can answer yes by tapping once. Two taps for no.'

'Can he write?'

'I'd prefer he was stressed as little as possible.'

'So would I, but can he write?'

'I see no reason why not.' The doctor handed him a notepad and a ballpoint pen. 'It wasn't difficult to anticipate. But don't push him too hard.'

Lacey took them from him gingerly to avoid contamination. He didn't know where the man's fingers had been, but he could guess.

'Thank you, doctor. I'll be as brief as possible.'

The doctor sniffed the atmosphere and looked at the full ashtray. He reached into the pocket of his white coat again for his handkerchief.

'There must, of course, be no smoking.'

'Of course.'

Lacey felt like prescribing a Beechams Powder and an early night for all their sakes, but he resisted.

They went into the next room.

Goodman had a surgical collar around his neck and

253

tubes running from his throat, but his eyes were open and they swivelled to the door in apprehension as they entered.

The starched white sheets were turned down at his chest and his arms lay on top of the covers. The hospital gown he wore had short sleeves and his arms were heavy and dark with hair. By his left hand was a bell push on a cord.

The doctor said, 'This is the man I was telling you about, Mr Goodman. The man who wants to ask you some questions. He found you and brought you to hospital. All right?'

Goodman moved his eyes from the doctor to Lacey. Then he tapped the index finger of his right hand on the bed . . . once.

'I'll be outside if you need me,' said the doctor, and left the room.

Lacey pulled up a chair so that he was sitting alongside the bed, facing Goodman.

'Hello, Martin. My name is Peter Lacey. As the man said, I found you. I'm with the Foreign Office.' Goodman was staring at him blankly. Lacey didn't expect a song and dance, but he had hoped for a more welcoming response. He could have twitched his eyes, or something. 'Martin, I'm with MI6. You're with the CIA. That makes us cousins and I'm here to help. OK?'

The man stared at him for a while longer, and, after due consideration, the finger tapped once.

'Good.' The bloke wasn't arguing. Maybe he wanted to talk . . . communicate. Lacey put the pad on the bed by Goodman's hand and placed the ballpoint next to it. 'You may need that. Can you use it?'

Goodman picked up the pen and wrote: *Yes.*

'OK. Now, I don't want to upset you, Martin, but there are questions I have to ask. I know you understand that.'

The finger tapped once and Lacey nodded.

'Now. The reason you tried—' there was no delicate way of phrasing it '— to kill yourself?'

The finger drummed the bedclothes furiously and silenced Lacey. Goodman picked up the pen again and wrote on the pad: *Not suicide. Murder!*

254

'Murder?' Lacey had been waylaid again. 'You didn't hang yourself?'

The finger drummed twice.

'Someone tried to murder you?'

This time it tapped once.

'To silence you?'

It tapped once again.

'Because you know about the VIP List?'

Goodman hesitated and then tapped once.

Lacey licked his lips. He felt uncomfortable, the hospital central heating was making him sweat and this was the most unnatural interrogation he'd ever conducted. His was the only voice and he didn't know whether to talk to the man or his finger.

'The list,' he said. 'Was it a fake?'

One tap.

'How many names were on it?'

The finger tapped six times.

He'd been expecting five. Shit, they'd got two more targets to protect, not one.

'Jacques le Gall?'

One tap.

'Frederik Hals?'

One tap.

'Michel Chodron?'

One tap.

'Franz Haber?'

One tap.

Lacey stared into Goodman's eyes.

'They're all dead. Did you know?'

The man gulped and tears welled up from nowhere and began coursing down his cheeks. Lacey wondered whether the man was crying for the dead or for himself.

Slowly, his finger tapped twice.

'Martin. I don't know the other names. Tell me who they are and we can save them.'

His finger rapped twice.

'You won't tell me?'

He wrote on the pad: *Henriks Jorgensen – dead!*

The name meant nothing to Lacey. It was a death that had not been claimed by Red Dawn.

'Jorgensen. This man was on the list as well?'

One tap.

'What was his nationality?'

Dane.

'What about the last name? Who is it?'

Goodman picked up the pen and wrote on the pad. Lacey leaned over the bed to read the name.

'Oh shit.'

The name was James Weldon, the Leader of the Opposition.

Chapter 33

Lacey used the telephone next to Goodman's bed to call Charing Cross Road. He got Malcolm.

'Where's Sam?'

'He's gone to the Reform. He asked me to play long stop in his absence. I can contact him.'

'Good. Tell him the list is confirmed fake. And tell him there are two more names. Henriks Jorgensen, Danish, deceased, and Jim Weldon. He'll know what to do.'

'Your word is my command, dear boy. Anything else?'

'Yes. You can also tell him our friend in hospital needs Special Branch protection. Immediate.'

'Will do. Is that it?'

'For now. If there's anything more I'll call back.'

'I can hardly wait. Wilko and out.'

After he had hung up, Lacey absent-mindedly felt for his cigarettes before he remembered what the doctor had said. He left them in his pocket. Goodman's throat was enough of a mess without chancing a coughing fit. He viewed the pipes and wondered where he could cough from? He also wondered about the doctor. With his cold, he could be more lethal than an assassin.

'You heard?' Lacey said.

One tap.

'I'll stay until Special Branch get here. Don't worry, you'll be safe.' There were many questions to ask and they didn't fit any order. 'Do you know the name of who tried to kill you?'

Two taps and Goodman also wrote on the pad: *Male. American.*

'An American.'

257

It didn't make sense. If the American had hung Goodman, why had he allowed him to live when the faked suicide went wrong? Unless Goodman's death would only have fitted into someone else's plot as a suicide and not a murder? And maybe there were other players in the game he didn't know about. Christ, if he stopped to think out every answer he'd get nowhere.

'Did he ask you questions before he hung you?'

Two taps.

'When did this happen? When did he hang you?'

Goodman wrote: *Sunday afternoon.*

That confirmed what the administrator had said. Goodman had spent the night on the barn floor, after the hook had broken loose.

'Let's get back to the list. Who did you make it for?'

He wrote on the pad: *Bill Woodward. National Security Council. He's dead.*

Lacey thought about it. Everybody connected with this bloody list seemed to end up dead.

'How did he die?'

Goodman wrote: *Chopper crash. With Jorgensen.*

'They died together?'

One tap.

Shit. Why couldn't the man talk. He tore a full page from the pad for him.

'You say Woodward was with the National Security Council?'

One tap.

'But you're with CIA.'

Goodman wrote: *He moved from CIA to NSC.*

'Woodward went from Langley to Washington?'

One tap.

'And he took the report with him?'

Two taps. He wrote: *Woodward had already moved to NSC. He called in a favour.*

'You did it as a favour?'

One tap.

'Did he explain why he wanted it?'

258

He wrote: *Blackmail*.

'There's nothing on file at Langley about the report. Were there any copies?'

Two taps.

'Woodward had the only copy?'

One tap.

And somehow, Lacey thought, that only copy was seen by others, including a Soviet agent and whoever was killing off those named.

'You came to Scotland three months ago?'

One tap.

'Why?'

Goodman hesitated before picking up the pen and writing: *le Gall, Hals*.

'When they were killed, you thought the list had been activated?'

One tap.

'Why didn't you tell anyone?'

Goodman's eyes widened as if Lacey was a fool. He wrote his own question on the pad: *Who?*

Lacey could see his dilemma. For all Goodman knew, the list could have been activated by his own side for reasons he shouldn't question. He had also created it as a favour, a point his director might not appreciate if he owned up to it.

'You came to Scotland to hide?'

The man's fat jowls began to quiver again, but this time he didn't cry. Instead, he reached for the pad but the page was full. Lacey tore off the top sheet, and Goodman wrote: *I was responsible. I didn't know what to do. I've never . . .*

He paused and the pen shook in his fingers before he steeled himself to continue.

. . . killed anyone. This wasn't supposed to kill anyone. It was sanctification. A hypothesized project.

He had filled the page and Lacey tore it out, but Goodman put the pen down.

Sanctification was a company term for blackmail. To influence people, the blackmail didn't have to be true; the

259

whole smear could be, and frequently was, a pack of lies. Just like the list.

At the very least, Goodman should have reported his fears, whether or not he got into trouble. It was an in-house project and if there was a chance of it being used by someone else for reasons that could damage the Company, he should have alerted senior management.

Goodman was supposed to be an expert; he would know that sanctions to kill were rare, that sanctification was almost always preferred and was far more profitable. He would know it was unlikely the killings would have received official approval.

He got up and moved the chair. He'd got what he needed and, anyway, Goodman wouldn't be going anywhere fast. If Beckindale wanted a chat, he could see him in the morning.

'Thanks, Martin,' he said. 'I won't bother you any longer.'

At the door he looked back. Martin Goodman might have a brilliant mind, but it wasn't a particularly strong one. He looked ready to blubber again and this time Lacey had no doubt. The man was feeling more sorry for himself than anyone else.

While he was waiting for Special Branch, he telephoned the office and again spoke to Malcolm.

'Sorry, to keep you late,' Lacey said.

'That's all right. I'm making a night of it. My neighbourhood is upwardly mobile with crime figures. I prefer the safety of the annexe rather than risk tubing it home at this time, all middle-aged, plump and defenceless.'

Lacey laughed.

'It's true, Peter. My only form of defence is to bleed profusely all over an attacker. And that would probably annoy rather than deter.'

'Well, look upon it as an opportunity to make new friends. Try Scrabble with the duty man.'

'Desperate Dan? I'll pass. I'll settle for the latest copy of *Hansard*. Perfect bedtime reading.'

'Did you get Sam?'

'Yes. I told him.'

'There's something else to tell him. The list was compiled for a bloke called Bill Woodward. He was a Company man who went to the NSC. He died in a helicopter crash with Jorgensen. He might like to ask Langley about him.'

'Right.'

'And that really is the lot. I'll be back tomorrow. Sleep tight, Malcolm.'

'You too, Peter.'

'I intend to do my best.'

Two Special Branch officers arrived within an hour and Lacey explained that Goodman had survived one murder attempt and there was a possibility a second might be made. They had come from Glasgow and looked as if they would welcome the sport.

Beckindale had phoned in with the name of his hotel and Lacey joined him. He had booked an adjacent room for Lacey, and said he was feeling improved enough for dinner. They just made it to the restaurant before the kitchen closed.

'Brief me while we eat,' he said.

Lacey told him the major features between courses, but left discussion until coffee.

'What about Bill Woodward, the bloke from the NSC?' Lacey said. 'Did you know him?'

'I knew him. He was a good man.'

'Was he involved in covert operations?'

'No. He was senior aide to the National Security Adviser. But I don't know what he did at Langley. I'll call Washington and find out.'

Lacey lit a cigarette, and Beckindale continued.

'I guess Goodman was running scared when he came to Scotland. Wanted to stick his head under the bedclothes and come out when somebody told him he'd had a bad dream. By keeping quiet, he's flushed his career down the toilet.'

'What about the American?' Lacey said.

'Don't make assumptions. Anyone can adopt an accent. But his behaviour was weird. Why didn't the guy kill Goodman when he came back? Why didn't he kill us? Who the hell is he working for?' He took a drink of coffee. 'Of course, there's still the possibility that Goodman's lying.'

'I don't think so.' Lacey lit a cigarette. 'The man's too scared and too much a coward to lie. Go see him yourself. He's a wimp.'

'That makes him malleable.'

'Jesus, Dan, someone hung him from a beam and damn near killed him. That made him so malleable he shit himself. If he was any deeper involved than he admits, he would have been looking for deals. He wasn't. He was looking for a confessional.'

'Maybe you're right. At least Jim Weldon won't be such an easy target.'

'I'm not so sure. Weldon is one of those man-of-the-people politicians. He doesn't like high-profile security. Believes in being accessible.'

'He'll have to be persuaded.'

'Yes, well. I've left that to my section head.'

Lacey stubbed out the cigarette and said, 'There's something else to consider.'

'What?'

'Was Capaldi the hit man? Maybe we've been making wrong assumptions all along?'

'Capaldi was *a* hit man. My network told me that, your Russian friend told you that. But maybe there was more than one.'

Lacey was fed up with the complications. He shook his head.

'I'm going to have a few beers to settle my brain,' he said. 'How about you?'

'Sure. It might take our minds off one other point that hasn't been mentioned.'

'Go on. Make my day.'

Beckindale said, 'The timing. The assassinations have happened at four-week intervals. The last one was over three weeks ago. If the pattern stays the same, we've only got a few days to find the guy who plans to do it.'

Chapter 34

For once the hangover didn't work. Lacey blamed the failure on tiredness. He'd been too tired to drink enough the night before. Instead of achieving temporary lobotomy, he simply had a fuzzy head that was no match for a brace of paracetamol.

He called the office after breakfast and got Malcolm.

'Peter, you sound healthy.'

'Don't rub it in. I don't understand healthy.'

'It's an aid to clear thinking.'

'I prefer stumbling through the pain barrier. It can give a new perspective on things. Where's Sam?'

'He's across the river. He has an appointment with HRH at ten. He wasn't looking forward to it.'

'I'll bet. Any message?'

'Yes. Get back soonest.'

'I'll be in the office this afternoon.'

Lacey found Beckindale still drinking coffee in the dining-room.

'I'm going back to London.'

Beckindale nodded.

'No sweat. I'll stick around. Check out the farmhouse, see if Goodman has improved any. Special Branch know about me?'

'You've got access.'

'Right.' He handed him the car keys. 'Take the hire car. I'll get another. Call you later.'

Someone had rolled the clouds back from where they had been tucked into the chin of the Midlands. The sun shone all the way to London and beyond. It brought out the

264

tourists in droves, to clog the underground and force Lacey off pavements. They were one of his pet hates.

He bought a corned beef sandwich at a delicatessen near the office before going up to face Bryson. He was taking no chances on missing meals this time. When he got there, Bryson still wasn't back. He ate in privacy in his own office and drank black coffee and wondered when the break would come.

There had to be a break. If there wasn't, Weldon could end up dead. Worse, one of the convoluted plots he and Beckindale and Bryson had discussed might declare itself to international embarrassment, distaste and anger, and possibly cause the downfall of Mikhail Gorbachev.

Shit.

He wished he'd had more success with his hangover. If his head had been aching he might not have been this rational. There was always Jim Beam, of course, a legacy of another American collaboration. He leaned back in his chair and pulled open the filing-cabinet drawer just to check Jim was still there and to test temptation.

Bryson arrived half an hour later, came straight into Lacey's office and sat down in the chair for visitors. The bourbon bottle was still intact and Lacey was pleased with himself. Bryson spoiled it by getting back to reality.

'I saw Rossington-Hall.'

'Yes.'

'He was not pleased.'

'Who the hell is?'

'And I've just had lunch with Roy Selwyn.'

'Ah.'

Lunching with the Foreign Secretary in these circumstances could not have been a happy experience.

'He wasn't pleased, either.'

'Why? Because we've discovered something nasty?'

'Rossington-Hall seems to think we're responsible.'

'What?'

'He's worried about his knighthood and he's looking for someone to blame.'

'The little shit.'

'Selwyn's worried, too. For his career, as well as anything that might happen to world politics.'

Bryson reached for his pipe and Lacey reached for his cigarettes and they started another smog.

Lacey said, 'Why the panic?'

Bryson replied between puffs to get the pipe going.

'Rossington-Hall took care to lay some of the responsibility off on to Selwyn right at the beginning.' He held a matchbox over the bowl and sucked. 'When Devere and the Mathieson woman were killed, HRH was delighted at how easily he'd made her a heroine. It appears Selwyn was quick to claim his share of the credit, too, and did some heavy-duty whispering to the Prime Minister. He's now beginning to wish he hadn't been born. If the mess we've uncovered begins to smell, the PM will have his balls removed and served with garnish.'

'He hasn't got any balls.'

Bryson waved his pipe.

'Academic. They're both running scared at the possible repercussions.'

'If we find who it is and stop them before they kill Weldon there won't be any repercussions.'

'Quite. Which makes it all the more important to persuade Weldon to accept protection.'

'He's turned it down?'

'Yes. Says he doesn't believe us.'

'The man's mad.'

'No. He's a politician with an image. And he's less than controversial. He's not the type to attract assassination attempts. As Leader of the Opposition, he had a protection team at the last election, but he's had none since. Don't forget his mining roots. He feels he can look after himself.'

'Maybe from a loudmouth in a restaurant, but not from a bullet.'

'Anyway, last night he told Special Branch no. Our problem is how much we can tell them or tell him. This whole operation is booby trapped with potential.'

'We can tell him about the list. That five people are already dead.'

'The Foreign Secretary would prefer it if we were not so specific.'

'Why?'

'Politics. It would be difficult to explain to Weldon that he was on a list that had been devised by the CIA for the purposes of blackmail. If the man had been smeared three years ago, it wouldn't have damaged Britain, but it would have wrecked the Opposition, just when they were starting their fight back. A cynical party leader might even suspect government collusion. Wouldn't you?'

'The thought might cross my mind.'

'And if he knew of it, and chose to reveal it, even though the government is totally innocent, the effect could still be catastrophic internationally.'

'He wouldn't do that.'

'It could be an election winner?'

'Weldon has principles.'

'He may have principles, but perhaps some of his colleagues don't have. It's a risk we can't take.'

'Why is Weldon on the list, anyway?'

'Future planning. Look at the Labour Party's unilateral disarmament policies of the time. If Weldon ever became Prime Minister, the Americans could hold his Government in check with a good grip on his bollocks.'

'So what do we do about getting him to accept protection?'

'Both Selwyn and HRH are going to speak to him personally. Say the information is from a top source and lay the blame on Red Dawn. And they're going to stand by the story that the Mathieson woman was a British agent.' He coughed with embarrassment. 'You may have to do your bit, too, Peter. They may want to present you as the star witness to convince him he's in danger. You may have to be economical with the truth.'

'Jesus Christ, it gets better. We're in danger of drowning in lies. I've already forgotten what the truth is.'

Bryson said, 'Truth is elastic.'

'Too bloody elastic, Sam. We stretch it to accommodate conscience and expediency. Repeat the new version a few times and begin to believe it. Stretch it again and repeat the process. The beauty is, by the time we've finished we can convince ourselves it's still the truth, even though it stretches from here to hell.'

Bryson took refuge for a few moments behind a cloud of smoke.

'You're probably right. But I'd be grateful if you stopped short of hell. Besides, what motivates the likes of Selwyn and H R H may be venality, but our job is to ensure a balance that doesn't tilt out of control. Sometimes we have to stretch the truth to do it.'

Lacey accepted what Bryson said. As far as they were concerned, politics didn't enter into it. They had to safeguard against a scandal that might destabilize governments.

'All right. If needs be, I'll see him.'

'Thank you. At the moment, he's being watched by a team of pavement artists. It's a protection he doesn't know about, but it would make the job a lot easier if he agreed to it officially. Now that Parliament's in recess for a week, he's going north tomorrow. He has a cottage in the Yorkshire Dales. Special Branch might have difficulty with only cows and sheep for crowd cover.'

The thought was a pleasant diversion.

'What about Bill Woodward?' Lacey said. 'He had the damn list drawn up. Dead or alive, he has to provide some answers.'

'I called a friend at Langley. He called back this morning. They want to see you. Just you, without Dan Beckindale.' He puffed smoke. 'They know the two of you are working on something and suspect they're involved. They're sensitive.'

'Only sensitive? Wait till they hear the full story.' He stubbed out his cigarette. 'When and where?'

'They'll make contact.'

'Not tonight, I hope. I'm going home.'

As he said it, he realized he hadn't called Susan. She didn't know he was going home. He hoped this wasn't the night she was seeing corduroy Michael.

Chapter 35

Lucy had insisted on running the shop herself so Susan could go for lunch with Michael. A promise was a promise, Susan had kept reminding herself. She was the only friend Lucy had.

Michael turned up in neatly pressed jeans and a corduroy jacket. She hoped he didn't take her somewhere she was known. If aquaintances thought she was having an affair, she would prefer it was with someone who was a bit more presentable.

He made the mistake of choosing a pub in the country where she and Peter sometimes went. It had special memories for her, and, at first, it caused her to be distant towards him.

Their conversation was stilted, anyway, until Michael was halfway down his second pint of lager. It relaxed him sufficiently to show more than a passing interest in a girl in a low-cut blouse at the next table. Perhaps Peter had been right about him being a closet chauvinist.

'You know, Susan, families can be very stifling, very demanding. I love my children, but I'm frightened that by remaining in an environment situation that is so draining, it could turn me against them. I mean, I could end up blaming them for the trap I've built and haven't the courage to break out of. Do you see what I mean?'

Susan saw what he meant and already regretted coming. He was a pretentious bore who had suddenly discovered life was passing him by and didn't know what to do about it except moan.

'What would you do, if you did break out?'

'Oh, new experiences, new challenges.'

'Like what?'

'Well, it's hard to say, just like that.'

'Do you have any burning ambition to fulfil?'

She had put him in a corner because she suspected Michael's ambitions had ended when he got schoolchildren to call him sir. He'd lived all his life in education and had never had to come out into the real world, except as a paying customer.

'Well, of course, there's the book.'

'The book?'

'I started it at college. Just a collection of notes then. And poetry.' He took a gulp of lager. 'But it's been developing over the years. It's all there.'

'All where?'

Susan was beginning to enjoy being obstinately direct while he waffled.

'It's there.' He waved a hand. 'In my head.'

'Oh, it's not written, then?'

'No. That's the point. What with Lucy and the children and my career. There's been no time.'

'So that would be an incentive to leave home?'

'Yes.'

'Even though you'd probably have to make do with a grotty bed-sitter?'

'Surroundings don't matter, Susan. I've often crashed in my sleeping-bag on someone's floor.'

'That was twenty years ago, Michael. Your bones might not appreciate it at your age. Nor you friends.'

He took another drink.

'I'm not totally over the hill, yet, Susan.'

She would have liked to have told him he'd been over the hill at twenty but resisted.

'So. You've got the incentive. But you're still living at home. Lucy still does your ironing. All you've done is move into the spare room. That's hardly breaking out.'

He grimaced.

'I suppose I'm a fool to myself. It would be a lot easier to move. But it's Lucy. I'm worried about her, and, believe it

271

or not, that's the only reason I'm still there.'

'Do you still love Lucy?'

'In a way.'

He tried to make it sound affectionate, but his attention was diverted by the girl in the blouse bending down to pick up her handbag.

'Do you still find Lucy attractive?'

'Mmm . . . ? Well, she's had two children. It takes it out of a woman.'

'Do you?'

'I suppose, if I'm honest, I have to say, not as attractive as she used to be. But,' he held up his hand, anxious to explain further, 'that's not the reason for our . . . problems. I'm not the sort of man that reacts to stereotypes. I hope you give me credit for seeing beyond physical appearance to the real worth of a person. And, I'm the first to admit, that Lucy is a marvellous human being.'

'But you don't fancy her?'

'You make it sound crude, Susan. It's not crude, it's complicated, it's . . .'

'It's basic, Michael. There's nothing wrong in admitting it.'

He finished his drink in embarrassment and went to the bar to get more but, when he came back, Susan continued.

'Are you having an affair?' she asked, surprising even herself with the question.

He was surprised, too, his eyes widened and he sat back, dropped his chin on his chest and gave her a disapproving look.

'I didn't expect that from you, Susan.'

'But are you?'

'No.'

'Would you like to have an affair?'

It was fun making him uncomfortable.

'Look really . . .'

'No, seriously. You no longer find your wife attractive, you're in reasonable shape and condition, with all the normal desires of a male—' she dropped her voice to a whisper

'—you do have the normal desires of a male, don't you?'

'Of course.'

He snapped the reply.

'Then I would think it perfectly natural you would consider having an affair. Particularly working with all that temptation every day.'

'Temptation?'

'Nubile young girls. I suppose you have to be very careful? I mean, you read about it in the papers.'

'Nothing untoward has ever happened between myself and a student. Good God, it's a basic trust.' The girl in the blouse was now staring at him because he had become pompous. 'I don't know how you could suggest such a thing.'

'I didn't. I said they must be a temptation.'

'It's the same thing.'

'No, Michael, it isn't.' She tried to calm him with a conciliatory tone, and touched his hand. 'What I'm saying is that it's natural for relationships to go through difficult periods for all sorts of reasons. People change, expectations change. It's normal to get bored with what you've got and, maybe, to want to try something else.'

She felt a hypocrite because she wanted to tell him to grow up and recognize that what he had got was as good as he was going to get, but she had promised Lucy and Lucy still wanted him.

'Maybe you should, try something else, I mean, just to discover it's not as wonderful as you imagined,' she said, at the same time wondering who, in their right mind, would consider an affair with a stuffed corduroy jacket.

'I also think that relationships that have lasted as long as your's and Lucy's are worth trying to save. Maybe you should both try to see the change that's happened in each other, and adapt to it.'

She shook her head and brushed hair from her eyes.

'I'm probably saying this all wrong, but I want you to know I'm a friend and that I want to help. I'll talk to Lucy, too. Try to get her to throw away those boilersuits she's so

273

fond of. Maybe try to get her looking a bit more feminine? What do you think, Michael? Is it worth a try?'

He thought about it and smiled with a condescension that Susan would have liked to kick.

'Perhaps it is. Perhaps you can help.' He stretched his arms in a helpless gesture and spilled some lager. 'After all, I'm only a poor male.'

Susan tactfully offered to drive on the return journey but he declined. She gritted her teeth, fortified by only two gin and tonics to his three pints and a Scotch, while he aimed them towards her house where they were to meet Lucy.

He made it, but that was about all she could say about the experience. Michael and strong drink did not appear to mix.

The front door was unlocked but there was no reply when she shouted for Lucy. Instead, she found two notes. The first said Peter would be home in an hour, and the second said the child-minder had rung in a panic after one of the children had painted his hair green and would Michael bring home a bottle of turpentine.

Susan found Michael in the study holding a large Scotch which he had poured himself. She handed him the relevant note.

'Domestic crisis. I think you should go home.'

He glanced at it and put it in the pocket of his jacket.

'No rush. Lucy can cope. She always copes.'

'Michael, I don't want to be rude, but do you really need that drink?'

He smiled and she saw he was more drunk than she had realized.

'Why? What did you have in mind?'

'Pardon?'

He lurched towards her, his arm going around her shoulders, and pushed his face forward in a clumsy attempt at a kiss. She slipped out of his grasp and his lips brushed her hair.

'I think you've had too much.'

She said it in her best prim and proper voice, but inside

274

she was nervous. The house was empty and she felt vulnerable.

'Oh, come on, Susan. Your pep talk? Yes, of course I fancy an affair. I fancy you, too. Have done for years.' He straightened and dropped his head on his chin again, to stare appraisingly at her. He no longer looked so funny. 'Those skirts that swish? Those high heels?' He took a gulp of the Scotch. 'There've been times when I've . . . *been* with Lucy, when I've imagined it was you.' He finished the drink. 'There were times when it was the only way I could do it with Lucy.'

'I think you need fresh air, Michael. This is all very silly.'

She walked out of the room and he followed. The nearest outside door led into the garden and she automatically turned that way, immediately regretting the direction she had chosen. She would have felt safer at the front of the house.

God, but how had she got herself into this situation? What had she said that he had interpreted the wrong way? And, most of all, why was *she* feeling guilty?

Susan walked on to the lawn at the side of the house to put distance between them and turned so she could watch him. He had stopped in the doorway and was looking at her with a smirk on his face. No, he wasn't looking, he was staring. The sun was behind her, outlining her body through the cotton dress. She flushed and walked towards the front of the house. Would he think she was flaunting herself?

The lawn ended at rhododendron bushes which meant she had to walk back to the path that ran alongside the house. Michael moved to cut her off.

She stopped and faced him, shaking with anger.

'Michael. Go home now before you do something you regret.'

'Susan.' His smile was a leer. He thought he was being seductive. 'Just a little affair. I won't tell Lucy. You don't tell Peter.'

He moved with surprising speed and was close to her before she could take evasive action. But what evasive action should she take? She was trapped in her middle-class upbringing and couldn't picture herself running down the drive shouting for help. Right up until now she had thought she could cope. After all, this was a family friend she was helping over a crisis. Christ. Even as he grabbed her arm, stupid facts and figures filled her head from something she'd read about most rapes and assaults being committed by people the victims know.

Suddenly, she was a victim.

'Michael. Let go.'

'Susan. Don't be silly.'

His face was red and his breath smelled of alcohol and he pushed her hands away and tried to kiss her again and his beard grazed her cheek. Now he was close, he released one of her hands to put his arm around her waist and pull her against him. She tried bringing her knee up, but he blocked the movement and now the struggle was becoming a fight.

'Fuck off, you bastard. Fuck off!'

The language was as violent as she could be.

A hand dropped over her buttocks and his breathing became ragged. She was panicking at his strength and screaming inside her head but knew she would never scream out loud, when, without warning, he released her and stepped back.

Susan fell on to the lawn and watched Michael dance. Her feelings were still unreal and it took a second to connect the irregular jerking of his legs with the man who held him from behind.

She didn't recognize the man and hadn't heard him arrive but was grateful that he had. He held one of Michael's arms high in the small of his back while his other hand held him by the hair.

'Let go, let go.'

Michael was whimpering in pain.

The man let go and kicked Michael's legs from under

276

him. He fell face down and braced his hands to raise himself. The man stamped hard on the fingers of his right hand.

'Stay face down and spread 'em.'

An American. She had been rescued by an American.

Michael stayed down and, when the American nudged his hands and feet with the toe of black leather shoes, he spread them.

'What do you want to do with him, ma'am? The police?'

He spoke quietly and with a matter-of-factness that implied he knew all about violence. She was still breathless but the suggestion brought her voice back.

'No. Not the police. He's—' she gulped for saliva '—he's the husband of a friend. He . . . he . . .'

'He owes you an apology, ma'am.' He stood between Michael's legs and nudged him with his toe. 'Apologize.'

'I'm sorry, I'm sorry, Susan. I don't know what . . . please, don't tell Lucy.'

'Just go home, Michael. And stay there.'

'I will. I will.'

'OK, ma'am?'

'Yes. OK.'

'Then you'd better go home, Michael.'

The American waited until Michael was on his hands and knees before he kicked him between the legs. Michael yelped before rolling over in a ball and retching into the rhododendron bushes.

The act shocked Susan and she hesitated before accepting the American's hand to help her to her feet.

'Thank you,' she said.

She smoothed her dress for something to do. The panic had gone but she still felt guilty, as if she had been culpable of incitement to misbehaviour, simply by being a woman. Michael still writhed in pain and she was suddenly glad. My God, she hoped it hurt.

The American moved back towards him and he adopted the foetal position and made a noise like a sick dog.

277

'Move, buddy. You're hurt but you're not damaged.'

Hesitantly, Michael got up and walked crab-like to the path that led to the front of the house and his car. He didn't look back.

This was a new embarrassment. The American had rescued Susan, but what would he think?

'Ma'am. I've come to see your husband. I guess he's not in, right now. I'll quite understand it if you prefer me to wait outside.'

'No. No, of course not.' As she said it, she realized she was again taking risks. 'You'll wait in the house. I think we could both do with a strong cup of tea.'

'That sounds fine, ma'am.'

No. She was taking no risks. She recognized the type. This man was in the same line of business as her husband and Dan Beckindale and others she had met. They might kill people, but they didn't take advantage of women. It was amazing that she should feel safer in their company than with the corduroy Michaels of this world.

'Thank you, again.' Her smile twitched nervously and she held out her hand. 'I'm Susan Lacey. I don't know what you must have thought . . .'

'I think the guy got off light.'

They shook hands.

'I'd be grateful if you didn't tell my husband. He might . . .'

'I won't say a word. I guess Michael won't, either.'

'No.'

She smiled with more confidence now. He made her feel at ease. She could tell he wasn't blaming her, and having a witness who tacitly accepted her innocence was a help.

'I'm sorry. I was talking. You didn't say your name?'

'Fowler, ma'am. Amos Fowler.'

Chapter 36

The brief taste of summer had been a tease. Heavy clouds were now massing and, as Lacey paid the taxi-driver, there were distant rumbles to the west.

'World War Three's started,' said the taxi-driver.

'Yes,' said Lacey.

He noted the Ford Orion Ghia parked next to Susan's Citroën in the drive and assumed one of her friends had called. At least it wasn't Lucy. He let himself into the house and followed the sound of voices towards the kitchen. Susan was laughing.

He pushed open the door and froze.

The American he had last seen in Scotland was sitting in a chair, sharing a pot of tea with his wife.

Susan turned and smiled.

'Hello, darling. You've got a visitor.'

The man got to his feet. He was amused at Lacey's surprise.

'Mr Lacey. My name is Amos Fowler. I think we have things to talk about.'

At least this time he wasn't holding a gun.

'Yes.' He was temporarily lost for words. 'I think we do.'

He went to Susan, squeezed her shoulders and kissed her cheek. She reached up and held his hand.

It worried him that she had been alone with a man who, in cold blood, had made Goodman attempt suicide. The man had known his name in Scotland, so it followed he would be able to find out where he lived, but it had never occurred to him that he would come here or that Susan would be at risk. She had been at risk once before and he

279

would never forgive himself if anything ever happened to her again. It was also important she shouldn't know she had been at risk. He didn't want her worrying.

He smiled at her.

'I'm sorry, sweetheart. This is important. We'll be in the study. OK?'

'Of course.' She had caught something of his reaction and tensed up a little but, she too, was trying not to show it. 'Do you want tea, or anything?'

'No, I don't think so. You don't want more tea, Mr Fowler?'

'No, thank you.' The man smiled at Susan and bowed his head. 'That was very nice, ma'am.'

Lacey stepped back to the door.

'The study's along here.'

He led the way, still unsure at having the man behind him, still wondering why he was here. Once in the room, Lacey found himself slipping into normal social modes of behaviour.

'Would you like a drink?'

It was ridiculous. He was offering hospitality to the bloke.

'No, thank you. Not until we've gotten some things straightened out.'

Well, at least he had sensibilities.

Lacey resisted the temptation to drink alone and they sat in armchairs facing each other across the room.

'Amos Fowler?' he said.

'I've used others, but that's my given name.'

'The last time we met, you didn't use any.'

'The last time we met, there was no need.'

'Now there is?'

'I believe so.'

Lacey evaluated him and came to the same conclusion as he had the day before in Scotland. Fowler was a professional who obviously had been around a long time. To achieve that, he hadn't made many mistakes. If he had come here to kill Lacey, he would have done it already, as

280

Lacey had stepped through the front door. That meant he really had come to talk.

'All right. Why do I need to know your name?'

'Because you have to trust me, and I have to trust you.'

'Why?'

'So we can sort out this son-of-a-bitch operation.'

'Which operation?'

'The one that's had the both of us chasing round Europe with our heads stuck up our asses.'

'I like your turn of phrase, Mr Fowler. You mean Red Dawn?'

'That's what it started as.'

'And what's it become?'

'That's what I hope we can work out.'

Lacey felt as if somebody else was pulling his strings. He'd had so many private and confidential conversations with different people in the last few days, he was beginning to lose track of what was private and confidential. What secrets did Fowler expect him to impart?

'Who are you working for?'

'The Company. You were supposed to expect me.'

Lacey didn't respond immediately. He had half-expected the reply and sensed there were a lot more surprises ahead. He'd hear them all before making judgements.

'You don't look like a Company man.'

'I'm not. I'm freelance. They hired me for this one.'

What luxury. Lacey wished Six had hired someone for this one as well, instead of giving it to him.

'I think I should make a phone call.'

'Go ahead.'

He left the room and used the telephone in the hall to call the office. Sam Bryson was still there.

'I have a visitor,' Lacey said.

'I know. I was told after you left.'

'Do you know his name?'

'Amos Fowler. He used to be CIA, but left years ago. They're using him because he's unofficial and he knows his way around Europe.'

'How do I know this is the right Amos Fowler?'

'There's a control question. Ask him if he reads Graham Greene. He'll tell you his favourite book is *The Quiet American*.'

'Jesus.'

Lacey hated cloak and dagger.

'Anything wrong?'

'I could have been a teacher, you know?' he reminded Bryson. 'Long holidays with pay?'

He remembered corduroy Michael. No, he couldn't have been a teacher.

'Just ask the question, Peter. I'll be staying late tonight. Call me.'

'All right, Sam.'

Lacey went back into the study and stopped in the doorway. Fowler didn't appear to have moved.

'Graham Greene?' Lacey said.

Fowler smiled thinly.

'*The Quiet American*.'

Lacey felt foolish and shook his head at the absurdity of his profession. He resumed his seat.

'OK. How do we sort it out?'

Fowler said, 'I'll tell you what I know. Then, maybe, you'll tell me what you know.'

'I've already got a partner. I've been working with Dan Beckindale. You remember Dan Beckindale?'

'I know Beckindale. He treats a covert operation like Iwo Jima.' He shrugged. 'I'll tell you anyway. Then I think you'll want to tell me what you know.'

Lacey pulled out his cigarettes, looked at the packet and put them on a nearby table. His throat hurt from the afternoon session with Bryson. Maybe it was time to cut back.

'Go ahead.'

Fowler crossed his legs and looked at his shoe while he considered where to begin.

'I've operated in Europe, periodically, for six years. My intelligence is good. I pay well, because I get paid well, and I make no judgements.'

Lacey found himself sitting forward to listen because Fowler spoke so softly.

'Langley asked me to check Red Dawn after the first two hits. The Frenchman and Dutchman. European stations were getting nothing. Red Dawn's security was so tight it worried them. Their security was tight because they didn't exist. It didn't take long to find that out, and only a little longer to finger Aldo Capaldi as the trigger-man.'

He smiled.

'Did you know Aldo's nickname was Stiff? Stiff Capaldi. An American lady gave it him. Because he was always stiff? I guess now it's permanent.'

'I guess it is.'

'Anyway, I cut tracks with you and Beckindale after Sarah Mathieson got killed. She'd been Capaldi's woman since before the Frenchman was hit in Athens. When she was taken out, I guessed she'd been more than a lover. I figured she'd been a courier, the link between Capaldi and whoever was running him. I figured that if she'd been silenced, maybe Capaldi would be next, and I wanted to talk with him first. I got there too late.'

Lacey said, 'Sorry about that. I'm afraid Dan and I beat you to Capaldi.'

'I know. I was in the bar in Arras the night you came in like it was the movies.'

'You . . . ?'

'Yeh. It's amazing what a chunk of foam in your mouth can do. It won Marlon Brando an Oscar. Anyway, who notices drunks?'

He was right. Lacey remembered stereotyping, and then dismissing from consideration, the bystanders in the bar. He had been hyped-up and looking for a shoot-out.

'You caused quite a war. It was less than subtle.'

'It got out of hand. Capaldi thought he was in the movies, too.' He had a sudden thought. 'Maybe, that night, you thought I'd been running Capaldi?'

Fowler nodded.

'It crossed my mind. But I knew Beckindale. I knew he was Washington.'

'How come Dan didn't know you?'

'I saw him in London. I met head of station at an apartment near the Tower. The Colonel had the next apartment. He was coming along the corridor as we were leaving. I stayed inside until he'd passed, but the guy I was with said hello. I saw him through the crack in the door.

'After Arras, I came back to London and asked for all traffic between Europe and Langley and the Security Council involving Beckindale. I didn't get it. Langley said there hadn't been any and the NSC told me to go screw. Still, I had you, and I guessed you might see Beckindale again. I spent a couple of days being a tourist near the apartments. There's a very good pub there? On the other side of the dock?'

Lacey nodded. He knew the pub.

'I saw you visiting and took pictures. London Station gave you a name and a pedigree.'

Lacey said, 'How did you know about Martin Goodman?'

'The NSC made a request to Langley about an operation called the VIP List. They said it was past its sell-by date and it didn't seem too important. But Langley noticed the request originated from Beckindale's outfit, the Anti-Terrorism Unit. All they found at first was the code-name listing, and the guy who'd been assigned it, Goodman. Then they discovered Goodman was in Europe. They remembered my request, thought it might add up to something, and sent it to CIA London as well as the unit.'

Lacey said, 'How did you make a connection?'

'It was a reasonable guess. A load of important people get bumped off around Europe and all of a sudden Beckindale's outfit is asking about a VIP list.' He smiled. 'Besides, Langley kept looking, and they found more. The number of the code-name had been cross-referenced and they traced it to Bill Woodward. He used to be a Company baron.' Fowler raised his eyebrows. 'You know the system?'

'Remind me.'

'Barons are division chiefs. Woodward had Europe. A good operator could run his division with total control, as long as no one messed up. The Director, even the Deputies, didn't know what was happening. Goodman had worked for Woodward before. It was Woodward who'd brought him from Columbia.

'A lot of his stuff was one copy, eyes only. He submitted it as a document and on computer disc, so that Woodward could destroy the disc himself. But when this file was opened, Woodward had already gone to Washington and maybe Goodman got a little careless. He took the disc, but he forgot to wipe the file from the memory bank of the central computer. It took some finding, but it was still there. It was not sent to Beckindale's unit at the Security Council. First reaction was to protect ass.'

Fowler had said earlier that he didn't make judgements. He'd implied he just got on with his job and collected his fee. Lacey wondered if, in the same position, he would have been able to maintain the same indifference as he picked his way through the facts that led towards a distasteful confrontation north of the border.

'So you went to Scotland?' he said.

'That's right.'

'And made Goodman hang himself to protect the Company.'

'No. I didn't do that.'

The man's final prevarication angered Lacey.

'Then what the hell were you doing?'

'Saving Goodman's life. Colonel Dan Beckindale was trying to kill him.'

Chapter 37

Lacey could think of nothing rational to say. He stared at Fowler and Fowler stared back. The man's expression remained the same. The statement had not been a dramatic revelation made for effect, it had simply come in the chronological order in which he was telling his story, and it had been said in the same quiet, but authoritative, way he had said everything else.

'That's crazy.'

'Sure,' Fowler said. 'It's crazy.'

'Perhaps you can explain . . . exactly what you mean?'

'I think I was pretty specific the first time, but OK. When you and Beckindale found Goodman in the barn, he sent you for an ambulance. I was outside, looking in. As soon as you left, he tried to kill him. He held his hand over his nose and mouth.'

'Are you certain?'

'It sure as hell was not resuscitation.'

Lacey got abruptly to his feet.

'I'm going to have a Scotch.' He went over to the drinks. 'How about you?'

'Sure. Why not?'

Why not? Why anything? The new perspective had arrived, the missing link they had all been waiting for, and it was demanding new questions and answers. Jesus Christ, Fowler had to be mistaken.

He poured one drink and stopped, his mind in fast-forward, scanning for bits that didn't fit. Still holding the bottle in one hand, he turned to Fowler.

'Did Dan try to jump you in the car?'

'He couldn't. He was driving and I had a gun on him.'

286

'Did you hit him with the gun?'

'There was no cause. Did he say I did?'

Lacey poured the second Scotch and carried the two glasses across the room. He handed one to Fowler.

'Yes. He said you did.'

'Can you think of why he said that?'

'Yes. I can.'

Shit. This couldn't be. It was fantasy breeding fantasy. They were chasing theories into Disneyland and making them sound real.

'Tell me.'

Lacey shook his head, still unwilling to betray Beckindale. Instead he asked a question.

'When did Dan find out Goodman was in Scotland?'

'The information was sent to the Anti-Terrorism Unit in Washington on Saturday night. Beckindale has his own communications system with a direct link to the Old Executive Building. He could have received the information late Saturday night, London time, or early Sunday.'

'When did you find out?'

Fowler smiled.

'I was in Europe, Saturday. I didn't get back until past noon on Sunday.'

Lacey's mind was overloading with theories and none of them were the sort he wanted to consider. He got up and walked to the window and looked out at the cars parked on the gravel drive. They were normal. They each had four wheels and an engine and operated on a logical principle. They made sense. But nothing he had heard in the last few minutes did. At least, not an acceptable sense.

How did he evaluate this? And who the hell was Fowler anyway, apart from a Graham Greene fan?

He walked back to his chair. Maybe by sitting down he could hide his agitation. Fowler had moved very little during the exchange. He still looked as neat as a Mormon. Lacey picked up the cigarettes and lit one. This was no time to consider quitting. He took a deep draw on the Gitanes and let the fumes bite.

'OK,' he said, exhaling smoke. 'Dan Beckindale had the time to go to Scotland on Sunday and make Goodman hang himself. If he did that, it would have been a shock to find the man still alive on Monday. If Goodman regained consciousness, he would have identified Beckindale. That's why he tried to kill him a second time. He invented the head wound to avoid having to see him at the hospital.' He sighed. 'Is that how you read it?'

'Sounds about right.'

'Why did you take Dan with you in the car, when you went to call an ambulance?'

'I figured Goodman would be safe with you and I wanted you to hear what he had to say.'

'But what if Dan had come back and killed us both?'

'That would had been a clear-cut answer to what was still a suspicion.'

'Thanks.'

Fowler sipped the whisky.

'Also, I wasn't totally sure about you.'

'Are you now?'

'Yes.'

'Why?'

'Your guy Bryson. He called a friend at Langley. From what Bryson said, it was obvious you were straight.'

Lacey sat back in the chair and sipped his own drink. As far as he was concerned, they were still playing with theories. He still had to be convinced.

'Why?' he said. 'Why did Dan try to kill Goodman?'

'I don't know why. But I know some more crazy things. Let's talk about Arras.'

Lacey felt in no hurry. Maybe he was in shock?

'OK.'

'Who killed Jo-Jo?'

'Dan. Jo-Jo was going to kill me. He came back when I was searching the house.'

Fowler said, 'Capaldi was tipped off someone was in his house. Jo-Jo was supposed to phone him after he had checked it out. That's why you got an ambush in the town square. Capaldi knew things were going badly wrong.'

'How do you know this?'

'I was in the bar when Capaldi got the call. I also had words with François Rocard. The owner? I went back to Arras after the police let him go, and persuaded him to talk.'

'Will he talk to anyone else?'

'No.'

Lacey didn't ask him to elaborate. His thoughts were back in the farmhouse in France, with Jo-Jo getting ready to shoot him. Dan had said he hadn't been able to warn him because there had been a fault on the walkie-talkies. He had shot Jo-Jo instead, right at the last minute.

Had there been a fault? Or had it been calculated to provoke a shoot-out so there would be no chance of interrogation? Had he used Lacey as both bait and witness?

Fowler said, 'Does it add up?'

'Yes.' Lacey said it reluctantly. 'It adds up. But where the hell is all this leading us? Dan has been operating with the approval of the National Security Adviser. He has access to the president. He was in Washington last week about this.'

Fowler shook his head.

'Colonel Beckindale hasn't been to the States for two months. Last week he was in London. On Thursday he had lunch at the House of Commons with James Weldon.'

Lacey had talked to Dan's loyal and protective secretary; Dan had called him back. Dan had even remembered to put the transatlantic pauses into their conversation.

'Jesus Christ.'

He was beginning to accept it. He could do nothing else.

'I looked at the reports of the Sarah Mathieson killing,' Fowler said. 'Whoever did it knew the woman well enough to have keys and codes for the doors. Colonel Beckindale knew her, had done for years. He was at a house party with her, the day Capaldi killed Haber in Vienna. The day before you took her in. Does it fit?'

'It fits.'

289

Of course it fitted. Sarah and Dan and HRH all cosy at the house party. Dan would have seen the other two leave together under abrupt circumstances. When he didn't get a call, he would suspect something was wrong and rectify it.

Fowler said, 'I wasn't a hundred per cent sure. That's why I came. Now, I'm sure.'

'Have you thought this through? What it means?'

'Mr Lacey, I don't give a shit. I'm doing the job I was hired to do. When we've finished here, the Company will get my report. It's up to them what they do with it. It's up to you to protect Weldon.'

Chapter 38

In training, they told you waiting was a major part of the job. Knowing that didn't make it any easier.

Lacey was back at Charing Cross Road and facing Sam Bryson across a clouded desk. Bryson had joined him after making a telephone call from his own office to a friend in high places – former Air Force General Andrew Hirst, now military aide to the Deputy National Security Adviser.

They were waiting for the General to call back.

Lacey said, 'I think this is the one I'll retire on.'

'You're just tired,' Bryson said.

'No. I'm not tired.' He gave him a crooked smile. 'I think I'm disillusioned. Can you believe that?'

'You never had any illusions, Peter. That's what makes you good.'

He went back to puffing the pipe and Lacey leaned across the desk. He had run out of cigarettes so he inhaled the pipe smoke second-hand.

Beckindale had checked out of the hotel in Stirling and was on his way back to London, being tailed by Special Branch. Lacey had spoken to him on the telephone before he left. It had been a difficult conversation.

'I'm spending tomorrow at Century House,' Lacey had said. 'Collation and assessment of current status of all known assassins, mercenaries and terrorists in Europe. It's boring, but it sometimes pays off.'

'I'll say a prayer for you.'

There had been a lightness in his voice, but Lacey suspected he was serious.

'You mean that, don't you?'

'Yes, I mean it, Peter.'

'Say one for yourself, too, Dan.'

'I always do.'

'I'll call you tomorrow.'

When he hung up, Lacey had laid his head on his arms on the desk in front of him and begun doubting all over again. When Bryson had asked him how the telephone call had gone, he had said it had gone fine. If it had, why did he feel like Judas?

There had been nothing to do but wait and renew aquaintance with an old friend. He had opened the bottle of Jim Beam.

'This is a shit job, Sam. No one trusts anyone. No one knows where to draw the line. Langley suspect Dan is involved in the Red Dawn killings, but they don't know if he's rogue or acting with authority.' He snorted. 'And they daren't ask Washington because they think he might have authority. They think this could be official.'

Bryson took his time before replying.

'It could.'

'Oh, come on, Sam. You can't think this is a plot hatched in Command Group Alpha of the National Security Council? Or that the President wished Dan God speed?'

'No, I don't. I just said it could be.'

'Why can't Langley just ask?' he said, in exasperation.

'You know why. The reason's the same the world over. The CIA and the NSC don't trust each other. It's the same here. Five don't trust Six, Six don't trust Five, and Special Branch think we're all wankers.' He blew more smoke. 'We all have secrets and sometimes the last people we want to share them with are our own side.'

They had drunk a quarter of the way down the bottle of bourbon when Andrew Hirst telephoned on a secure line from the crisis management centre of the Executive Office Building in Washington.

Bryson took the call in his own office and Lacey listened to the hum of the air-conditioning that had been installed for the sake of the computers. He poked around his ashtray, but couldn't find a cigarette-butt worth lighting, and considered another drink but rejected the idea. He put the kettle on for coffee.

He was pouring boiling water into a cup when he heard Bryson emerge from his office. The call had lasted less than ten minutes.

He shouted, 'You want coffee, Sam?'

'No thanks. I need to sleep tonight.'

Bryson walked slowly through the outer office to Lacey's door.

'Well?' Lacey said.

'We'll get some answers tomorrow. Andy Hirst is coming to London.'

Maybe the coffee had been a bad idea. Lacey didn't sleep too well. He was tired enough to let his mind have its own way, but instead of settling down for a rest, it slipped into overdrive and spent the dead hours before dawn darting around his head without rhyme, reason or control. It was a phenomenon close to hallucination. Susan had said she also suffered from it on occasions when she was overtired, overstressed or had the 'flu. She called it the whacky races.

By five o'clock he'd had enough and got up. He made black coffee but it tasted bitter. The office was dark and it was easy to imagine the murmur of the air-conditioning was ghosts talking. He found himself standing by the desk that had been Roland Devere's. The drawers were empty now; he'd had the job of clearing them and the well-safe that had been allocated for his use. Lacey remembered when he had been the new boy in the department and had been given a safe. It had contained a box of fruit gums. He had figured only a dead man didn't return for his fruit gums.

The windows in the room were double-glazed, wire meshed and painted to allow only vision out. Incongruous net curtains hung at them. The office was supposed to be secret, but these were all devices to foil any attempt to eavesdrop by someone using a sonar laser-beam to pick up voice vibrations from the glass. A side effect was that light from outside was permanently subdued, even when the sun shone. It was raining heavily enough for him to hear, despite the insulation, and he could tell the day was about to begin.

The rain reminded him of the funeral at the hillside church and of the two women by the grave: Devere's mother and the girl whose eyes had been wet enough to drown in. He wondered if their grief had diminished yet. His hadn't. He sat in Devere's chair and ran his fingers over the desk top.

Dawn on a rainy day was a perfect time for melancholy but it didn't devalue what he felt. His grief was not personal, like the grief of the two women. It was not grief for Roland Devere as a friend, because he hadn't known him as a friend; he had consciously avoided the pitfalls that led to friendship. It was grief at the waste of a man so young, so alive and for such a stupid reason. It was grief at his own recurring guilt.

He went into his office and got the bottle of bourbon from the filing cabinet. Jim Beam would understand, he always understood. He poured a large one and took it back into the outer office. At the far end of the room, one of Harry Ryburn's computers purred as it accepted an in-put of information along one of its umbilical cables. If Harry had been there he would have stroked it.

The bourbon burned through his smoke-deadened taste-buds and he raised the glass to the absent Devere and drank again.

Maybe next time it would be him. Maybe next time Sam Bryson would be sitting here toasting Lacey's memory with the remnants of Lacey's bourbon. The thought didn't worry him, it wouldn't worry him until the last second of the last minute when he realized that this really was his turn.

Playing with destiny was part of the compulsion. Life and death were the only stakes that meant anything and he was hooked.

294

Jesus Christ, he enjoyed it, and that was why he felt guilty, because he couldn't work out whether Devere had been a player or a pawn. Friendship would have made him a partner, but Lacey had denied that possibility and had used and sacrificed Devere, the same way he, Lacey, had been used by Dan Beckindale.

All these silent service games were supposed to be challenges to cerebral ingenuity, but the concept invariably got fucked-up by relationships. The first fuck-up was in not having a relationship with Devere, the second was in allowing one to develop with Dan Beckindale. Even though it was built on false pretences, it was still effective.

It seemed likely that Beckindale had been the executioner in Sarah Mathieson's apartment, but even that didn't invalidate the friendship. Lacey didn't know the circumstances and could make no judgements. He didn't know what role Sarah Mathieson had played or how close to terrorism she had been.

If Beckindale was a lone wolf, he could have become paranoid about security. If he had had any doubts about her, he might have decided there was no alternative but death in cold blood. Once that decision had been made, Devere would have been a complication, but not a consideration.

Lacey understood paranoia and the single spy. Perspectives changed when you were backed into a corner at the tail end of an operation that was in danger of being compromised.

He felt guilty at understanding Beckindale's actions, even if he didn't condone them, finished the drink and went back to his office and replenished the glass. If he was putting himself on trial, he couldn't do it sober.

Back in the main office, he walked down the room to Harry Ryburn's computers and gave them a stroke. Ryburn had a lot of sense. He only had relationships with his wife and computers.

Moments like this, when the world outside stood still, were dangerous. They encouraged evaluation of ethics that didn't really exist. How could execution be justified? How could the game be justified? Even the names they used for it were obscene misnomers. The game. The looking-glass war.

They spent their lives infiltrating and disinforming, living in a shadowland where reality often ceased to exist. They were the begetters, procrastinators and propagators of their own world. The world of the conjurers. Using child names for a profession of lies.

He gulped half the drink and coughed when it hit the back of his throat.

Never mind, normality would be back at nine o'clock with Natalie and Harry and Malcolm. The machines would buzz, the lights would be high and doubt would be dispelled by activity and people playing people and he would slip back into character and smoke French cigarettes and pretend he didn't care.

Andrew Hirst, military aide to the Deputy National Security Adviser to the President of the United States, would be here hot-foot from Pennsylvania Avenue to reveal all about a hero-gone-rogue who was causing an embarrassment in Europe.

The cosy covert world would be put to rights around a table where the discussion would be sincere, the consequences would be faced, and the decision would be made to remove the embarrassment.

Lacey had a premonition about the outcome. He suspected he would be asked to remove the embarrassment.

Chapter 39

General Andrew Hirst had a bull neck and a front-line way with words.

Bryson introduced him to Lacey. Hirst shook hands, appraised him, but made no comment. Lacey wondered if he'd passed muster.

'Good flight?' he made the mistake of asking.

'No. It was shit.'

They went into Bryson's office and sat around the desk. Hirst put a large metallic briefcase on it that looked as if he was on a picture assignment for *Time* magazine. He opened it and took out a cardboard file, that had across it a wide blue strip to designate its high-security rating, and a plastic box that contained three eggs.

'You got any coffee, Sam?' he asked.

'Certainly, old chap. I'll arrange it.'

'Black, strong and sweet.'

Bryson left the room.

Hirst held up the box to show Lacey.

'Lunch. Flying fucks up my metabolism and flight food fucks up anybody. I take my own. Hard-boiled eggs. That way I know what I'm getting. You can't fuck about with an egg.'

'True.'

Lacey reached for his cigarettes rather than attempt further conversation. Hirst watched him.

'No offence, son, but smoking is unhealthy.'

'It's my health.'

'In this room, it's my health, too. I'd be obliged if you postponed your death-wish until after we've finished.'

297

Despite everything, Lacey liked the man. He put the cigarettes back in his pocket.

Bryson returned with the promise that the coffee was on its way.

'It's good of you to come, Andy,' he said.

'Shit, I had to come. Somewhere along the line, this latrine has to be cleaned out before it overflows. I guess it's down to us.'

'Has it gone to the President?'

'Not officially. But Hegginbaker and O'Connell saw him last night.'

Roy Hegginbaker was the National Security Adviser and Michael O'Connell, his deputy. Hirst was military aide to O'Connell.

A knock at the door announced the arrival of Malcolm with a tray containing three mugs of coffee. After he had gone, Hirst cracked an egg and peeled off the shell.

'Maybe you can tell me where we're at, while I eat,' he said to Bryson.

'Peter's better placed to tell you.'

'OK.' He bit into the egg. 'Go ahead.'

Lacey shuffled in his chair and waited until Hirst had taken a slurp of coffee.

'When I met Dan Beckindale, I believed he had the highest authority from Washington. He was well connected. He knew all the right people, including the Deputy Director of Six. When he said Sarah Mathieson had been working undercover for him, it was a relief to senior people here. No-one argued. He also appeared to have good intelligence in Europe, which supported his claim that he was infiltrating the terror networks.

'He set up the caper in northern France very professionally, with a car switch, equipment and a safe house. He was no slouch when it came to action, either. All in all, if you're in a tight spot, you couldn't have anybody better as a partner.'

Hirst nodded and Lacey sipped his coffee before continuing.

'Dan stage-managed the hit in France so there would be no interrogation of Capaldi. He even tipped the guy off we were looking for him.' He shrugged. 'It was foolhardy, but he enjoyed the action, he enjoyed battle. Maybe he preferred doing it that way.

'Afterwards, he would have been happy if I'd gone home and closed the file. When I told him I had doubts, he came up with his KGB plot against Gorbachev.' He smiled. 'He's very persuasive. Besides, the KGB haven't suddenly become boy scouts. They've assassinated people before and they'll do it again and it was plausible. Anyway, it prompted me to go to Vienna to stir up a reaction. What I got was the VIP List and the ball thrown back into the West. Dan, in a way, had provided us with our first lead.'

Hirst held his hand to his mouth and burped softly.

'That lead was Goodman?' he said.

'That's right. Goodman gave us the names of the final target and Bill Woodward. I still didn't suspect Dan. That only happened after Amos Fowler called. All of a sudden, things didn't add up any more.'

Hirst nodded and tapped the file.

'OK, son. Bottom line. What do you think Beckindale is guilty of?'

'I think he directed Capaldi, through Sarah Mathieson, and paid him to kill four times in Europe. I think Dan himself killed Sarah Mathieson and Roland Devere. He tried to kill Martin Goodman, and I think he's going to try to kill James Weldon.'

'OK, one more question. Do you think he had authority to do all this?'

'I hope not.'

'That's not an answer. Do you think this was sanctioned by the President or the National Security Council?'

It was unthinkable.

'No, sir. I don't.'

'Well, thank God for that. You show more faith than the CIA. Those bastards are still not sure.' He picked up the file. 'Shit, after reading this, I don't blame them. Beckindale has been allowed to become a one-man task force and the conscience of America.'

'How?' Lacey said.

'Through patronage, weakness and secrecy, but mainly because the guy had the balls to pick up the ball and run.'

Bryson said, 'Your turn, Andy.'

Hirst snorted.

'Before telling you about Beckindale let me tell you about Hegginbaker. The guy is a great Republican. At the last election he raised millions of dollars and secured a marginal state for the President. After inauguration, the shitbags who'd helped put the President in the White House queued up to be paid off. Some were sent as ambassadors to Australia, New Zealand, the Bahamas. Hegginbaker didn't want to travel. He got National Security.'

Hirst shook his head.

'It's a fact of life and it stinks. Hegginbaker is great at budgets and lousy at defence. When it comes to running the NSC he's a dickless dwarf. He's the reason we're all standing in a latrine. He has no grasp of the job and he's ready to give subordinates an excess of power because he doesn't understand what they're doing. He also has access to the President and he's in the habit of taking into the Oval Office the best of *his boys*.

'With so much dead-wood in the department, Dan Beckindale became one of his top boys. He likes the way he gets things done, the way he presents reports in a way he can understand.' He shook his head. 'Well, he's let this one go too far. It's become a one-man bay of pigs. The only good thing about it is Hegginbaker will go. Maybe he'll become a diplomat after all. Libya would be nice. Shit. Even last night he didn't want to see the President. O'Connell had to make him. He was still thinking career.'

'We have people like that here, too,' Bryson said.

Hirst opened the file on his knee.

'OK. That's enough background. The rest should

300

make sense.' He looked at the papers. 'Dan Beckindale. Born 1947 in Portland, Maine. An only son and he has two younger sisters. Both his parents are dead. His father was a lawyer, Myron Beckindale, who served in the Army in Europe during the Second World War with the rank of captain, although he never saw action.

'His mother was a refugee who came from Eastern Europe at the end of the war. She was a charmer and she doted on her son. She instilled in him patriotism and a distrust of Europeans. Germans had killed her brothers and Communists had driven her from her homeland.

'They were a close family, saluted the flag, ate apple pie and went to church every Sunday. Dan Beckindale went to college and studied languages, but he really wanted to be a soldier. He graduated at West Point, trained at the Special Warfare Centre at Fort Bragg and attended the US Army Command and General Staff College at Fort Leavenworth. He served three tours in Vietnam, two of them with Special Forces, and was involved in the Unconventional Warfare Campaign in Cambodia. Later, he trained with the US Rangers and took part in the invasion of Grenada, ostensibly as an observer. He's been decorated seven times and wounded three. He left the service after a two-year secondment with the National Security Council to make Washington his full-time career.

'Along the way, he found time to get married and have a son, but the marriage didn't work out. His wife divorced him two years ago and she has custody of the boy.'

Lacey said, 'They're alive?'

'Sure they're alive. Alive and well and living in California.'

'Dan said they were dead. Some kind of accident.'

'Nope. They're fine. But the divorce hit him. He had some kind of breakdown, although it was never called that. If it had been, his career would have been finished. He took two months' leave to get over it. Afterwards, it was as if they were dead. He didn't talk about them. The subject was taboo. He'd always been a workaholic and

301

that had been a major problem with the marriage. His wife and son never saw him. It was while he was getting over the divorce he rediscovered religion. It became his new motivation and he worked even harder.'

Hirst turned a page and read a few lines to remind himself before continuing.

'Beckindale had a stroke of luck when he arrived in Washington. He met Bill Woodward. Woodward had come to the Security Council from the CIA. He'd also been in Special Forces, although the action stopped when he was recruited to Langley. He was strictly desk-bound. But he and Beckindale shared the same get-things-done attitude, along with a strong suspicion of anything Liberal.

'Woodward was ten years older than Beckindale, introduced him to the right people and promoted his interests. His area was Western Europe and eventually Beckindale went to work for him, although he was soon a star in his own right. He was the guy you took problems to and who sorted them out, even if it meant working twenty-six hours a day. He became indispensable and his authority grew. Shit, responsibility was lying around waiting to be picked up, all Beckindale did was accept a work-load no-one else could match, and carry the responsibility back to his office in a dump truck.

'Woodward got him appointed to the Anti-Terrorism Unit and it was Beckindale's idea they tighten its efficiency by creating Command Group Alpha, a three-man committee with power to react in an emergency. Beckindale became the button man.

'A year ago, Woodward died in an accident in Jutland. He was a passenger in a helicopter piloted by Henriks Jorgensen. They were both killed. Jorgensen was a Danish politician with a big reputation. As a young man, he'd been a war hero, a member of the Churchill Club that fought the occupying Nazis. His sister-in-law married an American and he was known to like America even though he didn't like our NATO policies.

302

'Woodward became friends with Jorgensen to try to soften the line he took against us. The cause of the crash that killed them was pilot error. They had both been drinking heavily – beer and akvavit.'

He paused and massaged his crutch with his left hand.

'The death shook Beckindale. Bill Woodward was a fine man, and Beckindale owed him a lot. He'd helped him when he'd first arrived in Washington and he and his wife Mary had helped him get over the divorce. He'd been their house-guest for a month. Bill and Mary were also strongly religious and it was through them he'd found God.

'It seemed appropriate that Beckindale was the guy to clear Woodward's desk and safe at the department of personal documents, and to retrieve secret data from his home.' He shrugged. 'We guess that was when he found the list.'

Lacey said, 'He believed it to be real?'

'We presume so.'

'And he came to Europe and set up a killing operation to eliminate the people on it?'

'That's the way it looks.'

'Why? If the chopper crash was an accident?'

'Maybe he thought the Soviets had rubbed out Woodward because he'd broken a spy ring. Maybe he thought they'd sacrificed Jorgensen because he'd been compromised. Maybe all he was after was pure revenge. Make up your own reason, it doesn't matter a shit why he did it, just that he did it. And he did it because Dan Beckindale was a bomb waiting to go off.'

Lacey raised his eyebrows.

Bryson said, 'Go on.'

'I've had a preliminary profile done but we've just scratched the surface. Colonel Dan Beckindale is the true American hero. Brave, courageous and bold. He's action-orientated in a department that isn't. His authority is out of proportion to his rank or experience. He has an overwhelming belief in himself and that the enemies of his country should be smitten where it hurts. He's also unbalanced.

'He saw a psychiatrist after his divorce. Mary Woodward tells us he refused to accept the blame for the marriage breaking-up. The best he would accept was that his duty had caused the rift. Privately, he told the Woodwards the Soviets were the cause of the long hours he worked, therefore his marriage had been a casualty in the battle against Communism. Religion fuelled his obsession. It gave it divine approval. His minister says everyone has a mission in life and that Dan Beckindale took his mission very seriously.'

Hirst ran a finger down a page and read some more.

'Beckindale has urged pre-emptive action against known terrorists or those planning or aiding activity against United States citizens or property. It's been tried before, and it didn't work then. The CIA trained a bunch of Lebanese who missed their target and killed sixty civilians with a bomb.

'President Reagan also had something to say about political killings. The 1981 Reagan Executive Order 12333 says, and I quote: No person employed by or acting on behalf of the United States government shall engage in, or conspire to engage in, assassinations. End quote.

'This time, Beckindale targeted four guys he believed to be agents of influence, and used a freelance assassin to make the hits. We guess he'll try to get Weldon himself. He's on record as saying success overcomes moral indignation. To him, this will be a success if he nails Weldon, despite what Reagan said.'

Lacey said, 'Even though the list is phoney?'

'He doesn't believe that. He can't believe that. To him, that's KGB propaganda.'

Bryson said, 'Was the list ever used for persuasion?'

'No. It wasn't used and it wasn't known about until four days ago.'

'How was Dan able to run the operation without anyone at the NSC knowing?' Bryson said.

'Simple. He dealt in secrecy and he was Hegginbaker's blue-eyed boy. He didn't have to tell anyone.'

Lacey said, 'What about funding? The help we had in France?'

'He came to Europe with a budget. We don't know yet if he exceeded that, or if he used other funds. There were two Swiss accounts he could have used. I don't know about the help you got in France. Maybe the embassy in Paris, maybe not. But Beckindale has pull and a reputation for getting what he wants with no questions asked. If some secret service guy from Paris did help, he sure as hell won't have filed any reports after what happened in Arras.'

'It's incredible,' Lacey said. 'That one man can acquire the power to run such an operation through official channels and get away with it.'

'He's not got away with it,' Hirst said. 'He can't be allowed to get away with it and he can't be arrested and put on trial. He's too close to the President. Can you imagine what a congressional hearing would make of this? For fuck's sake, the President has been photographed with him. He's called him a national fucking hero.'

Lacey got out his cigarettes, regardless of what Hirst had said earlier. He sensed what was coming and he saw that Bryson had, too. He left it to his section head to pose the question.

The silence stretched until it became uncomfortable. Hirst closed the file and put it back in the briefcase. He stared as Lacey handled the cigarette packet without taking one out, but said nothing. Bryson reached for his pipe and began methodically to fill the bowl with tobacco, as if the balance of propriety had changed.

Bryson said, 'I think we understand what you're saying, Andy. It's something we've obviously considered ourselves. But I think we'd still like you to be a little more . . . specific, about what you propose we do with Colonel Beckindale.'

'There's no point avoiding the issue. Beckindale has to

305

be removed. He has to die. Preferably, as a hero.'

Lacey took out a cigarette and looked at Hirst.

'Who's going to kill him?' he said.

'You are, son. You know that.'

Lacey lit the cigarette. The general didn't object.

Chapter 40

Special Branch lost Beckindale between Heathrow and Grosvenor Square. He had taken the tube from the airport as if he were going to the American Embassy, but somewhere along the line he had dropped out of sight.

He had finally gone undercover for the last hit. It might make him more difficult to stop but, Lacey reflected, it would make him easier to kill.

Bryson telephoned Jim Weldon at his country retreat in Yorkshire and Lacey took the first train north, hoping his section head would be able to impress upon the politician the seriousness of the situation.

The train journey gave Lacey more time to reflect. He wasn't grateful. His recurring thought was that maybe it was time to retire.

The weather matched his mood. Dark skies prematurely aged the day and rain machine-gunned the train in heavy bursts. A siege mentality pervaded the carriages, as if the passengers were enduring warfare.

Perhaps the British spirit didn't come from being an island race defying all odds. Perhaps it came from surviving the weather.

His throat was beginning to hurt from the number of cigarettes he had smoked.

Jesus Christ, what was wrong with him?

His mind was adopting retirement attitudes in anticipation. This was no time to change his life. In the next few days, he might find he didn't have one.

He shifted in the seat. The shoulder holster of the Browning pistol was uncomfortable. He wasn't used to wearing a holster and he wasn't used to the Browning, but his own Heckler and Koch was at home and there had been no time to go and get it.

The change in armament didn't really bother him. It would have bothered him if he hadn't been armed at all. He was only too aware of his physical shortcomings, but he was proficient with guns. The Browning was a stopper and its magazine held thirteen rounds. It was just bloody heavy for a three-hour journey to Leeds.

He watched the rain and the passing housing estates and towns and snarled traffic on congested roads and wondered about having an ordinary job. Nine to five, a social life, sex twice a week and tailing off as boredom with routine set in.

If he asked for a move within the Firm he'd probably end up back in Century House with an in-tray and an out-tray, making faceless assessments. If he left, he didn't know what he could do. His qualifications were unusual. Foreign languages and bloodshed. Maybe he *should* become a teacher?

A Special Branch sergeant met him at Leeds and drove him to Weldon's country cottage. The man was in his thirties, needed a shave and was less than loquacious, as if he resented being a chauffeur to a clever dick from London. For the first thirty minutes they drove in silence, out of the city and through suburbs. As they approached a major roundabout, the man was moved to speak.

'Harry Ramsden's,' he said, nodding towards a large circular establishment. 'Biggest fish and chip shop in the world.'

Lacey felt duty-bound to look and noted the extensive take-away section and chandeliers in the restaurant. Fish and chips and chandeliers? No wonder northern pride had overcome the man's reticence.

'Very nice,' he said.

They swished through the spa town of Ilkley that sat beneath moors that were entitled to brood in this weather, turned off the main road and were suddenly in beautiful, if rain-drenched, countryside.

308

'Not far now.'

'How's Weldon taking it?'

The man shrugged.

'He thinks we're playing games. This shitting weather, and he thinks we're playing games.' The man looked at Lacey. 'We're not, are we?'

'It's no game.' The fields were lost in mist as they rolled up to meet the hills, and the road dipped and swerved. 'Is the cottage isolated?'

'Aye. Desirable detached property with two-car garage and stables.' He grunted and Lacey interpreted it as a laugh. 'Calls himself a socialist, an' all.'

'How are you placed?'

'One in the house. Cars staking out the road in both directions, and some poor sod in a potting-shed at the bottom of the garden. I hope you're expected. You might be sharing the potting-shed.'

'I'm expected.'

Before they reached their destination, the driver used a radio-phone to call ahead.

The car stopped by a five-barred gate. A smaller gate for pedestrians was alongside it. The cottage hadn't been visible from the road until now, because of high hedges. The gates led on to a gravelled car-parking area in front of the house. The word cottage was a euphemism and Lacey could understand the sergeant's bile. It was the sort of property to set estate agents drooling with adjectives.

He grabbed his bag from the back seat, pushed through the side gate and ran across the gravel. The door opened as he got beneath the cover of a porch, and a young woman grinned at him.

'You look like a drowned rat.'

She opened the door wider to let him inside.

'Thanks,' he said.

She had short blond hair and wore jeans, white leather training-shoes, an open-necked shirt and a cardigan. Her age was late twenties.

'I'm Lacey,' he said.

309

'I know. I'm Helen Sykes, Special Branch Protection Squad.'

He widened his eyes.

'You're a surprise.'

'Don't be sexist.'

She smiled when she said it.

'I wouldn't dream of it. But you're still a surprise. A pleasant one.'

'Flattery I don't mind. Even sexist flattery.'

He grinned and looked round. They were in a hall with a staircase and two corridors. One corridor went straight ahead and the other led off to the right.

'Impressive,' he said.

'Very. He bought it for a song years ago and had it renovated before property prices went through the roof.'

'Lucky man. How many are staying here?'

'Weldon, his wife Margaret, and her sister, Pat Bennett.' She nodded up the corridor to the right. 'I'm in the breakfast room, out of sight and out of mind. I'm night-shift, here until six in the morning.' She grinned. 'We never sleep.'

'How's Weldon?'

'He thinks we're an intrusion, but he's putting up with us.'

'What about his wife and sister-in-law?'

'His wife's smashing. Her sister's a bit snooty. Intellectual, twin set and pearls. The widow of a college lecturer. I think he died of an inferiority complex.'

Lacey laughed.

'I can hardly wait.'

'Weldon's son arrives tomorrow. He's at medical school. Come on.' She walked down the corridor facing them. 'I'll introduce you to Jim.'

He left his bag and followed. She took him to the furthest door, knocked and looked in.

'Jim? Peter Lacey's arrived.' As she moved back, she said to Lacey, 'Mind the steps.'

Three steps led down into a large sitting-room with wooden beams in the ceiling and an open fireplace. French windows looked into a garden that fell away with the slope of the hillside to a tree-line fifty yards away.

The room was furnished with overstuffed chairs and settees that were covered in floral print material. Two of three small tables were stacked with books and magazines. A writing-desk was beneath one window and a baby grand piano filled a corner to his right. *Home and Gardens* would have been delighted.

Weldon put down a book and climbed out of an armchair. It was always odd, and quite often disappointing, to meet a media personality. Weldon looked different from his usual image because he wore dark blue levis and sweat shirt. They made him appear leaner and younger than his fifty-four years.

He smiled as he walked to meet Lacey and held out his hand. It was a proper handshake. Lacey had been expecting the finger-grip so often adopted by public figures and freemasons.

'Mr Lacey. It's good of you to come, but quite unnecessary. I don't know what the fuss is about.'

The voice was educated and well-modulated, as if trained for public speaking, but a hint of his native North-East accent remained to give it a Socialist edge.

'I'm sorry for the inconvenience, Mr Weldon. But I think it is necessary. Our intelligence is good. If we're right, an attempt may be made on your life in the next two or three days.' He smiled. 'I don't want to alarm you, and I hope we're wrong, but if we're not, we're well placed to stop it being successful.'

Weldon was not as unconcerned as he pretended. Lacey noticed a twitch in his right eye that suggested nerves.

'All right. But for God's sake don't scare Margaret and Pat with unfounded rumour.'

'I won't. But they know about the threat?'

'Yes. I could hardly pretend we'd taken on a maid and a gardener when Special Branch insisted on moving in. By

311

the way, it'll make life a lot easier if we drop the misters. I'm Jim. I believe you're Peter?'

'That's right.'

'Good. Margaret and Pat are out at the moment, but should be back any time. Let me show you round, then you can dump your stuff in your room and settle in.' He grinned. 'By then it'll be time for a drink before dinner.'

'That sounds extremely civilized.'

Margaret Weldon was a good-looking woman in her late forties, her hair styled, and lightened with blond tints. She was bright, intelligent and good company. Her sister, Pat Bennett, was ten years younger and as good looking, but in a different way. She wore her naturally-blond hair long and straight, a style which was very English. When she shook hands with Lacey, her mouth twitched. It was the sort of middle-class excuse for a smile that was bestowed upon people who didn't really count. Her one saving grace was that she smoked. It stopped Lacey feeling like a pariah.

They gathered in the sitting-room and Weldon steered the conversation in directions where everyone could contribute. They talked about travel and foreign places, about the differences between the North and South of England, and about the Dales countryside.

'Of course, I haven't seen much of it yet,' Lacey said, indicating the rain that still lashed the windows.

'You'll see it tomorrow,' Weldon said. 'We'll walk. Did you bring any boots?'

'Er, no. I'm afraid not.'

Cross-country walking was something he hadn't considered. Christ, the man was under threat. Lacey would have preferred to lock him in the cellar until Beckindale was stopped.

'Never mind. We'll fix you up. What size do you take?'

'Eight.'

'No problem. There's a pair of eights in the garage.' He grinned. 'We could start a hiking shop with the gear people have left.'

312

He would have private words with Weldon and try to dissuade him. Apart from the danger, he hated bloody walking.

Dinner was unpretentious steak and salad and was very enjoyable. It was cooked and served by Margaret and with it they drank Sainsbury's claret. Afterwards, he and Weldon went back to the sitting-room while the women cleared the table. Weldon poured them both brandies and lit a slim cigar.

'One of my secret vices,' he said.

'Another is walking,' Lacey said. 'It's not on, you know. Tomorrow's jaunt.'

Weldon exhaled smoke.

'You know, for most of the year, I'm on public display. I'm public property. It makes those moments when I escape all the more precious.' He held up the glass and the cigar. 'A drink and a smoke without a camera recording my licentious behaviour.' He smiled. 'A walk in the Dales. I understand your dilemma, Peter, but I'm going walking in the morning. You're welcome to come along.'

The argument was ended. Maybe that was why he was the Leader of the Opposition.

'You'd better give me the route and I'll make arrangements with Special Branch.'

'Certainly. But they're not coming too.'

Weldon got an Ordnance Survey map from one of the shelves and unfolded it and explained the route to Lacey. He said it was a comfortable morning stroll.

The women rejoined them and Weldon poured them drinks and they sat around in the overstuffed furniture like characters in a drawing-room who-dunnit. Pat Bennett, mindful that Lacey was from the Foreign Office, talked about her work with the United Kingdom Immigrant Advisory Service, and a fact-finding trip she had made to Pakistan.

'Have you been to Pakistan?' she asked Lacey.

'Many times.'

'On business?'

'Yes.'

'And what impressed you most about the country?'

She was setting him up and he and everyone else knew it. Margaret Weldon was uncomfortable, but Jim Weldon seemed to find it amusing. Lacey looked thoughtful and only spoke after due consideration.

'There are the queues at the British Embassy, but overall, I suppose what impressed me most was the price of beer.'

Jim Weldon laughed and Margaret smiled. Pat went red.

'Didn't the plight of the people impress you? The poverty?'

'People are in plights all over the world and there's nothing impressive about poverty. There's no dignity in it, either, despite what you read in the papers. If you want a discussion on immigration, I'm afraid I can't oblige. I'm a civil servant. I'm not allowed to have a political view.'

Jim said. 'Quite right. We should have barber-shop rules for the duration of Peter's visit. You know what they are, don't you, Pat?'

Pat took a drink rather than answer.

'No politics, no religion. They drive customers away. That's what my barber used to say when I was growing up in Chester-le-Street. Of course, you were on sticky ground with football, too. That's always been a religion in the North East.'

Margaret Weldon said, 'You left County Durham when you were twelve. I'm amazed you can remember.'

'Hah. My conscience speaks.'

'He goes back periodically to brush up the accent,' she confided to Lacey.

Lacey grinned.

'I could never divorce the woman,' Weldon said with a smile. 'She would sell my secrets to the tabloids.'

'He likes to pretend he's working class,' Margaret continued.

'My father was a miner.'

'He was a colliery manager. You never went short.

Anyway, you were an opportunist from birth.'

'Hush woman. You're destroying my credibility.'

'That's all right. Peter's neither a constituent nor a journalist. You can be honest with him.'

Weldon laughed and Lacey guessed this was a variation of a comfortable routine in which they occasionally indulged.

Lacey said, 'I went to university in Durham. That's where I met my wife.'

'It's a lovely city,' Weldon said. 'And a fine university.'

'I believe you went to Cambridge?' Lacey said.

'That's right.' He smiled and his eyes hit middle distance as he remembered. 'I had a marvellous time. It was a great leveller. Until then, I'd been guilty about missing out on the hardship I'd seen in the North East. Margaret's right. I never went short as a youngster, but many of my friends did and I saw how poverty builds barriers. Cambridge helped me identify needs, directed my energies. I met an incredible cross-section of people there.' He sipped his drink. 'Great minds, influential men.'

'It made you want to change the world?' Lacey said.

Weldon laughed.

'Something like that. You know, politics is an odd business. You start off fired with altruism and end up a salesman. I might have the greatest policies of all-time, I might have the secret of the universe, but without the right help and the grooming and the packaging, no bugger will listen to me. Being sincere isn't enough. I have to be bloody media-friendly, too.'

Margaret said, 'Remember the barber-shop rules? No politics.'

Her husband smiled.

'No politics. What a world that would be.'

Chapter 41

The rain had stopped by morning but the sky was angry and threatened more. Weldon drove them in a red Ford Escort for twenty minutes. They went past a pub and hotel called the Devonshire Arms where Lacey imagined they were serving breakfast, and along a narrow road that ran beneath arched ruins that a sign said was Bolton Abbey.

'Twelfth century,' Weldon said. 'But it wasn't an abbey, it was a priory. What survived the dissolution is now the parish church.'

He turned off the road on to a track that went down towards a river in a valley. Fells rose from the far bank, their only occupants sheep, who seemed oblivious to the cold wind.

Weldon parked by a footbridge that crossed the river. A wooden pavilion café was closed and there were no other vehicles in the parking area. Lacey was not surprised. It was seven-thirty and the weather was lousy.

They got out of the car and began putting on walking boots. Lacey wore jeans and a borrowed wind-cheater. With two pairs of socks, the boots were a reasonable fit. At least he looked the part, even if he didn't feel it. He resisted the temptation to light a cigarette in case it ruined the illusion.

Weldon wore elasticated walking trousers covered with zips, that ended below the knee where they tucked beneath socks, a patterned sweater and woollen bobble hat. From the boot of the car, he took two back-packs and a hand-carved walking-stick. He looked as if he was ready to hunt edelweiss.

He handed Lacey a back-pack.

'Waterproofs, flask and sandwiches.' Also from the boot he took two sets of leggings. 'It's likely to be muddy, after all the rain. We'll need these.'

Lacey became lost in the intricacies of straps and hooks and needed Weldon to fasten the leggings for him. So much for the illusion.

The previous night, Weldon had described the walk as a gentle ten miles, but Lacey was no longer so sure. It had looked different on a map. He hadn't been able to see the hills.

Weldon had the Ordnance Survey map, folded at the correct section, in a plastic case that hung around his neck. He had provided Lacey with a small footpath map and guide of the area that was not to scale, but which provided all salient landmarks.

Lacey glanced back the way they had come and noted the first Special Branch car parked near the road. The map followed the contours of the River Wharfe. There would be another car four miles up river at the hamlet of Howgill. Their route went across the river, through a place called the Valley of Desolation, and hiked over fells to Simon's Seat, a 1,550 feet vantage point. From there, it wound down to Howgill where they would rejoin the river and walk back along its banks.

He took a two-way radio from the back of the car, extended the aerial and pressed the call button.

'We're leaving now,' he said into it.

It crackled briefly before the car on the hill replied.

'Have a nice day.'

Lacey stowed the radio in the back-pack and they set off.

They didn't speak for the first half-mile, while they found their rhythm. At least, Weldon found a rhythm; Lacey concentrated on staying with him. They followed the river, which was easy going, before they turned off right and began to climb.

Over a hill and far away, Lacey kept saying to himself. A bloody long far away.

On the other side of the hill they came to a tributary of the river they had left behind. They should have used stepping-stones, but they were covered by a fast-flowing current. Lacey didn't think for one minute they would turn back. He was right.

Weldon walked further on and pointed. A tree, that had fallen in some past storm, spanned the water. Before Lacey could voice any objection, Weldon climbed on to the trunk and started across on hands and knees.

The water was running fast, but it wasn't deep enough to drown in. Weldon's life was not in danger, but Lacey's image was. He'd never been any good on the assault course at Fort Monkton, but he was supposed to be Weldon's bodyguard. In the movies, Lacey would leap on to the tree trunk and run across. He climbed on to it with great care and crawled.

Weldon laughed.

'I thought you were supposed to be an action man.'

'Let me assure you I'm deadly at pushing past old ladies on the tube. The urban jungle is my game. This is just too, too . . .'

'Real?'

Ferns grew as tall as a man in the Valley of Desolation. The only sound was the water. Pterodactyls and the occasional caveman would not have been out of place. He slipped a hand inside his jacket to check the accessibility of the Browning. If Beckindale had somehow anticipated their walk, this was good country for a killing.

He was sweating, despite the cold wind, and his legs and lungs ached. The path left the valley and entered a forest, still going upwards. Lacey was surprised to discover that he, too, had found a rhythm.

They rested briefly when the forest ended and the fells began. It looked an awful long way to their destination. The gorse rose in layers as if a giant had casually folded a blanket. Spaced on the hillsides were man-made camouflaged shelters that blended into the background.

'What are they?' Lacey asked.

318

'Hides. It's grouse-shooting country.'

The path they were to follow wandered through the middle of them. They would be targets on a shooting range. This was another great place to kill someone. He was beginning to think the Special Branch officer who had called him a stupid twat had had a point.

Lacey was too out of breath to talk, but he listened to Weldon as they continued walking. The politician reminisced about university, about meeting Margaret at a party and knowing immediately she was the woman for him, and about his son and two daughters. He talked a lot and gave Lacey a potted biography full of amusing anecdotes. It passed the time and took his mind off the soreness of his feet.

'I joined the Labour Party when I was still at school, you know. My father would have killed me if he'd known. I knew, even at that age, that I had to be involved, had to try to change things. I've worked all my life towards that ideal. Sacrificed a lot, too. Seen many changes, some for the better, a lot for the worse.' He shook his head. 'But they'll get put right next time. We're going to win next time. And nothing's going to stop us.'

Weldon, he began to believe, was a good man. A man who valued loyalty and principle. Perhaps even someone worth voting for.

They were in an exposed position for weather as well as assassins and the wind chased the clouds across an Olympic-sized sky. June had started with extremes, winter following summer within the space of a few days.

The up-hill slog became painful and Weldon noticed his limp.

'Not far now,' he said, and pointed to the pile of rocks on the skyline that was Simon's Seat. 'We'll rest there.'

Lacey cursed his feet and his burning lungs and kept going. At last, they reached the landmark.

The rocks were twenty to thirty feet high. They took off their packs and Weldon led the way through a gap to look at the view on the far side. They stood at the edge of a steep drop. A route led down, but it would be a climb rather than a walk for maybe a hundred feet.

Weldon pointed at the dales and valleys spread before them.

'Worth the walk?' He had to shout. They were standing in an exposed position and the wind snapped the words away. 'Makes you realize what fools men are.'

Lacey nodded. He could appreciate the country and he could appreciate what Weldon meant, but he still preferred taking a taxi to a two-hour walk on aching feet. The sensible way of appreciating the beauty of nature was the way he had done it in Scotland: from a comfortable armchair with a malt whisky in his hand.

The village of Appletreewick was in the valley below. White cottages strung along a narrow lane near the river. Lacey imagined stone-flagged pubs, pints of ale and home-cooked food. They could have driven there and enjoyed rural England at its best without walking round in circles for bloody hours.

They went back through the gap to the other side of the rocks, out of the wind.

'You're limping,' Dan Beckindale said.

For a moment, Lacey looked at Weldon to see if he had spoken, but Weldon was turning round to stare behind them. Lacey turned, too.

Beckindale was standing in an alcove, dressed in walking gear. A pack lay at his feet and he was smiling.

Weldon said, 'Dan. How clever of you to find us.'

He walked to him and they shook hands.

'Hello, Peter,' Beckindale called.

Lacey nodded and said, 'Dan.'

'You're limping,' he repeated.

'Too bloody true.'

Weldon said, 'Take your boots off. I've got some plasters. Your feet need more air. Leave a pair of socks off.'

Lacey sat down and did as he was told and watched Beckindale as Weldon put plasters on two blisters that were starting on his right foot.

'How did you know where we were?' Lacey said.

'I saw Jim last week. He's enthusiastic about this country. Told me his favourite walk.'

He said it as if it all made perfect sense, even though it didn't, and Lacey couldn't push him too much because he didn't want Weldon to discover they had been joined by the man who intended to kill him.

When Weldon had finished, Lacey did as suggested and put on only one pair of socks. The boots felt better, but his right foot remained tender. He joined the other two, sitting in a sheltered area, and they unpacked food and coffee from the bags.

Weldon said, 'I take it you don't do much walking, Peter.'

'Only round London.'

'You should do this more often. It's as close to religion as you can get.'

Lacey leaned back against a rock, the earth beneath him and clouds scudding almost around him.

'I know what you mean, but basically I'm idle. I sleep late on Sunday mornings, too.'

Weldon smiled, and he looked at the sky.

'I used to get up in time for church every Sunday. My mother made sure of that. But I used to skip the service. I preferred the communion of the hills to the communion of bread and wine.'

Lacey bit into a corned beef sandwich. His appetite had been sharpened by the walk and he had never tasted anything so delicious. It was as close as he'd ever been to a religious experience.

Beckindale asked Weldon, 'You never found God?'

'I found God, all right. But not your God. What I found was that spark in every man and woman that makes them special, that makes them individuals. The spark that makes the pauper the equal of a prince. The God you find in churches and temples is a senior civil servant. Mine worked in shipyards and down the pits.' He smiled, sadly it seemed, at Beckindale. 'Socialism, Dan. Socialism became my God.'

Short of taking out the Browning and shooting Beckindale, Lacey couldn't think of any way of stopping him from joining them for the rest of the walk.

He couldn't understand what game his former friend was playing. Beckindale had guessed their route and could have ambushed them without trouble, but this was adding to his problems. Maybe he would provoke a battle, as he had in Arras, preferring a fight to murder in cold blood. Or maybe he'd decided he'd gone as far as he could and was now easing his way back in. Maybe he hadn't even noticed Special Branch tailing him from Scotland and they had lost him through ineptitude, and he still didn't know he had been rumbled.

Before leaving, Lacey had to check in with the car at Howgill by two-way radio. He held it up for Beckindale to see.

'There's a car down in the valley,' Lacey said.

'Sensible.'

He flicked the call switch.

'This is Lacey. We're about to leave Simon's Seat. Also, there are now three of us. We've picked up a friend. No need for alarm. I repeat, we've picked up a friend.'

An officer responded and acknowledged the call.

They climbed down the steep north side of the fell without mishap and followed a path through heather. The going was all downhill and Lacey's feet now began to hurt from different pressures.

As they reached a lane in the bottom of the valley, the threatening rain kept its promise and they stopped to don waterproof cagoules. Lacey was prepared for the technicalities of garments in layers. He left the wind-cheater open and fastened the cagoule down the front with only press studs instead of the zip. The shoulder holster was easy to get at.

They by-passed Howgill and after another mile, the road converged upon the river and they took to the bank. The weather had kept most other walkers at home, although they had passed a couple on the road. The riverside was deserted. There were no more hills to climb and the turf was an improvement to feet that had gone through the pain barrier.

The river, that had been running fast and wide, narrowed at a bend ahead.

'The High Strid,' Weldon explained.

They could hear the noise well in advance as it pushed through the gap, causing white water to foam beyond it. The river dropped through a gorge here and was enclosed with trees that grew tall up both sides. Rocks filled the river bed and caused rapids. The roar got louder still further ahead, the sound echoing from the giant boulders.

The river widened briefly, as if to catch its breath, before thrusting again between ancient black stones. Weldon led the way across a giant's causeway of rock slabs to stand at the very edge of the pincer through which the water gushed.

He turned and smiled at them, as if proud of the nature he had described as being close to religion. This example was pagan in its fury and power.

The gap was only a few feet wide, the outcrop of rock higher on the far side than where Weldon stood, the water splashing his boots.

It foamed and roared, a giant jacuzzi tumbling into a deep basin where it moved treacle-black and deadly, before pushing on through a narrow channel of rocks that jutted both beneath and above the surface.

Lacey knew this was the place. The bends, both above and below them, made it private. It was a glorious setting for Dan Beckindale to complete his divine mission.

'The Strid,' Weldon said, taking off his pack and dropping it behind him.

Lacey climbed on to a rock two yards downstream from Weldon and pulled open the press studs of the cagoule. Beckindale was four yards away to his right and would have to come past him to get to Weldon. Lacey casually put his hand inside the jacket.

Weldon continued.

'Country lads used to jump the gap to prove their manhood. That's how it got its name. It looks no more than a stride, does it?'

Lacey glanced at the gap. A jump from this side would be close to suicide. It would be possible from the other side because the height of the rocks gave an advantage.

'Personally, I'd walk round,' Lacey said. 'Even with my feet.'

Weldon laughed.

'A lot didn't make it. A lot still don't. When the water's running high, like now, chances of surviving are slim. It's deep and it's turbulent. If you don't drown, you get battered to death.'

Beckindale began to take off his pack and Lacey watched him closely.

'Shouldn't we be moving on?' he said.

'In a minute.' Weldon turned to look at Beckindale. 'You promise, Dan?'

'I promise.'

Promise what?

Weldon stepped off the rock into the Strid.

'Jesus . . . !'

Lacey began to move towards the gap before he realized rescue was futile. His boots slipped on the wet rock and Beckindale grabbed his arm and stopped him sliding in as well. They stared into the water.

For a moment, there was nothing to see, then Jim Weldon's legs were thrown to the surface, although his trunk remained submerged. The body half turned, almost lazily, before being pushed towards the fast-flowing gorge and the waiting rocks.

They watched it smash from one side to another, turning, diving, bludgeoning its way to the open water at the bend.

324

Lacey turned his head, aware now, that Beckindale still gripped him and was glad of it.

'Why?' he said.

Beckindale's face was only inches away and he could see the sadness in it.

'Because, Peter, the list is true.'

Chapter 42

Lacey moved away from the edge, removed the pack and sat on a slab of stone. He lit a cigarette and, on the second drag, used the two-way radio to call the car near where they had parked.

'There's been an accident. Weldon is in the river.' He took another pull on the tobacco. 'His body needs recovering. Over.'

'He's dead? He's fucking dead?' The voice was incredulous. Lacey let the static crackle until the voice came on again. 'I asked if he was dead?'

'He's dead. We're about a mile upstream. He'll be with you shortly. Over and out.'

He was in no mood to exchange obscenities with angry police officers and he didn't give a toss what they thought.

Beckindale sat opposite, his back against a rock and the river behind him, and poured coffee from a flask into a plastic cup. He offered it, but Lacey declined.

The two men stared at each other. When the cigarette burnt down to the end, Lacey lit another from the stub.

'Maybe I should explain,' Beckindale said.

Lacey nodded but didn't speak.

'When Bill Woodward was running Western Europe for the company, he made a point of meeting people. He didn't stay at Langley, he toured the European stations, went to embassy receptions, made contacts. You know how the reception thing works?'

Lacey knew. He'd attended them. Secret-service third secretaries and cultural attachés from opposing sides swopped disinformation while trying to spot possible targets for blackmail and defection.

'One of the guys he met in Bonn was a KGB officer. Volodya Murashev. Three years ago, Murashev got in touch with Bill. He said he would only deal with him, because he wanted personal guarantees from someone of his seniority.

'Bill met him in Hamburg and Murashev gave him the names of six sleepers. They were a down payment and he gave him just the names, no details. He promised the names of more sleepers and agents of influence. They fixed another meeting, but the guy never made it. He fell out of a seven-storey window.

'All Bill had were the names. He didn't tell anybody else because he didn't want it known he'd even seen Murashev. But he worked out two possibilities. He could try to turn them and create a VIP set of double agents, or he could expose them to their own governments. Trouble was, he had no evidence. That's where Martin Goodman came in.

'He gave Goodman the names and told him to create a case against each of them. Dates of visits to Eastern bloc countries, influences, friends, attitudes, political tendencies, and any dirt, sexual or financial. Bill wanted documentation for the VIP List. Something he could maybe wave at the sleepers if they said prove it, or take to their governments to force them to mount an investigation.'

Beckindale sipped coffee.

'He activated it when Gorbachev started winning all the moves. NATO was a mess. He started with Jorgensen. Jorgensen took some persuading, but he agreed to become a double when Bill told him about the list.' He shrugged. 'Then they both died.'

Lacey continued to work his way down the cigarette. He still said nothing, but waited for Beckindale to continue. After another drink of coffee, he did.

'Bill told me what he was doing. He rated its security so high he told no-one else. The targets were prominent. It was a one-man operation. Besides, he didn't trust the

Company any more. They bad-mouthed anything that came from the NSC.'

Lacey could see reasons other than security and love of country behind Woodward's one-man show. It would have been a tremendous personal coup to take next door to the White House and deliver to the President.

He remembered what Andy Hirst had said about the way the National Security Council had been operating. Achievers in an amorphous department could make the whole damn thing work for them, and mount whatever clandestine operation they wanted. He wondered what else might have been originated by mavericks like Woodward and Beckindale?

Lacey said, 'If Woodward was trying to turn them, why did you kill them?'

'The operation was blown. The Soviets knew what we were doing. There was only one thing left to do.'

'An eye for an eye?'

'Not as blatant as that, but the Lord's message is there. They took out Bill, so I took out their agents. It tells them we're vigilant. It tells them we don't take shit. I fulfilled Bill's mission, but in a way that made sense. Killing them was retribution and a warning. It's straightforward, Peter, whether you read scripture or the *Wall Street Journal*. It's good against evil, and those sons-of-bitches don't suddenly become good because they're pitching for a new economic deal.'

Woodward had been a Green Beret who had found himself desk bound. This had been a chance to get out in the field, even though he had no espionage experience. Lacey could imagine him waving his VIP List under Jorgensen's nose and the Dane realizing the evidence was postulation rather than fact.

The outcome suggested the Dane had reported to his Soviet control. The rest was speculation, but it didn't take a great mind to work things out. Jorgensen would have been told to find out as much as possible from Woodward. When he had, they had both been silenced for safety. It explained how Sutherland knew the name of the list and that its evidence was fabricated. It also explained why he hadn't known the other people on the list.

The Soviets had many agents lying fallow, and all Sutherland had been able to do was tick off the sleepers as they were killed. When Lacey had gone to Vienna, he had known five were dead and one remained a target, but which one, he didn't know.

There had been a chance of stopping the killings and saving the life of an agent by giving Lacey the name of the list. It had also been a way of safeguarding perestroika by laying the blame on the Americans. They had created such confusion, no-one dare take advantage of any of it. Hell, it was so confused, the only reason Lacey now believed he was getting the definitive story was Weldon's suicide.

Lacey lit another cigarette. Jim Weldon's reminiscing now made sense. It had been a reprise of his life.

'What about Weldon?'

'I told him last week. Funnily enough, he admitted it without too much pushing. I gave him an option. He could defect or I'd expose him.'

'Not kill him?'

'He was the most important on the list. The publicity would have been worth it, let people know the Soviets still have their spies in high places, and it would have been unrelated to the Red Dawn killings. Besides, I couldn't risk taking him out in case anything went wrong. An American killing a prominent Brit would not help Anglo-American relations. He asked for time to consider. He had until today.'

'Did you know he was going to jump?'

'I guessed. He suggested an accident as an honourable alternative if I promised to say nothing.' He threw the dregs of the coffee from the cup and chewed his lip. 'He was an honourable man who chose the wrong god, a man who didn't want his family or his party to suffer.'

Beckindale was right. Weldon knew the revelation of his secret would have destroyed his family and all he had

329

worked for. His party would have been back in the wilderness. Everything he had said to Lacey, that morning and the previous night, corroborated his intention.

But what of Beckindale himself? The man was fired by belief, but was he a madman? Lacey began to wonder whether he was as unstable as Andrew Hirst had made out. So what, if he said his wife and son were dead or victims of communism? Lacey had got used to the way Beckindale used God and grand concepts. Losing them had broken him up; the easiest way to avoid talking about them was to tell people they were dead. Maybe Andrew Hirst was covering ass, too.

'When did you know it was coming apart?' Lacey said.

'When you started asking questions and I started throwing screen passes. But I guess when I heard about Martin Goodman.'

'You tried to kill him?'

'I was buying time. I couldn't let anything stop me.'

'And you shot Sarah Mathieson and Roland Devere.'

'I had to.' He locked eyes with Lacey. 'I regretted it, but it had to be done.'

'How did Sarah get involved? Did you recruit her?'

'In a way, she volunteered. She was bored and looking for amusement. I needed a courier, but she became Capaldi's lover. That was her choice. Morality was not her strong point. At the beginning, she didn't know he was an assassin. I don't know about later. I think she sensed the danger and enjoyed it. But towards the end, she was becoming strung out. Excitement was one drug too many. She became a liability and I had no choice. I thought she was alone and when I found your man there, I had no choice about him, either.' He licked his lips. 'I prayed for them. Like I've prayed for you, Peter.'

'Why? Do you plan on killing me, too?'

'No. Do you plan on killing me?'

This was the question he'd been waiting for, because he hadn't known the answer. Now he did.

'No.'

He drew smoke deep into his lungs and felt its damage. Why the hell should he remove an American embarrassment? His training had stressed that killing for revenge was futile and dangerous. Besides, if he hadn't got involved because of Sarah Mathieson, Beckindale would probably have completed his mission without anyone being any the wiser and the Soviets would have lost five very well-placed agents. Lacey, and that poor damn photographer Jim Brady, had caused all the complications.

Lacey suspected Beckindale had never got over his breakdown. Valium would be more appropriate than a bullet.

'You never had any authority, did you Dan?'

'There was no finding. There couldn't be.' Lacey could understand that. A finding was a formal intelligence order signed by the President that authorized a covert operation. They had to be presented to the Senate and House Intelligence Committees. A finding that sanctioned five killings would have caused more than a ripple. 'The President can't always be specific,' Beckindale said.

'President Reagan was specific. He banned assassination.'

'Sure. He banned jay-walking, too. The President is the head of a nation that believes passionately in freedom and the law. Every covert operation undertaken breaks the law. It's best the man at the top doesn't always know.'

'That's a split definitive the public wouldn't understand.'

'I think they'd understand removing five KGB agents. And I think they'd approve. Anyway, they'll never know. Nobody's going to make a song and dance about this. Nobody can afford to.'

Beckindale was right about covert operations. Dissect any operation mounted by British or Americans and there would be enough dirt for the Press and public to demand criminal charges be brought against those involved. Protecting the freedoms of the West was an underhand and thankless business. But Lacey preferred at least to start

331

with an approved brief, even if the way he handled it seldom stayed within the Queensbury Rules.

Colonel Dan Beckindale's logic was faultless and flawed. Maybe, in the right circumstances, he would choose to keep the President clear of all blame by mounting a Third World War on his own initiative. Lacey reflected that heroes were great in the movies, but hell to live with. This one was a dangerous patriot into the bargain. Even so, he didn't feel inclined to kill him.

'We'd better get back,' Lacey said.

He threw away the cigarette-butt and got to his feet. There were traumas to face at Weldon's house and in London, and the sooner he got them over with, the sooner he could go home to Susan and forget.

Beckindale stood up, stretched and stiffened in surprise. He crumpled sideways in a heap and Lacey dived behind the rock the American had only seconds before been sitting against.

He pulled the Browning from its holster and peered across the river at the trees, but knew he was only going through the motions.

'Dan!'

As he grabbed Beckindale's arm, another bullet hit the lifeless body and helped roll it into the dip where Lacey lay.

Fowler. The freelance killer had been given his orders, too, and had carried them out with a silenced rifle for Company pride and a pay cheque.

Lacey looked back at the trees and knew he wouldn't get a target. Even if he did, the range was too great for the Browning.

He turned and sat in the same protected position where Beckindale had sat, lit his last cigarette and told himself this was a good time to stop. He listened to the river and the wind in the trees, inspected the dirt under his finger-nails and wondered if any would stick to Rossington-Hall in London and Hegginbaker in Washington. Probably not.

When the cigarette was finished, he got to his feet, but

no-one shot him. Fowler would be long gone. He took Dan Beckindale by the shoulders, dragged him to the river and tipped him in.

He used the two-way radio and, after a while, got a response.

'There's another body in the river,' he said. 'This one's a hero.'

Chapter 43

The Leeds-Bradford Airport was cosy, convenient and had a flight to Heathrow that left at 6.45 p.m. Lacey concocted his last lies for the police and grieving widow and made it with thirty minutes to spare.

He called Susan.

'It's me. I'm coming home,' he said.

'I've just seen the news on television. Were you there?'

'Yes. I was there.'

'Are you all right?'

'I'm . . . tired.'

She paused before saying, 'I'm sorry, Peter. I know you liked him.'

'Yes.' He lit a Gitanes. 'Look. This thing I've been working on is finished. I'm taking some time off. I thought we might go away somewhere. What do you think?'

'I'd like that.'

'What about the shop?'

'Lucy can manage.'

'What about Lucy?'

'She's promised to wear frocks and Michael's renewed his vows.'

'So, it's a happy ending?'

'Sort of.' Amos Fowler had made it a happy ending, but she daren't tell him that. 'When and where are we going?'

'I'd like to go as soon as possible. Tomorrow?'

'Can you fix that with the office?'

'It's fixed. How about you?'

'No problem. So where?'

'Somewhere with sunshine and no telephones.'

'Sounds good. How about a Greek island?'

334

'How about we just go to Heathrow and catch a plane?'

'Sounds better.' They shared silence for a few moments. 'Are you sure you're all right?'

He laughed.

'Yes. I'm all right. I'm just in the mood for dramatic gestures. Maybe tomorrow I'll take you back to Brighton instead.'

'Anywhere will do, Peter. You know that.'

'I know.' He took a drag at the cigarette. 'Look, I have to go. I'll see you in a few hours.'

'OK. I love you.'

'I love you, too.'

He went to the bar and ordered a large Scotch and a bottle of Beck's and considered that if Jim Brady hadn't snatched a photograph in Vienna a month ago, he wouldn't be in Yorkshire considering his future, and if Amos Fowler hadn't shot Dan Beckindale and done his job for him, he might not have a future to consider. Fowler's action had brought relief to those in authority who had been running scared, and provided a scenario that would cause least damage to everyone concerned.

James Weldon, Leader of Her Majesty's Opposition, had slipped and fallen into a dangerous part of the River Wharfe while walking in the Yorkshire Dales. His friend, American Colonel Dan Beckindale, had jumped in after him, but had been unable to effect a rescue. Both had drowned.

The Press would like it, the President and the Prime Minister would like it, even Rossington-Hall would like it and maybe Beckindale would get another medal for bravery. Only Lacey didn't like it.

His refusal to kill Dan Beckindale had been a way of provoking personal change without having to seek it. It could have caused change to be thrust upon him. Now he was left with a success of sorts and no decision about where he went from here, apart from back to Susan.

He needed a break and he needed to think things out. He needed time and distance and distraction. Then maybe he wouldn't have to make a decision. Until the next time.

Maybe he would just remember the good times. The good times? Like happy endings?

His flight was called and he raised his glass in an ironic toast to the Quiet American.

To Amos Fowler, and happy endings.